FALLING SEVEN TIMES

MARK G. WENTLING

ARCHWAY PUBLISHING

This is a work of fiction. All of the characters, names, incidents, organizations, and dialogue in this novel are either the products of the author's imagination or are used fictitiously.

Archway Publishing books may be ordered through booksellers or by contacting:

Archway Publishing
1663 Liberty Drive
Bloomington, IN 47403
www.archwaypublishing.com
844-669-3957

ISBN: 978-1-6657-6321-9 (sc)
ISBN: 978-1-6657-6323-3 (hc)
ISBN: 978-1-6657-6322-6 (e)

Library of Congress Control Number: 2024914662

Print information available on the last page.

Archway Publishing rev. date: 08/28/2024

Dedicated to my beloved wife Almaz

Based on a True Story

Proverbs 24:16

"Even if good people fall seven times, they will get back up. But when trouble strikes the wicked, that's the end of them."

(Contemporary English version of the Bible)

CONTENTS

CHAPTER ONE

Raindrops

THE PITTER-PATTER OF THE GENTLE rain falling on Alya's tin roof roused her in the middle of the night. She got up slowly from her sleeping mat, taking care not to disturb the other members of her family who were sleeping soundly in spite of their woes. In the darkness, she touched the walls of her ramshackle dwelling to find an old plastic bucket sitting just outside her open front door.

She wanted to light a candle but decided to conserve their dwindling supply of matches in case they obtained some food to cook. Although she could not see clearly, she rinsed the cracked plastic bucket in a puddle of water and placed it to catch rainwater flowing off her rusty roof. She thought to herself, "We may not have any food to eat tomorrow, but at least we'll have fresh water to drink."

To keep their sleeping room warmer, she shut the door behind her even though it provided little security as its latch had worn out long ago. She returned to her sleeping place, but the noise made by the rain falling on the roof kept her awake. She wanted to doze because sleep was the only recourse to escape the desperate reality that she and her family faced. Her thoughts were dominated by how they would find food to get through the next day when the sun rose.

Their poor neighbors living in the makeshift hovels next door were full of ideas of what she could do to earn the money she needed to buy food, but all their suggestions took time to realize. She did not have the luxury of time. Her family needed to eat now. She was worried deeply about how they would get through the day. It made her angry when her neighbors told her things that would take days to achieve, if ever. Her problem was more immediate. It was useless and insulting to talk to her about what could be done tomorrow or next week. Her present needs outweighed any satisfaction of her future needs. She knew she was in a deep hole, but who would reach down and give her the help she needed to dig her way out and stay out? Her life, and the lives of her infant daughter and the rest of her family, depended on her finding today a way to make some money.

There were no jobs available which paid a livable wage. The whole country had been upset by the previous violent communist regime, which harshly ended the royal reign of a thousand years and fought a lengthy war against rebels from a remote northeastern province. Everyone was happy when the rebels prevailed and the bloody dictator was obliged to flee the country. But then they had to submit to the hegemonic rule of a minor ethnic group. Their country was becoming undone by ethnic conflicts and a high population growth rate. Fighting a nonsensical war with a neighboring country killed many soldiers and sapped the national treasury, leaving no money to undertake needed public works and social safety nets. There were certainly many more people searching for jobs than there were jobs. Even if one were lucky enough to find a job, it paid less than was needed to survive. For the vast majority of the population, times had become worse and this situation was eroding the social fabric of the country.

Alya spoke to a neighbor lady who was in a similar situation and all she could say, "We must leave this country if we're to survive. There's nothing here for us. Are you coming with me?"

Alya had no idea about what her neighbor friend was talking about, but she returned to her house to tell her elderly grandmother she was going out with a neighbor. They wore traditional habesha kemi robes which extended to their ankles. They wrapped their heads and shoulders with netelas made of two layers of white hand woven shemma cotton. They wanted everyone to think they were going to their orthodox church to pray, but in reality these were the only sets of going-out clothes they had.

During their long walk across Addis Ababa. They passed by numerous food and arabica coffee stalls, which only served to accentuate their hunger pangs. In particular, they suffered when they smelled people scooping up heaps of a spicy variety of Ethiopian condiments with pieces of injera. A common saying in Ethiopia is, "If you have not eaten injera, you have not eaten." They were afraid to admit that they had not eaten injera in days. The aroma of coffee reminded them that Ethiopia was the birthplace of arabica coffee and it remained an important export. It was also embedded for centuries in Ethiopian culture and no social gathering could be complete without having a traditional coffee ceremony. The smell of the coffee being poured into small porcelain cups by women holding antique clay pitchers (jabenas) and the burning of incense by the coffee makers was overwhelming. They wished they could be farmers with a large field of teff so they could have a plentiful supply of the grain needed to grind into the flour used to make injera. They pictured in their minds living in the mountains with well-watered fertile fields and patches of coffee trees to harvest. Their bodies were so agitated when they encountered food stalls that they held their noses. After several hours of traipsing through squalid neighborhoods, they reached their destination—a non-descript, run-down building from a forgotten era. Alya's friend, Tigest, announced in a weak voice, "This is the place I was told about."

Alya reacted as if she were hurt by what she saw. “There’s nothing here. Are you sure this is the place?”

With an anguished tone, Tigest uttered quietly, “This is the place I was told to go. There is no one here to ask anything.”

Suddenly a young man dressed liked a farinjé (foreigner) appeared in front of them and said, “Are you here because you want to work abroad?”

They both nodded in the affirmative and the man said, “Okay. Show me your passports.”

Their hearts sank. They did not know they needed passports. As Tigest was older than the diminutive Alya, she spoke first. “We didn’t know we needed passports.”

The man laughed and said emphatically, “Of course, you need a passport so I can get you a visa. For all that and traveling abroad and finding you a job you have to pay me. Come back when you have passports and some money. There’s a big demand abroad for Ethiopian maids.”

Alya and Tigest looked at each other with the saddest faces. They both wanted to cry and sit down after their long walk. The man stood by and took pity on them. He could see they were suffering and well-intentioned. It was a risk but he trusted them. Reaching into his pocket, he withdrew a roll of birr and said, “Here’s some money. This should help you get something to eat and your passports. I will deduct this amount from your first salary payment, so be sure to come back.”

Both of the young women thanked him profusely with tears in their eyes. Tigest said, “Thanks so much. Don’t worry. You can count on us. We’ll be back when we’ve got our passports. Right now we need to eat so we’ve enough strength to walk home. We’ll rest here for a few minutes and talk over our plans.”

After a few minutes, Alya said, “Let’s go eat and then go to church to thank God, Jesus, and Mariyam for getting us this far.”

They walked slowly, looking for a roadside food stand. They found a stand managed by a woman who was dishing out small tin plates of injera topped with a spicy sauce called doro wat and dashes of sour cream. The line for the food service was short and moved quickly. Tigist had some money ready and quickly asked for two plates and handed a few birr over to the server, thanking her for her good work.

Alya and Tigest quickly devoured the food on their plates, which were then quickly taken from them by a little boy. They looked around and saw people taking turns drinking water from a public faucet. After they had taken a few gulps of water from the faucet, Tigest suggested they go to the nearest Tewahedo Orthodox church to thank God and ask Him for the strength and wisdom to pursue the process of obtaining their passports. They both agreed that their lives depended on the issuance of their passports.

Alya reacted forthrightly to Tigest's suggestion and said, "Yes, we should go to a big church and ask for the guidance and support of all the saints. Let's go to Saint George's Cathedral. There is no better place than this old and very holy church to get the blessings for what we are about."

Tigest did not hesitate to say, "I agree totally. This church has stood for decades as a bastion of our Christian orthodox religion, The church assured victory over the Italians in the battle of Adwa and was the place where our dearly departed former Emperor, Haile Selassie, was crowned. If it can do all that, surely it can help us get our passports and go abroad to work."

They did not know this part of the city and had to ask several times for the way to the cathedral. They reached the church and before going inside at the entrance reserved for women, they pried through the crowds and found a spot along the outer wall of the church where they could touch and kiss the wall while they kneeled and said prayers.

The female entrance was nearby, so when they finished their prayers on the outer wall they removed their sandals and walked barefooted into the cavernous church. People were packed closely together in the church which was filled with the odor and smoke of burning incense. They prayed fervently, asking God, Jesus, Mariyam and all the saints to guide, lead, and direct them as they pursued what they needed to go abroad for gainful employment.

A church priest (abuna) passed through the crowd and noticed how fervently Tigest and Alya were praying. He bowed down to them and whispered, "Your prayers will be answered. This is an ancient religion that dates from the writing of the Bible and when Ethiopia was known as Abyssinia. I can see that you're true believers and God always answers the prayers of those who believe in Him and his Son."

They left the solemnity of St. George Church to walk quietly home, arriving late in the afternoon. Tigest parted ways with Alya and went home to inform her family about her day. Alya's stern grandmother, Yeshi, was in the courtyard to welcome her and the first words out of her mouth were, "What did you bring us?"

Alya stammered, then held up a fistful of birr for Yeshi to see. Yeshi stepped rapidly forward and grabbed the grimy bills from Alya's outstretched hand. When Yeshi did that, Alya cried out loudly, "That was the money the man loaned me so I could get my passport. Without a passport I can't go abroad to earn money for this family."

While Alya was explaining why she was given the money, Yeshi was busy counting the money and said, "This is not enough to get a passport. Anyway, I need this money to buy food for your child and two sisters who live with us."

In reality, the two sisters named by Yeshi were her cousins, but Yeshi had raised them as her daughters. These two young women had lived in the same house with Alya as far back as she could remember. Alya understood why Yeshi was going to use her money in this way, but she still had to get a passport. She said in plain language to Yeshi, "What about my passport?"

Yeshi was quick to answer, "You need much more than this to get a passport fast. I'll have to borrow the money."

Alya asked, "Who will loan you money?"

Yeshi spoke as she had already thought of borrowing money from someone. "There's the son of my second husband who now runs a trucking business. I think that when I tell him you need money to get a passport, he'll be agreeable."

"When are we going to see him and what's his name?"

Yeshi replied, "Tomorrow and his name is Cherenet. Be ready to go first thing in the morning. If he loans us the money, we'll go straight to the passport office."

Alya could not help but to say, "I hope he lives up to the meaning (kindness) of his name. I'll be ready to go early tomorrow morning."

Later Alya hugged her two-year old daughter, Hiyab, and sat down with her two younger sisters, Belkis and Fana. She told them the news of the day, stressing her need to get a passport. Belkis wrinkled her face and said, "To get a passport, you need an original copy of your birth certificate."

When Alya heard her sister say these words, she immediately went to a corner of a side small room where Yeshi kept all the important papers in a large khaki envelope. She dug through the envelope and fished out her birth certificate. She rushed to join her sisters to show them she had a birth certificate. Fana looked at the certificate and said, "Yes, but you need a certificate that shows you're two years older so that you have the age of eighteen years as required to get a passport and travel abroad."

Alya could not believe her ears and said, "What do you mean? I have to get out of this country to find a job that pays a decent wage."

Fana continued by saying clearly, "No matter. You just have to get a new birth certificate that shows you were born two years earlier. With enough money, you can bribe officials and get a birth certificate with any date you want. You can start by going to church and asking for a baptismal card that shows the birthdate you want."

Alya was beginning to think she would never escape from poverty in Ethiopia. She asked her sisters to excuse her while she sought out Yeshi to explain to her why she had to borrow more money. She found Yeshi outside talking with a neighbor woman and waited patiently to speak with her. Yeshi finished her conversation and turned to face Alya. She informed Yeshi, "You have to borrow enough money to cover the cost of a new birth certificate for me as well as a passport."

Yeshi was consternated and said, "What about the birth certificate we already have for you?"

"I'll explain in more detail later, but please understand that the birthdate on the certificate we have makes me too young to work abroad."

Yeshi had a worrying look on her face when she said, "We have to be able to tell my adopted son all we need, how much it will cost and why. Let's talk about it with your sisters."

"First, let me go next door and explain to Tigist my difficulties and to see if she doesn't have the same problems. Maybe she knows something we don't know."

Alya quickly found Tigist and explained to her in rapid fire Amharic the problems she was already having in fulfilling the passport application process. Tigist immediately went into her house to check her birth certificate. She found that all was well with her birth certificate. She looked at Alya and said, "You're on your own. I'll let you know how it goes with me and if I learn anything that will be of use to you."

Alya refused to fall down and was more determined than ever to get her passport and travel abroad to work. Her survival and the lives of her child and family depended on the money she would send them from working in another country. For her, it was a matter of life or death.

CHAPTER TWO

Passport to Survival

YESHI AND ALYA ARRIVED EARLY at their old neighborhood church. They were impatient, but they had to wait until the early morning service was over and the priest was free to tend to them. They listened intently to the sermon of the priest as he delivered his homily in the ancient religious language of Ge'ez. When the priest finished with the religious services, he approached them. Yeshi said politely but with a sense of urgency in her mournful voice and her head bowed, "Your Holiness. My daughter needs a baptismal card so she can get a birth certificate and then a passport."

The priest looked at them from head to toe and could see they were serious. He softly instructed, "Follow me."

They followed him into a cramped office located beneath an open wooden stairs that led to nowhere. He withdrew a red card from his cluttered dusty tabletop that had not been organized in years. After wiping the filth off the card with the sleeve of his heavy black robe, he asked, "Name and date of birth."

Alya spoke feebly, saying, "Alya Tsehay Adal, June 24, 1985." She gave her real full name but a fake birthdate that would make her two years older than her real age.

The priest scribbled wildly on the card as she provided him the information he requested. He had to consult a special calendar to make sure he wrote the date according to the Gregorian calendar used in most of the world instead of the more ancient Julian solar calendar used in Ethiopia and by the Tewahedo Orthodox Church. The orthodox calendar was generally seven to eight days ahead of the Gregorian calendar. When he finished writing on the card, he handed it to Yeshi and with his head bowed said, "Your offering for this service will be eternally blessed by God." The priest got up and went into the church to tend to other parishioners. Yeshi and Alya walked toward the exit and left some money in the metal offering plate before they went out into the bright daylight. Yeshi immediately opened her umbrella to block any sun rays which would cause her to burn and turn her light-complected skin darker. Although Addis is located in a tropical zone in northeastern Africa, it is situated in a mountainous valley almost 8,000 feet in altitude. Sun burns were common on a bright day.

Once they were outside the church and Yeshi had adjusted her head shawl and umbrella, Yeshi said, "Let's go to our Kebele neighborhood government office. A relative works there and I'm sure he'll quickly issue a birth certificate for you upon presentation of your baptismal card."

They walked the short distance back to their neighborhood and through crowded passageways to find their local government office. What they could see of the dilapidated office through the compact group of people mulling about in front of the office told them this was an old building that had seen better days decades ago. Yeshi told Alya to wait behind while she weaved her way through the crowd to find somebody at the entrance who worked there. She found a middle-aged man guarding the front door and said, "My name is Yeshi and I'm here to see Haile."

The man pushed his lower lip out before yelling behind himself, "Haile, there's somebody here who knows your name and wants to see you."

Haile squeezed his way out of the tiny, packed office to see who was calling him. Upon seeing the elderly Yeshi, he expressed surprise at seeing a relative he had not seen in years and greeted her warmly, paying all respects due to a family elder. When he was finished with his greetings, he took her aside and asked, "Auntie, why are you seeing me?"

Yeshi had few words for him. She handed him discreetly the baptismal card and said softly, "My daughter urgently needs a birth certificate so she can get a passport to travel abroad. Our lives depend on her getting a birth certificate today."

Haile readily sensed the urgency of the matter and replied without hesitation, "Come back in a couple hours to collect your certificate."

Yeshi thanked him and said, "See you later." She then gently wove her way through the crowd standing in front of the office to find Alya waiting on the periphery of the mob besieging the office. Her advanced age saved her from being criticized by the more vocal members of the crowd. She said to Alya, "Let's go find a shady place to wait within eyeshot of the office. I want Haile to be able to see that we're waiting for him to show us your certificate."

They found a place under a leafy eucalyptus tree on the fringes of the office courtyard road which directly faced the office's front entrance. They spread their head scarves on the sparse grass covering the ground and sat down for the long wait. Yeshi leaned her back on the trunk of the tree, closing her eyes so she could get the rest her aging body needed. Alya was tired but kept her eyes focused on the office entrance for any sign of Haile.

The hours passed. The sun was high in the sky. There was no sign of Haile. The morning crowd of people had dissipated. Suddenly, Haile appeared with papers in his hand. Alya nudged Yeshi, as her heart raced. Yeshi struggled to her feet and wrapped her shawl over her head and around her shoulders. She moved forward as quickly as her age would allow her. Haile saw her coming and smiled. He was happy that he had been able to accomplish what his elderly aunt had requested of him.

Yeshi got near him and he extended his hand and said calmly, "Here's the paper you asked for along with your baptismal card. The certificate is all stamped and sealed. I paid out of my own pocket for the cost of the official stamps."

The ink on the birth certificate had not yet fully dried. Yeshi's heart was full of thanks and tears swelled in her eyes when she said, "I thank you, all our ancestors thank you, the Lord and all his saints … thank you. How much do I owe you?"

"You owe me nothing except your prayers and continued faithfulness to our church."

With those heartfelt words, Haile turned and entered his office. Yeshi trod back with the papers in hand to where Alya was waiting and proudly announced, "Here's your birth certificate. Now you can get your passport."

Joy surged in Alya's heart and she could not help but embrace her grandmother and say, "I can't thank you enough. My hope has been restored."

Yeshi surprised Alya by saying, "Which way is the passport office? While I'm out, I might as well try to keep going. The sooner you can get your passport the faster you can get a job abroad and send us the money we need to survive."

Although Alya was surprised by her grandmother's stamina and her willingness to go directly to the passport office, she was in total agreement that they had to keep pushing to get her passport as soon as possible. Alya had great respect for her grandmother who had raised her since she was an infant, and responded meekly, "Let's go that way and ask someone for directions."

Alya was afraid that her grandmother could not walk far, so she was relieved when they learned from a passerby that the passport office was not distant. After walking several blocks, they came upon a long line of people and asked. "What are all these people doing here?"

The reply they got was that all the people were waiting to go into the passport office. Although they were unprepared for a long wait, Yeshi and Alya got in the slow-moving line. They shuffled forward at a snail's pace in the line for a couple of hours and it seemed like the line had barely advanced. Their irritation with the slowness of the line was enhanced by their hunger and the need to relieve themselves. They did not notice him, but there was a young guy standing some distance from the line. This guy observed how their stress levels were rising. He came up near them and whispered, "I can get you to the front of the line for a small payment."

At first, Yeshi rebuked him in the strongest terms. Then he turned to Alya and made his offer again. Alya simply said, "We don't trust you, but how much?"

The guy replied, "One hundred birr. I only keep a small part of this amount. Most of it goes to the officials working inside."

Yeshi and Alya had heard the passport office was corrupt, but they did not know the corruption started before they had even applied for a passport. They were afraid of being swindled. Yeshi tried to negotiate the price with the guy, but he said bluntly. "Take it or leave it. For all I care, you can stay in line forever."

Yeshi turned her back and removed from inside her bra one hundred birr and handed the money to the man. Forthwith, he escorted them to the front of the line and wished them good luck. He winked at the man guarding the doorway and off he went.

Rapidly the man guarding the door instructed them to go inside and complete their business. They found in the inside room a jumble of people all vying for the attention of clerks hunched over worn wood tables with stacks of papers. They immediately saw the need to join in the competition for attention. A middle-aged woman beckoned them over to her table. She handed them a form and said, "Complete this."

Yeshi was not literate, so Alya studied the form, filled in the blanks in Amharic and English, and invented a signature to place in the designated block at the bottom of the form. She was thankful that post-sixth grade instruction in Ethiopia was in English and she had completed high school. Alya gave back the form with her birth certificate to the busy woman who thanked her and said after briefly looking over the form, "Come back in two weeks to collect your passport. By the way, you'll need two photos for your passport."

Yeshi quickly interjected, "I beg of you. We can't wait two weeks and where can we get photos?"

The woman said pleasingly in a low voice, "Well, you can pay me extra and get your passport within forty-eight hours. As for the required photos, we got a guy here who can take your photo for a price."

As the price of getting a passport was rising, Yeshi's became concerned about how the costliness of getting a passport for Alya would drain her meager financial reserves. All she could manage to say was, "How much?"

The woman politely said, "That's two hundred birr for me and another two hundred birr for the photographer."

Yeshi removed all the money from inside her bra and handed it over to the woman saying, "That's all I got."

The passport clerk counted the money, straightened the ragged bills out flat and then said with a sad face, "That's not enough but you seem like my sisters, so I will do you a favor and get all done with the money you gave me."

With those words, she signaled to a man across the room to come with his camera to take photos for Alya's passport. This guy guided Alya to a spot along the soiled wall near a window where he had hung a white sheet. He indicated to her to stand in front of the sheet and look at the small black camera he held. A few snaps were quickly taken and Alya returned to Yeshi who was still standing in front of the application table administered by the woman who said in a business-like manner, "Come back the day after tomorrow to collect your passport. No need to wait in line. Just address the man at the door that you are here to get your passport from Mahi. Good day."

Yeshi and Alya shoved their way out of the jammed office and walked to a shady place where they could take a deep breath and figure out their next move. An exhausted Yeshi told Alya, "You go home. I'm out of money. I got to go see someone from my royal past about lending me some money."

They parted ways. Alya ambled in the direction of their home abode. She understood that Yeshi knew people from her illustrious past and she had to see them alone. Alya was surprised that Yeshi still had connections with people she knew from the old Ethiopia. Anyway, she wished Yeshi well and hoped these connections from the past were fruitful in terms of loaning her the money they needed to live.

Yeshi found her way through winding roads to the old neighborhood of her childhood to see if any of her old family relations still lived there. It had been many years since she dared return to this crumbling place. The age of the buildings reminded her of the glory days of Ethiopia when an emperor still sat on the millennium throne and royalty thrived in a feudal system. She recalled her pampered life and her personal servant. Back then she never thought that the easy life she knew would come to an end with the takeover of her country by a communist dictator. The murder of the emperor over thirty years ago ended a Solomonic dynasty which had existed since Biblical times. The ancient history of Ethiopia is intertwined with the old testament of the Bible in which Ethiopia is referred to as Abyssinia forty-three times. Yeshi had been told of this history, but what counted for her was the disappearance of her expensive royal life with the death of the emperor and the harsh abolishment of the royal family and the seizure of all their property.

This situation quickly led to the destitution of Yeshi and her family. The millennia succession had been turned on its head and she and other members of the royal family were lucky to avoid being killed. She had survived by living poor in one of the poorest neighborhoods of Addis. She changed her name and joined the struggle of the poorest of the poor to survive in these unstable times. Most of her relatives had emigrated to other countries to become part of the large Ethiopian diaspora. Yeshi was a survivor, but she did not talk about her past. Fear of being identified with the royal family haunted her. Also, she knew that her royal past had no relevance in the present and could be a handicap to trying to survive among the poor masses. She forced herself to learn how to dress, eat and talk like the poor woman she had become. The past was past and it would never be repeated.

She wandered through the old passageways of her youth. Nothing was like she remembered it. Everything looked much older and smaller than she remembered. Also, the streets were so empty she did not think she would see anyone from the old days. In particular, she did not think she would find her cousin Addisu. And even if she did find him, she was not sure he had any money to loan her.

Yeshi arrived at the house in which she thought Addisu lived. She knocked lightly on the front gate. There was no response, so she knocked again more loudly. When the gate flew open forcefully, she was startled and fearful to respond to the question, "What do you want?

It took Yeshi a couple of seconds to find her voice and utter, "Addisu?"

The burly man who opened the gate so roughly said in an angry voice. "Who wants to know?"

Yeshi took a few seconds to study the face of the wrinkled man facing her and said softly, "Addisu is that you? It's Yeshi."

The man at the gate stood still while his eyes examined Yeshi from head to toe and then exclaimed, "Yeshi, my cousin. Come in. You're welcome in the house of Addisu. God is good."

Yeshi followed Addisu to a shady place in a flowery courtyard. He asked her to please be seated on a cushioned chair. After they were comfortably seated, Addisu said, "My sister, I'm pleased to see you after so many years. It has been so long that I thought you had died. Tell me, what brings you to seek me out now?"

This unusual encounter with a close family member from the glorious past left Yeshi speechless. It took several minutes before Yeshi could find any words to say. After a long pause, she said, "Dear cousin, my brother, I'm so happy to see you in your old house that I'm lost for words. If I knew you were still here, I would have visited you long ago, in spite of my distant and impoverished state. Desperation obliges me to come awkwardly here today. I have nothing and I was wondering if you had anything to help me get on my feet."

Addisu was quick to reply in a sympathetic manner, "My sister, I have next to nothing but the little I have is to be shared with you."

Tears swelled up in Yeshi's eyes. She was deeply thankful that her long walk to Addisu's house in her childhood neighborhood had not been for nought.

CHAPTER THREE

Waiting to Go

THE WAIT FOR HER PASSPORT was unbearable. Alya sat with her one-year old daughter, Hiyab (Gift of God), on her lap among her two younger sisters (cousins), Belkis and Fana, and her grandmother, Yeshi, with tears in her eyes. She was afraid to travel to another country, but she was also afraid to stay. She did not want to go, but her family needed money to live and she was their only hope. Alya especially did not want to leave her daughter, but if she remained at home there would be no money to give her all the things she needed. She had her daughter out of wedlock. Her daughter did not know her biological father who had left a long time ago for Australia. The rumor was that he had married an Australian woman and was raising a family of his own. His family which was remaining in Addis did not have the means to provide the kind of support her daughter needed.

She tried to relieve her agony by going to church with her grandmother every day in the early dawn hours. In the dimly lit interior of the church, they searched for a seat in the pews or on the carpeted floor. They spent all morning in the church, receiving the service administered continuously each day by the priests and praying to all the Orthodox saints, especially to Mariyam, the earthly mother of Jesus, the immortal son of God. The church was filled with smoky Holy incense that was dispensed from thuribles the priests were constantly swinging. Huge colorful religious paintings depicting Biblical scenes were hung on the walls and ancient relics were on display at the front of church. The priests read the liturgy in Ge'ez and blessed the congregation, which mouthed their parts of the lengthy but thorough religious ceremony, crossing their chests with much fervor at the appropriate times.

Every day she would buy for a few birr a small candle from the church's store to place near the altar and light it, illuminating her need for religious support of her trip abroad for a job that paid a livable wage. Alya knew that the sacred tabot, a replica of the Ten Commandments stored inside of Ark of the Covenant, which established her church, was covered by an ornate cloth and placed on the altar. Only an ordained priest could touch the tabot which is paraded monthly with great ceremonial fanfare around the church on the divine Kirkos saint day. On this auspicious and colorful occasion, there is much joyous chanting and drum beating. An even greater religious procession would occur once a year when all the priests of all the churches in Addis Ababa and every town in Ethiopia would join together with the tabots to praise God, Jesus and the Holy Spirit. People from the crowds of the faithful would vie to approach the blessing of the sanctity of the tabot and kiss the holy golden crosses carried by the priests. The multitudes of people would all busy themselves with moving their hands in a waving motion to bring the holy incense smoke toward them so they would be blessed and their prayers would rise to heaven. This impressive annual religious festival in Ethiopia is called "Timkat" to commemorate the epiphany, the baptism of Jesus in the River Jordan.

She did everything she knew how to do to beseech the holy blessing of her planned travel to an unknown country for gainful employment. With a full spiritual uplift, she was confident of being carried successfully through her solo journey into the unknown. Her belief in the holy power of her church and all that it stood for was unsurpassed. The patron saint of the century-old church was Kirkos, infant son of Saint Julietta. They had both had been put to death centuries ago for their firm Christian beliefs. The church was built of blocks of brown stone in the time of Emperor Menilik II, descendant of legendary Menilik, son of King Solomon and Queen Sheba, who existed centuries ago. It was the ninth church built in the fast-growing capital city of Addis Ababa. It was constructed in an oblong form in the image of Noah' s Ark. Hundreds of worshippers could be accommodated inside the church and many more would worship in the extensive courtyard surrounding the church and its separate bell tower.

Alya made sure she obeyed all the church's requirements of the faithful and pure of heart. She seriously adhered to all the many 250 fasting days practiced by the church, abstaining from eating meat and any animal products, and refraining from any sexual activity. Assiduously, she removed her shoes before entering the church entrance reserved for women. With head covered, she joined the women on the right side of the congregation facing the abuna. She would always check if the small wooden cross blessed by and given to her by the abuna was dangling by a heavy black thread around her neck. She never took off this holy necklace. She dared not enter the church when experiencing her monthly menses and during this time prayed in the church's courtyard. She believed deeply that a strong religious conviction would bold well for obtaining her passport and traveling abroad. She was convinced that her faith would bless her trip and time abroad. With God, Jesus, and all the saints on her side, she strongly believed she could not fail in her desperate survival mission.

Forty-eight hours had expired and it was time for her to go alone to collect her passport. She approached the passport office with much trepidation. The people in the long line wanted to complain about her passing by them to go to the head of the line, but they could see the deep reverence etched in her face and refrained from interrupting her serious progression. She was stopped by a man guarding the front door of the office and said in a weak but determined voice, "I'm here to see Mahi."

Upon saying these simple words, she was immediately allowed to enter. She wove her way respectfully through the crowd in the small office room until she found Mahi's table. The brief wait for Mahi to recognize her seemed to last an eternity. Her stress levels rose and she began to perspire. Mahi saw her and immediately reached into a small table drawer to retrieve a small booklet and said in a matter-of-fact manner, "Here's your passport."

Alya gently grabbed the passport and was beginning to thank Mahi profusely when Mahi told her, "No need to thank me. Now, be off with you before somebody notices our business." With Mahi's crisp words, Alya quickly realized she should hide her passport and get out of the office and far away from the crowd of people gathered there, acting as if she had been rebuffed. Nobody should notice that she had gotten her passport. She did not want to incite the ire of the crowd of people who were trying to obtain a passport legitimately.

Her first impulse was to run home and show her family that she had indeed received her passport. But, in spite of her excited state, she tried to rein in her emotions and take the long walk to see the man who brokered job trips abroad. With her passport safely tucked inside her clothing, she damned her exhaustion and took off in the direction of the job broker. Although her body was weak and her throat parched, she arrived after walking a couple of hours to the spot where she had last seen the broker.

She found only two old ladies sitting on low wooden stools at this spot and she managed to ask, "Where's the person who arranges jobs abroad?"

One woman got up and went to the small building adjacent to the road and knocked on its metal door, saying, "There's somebody here to see you."

The door was quickly flung open and the guy she had seen before stepped out. He walked the short distance to where she stood and said stiffly in a business-like manner, "Do you have your passport?"

Alya promptly retrieved her passport and managed to say with an air of excitement in her squeaky, dry voice, "Here it is."

The guy studied her passport and flipped through the pages, saying, "Very good. Here's a pen. You have to sign on the photo page for your passport for it to be valid."

Alya took the pen and passport handed to her and hesitated because she did not know how she should sign her name. The guy noticed her hesitation and said, "Sign the same way you did on your national identity card."

Alya did not want to admit she was not old enough to obtain a national identity card and quickly scribbled her signature on the line provided on the face page of the passport. When she finished signing the man said, "Now, you can give me back your passport, so I can make the necessary arrangements for landing you a domestic servant job in Dubai. Come back here in a week for my final instructions."

The broker's words should have been welcomed by Alya, but they were not. She wanted to show her passport to her family and she could not do that if the broker had her passport. Moreover, she did not trust the broker. She did not know what to do. If she did not give her passport to the broker, he could not arrange for her a job abroad. With misgivings digging deeply into her heart, she had no option but to count on the broker and said quietly, "I'll be here at the same time next week without fail."

Before the broker turned to return to his house, he tried to encourage her by saying, "Trust me. You're going to Dubai to work. Start getting your affairs in order for travel to Dubai and a long stay there."

All Alya could say was, "Thank you."

The broker had a few more words to say. "Next time, Alya Tsehay Adal, ask for me by my name, Lami."

Alya nodded her head in the affirmative, but doubts swirled in her head when she heard the broker's name. His name indicated that he was an Oromo and she wondered if he would treat her favorably. She did not think her Amara ethnic identity would make any difference. There were many ethnic groups in Ethiopia and normally they all lived in harmony.

It took Alya most of the rest of the day to return home on foot. She was famished, but she had no money to buy food. When she arrived home, her family immediately started to pelt her with questions about her quest for a passport. Alya wanted to address all their questions, but she was too hungry to talk. Yeshi saw that she was exhausted and brought her a hot plate covered with injera smothered in chiro sauce, and a big mug of water. Alya sat down with her family and attacked her plate of food as only a starving person could do. Although it was difficult to contain their level of excitement, her family sat patiently around her, waiting for her to finish eating and drinking. They knew when she ate the last bit of food, washing it all down with water and recovered some strength, she would tell them the details of her day. Their patience originated in their knowledge that Alya was the only member of the family who could support them.

As Alya swallowed the last bite of her sumptuous dish and drank some more water, her family edged closer to her, eager not to miss a word she said. Alya smiled, cleared her throat and said, "I have good news. I got my passport."

All her family members clapped loudly and chanted wildly upon hearing this news. Yeshi had tears in her eyes. Baby Hiyab did not know what was happening but could see that everyone was happy, and she too joined in the clapping and amused her family by trying to do a little jig. When these joyous antics subsided, Alya continued to recount what she did after she got her passport. "I walked from the passport office to where the job broker lives."

Yeshi interrupted at this juncture to say, "I was hoping that was what you did because you were gone so long."

Alya described her meeting with the broker and informed her family that she reluctantly turned over her passport to him and he told her to return in one week. Yeshi again interjected, "I hope you can trust him to use it wisely and to keep your passport safe."

Alya quickly interjected, "That crossed my mind, but I had no choice but to trust him."

Yeshi said, "I understand. We must pray more fervently to all the saints at church for the successful conclusion of this critical effort to go abroad and work."

They spent the week mostly in the church. Other than that, Alya moved ahead in the belief she would be traveling soon, arranging the few things she wanted to take with her. She also tried to spend more time with her child who she would leave behind in the care of her grandmother and sisters. During this week, Alya looked at her grandmother Yeshi with the realization of the deep love she possessed for this gray-haired woman. She would miss Yeshi, but it was mainly because of her that she was taking the risky step of going abroad. She knew she would miss her family profoundly, but she had to get money for their survival. Her sacrifice was for them.

Almost before she knew it, a week had gone by and she found herself on the long walk back to where Lami did his broker business. She arrived in front of his room and knocked, but nobody answered. Not knowing what to do, she spread her netela on the ground and she sat down, waiting for Lami to appear. She sat for a couple of hours before Lami came marching up to her and said, "I'm glad you made it. I got good news. You are booked on tomorrow night's Ethiopia Airlines flight for Dubai. Here's your ticket and passport."

Alya stood up quickly. She wanted to speak, but her excitement over Lami's news had tied her tongue in knots. She took the ticket and passport that Lami proffered and managed to emit emotionally to Lami a big, "Thank you."

Lami was happy that she was happy and said with a tinge of gaiety in his voice, "Be sure to be at the airport at least three hours before your flight takes off. One of my colleagues will be at the airport. You'll recognize him by the sign he is carrying with your name written on it."

Alya was breathless. Things were happening too fast for her. She thanked Lami again and said, "This is much welcomed news for me and my family. You can count on me. But how do I get to the airport? I've never been there before."

Lami chuckled and said, "Take a taxi to the airport. I assume you do not have the money for a taxi so I will give you now a loan advance to cover that expense. All the money I give you will be deducted from your first salary payment."

The taxi money was handed to Alya who took it and placed it with her passport and ticket and carefully hid them inside her shemma clothing wrap where nobody could see them. Having secured these precious items, she extended her profound gratitude to Lami again and bid him farewell.

Lami said, "Good luck with this new adventure."

Alya gently waved goodbye to Lami as she set off on her long walk back home.

As she walked, she felt like a new person. The promise of traveling to a new job that paid a decent wage made her step more gingerly. She arrived home earlier than expected and remained silent. Her silence was duplicated by her family. This silence was broken by the ruckus that occurred after Alya produced her ticket and passport for all to see. Yeshi fell immediately to her knees and thanked God for His blessing of Alya's trip.

After the noise died down, Alya told her family, "My flight is for 2 a.m. tomorrow night. I need to arrive at the airport at least three hours before that. I've been loaned money for the airport taxi, which I need to arrange now."

Yeshi's rejoicing had subsided and she said firmly, "We'll go with you. I have to see you for as long as you're here. You can use my old suitcase. Now, I have to tell the neighbors of our good news."

Alya spoke up, "That reminds me. I have to tell Tigist."

Yeshi quicky said, "Don't you know? Tigist has already departed for Lebanon. Her family has been quiet about her departure because they didn't want her to go."

This news about Tigist was puzzling to Alya and her first reaction was to say, "I'm glad I'm not going to Lebanon but I'm going to Dubai no matter what."

CHAPTER FOUR

Dubai Beckons

ALL HAD BEEN ARRANGED FOR Alya's first trip to the airport, but the heavy rain did not make things easier. She and the family members accompanying her decided firmly that getting wet was a small price to pay for Alya's departure. After all, it was not unusual for a downpour to occur during the month of August at the height of the rainy season. They were praying, however, for a brief break in the seasonal rains so Alya would not have this added burden of traveling to Dubai.

Going to the airport was unusual for Alya and boarding a flight to Dubai was beyond her imagination. She did not know anything about the country she was going to and in which direction her plane would be flying. All she could think of was getting there and starting work so she could send money to her family. She did not care to know anything about the country and her first plane ride. All that mattered was her job and salary.

She and her family were too excited to sleep. They stayed up talking to one another. Alya's family wanted to enjoy all the time they could with her before she left for a long sejour working in Dubai. Their words masked their anxiety over Alya's departure. They did not want her to go, but they accepted that she had to go.

They had paid half the fare in advance to get a taxi man to come to their dwelling with his beat-up old Yugo car. Like all taxis in Addis, it was painted blue by hand. The taxis were a leftover from the communist Derg regime that had put a bloody end to the long glorious thousand-year reign of the imperial government. This authoritarian military regime adopted a Marxist-Leninist ideology and initiated a period of "Red Terror" in which tens of thousands of Ethiopians were executed. This regime ruled Ethiopia with an iron-fist for seventeen years before being ousted in 1991 by popular armed rebel forces.

Alya did not care about this past history of her country as she placed her small suitcase in the back of the Yugo taxi. She did not care about her taxi being manufactured in a country that no longer existed, and that it was something of a miracle it was still in use. All she wanted was a taxi that could get her to the airport in plenty of time to make her flight to Dubai. It was the year 2003 and the past was past and long gone. She was hoping and praying for a new and better future for her and her family. But all depended on going to Dubai to get a job that paid a decent salary.

It was slow going as they made their way the three miles to the international airport in a rainstorm. Alya sat next to the driver and Belkis sat with Yeshi in the back seat. Fana had stayed behind to care for Hiyab. The old cardboard suitcase that had been given to Alya by Yeshi for her trip was in the car's tiny trunk. The taxi's windshield wipers did not work and its dim headlights barely penetrated the dark night, so the driver had to go extra slow as he took care to stay on the road and not to run into other cars. The taximan wanted to stop on the side of the road and wait for the rain to subside, but Alya insisted that he keep moving toward the airport.

They arrived at the departure entrance of the huge international airport building in blinding rain. They could not see much because of the heavy rain, but Alya could see enough to know that many people were jostling to get into the airport. She wondered if any other Ethiopians would be on her plane with her. Yeshi and her sister planned to go into the airport with her but because of the rain she pleaded with them to go back home in the same taxi. She awkwardly reached behind her seat to embrace her grandmother and Belkis, saying, "I'll be in touch once I get settled in Dubai. Pray for me."

Yeshi was the first to weep, but she was immediately followed by Alya and Belkis. The taxi man briefly observed this sad threesome, but said in an irascible voice, "Enough. You got to get going in spite of the rain. I wish you well, but we can't stay parked here forever."

With the taximan's words, Alya released her hold on Yeshi and Belkis and said firmly to the taximan, "Get my bag. I'm getting out now."

Braving the rain, both Alya and the driver got out of the car. The driver unloaded her suitcase and hustled to hand it to her before running back to get into his battered taxi. Alya grabbed her suitcase and walked quickly to get under the cover of the airport entrance canopy. Once she was protected by the airport overhang and not being soaked by the downpour, she turned to wave goodbye to Yeshi and Belkis, but the taxi had already vanished. At that moment, Alya felt all alone. She was scared by the realization that she was on her own and the path ahead would be a solidary one.

Alya immediately realized she was in a compact crowd of people vying to enter the airport hall. The crush of the crowd made it difficult to hold on to her flimsy suitcase. The crowd around her pressed forward to the open gate and the officials checked passports and tickets before allowing entrance into the hall. She struggled to carefully remove her travel documents from her small purse that was strapped tightly over her head. Although of small stature, she was able to use all her strength to maintain her place in line. As she moved closer to the entrance, she could smell the body odors of the people forced upon her. It was obvious that some of the people had not bathed in days. Other people smelled like the incense that had saturated their clothes. Alya wondered if they had been immersed in incense as part of a traditional coffee ceremony or had come to the airport directly from church. Whatever the case may be, she had a passing thought that the smell of incense was a good way to cover up the smells of poor personal hygiene. Alya knew her netela smelled of incense because she wore her only shawl at all times. Now it served to cover her travel clothes—blue pants and a white blouse. One thing she had in common with the other people moving slowly toward the gate was that she was wet and cold. She appreciated the warmth emanating from the bodies pressed up against her but was hopeful of drying off once inside the airport.

After about an hour standing in the packed line, it was her turn to present her passport and ticket. She tried to maintain her calm and do as she had observed others do before her. The officials studied her and her documents. She functioned as if she was used to dealing with the airport. After a brief interlude, an official handed her documents to her and waved her forward.

Alya breathed easier once she was inside the airport but after walking a short distance, she stopped and wondered what she should do next. She felt lost in a place that she had never been before. She looked around at all the commotion and was undecided as to where she should go next. The ongoing bustling activity in her new surroundings was mesmerizing. She had never seen so many busy people at this time of night.

Across the wide airport lounge, standing among a bunch of people, was a man holding a white sheet of paper. Seeing this paper, jogged Alya's memory. She recalled that Lami had told her that there would be his colleague at the airport holding a white sheet of paper with her name written on it. She slowly walked toward the man holding the paper and saw her name was on it. As she got closer to the paper, she could see her name, "Alya," appearing in big block letters on the paper. Once she clearly saw her name on the paper, her step quickened and she arrived in front of the man holding the paper. She looked at the man and he politely said, "Are you Alya?"

"Yes. I'm the person whose name is written on your paper."

"Very good. Let me see your travel documents."

A nervous Alya handed her passport and ticket to the man and waited patiently while he determined if all was in order. To break the silence, Alya said, "You know my name, what's yours?"

The man smiled and said, "Yafet."

It was Alya's turn to smile as his name in Amharic meant 'handsome.' She thought that his physiognomy definitely fit his name. He had attractive features and he was only a shade darker than Alya's golden-brown complexion. Suddenly, Yafet handed back to Alya her travel documents and pointed straight ahead and said, "You see the Ethiopian Airlines counter straight ahead. That's where you check your suitcase and get your boarding pass with your seat number. Then, over there are the booths of the immigration and security officials. You have to pass through these checkpoints to get to the waiting lounge. They will stamp your passport and boarding pass. You have plenty of time. Find your departure gate and wait for your flight. I will stay here until you have entered the waiting lounge. Any questions?"

Alya had some questions, but she did not want to sound dumb and inexperienced by asking them, so all she said was, "Thank you so much."

The line for the ticket counter was nearby, but for Alya it was a distance she had difficulty covering. She knew in her heart of hearts that once she got her boarding pass and went through the immigration and security checkpoints, she was nearing the point of no return. There was no relaxing and her throat was so choked that by the time she handed her passport and ticket to the attendant, she was in a daze, struggling to understand what was happening to her. The airline attendant had to repeat her words several times before Alya heard what she was saying. She could see from the attendant's name tag that she was called Fana, meaning 'light,' but there was no light on Alya's situation. Fana repeated, "Place your suitcase on the scales so we can weigh and collect it. Do you want an aisle or window seat, and what row do you prefer?

Everything Fana said was new to her. Alya had never thought of any of this, but she did not want to act like a novice, so she said, "Window and a middle row."

Alya could sense the people behind her in the line were becoming impatient with all the time she was taking and quickly took from Fana her passport, ticket, boarding pass, and luggage tag. She thanked her and headed with heavy feet toward the immigration booths. Then the thought crossed her mind. "Where's my suitcase?" She spotted her suitcase on a conveyor belt and her first impulse was to rush and fetch it. But that would be awkward and nobody else was doing it, so she move back up to Fana's counter and asked excitedly, "When do I get my suitcase back?"

Fana laughed. She could see that this was Alya's first time for air travel. Although she was serving another passenger, Fana politely replied, "You'll get your suitcase at the baggage claim area at your destination. Excuse me now while I deal with another passenger."

All eyes were staring at Alya, demonstrating their annoyance at the delay her ignorance of traveling by air had caused. Alya was embarrassed and kept her head down as she headed toward the immigration checkpoint. When she arrived in front of the agent at this first formal checkpoint, she handed the agent her passport and boarding pass. The agent quickly looked at her and the photo in her passport. He stamped her passport and boarding pass and motioned for her to move forward to the security checkpoint. The security agents wasted no time in waving their Ethiopian sister through to the entrance of the waiting lounge. They were accustomed to seeing their fellow Ethiopians go abroad.

Alya felt like an innocent lamb being led to its slaughter. She exhaled forcefully to calm her surging anxiety. The many shops attracted her, but all she could think about was finding her departure gate and a place to sit down for the long wait for her flight. She wanted to escape and go to her Addis home but there was no going back. She redoubled her efforts to remember her mission and steady herself. She told herself that she had to do this for her family, especially for her baby daughter. She found her gate and a nearby seat. Her thoughts were muddled but the view of an Ethiopian Airlines 737 jetliner sitting on the wet tarmac fixated her mind on the pride she felt for her country that had had for a long time its own airlines. At least her maiden flight would be on her country's highly respected national airlines.

A middle-age Ethiopian woman sat down in the seat next to her. This woman turned her head to look at the young woman seated beside her and could see that her seat mate was another Habesha (Ethiopian). She greeted Alya in Amharic and asked, "First time to travel by plane abroad?"

Alya looked at her elder and said in a soft voice, "I cannot lie. This is my first time and I'm scared to death."

The woman responded, "My name is Zufan and I have made this flight to Dubai five times. I can always tell who's flying for the first time by how tight they hold their travel documents."

Upon hearing Zufan's words, Alya immediately noticed how tightly she was holding her passport and ticket. She immediately released her grip and put her travel documents in her purse. Zufan smiled widely and Alya asked, "Why have you gone to Dubai so many times?"

"Like all the other Ethiopian women you'll see on the plane, I work as a maid for a wealthy Arab family. Fortunately, the family I work for is agreeable and kind. There are hundreds of Ethiopian women working as maids in Dubai. Some of their experiences are not so agreeable. Anyway, the money they make is much more than anything they could make in Ethiopia, even if they can find a job in their home country."

Alya could see that what she was about was not novel and she would not be alone … many of her Habesha sisters were already doing what she planned to do. She could see that she could learn a lot about Dubai from Zufan, but she was not sure about what to ask her. After a brief interlude, she asked Zufan,. "What it's like to work as a maid in Dubai?"

Zufan lost no time to reply. "That's a big question. Mostly, all depends on the nature of your boss. If your boss likes your work and pays you on time, there's usually no problem. It's important that you keep in mind that you are their obedient and hard-working servant. Much depends on how you fit in with an Arab family and how that family relates to you."

Alya followed with another question. "What can you tell me about Dubai?"

"Very little. I get one day off each week, but I need that day to rest and get ready for another week of work. I mainly stay in my room.

Alya was curious and asked, "Are their many foreigners in Dubai?"

Zufan laughed and said, "Most people in Dubai are from some other country. I've never seen a local person do menial labor. They hire foreign workers like us."

They were talking about their flight when the public address system was communicating information. They listened and were pleased to learn that passengers for their flight to Dubai were being instructed to go to its departure gate. Zufan quickly asked Alya, "What is your row number and seat?"

Alya quickly looked at her boarding pass and said, "I'm in row 22, window seat."

As they got in the boarding line, Zufan said, "That's a long way from where I'm seated. So, I probably won't see you again. Don't worry. You'll do just fine. Good luck."

Nothing could help Alya now. She dutifully joined the long line leading toward her flight to Dubai. She and others in the line did not want to leave their home country, but their choice was limited to going abroad to make money. They were slaves to money and they did not like their situation, but they could not do anything to change reality.

CHAPTER FIVE

Dubai Bound

ALYA CONTINUED TO MIMIC THE actions of the more seasoned travelers. The airline agent looked at her boarding pass, then Alya quickly walked down the boarding jet bridge tunnel and to the plane's open door. After another boarding pass check with the hostess stationed at the plane's entrance, she was told to turn right on the second aisle. Alya found her row, seat letter, and slid past two seats into her window seat. She looked out the plane's small window and could see that the rain was still coming down hard. She feared the plane could not take off in such a heavy downpour. When every seat in the plane was filled, the plane's doors were shut. Her seat mates fastened their seat belts. Alya thought this was optional but was told by a passing stewardess to obey the seat belt sign. She looked up and saw a small, illuminated sign with the words, "Fasten Seat Belt." Alya struggled to latch her seat belt. This was her first experience with such a belt. The man sitting next to her noticed her trouble with the seat belt and reached over to help her, saying, "I had the same problem on my first flight."

Alya thanked him for his assistance and asked, "What are you going to for?"

The man answered, "I trained in Ethiopia as an engineer but work as a janitor at a large company in Dubai. Maybe we should be quiet now. The plane is backing up and then will taxi for takeoff. I always take this time to pray for a safe flight."

Alya wanted to ask if the plane could take off in the rain but the captain announced the flight details over the public address (PA) system, saying the plane would take off in a few minutes. Alya heard the groans of the plane as it moved into takeoff position. Her left hand tightly gripped the arm of her seat while she pressed in her right hand the small wooden cross strung around her neck. She also prayed for a safe journey. A brief glance out the window gave her a sinking feeling. More than ever she knew she was trapped in a new reality and it would be a long time before she saw her country and family again. This thought weighed heavily on her.

The plane took off into the night air and Alya opened her eyes to look out the window but all she saw was pitch blackness and the flashing lights on the plane's wing. The plane climbed to its cruising altitude and began to make more pleasant humming sounds. The lights in her cabin were turned down and the captain came on the PA system again to announce, "Welcome again to your non-stop Ethiopian Airlines flight to Dubai. There will be a flight duration of four hours. The time when we arrive in Dubai will be one hour later than Addis time. Therefore, our scheduled arrival time in Dubai is 7:00 a.m. in the morning. We've darkened the cabin so those who want can get some sleep. Thanks again for traveling with Ethiopian Airlines."

The captain's message was delivered in English and then repeated in Amharic. Alya wished she could see the captain and size up what kind of person who was in charge of piloting her first plane ride. She thought his suggestion of sleeping was a good one, but she could not sleep. Her excitement over actually being in a plane and flying to Dubai put her on edge. She was unable to sleep even a wink. She wrapped herself tightly in her netela, appreciating that it was made of two layers of spun cotton and handwoven. She closed her eyes, trying to sleep, but after a short while opened them again and examined her cramped location within the plane. She could see an illuminated sign indicating the location of restrooms but she did not know how she would get to the aisle leading to the restrooms without disturbing the two passengers asleep in the two seats adjoining hers. She decided to hold her urge to urinate. Unconsciously, she began to flip open and close the small ashtray embedded in the arm rest of her seat. Doing this made a clicking noise. She observed that this noise was annoying her seatmates, so she stopped playing with the ashtray and tried to pass the time by thinking of her family and life of growing up in Addis. Her mind was occupied, but she was not used to sitting for such a long time in one place. She wished she could get up and stretch her legs and not be like a frightened animal in a remote forest which could not remove itself from a snare.

Her senses were alerted to a the "ding" sound made when the "fasten seatbelt" sign was turned off. She saw a few people passing down the aisle in the direction of the restrooms. She wanted to do the same, but she did not want to disturb her two seatmates. The only option was to hold it a while longer. All of a sudden, the guy next to her got up and stepped into the aisle. She managed to unlatch her seatbelt and rapidly followed him and got in line for the restroom. For her, this line moved all too slowly. Finally, her turn came to enter the tiny room. She shut the door behind her and wrestled with her clothing and sat down on the toilet to relieve herself.

No sooner than she had sat down on the toilet, the door opened and another passenger tried to enter but saw her and said, "Excuse me. You need to lock the door." She quickly finished her business, pulled up her pants, and studied the inside of the door to figure out how to lock it. She saw a switching button protruding from the back of the door with the instruction to slide it one way to lock the door. She immediately locked the door and straightened her clothing and then explored the interior of the restroom, flushing the toilet which startled her with the vacuum roar it made. The small mirror above the stainless-steel lavatory gave her a chance to look deeply at her face. She could not refrain from talking to the face reflecting in the mirror. She said tearfully, "Alya, what are you doing to yourself?" She played with the faucet levers placed over the stainless-steel sink and withdrew several tissues from the slot in the wall and stuffed them into her purse. She was prepared to explore further the small room and all it offered when there was a loud thud on the door. The dull knocking reminded her that other passengers were waiting to get into the restroom. She quickly unlatched the door and exited with some embarrassment because of the longer than necessary time she took in her first visit to an airplane restroom. She passed the line of people waiting to get into the restroom with her head bowed, trying to indicate her modesty and apology for taking so long in the restroom. She wanted everyone to know that she was a shy, respectful person.

For a moment, she could not remember her row number. She had to retrieve her boarding pass stub to see that she was in row twenty-two. As she was slowly making her way in the darkened cabin to her seat, she spotted Zuhan sitting in a middle aisle seat and wanted to greet her but as she got closer to her, she could see that Zuhan was asleep. The plane was packed … she did not see an empty seat. It was a wonder to her that a plane could carry so many people.

The next novel problem she confronted was when she arrived at her row to find both of her seatmates fast asleep. She stood in the aisle in the hope that they would wake up and get up so she could enter her row and sit down. After a few minutes, the plane began to bounce and its wild movements made it difficult for her to stand. Her fear level mounted as the captain came on the PA system to announce, "We have encountered some rough turbulence. Everyone needs to sit down and fasten their seatbelts."

As soon as the captain stopped talking, the fasten seatbelt sign was turned on. A hostess approached Alya and instructed her to sit down and fasten her seatbelt.

Alya replied, "That's what I want to do, but my seatmates are asleep and blocking the way."

The hostess immediately tapped her seatmates on the shoulder and said in a firm voice, "Please allow your seatmate to take her seat and buckle up."

The two men quickly stood up and stepped out into the aisle, allowing Alya to pass to her window seat. Alya was full of apologies for disturbing her seatmates, but they groggily replied, "No problem. This is normal."

By this time, the plane was heaving with convulsions and Alya was frightened to the extent she was convinced they would crash and everybody on the plane would die. Tears began streaming down her face when she thought about leaving her family forever. She had not counted on the crashing of the plane among the many risks she was taking for the benefit of her family. Her close seatmate noticed her tears and said, "Don't fear for your safety. This kind of turbulence often happens. It won't last much longer. We'll arrive safely and on time."

His words served to calm Alya's nerves. She tried to act like nothing was happening. Suddenly, the plane was on a smoother flight path and the captain announced, "We have passed the turbulence zone and the fasten seat belt sign has been turned off. Please enjoy the remainder of your flight. We should be arriving as scheduled in about two hours."

Alya exhaled and tried to relax. There was nothing she could do but let the time pass, however the time passed all too slowly. She was beginning to think they would never arrive in Dubai when the lights in the cabin were turned back on and the hostess announced over the PA system, "A continental breakfast will be served. Please put your trays down. Enjoy your breakfast."

Her seatmates turned the small knob on the back of the seat in front of them. She saw what they did and she did the same. The hostess pushed her cart down the aisle and stopped at their row. She passed three small containers to her row and each of her seatmates took one. The man seated next to her passed her food to her. The hostess asked each of them if they wanted coffee or tea. Alya tried to pleasantly say, "Coffee please."

Alya observed how the man sitting in the seat next to her managed the food package and followed suit. It was only when the food was served that she realized the depths of her hunger. With the white plastic fork that accompanied her food, she devoured the scrambled eggs with cheese, and ate the bread slice, but she did not fiddle with the foreign packets of jelly and butter. She also savored her cup of coffee. Her plate was clean when the hostess reappeared with her cart. She saw her seat-mates arrange their empty plates and hand them to her. Of course, she did the same. It was obvious that the hostess was discarding them.

Shortly after eating breakfast, the man in the seat next to her got up and said, "I'm going to the restroom before we land."

Alya replied, "Good idea. I'll do the same."

She stood in line to the tiny toilet room, acting like she was accus-tomed to going to the restroom. Once inside she made sure she locked the door this time. While she needed time to marvel at all that was available in the cramped restroom, she sped through doing the necessary because she knew other people were waiting for her to finish. Also, she could feel the plane descending. As she stepped out of the restroom, she could hear the captain speaking again over the PA system. "This is your captain. We'll be landing in Dubai in thirty minutes. Please lock your trays in place and make sure your seats are in an upright position. Fasten your seatbelts and prepare for landing. Thank you for flying Ethiopian Airlines."

Alya rushed to regain her seat and do as the captain instructed. She could already see out her window in the distance the night lights of Dubai. Her adrenalin levels were rising. She did not know what to expect after the plane landed, but she was ready to deal with anything thrown her way. The man sitting next to her started fidgeting, so she politely asked, "What's wrong?"

The man softly answered, "Nothing. But landing is the most difficult part of flying and I always get nervous during this part of our flight. That noise you just heard was the sound made the landing wheels being lowered. If you pray, now is the time to pray."

Alya whispered prayers under her breadth as she saw the ground coming up quickly to meet the plane. Then suddenly her breath was taken away as the plane touched the runway with a jolt before smoothly coasting to a position where it turned around and headed at a slow pace to its designated place for deboarding. The successful landing caused all the passengers to applaud. They were all happy to arrive safely at their destination. The man seated next to her was all smiles now.

The plane came to a standstill and there was a loud dinging sound to indicate that passengers could prepare to disembark. The hostess announced over the PA system, "Make sure you have left nothing in the seat pockets or in the overhead compartments. Thank you again for flying with Ethiopian Airlines."

Alya had nothing to leave behind but upon hearing the hostess' words, she clutched her purse more tightly. Everything of value to her was in this purse. All she needed to prove her existence was carefully placed in this closed purse. In some ways, her purse contained her life and all its contents were needed if she were to live and work in Dubai.

The line of people trying to exit the plane moved slowly. The first thing she noticed when she approached the open plane door was the blast of hot air. Although it was morning in Dubai, it was hotter and dryer than anything she had ever experienced in Addis. In her home city the average temperature was around sixteen degrees Celsius whereas in Dubai it is twice that. She had not thought about the big changes in the weather and the stark difference in heat levels. She carefully stepped down the movable ramp stairs until she was firmly on the tarmac. Like the other passengers, she entered the nearby arrival lounge and took her place in line. A uniformed man walked up and down the line handing out immigration cards to complete. She did not have anything to write with, so she had to wait until the man next to her completed his card and asked him to borrow his ballpoint pen.

It was awkward to fill out the card while standing. She used her passport to write on the form, but this became difficult when the form asked for her passport number. She had just completed filling in her form when she was in front of the line. Anxiously, she arrived at the window of the immigration booth and slid her passport and form into the slot beneath the glass window separating her from the uniformed agent. The agent asked her questions and she had good answers for some of them. When he asked her, "How long will you stay in Dubai? She did not know what to say. At that point, a man standing behind the booth intervened and told the agent, "I will take it from here."

Alya did not know what was happening. She reluctantly followed the man to a small room across the hall behind the booth. They entered the bare room and the man said in Amharic, "My name is Biruk, I know your name is Alya. I'm responsible to escort you to a place you can wait for the Dubai man you'll be working for. Any questions?"

The man's words caught her off guard. She was relieved and reassured because he spoke in Amharic. She thought for a moment and said, "Yes my name is Alya and I have come to Dubai to work. I see that I need to trust you to do that. The sooner I can start working the better for all of us."

CHAPTER SIX

Dubai Doldrums

THE ETHIOPIAN MAN TOOK HER passport and escorted her to the baggage claim area. She immediately spotted her small old cardboard suitcase being carried around the baggage carousel conveyor belt along with many other suitcases. The man instructed her to go and collect her suitcase. She did as he said and lugged her flimsy suitcase to where he was standing with a boring look on his face. She then accompanied him as they exited the airport terminal.

They walked to a nearby parking lot and he told her to get in the back while he got behind the steering wheel. She was surprised that his car looked new. He said in Amharic under his breath, "We go to our office now. It is only a short distance. There, we'll call your patron on the phone."

For Alya, all was like a different planet. Unconsciously, she constantly fanned her netela shawl across her face in order to cool her body temperature. Although she appreciated the car's air conditioning, it was simply too hot for her and she was perspiring profusely for the first time in her life.

It was only a short ride to the office, a nondescript modern house. They entered to find another Ethiopian man seated at a simple wood desk. This man wasted no time in saying in Amharic, "Welcome to Dubai. You must be our newcomer, Alya. Make yourself at home while we call your patron to see when he's going to come to pick you up and take you to his house to begin work."

Alya sat down in one of the office chairs while a call was made on an old black telephone on the desk to her patron. Calling was not easy and the man tried calling several times before connecting with the right person. In good English, the man said clearly, "Is this Mister Ibrahim? Sir, your new maid, Alya, is here. When can you pick her up?"

Ibrahim responded and the Ethiopian man hung up and said, "Mister Ibrahim is busy today. He'll come first thing tomorrow to pick you up and settle your bill with us. You can stay the night in our spare room."

It was all too business-like to Alya. She was scared but she was not sure why. Did she have the jitters because she was in a completely different world that called for a behavior she had never practiced? Or was it simply because she would be sleeping over in a house with two Ethiopian male strangers. She did not know what to say but managed to utter these words, "It has been a long trip. I need to rest. Can you please show me my room now?"

The man seated at the desk indifferently said, "The second door on your left down the hallway. We'll bring you some food and drink a little later. Yes, get some rest because I'm sure your patron will put you to work as soon as you arrive at his house."

Alya found the right door and opened it to discover a well accoutered room with a big bed and its own bathroom. She locked her door from the inside and decided to take a bath and rest on the bed until her food arrived. She undressed and took a neatly folded fluffy towel from the top of her bed and wrapped herself with it. All this time prayers were circulating in her head, thanking God for a successful trip.

The shower stall in the small bathroom represented new challenges. She had never taken a shower before, relying on bucket baths, and did not know how to make the water flow from the shower head. Eventually, she turned one of the two knobs and cold water sprayed forcefully into the shower basin. She stepped into the downpouring stream of cold water and felt invigorated.

A bar of soap was conveniently placed in a space in the wall of the shower stall. The scent of the soap pervaded the stall. She grasped the bar of soap and washed with a sudsy lather her entire body, which had become accustomed to the cold water. She convinced herself that she was off to a good start. The welfare of her family weighed heavily on her mind, but in her current circumstances she had never had it so good.

The thick towel dried her body off with ease, comfort, and an efficiency she had never experienced before. Above the small white porcelain sink was a large circular mirror. She studied her face in the mirror and liked what she saw while she repeated softly, "I can do this. No matter what, I will do this. I have to do this for my family." She placed her suitcase on the bed, opened it and withdrew an habesha kemi, an ankle length gown made of shemma hand-woven cotton, and pulled it over her head. Fully dressed, she then lay down on her soft bed and wanted to sleep, but she also wanted to stay awake. She did not want to be asleep when her food arrived, so she sat up on the side of her bed and looked up to stare at the unsightly crack in the ceiling.

Suddenly, her boredom was broken by a loud knock and masculine voice that said, "Your food is here."

Alya unlocked and slowly opened the door. One of the Ethiopian men quickly entered her room and placed a big tray piled with food and drink on her bed. He said in Amharic, "Here's your food. When you finish, put your tray on the floor in the hallway. See you in the morning."

The man exited the room before Alya could talk to him. She wanted to ask him where he came from in Ethiopia and how long he had been doing this job. Evidently, he had no time to talk with clients or he had been instructed not to talk to her. Either way, he made her feel they were used to dealing with cases like hers and they were only doing what they did for the money. The small metal pots on the platter contained more food delicacies than she could possibly consume. Certainly, there was more and better food than she and her family would partake in any meal they were fortunate to have. There were ample heaps of rice and meat. Delicious tomato sauce with a dash of hot peppers. And there was fruit—oranges, bananas and mangoes—for dessert. There was no way Alya could eat at one sitting all the food that had been provided her, so she was already trying to figure out how she would stash some food to eat later.

Particularly appreciated was the large plastic picture of green iced tea. She could not drink it all, but she did not want to put it in the hallway with the rest of the food items. At the end of her sumptuous meal, she decided the sugary iced tea was too good to part with and placed the pitcher on the nightstand next to her bed. Minus the pitcher, she opened her door and placed the metal food platter on the floor as instructed.

Within a few minutes of depositing the food platter outside of her door, there was a loud knock and a voice which asked, "Where's the pitcher?"

Alya immediately responded in Amharic, "I'm keeping it next to my bed."

The man on the other side of the door then said, "No, you have to give it back so our inventory of dishes is correct and we won't be charged."

Upon hearing his words, Alya got up and rushed to open the door and handed the pitcher out to the man who grabbed it and rushed down the hall. Alya closed and locked the door and plopped down on the bed to get some sleep. She got under the bedspread to ward off the cool draft of the wall unit air conditioner. As much as she tried, she could not sleep. She thought it was because of the fact that she had never slept in a bed and room alone. Maybe she should turn off the electric light that bathed the pink walls of her room in bright light, but she was too afraid to sleep in the dark of her windowless room.

Her next worry was about how she could get up early the next day so she could be ready for the arrival of her patron. She did not want to rely on her caretakers to wake her, but in this instance she saw no alternative. Her sleep was long but intermittent. She tossed and turned, waiting for a knock on the door, signaling it was time to get up and ready to depart. After hours of this kind of torment, she got up and dressed herself and sat on the edge of the bed, waiting for someone to summon her. She waited for a long time. At last, the knock finally came. She quickly opened the door to find the same Ethiopian man who said, "Good morning. I hope you enjoyed your hot shower. Come to the front for a small breakfast and some coffee while we wait for your patron to arrive."

Alya thanked him, grabbed her suitcase and followed him to their office. Breakfast of bread and coffee had been placed on a rectangular low table. Alya sat down by the table and the Ethiopian man said assertively, "Eat. Your patron, Mister Ibrahim, should be here soon."

Alya asked, "You asked me to enjoy my hot shower. I took a shower with cold water. Where's the hot water?"

The Ethiopian man laughed aloud and said, "You must have turned on the cold-water knob and not also the hot-water knob."

An embarrassed Alya wanted to rush back to her room to see what he was talking about. She had always taken cold water baths and did not know there was such a thing as running hot water. This was another marvel of modern life that she was destined to experience.

Before she could finish munching on one slice of bread, a man dressed in a white robe with a white headscarf entered the office room, greeting the two Ethiopian men with the usual Arabic words, "As-Salamu Alaikum (Peace be upon you)."

The two Ethiopian men stood and immediately replied, "Wa Alaikum Salaam (and Upon You Be Peace)."

The Arab man quickly said, "Where's my new Ethiopian maid?

"She is right here, sitting in the corner eating her breakfast. Her name is Alya, but you can call her by any name you want. She's ready to go as soon as you pay us. We'll give you her passport as soon as we receive our money."

The overweight Arabic man approached the desk to scrutinize an invoice that had been prepared for him. This bill included the money advanced to Alya in Addis, as well as the hiring fee charged by the Ethiopian employment broker. The man saw the total cost and withdrew a large roll of dirhams from within his ample white gown and slapped some bills of money on the desk, saying, "This should be more than enough to cover all your expenses. Now, give me her passport and let me take away this young Ethiopian woman. My children can't wait to meet their new caretaker. We have a long drive ahead of us."

They shook hands heartily and touched their right hands to their chests as was done in the local Arab culture. The Ethiopian men were glad to conclude this deal, as they were in a hurry to prepare for the next one. They signaled to Alya to rise and walk obediently behind her new patron. Seeing that she had no other recourse, she dutifully followed her patron and sat in the back seat of his fancy car. It was too hot so she prayed that his car air conditioner worked well.

She did not turn to say goodbye to her Ethiopian handlers. Her eyes and mind were focused on the mysteries that lay before her. There were two things said by her new patron that disturbed her. He mentioned caring for his children, when she thought she would be tasked with keeping his house clean and organized. Also, he said they had a long drive ahead of them when she thought she would be working in Dubai City. The main question in her mind was, "What have I got myself into? He has my passport. I'm at his mercy."

Alya studied the foreign man as he entered the car, tucked his white traditional ankle-length robe beneath himself as he sat behind the wheel. She was to learn that this was the traditional dress of all Arab men in Dubai, and it was called a thobe or kandourah in Arabic. She would also learn that the traditional white head scarf was called a gutra and its black rope band was called an egal. It was obvious to her that she would have to learn some Arabic and about the local culture and customs to survive in this desert country.

Her patron, Ibrahim, drove fast out of town into the desolate desert. She did not know if it was proper in local culture for a woman to address a man, but she could not stand by silently while her patron drove deeper into the desert, farther away from Dubai City, and did not say a word. She weakly asked, "Where are we going? There is nothing out here?"

Ibrahim laughed and said, "Don't worry. I have a nice house in scenic Khor Fakkan, a coastal enclave located along the border with Oman between the Western Hajar Mountains, Shumaylians, and the Gulf of Oman. Khor Fakkan is part of the distant Sharjah Emirate which is located on the other side of Musandam Peninsula on the coast of the Persian Gulf. As you know, the United Arab Emirates (UAE) is composed of seven emirates and Dubai is just one of them. It's complicated. We have a map at our house that you can consult. By the way, it's one hundred kilometers to Khor Fakkan, so it'll take us a couple of hours to get there."

Alya immediately began to suffer from an information overload. She was discovering that she knew nothing about the country she was in and where she is going. She told herself that was okay and she needed to focus on her job. But what was her job? This question prompted her to ask meekly, "You mentioned the care of your children. Is that why you hired me?"

Ibrahim quickly replied, "Yes, that's why we hired you. We have two children, a toddler name Mariyam and an even younger toddler named Hammed. Also, madame is expecting our third child. Your job will be to care for our children as madame is working as a teacher and I'm away all the time for my police job."

All Alya could say was, "I understand. I'll do my best." Alya was worried. She had never taken care of small children before. She had a baby of her own, but her grandmother had always taken care of her baby. Taking care of a newborn baby and two other small children was more than she thought she could do. She worried that she was not up to doing this childcare job.

Ibrahim looked into the rearview mirror and saw the worried look on Alya's face and said, "Don't worry. All you have to do is look after our children. We have a Sri Lankan maid to clean the house and do all the washing and ironing. You'll be sharing a room with her."

Ibrahim words helped relieve some of her worries but introduced others. She had never met a Sri Lankan before. She could see already that they must get along for her to do her job well. And she did not know how sharing a room with a strange woman from a country she had never heard of would be.

CHAPTER SEVEN

Khor Fakkan

IT WAS A DAZZLING SIGHT for Alya. In her most fantastic dreams, she had never imagined such an enchanted place existed. Nestled in between low-lying—mostly bare—mountains and a sparkling ocean coastline, Alya thought she was arriving in a little-known paradise. If it were not for the stifling heat and the ferocious sunlight, this would truly be a hidden seaside paradise. Khor Fakkan was a small city but modern. It possessed everything one would need and was also something of a tourist haven. If you like pristine beaches and snorkeling, you would love Khor Fakkan. There were nicely manicured parks and modern shopping centers. Alya could not wait to see and experience everything this wonderland had to offer.

Ibrahim drove through the town to his upscale house and parked in the driveway, proudly saying in his stilted English, "This is my house. Let's go inside to meet my family and show you your room. Most importantly, my two children are eager to meet their new caretaker."

Alya was proud they taught English in the schools in Ethiopia from the seventh grade. She had a high school education, so she had a high proficiency in English. Now she could see the importance of knowing this international language. For the first time, she would actually have to use it in her daily life.

Alya fetched her suitcase and followed Ibrahim into his lovely home. She was nervous and fighting to control the emotions generated by her introduction to a new life in a different world. With her heart stuck in her throat, she had difficulty greeting all household members, including the two small children who were was assigned to her care. The oldest of the two children was a girl named Mariyam. She was three years old. The youngest was a boy named Hammed. He had just turned one year of age. The two children exhibited shyness in spite of Alya's expressions of kind tenderness toward them. Ibrahim saw how his children were acting and said, "Don't mind their behavior. Once they get used to you, they won't be able to get enough of you. Your job requires a close connection between you."

Alya nodded in the affirmative. Ibrahim proceeded to show her around the house. He pointed to one wing of the house and said, "My parents live on that side of the house. You'll probably never have to go to that side. Let me show you your room so you can freshen up and get to work with your two new toddlers."

She followed Ibrahim to the end of an obscure hallway where he threw open the door to expose a nice room with two twin beds. He pointed out that this room had its own bathroom. Alya was wondering who the other bed was for when Ibrahim said, "You'll be sharing this room with our other servant, Busha. You'll meet her soon and get to know all about her. As I said before, she's responsible for keeping the house clean but also washes the dishes and clothes, which she irons" A stream of thoughts were running through Alya's head. She could not wait to meet Busha. She hoped they could be good friends and that Busha could help with her orientation to this new life. A lot depended on what kind of relationship she would have with Busha.

Alya followed Ibrahim out of her assigned room into the central living area. She spotted a middle-aged woman with a lighter skin complexion than her golden-brown color hovering in the kitchen. She noticed that this woman had her head covered like a Muslim. Timidly, Alya asked, "Who is that woman?"

Ibrahim smiled and said, "That's Busha. She has been working for us for several years. You will be friends with her. Go and introduce yourself then occupy yourself with the children. Remember my wife is expecting another child in a couple of months. That'll give you three of our babies to take care of."

Alya did not want to say anything, but some words sprang softly from her mouth, "Where's your wife?"

Ibrahim said with the least concern, "She's at work at our local Arabic elementary school. You'll meet her when she comes home. Her name is Hadjara. Now, excuse me. I have to check on my parents and go to work at the local police department."

His white gown ruffled as he passed her by, brushing her with a slight puff of wind as he rushed to the other side of the house, leaving her standing with her mouth open as if she were prepared to say something. After taking a few deep breaths, she turned to go to the kitchen to introduce herself to Busha. She entered the kitchen and Busha stopped washing dishes, dried her hands on her dark blue apron and then placed them humbly over her chest to welcome Alya.

This was an awkward moment. Neither of them knew what to say. Finally, Busha said, "I'm Busha. I'm a Tamil from Sri Lanka. My Tamil name is Avira. But because of my Islamic faith I'm called Busha here. Busha means in English 'good news' and Avira means 'brave and strong.' My people are spread across the world, mostly doing low-level jobs like I'm doing here."

Alya was speechless. She did not expect Busha to introduce herself like this. She was getting used to Ibrahim's English accent and now she was hearing a different English accent spoken by the imposing Busha. She was intimidated by corpulent Busha, who was physically larger and much older than her. Particularly, the length of her black hair, descending from beneath her white headscarf to her waistline, made her lose her train of thought. With much hesitation, she said, "Pleased to meet you ma'am. My name is Alya. I'm from Ethiopia. My name in my native language, Amharic, means 'highborn.' This is my first job abroad. I hope to learn a lot from you. By which name should I call you? I see that we share the same bedroom. I hope you understand my English."

Busha smiled sweetly and said, "I think it is more appropriate in this Arab land that you call me Busha. Your name, Alya, is fine for here as it's a name in Arabic too. I don't know what to tell you but this is a good family to work for. You do your job well and you'll hear no complaints. Never forget that you belong to them now and you are thus obligated to serve them. They control our lives by retaining our passports. I appreciate that they have never missed a monthly pay date and take me to the local Western Union office so I can send a money order to my family back home. I admit that you'll have your hands full taking care of two toddlers. I don't know how you'll manage when the new baby arrives. I'm glad that I don't have your job."

Alya was coping with all the information Busha had voluntarily provided to her. She did not know what to say as a response to what Busha had said so forthrightly. After much hesitation, she said only a sincere, "Thank you."

Busha said, "I have to finish washing, drying, and putting up these dishes. I also have other housework to do. You should go find your two toddlers and start caring for them in the best way that you can. Good luck. See you later."

Alya was hesitant to ask anything more at this point but she had to ask, "When do you get time off?"

Busha laughed and said, "That's a funny question because there is no time off. My job and especially your childcare job is every day, night and day."

Again Alya thanked Busha and said, "I better go see the children and deal with their needs."

Busha grunted her assent and said, "Yes, you must bond yourself with the children for better or worse."

Alya searched the house for the children and found them hiding behind an opened hallway door. She spoke tenderly to them, assuring them they had nothing to fear. She feared that they did not understand her English, so she spoke to them in the most soothing words she could formulate. She slowly held out her hand to Mariyam who grasped it and told her, "Come out so I can see you better."

Hesitantly, Mariyam stepped forward and Hammed moved forward and took Mariyam's other hand. Alya asked, "Have you taken a bath?" Mariyam shook her head from side-to-side, indicating that they had not taken a bath, so Alya asked, "Where's the bathroom and where do you keep your clothes?"

As Mariyam and Hammed moved away from the door, Alya spotted on the smooth shiny brown vinyl floor a small pile of excrement. Evidently, little Mariyam was not wearing underwear under her house gown and decided to let her bowel movement flow. In spite of the bad smell emitted from this heap of poop, Alya told herself that she would deal with this later. For the time being, she asked in a soft and untroubled voice to Mariyam, "Show me your room? Let's get you and Hammed some clothes and towels and go take a bath."

Mariyam led them to her well-decorated bedroom and pointed to her ornate chest of drawers, indicating she had some clothes in the drawers. Alya looked in the drawers and withdrew some clothes for Mariyam. She asked, "Where's Hammed's clothes?"

"In his room. He's a boy so we've separate rooms," said Mariyam.

In her head, Alya was computing all the information she was receiving early on in her first day of work. She was hearing that the two children had their own bedrooms, making caring for them more difficult. Evidently, being of different sexes had something to do with this reality.

They proceeded to Hammed's bedroom, which was next to Mariyam's. Alya lifted Hammed into his baby bed and he immediately started crying loudly. In spite of the anguished cries of Hammed, she quickly pulled from his chest of drawers some clothes for him to wear after she had given him a bath. As she was going to lift Hammed out of the baby bed, Mariyam said in the best English she possessed, "Leave him there. He can't be in the bathroom while I undress and take a bath."

This kind of separation of the sexes of children for them to take a bath and get dressed was an unforeseen obstacle to Alya's mental plans for caring for these two toddlers. Maybe this had something to do with Arab culture. She certainly did not want to violate any household rules or cultural values. If this was the way things were done here, she would do it their way. But how could she care well for baby children when she could barely care for herself.

Alya left Hammed crying loudly in his baby bed and took Mariyam in one hand, her clothes in her other hand, and asked Mariyam, "Show me where you take a bath." Mariyam pointed to a hallway door. Alya opened the door to reveal a well-furnished bathroom. She closed the toilet seat and sat Mariyam on it while she ran lukewarm water in the plugged bathtub. When the water in the bathtub was about three inches high, she asked Mariyam, "Undress and step into the bathtub so I can wash you with this big bar of soap and clean washcloth."

As this was Mariyam's first time appearing naked in front of Alya, she shyly took off her clothes and stepped into the warm water contained by the bathtub. Alya acted as all was normal and told Mariyam, "Get down in the water and then stand up so I can wash you good. Don't be timid. You've got to be clean."

Mariyam did as instructed. She was trying to get used to Alya, who was determined to get used to her new childcare job in the Arab world. Alya scrubbed Mariyam's little, thin body from head to toe, and asked her, "Should I wash your hair?"

Without saying a word, Mariyam shook her head negatively. Alya said nothing about the smears of excrement she washed from her buttocks and legs. She was thinking this was an accident and would not occur again. A well-rinsed Mariyam stepped out of the bathtub and Alya took the fluffy towel wrapped around her little body and dried her off and slipped on her fresh white house gown. She found a hairbrush and comb next to the lavatory and used them to arrange her long silky black hair. She moved quickly because she wanted to fetch the bawling Hammed and wash him. She drained the water from the bathtub and cleaned the tub before plugging it and running into it some warm water. She was thinking how lucky Mariyam and Hammed were to have a bathtub and warm running water. These were modern luxuries she had never experienced in Ethiopia.

While the water was running into the bathtub, she rushed to get Hammed and take him for his bath. He was easier to deal with and held on to Alya tightly as she carried him to the children's bathroom. Alya quickly undressed him and placed him in the bathtub. Mariyam had already left the bathroom and was waiting in the hallway behind an opened door. Alya worked to finish bathing Hammed quickly so she could attend to Mariyam and the mess she left behind the hallway door.

She dressed Hammed quickly in his gown and combed his black curly hair. She found that he was a sweet little boy who was greatly attached to his older sister. She swung the bathroom door open, expecting to join Mariyam and go to the kitchen to eat something, but Mariyam was not there. She lifted Hammed and began to search for Mariyam.

Alya carried the overweight Hammed in her arms as she looked everywhere for Mariyam, calling her name. As little as Hammed was, he pointed to the door at the end of the hallway. Alya told herself that Mariyam could not possibly be there … that was the spot where she had already left an odoriferous dump of her excrement on the floor. In spite of her thinking, she partially shut this door to find Mariyam with a big smile on her childish face.

Alya asked Mariyam, "Come out of there. That's no place for you to be."

Mariyam stepped out and Alya spied on the floor a fresh poop on top of the old poop. Her first impulse was to rub Mariyam's nose in the poop and tell her sternly to not do such a dirty thing again. On second thought, she recognized these were her bosses' children, and she could not do that if she wanted to keep her job. She settled for turning Mariyam around and saying firmly, "You see that? You should not do that again. You should do that by sitting on the toilet in the bathroom. Understand?"

Mariyam responded by smiling and saying in a gay manner, "Okay."

Alya's arms were tired from carrying the chubby Hammed. She told herself that she had to clean the excrement up quickly. She thought the best time to do this ugly task was when her two charges took their nap, so she asked Mariyam, "When do you take a nap?"

Mariyam quickly responded, "What's a nap?"

"That's a daytime sleep. When do you do that?" an irritated Alya explained.

"We only sleep at night," replied Mariyam who continued by saying, "Let's play."

Alya could not help but chuckle when Mariyam said that in her small child voice and replied by saying, "No playing until we eat something and clean up the mess you made. Let's go see Busha in the kitchen."

With Hammed in her tired arms, she took hold of Mariyam's hand as they walked toward the kitchen. Busha was there as usual and she asked as Alya and the two toddlers approached, "How's it going with you and your two charges?"

A worried Alya replied, "It's only been a couple of hours with them and I'm already exhausted."

Busha solemnly replied, "You better get used to it as you have many more months to go and there is another baby on the way."

Alya thought for a moment and then described to Busha what Mariyam had done behind the hallway door. Busha laughed and said, "She does that all the time. You'll need to get used to cleaning that spot. Make that part of your job. Use the dustpan and dump the mess in the toilet, and then use toilet paper and soap to clean the dustpan and the floor, flushing all down the toilet. It will be quite an achievement if you can break her of that habit."

Alya's first day on the job had just begun and she was deeply depressed. She did not think she would ever be capable of caring for her two toddlers, and when the baby arrived that could be the last straw. The main question reverberating in her head was, "Should I try to quit today, this week or try to go on in my new job for a while longer?"

But she was committed to helping her Ethiopian family. She could not get away from the thought that she was like a sacrificial lamb being led to her own slaughter. This was a serious matter that required much prayer. She could not wait to retire to her room so she could pray to God, Jesus, and the Holy Spirit and, particularly, the Virgin Mary.

CHAPTER EIGHT

Childcare Calamities

"OKAY," SAID MARIYAM.

No matter what Alya said to Mariyam, she always said, "Okay."

Then it dawned on Alya that was all Mariyam knew how to say well in English. She asked herself why she had not thought of this before. Mariyam's language was Arabic and that was the only language she understood. More than ever, Alya knew that she had to learn how to speak some Arabic to do her job.

Alya observed Busha and rushed to ask her, "Do you speak any Arabic?"

Busha replied, "I learned only the words that I have to do my job. Your job requires more words in Arabic than I know."

"Please you can start by teaching me the words you know, but tell me where I can learn more words," said an exasperated Alya.

Now it was Busha's turn to say, "Okay, here are some of the words I know in Arabic. Maybe you need a notebook to write down in your way these words. I have a small notebook in our room that I can give you, but we'll have to wait until bedtime to give this to you and tell you the little Arabic I know. In the meantime, be thinking of the Arabic words you want to know how to say."

A fretful Alya said, "Who can teach me Arabic? My salary depends on learning Arabic, and without my salary my family back home will suffer."

The older Busha interjected, "You'll learn from the children. Also, when our madame has the time, you can learn from her. As you know, she's a good teacher. Now, go. Your kids need you."

Alya found her two toddlers watching their large, big-screen TV in the living room. They were watching an English version of cartoons filled with action characters and much amusing music. As they were too close to the TV screen, Alya moved them farther back onto the living room carpet. No sooner had she moved them back, than they moved to their original positions. She wanted to scold them for sitting so close to the TV, but she did not know how to do so in Arabic.

The children were transfixed by the colorful images and musical sound emitted by the TV. Alya was also interested in seeing cartoons for the first time on such a large-screen TV, so she sat down on a nearby sofa. She could see that watching TV was a good way to pass the time with the children. And it was a time she enjoyed. Anything that kept the kids occupied in a safe environment was a good thing, especially as she had no good idea about what to do with them other than making sure they ate, bathed. dressed and went to bed on time.

She asked herself, "What's a good bedtime?"

The clock on the kitchen wall told the local time. Alya had to learn how time was told in Khor Fakkan because they told the time of day and night differently than her native Ethiopia which uses a twelve-hour clock, with twelve hours from 6 a.m. to 6 p.m. and another twelve hours from 6 p.m. to 6 a.m. in the morning. She thought 8 p.m. local time would be three o'clock in the afternoon at home in Addis Ababa.

Alya also had to learn how to read the international calendar pinned on a wall of the kitchen. In her country, they used a solar Julian calendar which was seven to eight days ahead of the lunar Gregorian calendar commonly used, and the new year in her Ethiopian world started at a different date, several months ahead of the international community. Alya had been transplanted to another planet that used a different calendar and way of telling time than she had been accustomed to her whole life.

She was excited to learn that Mariyam was learning some English from watching cartoons on TV. This would make it easier for her to communicate with Mariyam, who would speak Arabic to Hammed whose speaking ability was limited to a few Arabic words. When Mariyam told little Hammed something, Alya would learn some Arabic. In this way, over time she would learn most of the Arabic she needed to do her childcare job.

The day passed without any major event except for the time Alya spent cleaning up Mariyam's mess behind the hallway door. She scoured the floor the best she could and dumped all in the toilet and flushed it several times. It was a delight to her to see a flush toilet work so efficiently. This was something she had never seen. She wondered where all the stuff flushed down the toilet went.

Alya heard the front door open and close. This sound notified her that she was about to meet her madame, the mother of her two toddler charges. She said, "Let's go see your mother. I'm sure she'll be in a hurry to see you."

The two children ran away screaming at the top of their lungs, "Umm."

Alya quickly learned that Umm was the Arabic word for mother. She followed the children as she was eager to meet her new madame, Hadjara, who hugged her two children and asked them in Arabic where her new childcare maid was. The kids pointed at Alya and said, "Al."

Hadjara was dressed in a black abaya, a floor-length cloak, which covered her everyday clothing. It was decorated with sparkling sequins and the edge of its sleeves were stitched with a colorful embroidered pattern. She covered her head with a matching silk hijab scarf and her face was covered with a traditional black niqab. Her tall physical frame and milky-white, smooth skin and long black hair distinguished her.

As soon as she entered her house and was out of public sight, she quickly removed her head and facial coverings. She approached Alya and said politely in perfect English, "I'm happy that you have arrived and met my children. As you know my name is Hadjara and I'm their mother. As you can see from my midriff bulge, I'm expecting a third male child in two months. Do you have any questions for me?"

Alya was so stunned by Hadjara's glamourous personage and the royal delivery of her words, she had difficulty responding in a mature manner to her question. Too much time was passing, so she simply said, "Pleased to meet you. I believe all is going well on this first day of working for you. Maybe you can ask Mariyam in Arabic to see what she thinks of me and my work."

Hadjara turned to Mariyam and directed a stream of Arabic words toward her. Mariyam replied with a smile, exposing some of her new teeth, and said a few words in her small child's voice. Hadjara turned to Alya and said, "Mariyam has nothing to say about you and your work. Maybe she's too young to understand all that I'm saying. I see they are referring to you as "Al." I hope that's all right. Anything else before I go and cook dinner?"

Alya felt obliged to say what was on her mind and said, "Madame. Excuse me, but can you teach me some Arabic so that I can communicate better with the children?"

Hadjara lost no time in replying, "Of course, just let me know what you want to say in Arabic. It's only fair and right that you learn our national language. Our second language is English, so I hope my children will learn some English from you. Anyway, let me go change my clothes and then get busy in the kitchen. I want to prepare a grand mezze in honor of Alya, or should I say 'Al,' joining our family."

Hadjara disappeared into the back of the house. Alya returned with the children to watch TV in the living room which adjoined the kitchen. Busha was waiting for Hadjara's return, always prepared to do her bidding. Everybody was hungry and ready for Hadjara to work her culinary magic in the kitchen.

Hadjara returned. She was dressed in an attractive long, red modern dress. She entered the kitchen with a flourish, donning a simple white apron that was hanging on the wall. The kitchen was divided from the living room by a granite countertop, so Hadjara could see Alya and the children watching TV. She called out to Alya, "Come. I can teach you some Arabic while I prepare our meal, or should I say in Arabic, 'wajabaat.'"

Alya obediently walked quickly to the kitchen to join Busha at the entry way. Hadjara looked up and said, "I will remove various plates of taa'am from the fridge and say the name in Arabic of each plate as I hand them to Busha for placement on the dining table. In that way, you can start learning the Arabic names of different foods."

"Taa'am is the Arabic word for food," whispered Busha to Alya.

Alya listened intently to Hadjara's Arabic words as she withdrew the plates of food from the fridge, warming as needed some of their plates in her spiffy large microwave oven, before handing them to Busha for placement on the large, well-lacquered big table in the dining room that was located across the hallway from the kitchen. Alya found this a good way to learn the Arabic words for food items, but she did not know how this would help her communicate with the children.

She did note that all the food plates smelled delicious. The aroma of the spices used in each dish was a new experience for her. They had many exotic spices in Ethiopia, but she was smelling for the first-time spices unknown to her. She could not wait to taste each of the mysterious dishes.

The dining table was all set and Hadjara went about the house clapping her hands and calling for all in the house to come and eat. She was hoping her husband could join them at the table, but often his work kept him occupied until late in the night. The children came and were lifted into their highchairs. Ibrahim's elderly parents joined them. Alya was ready to advance toward the table when Busha gently said, "We wait until they've finished, then we make a plate for ourselves as we remove the plates from the table and place any leftovers in the fridge. We eat on the countertop and never at the table. This is how servants do. The table is reserved for family."

Alya nodded her understanding and said, "I can see you can't learn all the ways of this household in one day."

Busha chuckled silently and muttered under her breath, "You've got that right. You have a long way to go and going the distance will require much discipline and persistence. Always keep in mind that you're putting up with all this for your family back home."

Tears swelled up unexpectedly in Alya's eyes. She did not know why she was teary eyed. Maybe it was because of her doubts about her own capacity to stay the course and become an obedient servant and childcare professional. She was fearful that she could not do this job for a long time. She wondered how she would get out of this job when the time came and return to her family in Ethiopia. This was her first time to be away from her family and she was experiencing profound culture shock. Alya struggled to suppress her strong desire to go home. She knew she had to endeavor to become accustomed to her new situation far from home. She blamed herself and her eagerness to earn some money to send to her family. Running away was not an option. For better or worse, she was stuck in this house in a foreign country. She felt hopelessly trapped.

Busha noted Alya's quietness and could see that she was preoccupied with her thoughts. She soothingly said to Alya, "Don't worry so much. Give it some time. You'll become used to this life of servitude."

Alya told herself that she would never get used to her new life but if Busha could adapt, so could she. She prayed silently to her Orthodox Christian God and saints for the strength and intelligence she needed to endure in her first overseas job. Her prayers were interrupted by Busha's reminder, "Be prepared to bring dishes from the dining room to the kitchen. They're almost finished eating and drinking."

Alya stood ramrod straight on full alert. She was prepared to help Busha carry the dishes to the kitchen and clean the dining room. For certain, she was hungry and thus eager to eat this new food. Her plan to help Busha was upset when Hadjara came up to her and said, "Al, my dear, please take my children and prepare them for bed. I'm tired and wish to retire to my bedroom."

Hadjara turned to go to her bedroom, leaving Mariyam and Hammed with Alya who quickly said to Busha, "Please save a plate for me while I put these two children in bed."

Alya took the hands of the sleepy children and led them to their bedrooms. She first went to Hammed's bedroom and undressed him on a spare bed. She powdered him and put a fresh nappy on him. She dressed him in warm pajamas she found in the chest of drawers. He was already asleep when Alya placed him in his big crib and tucked blankets over him. She wanted to ask Mariyam if she had done everything right with putting Hammed to bed and if he slept through the night, but she did not possess the Arabic words to do so. She took the somnolent Mariyam in hand and went out the bedroom door, leaving it slightly open so she could hear if Hammed woke up. They walked down the hallway to Mariyam's bedroom which was located next to Hammed's.

Mariyam showed Alya her sleeping gown and undressed herself to put it on. Mariyam made a curious gesture which Alya interpreted correctly as a desire to urinate. They walked across the hall to the bathroom and Mariyam sat on the toilet to relieve herself. When she was finished, she flushed the toilet and clasped Alya's hand as they walked across the narrow hallway to Mariyam's bedroom.

Mariyam hopped into her child's bed and covered up. To Alya's surprise, Mariyam hugged her tightly and then said softly, "Shuran. Tisbah 'ala kheir."

There was nothing like a child's sweet hug to cure all that ails one. She did not know what Mariyam said in her kiddish Arabic, but her kind gesture brought tears to Alya's eyes. Mariyam had made her forget all her worries and to give thanks to God for surviving her first day on the job. She tip-toed out of Mariyam's bedroom and closed the door softly.

She hurriedly went to the kitchen to find Busha waiting for her with her plate of food. Busha said, "Hurry eat your food. It's time to bathe and go to bed. What would you like to drink?"

"Just water please," said Alya as she examined her food plate mixture.

Busha took a clean glass from the overhanging cupboard and went to the kitchen sink to turn on the cold water tap to fill the glass. Alya saw how she was filling her glass with water and asked, "That's something we can't do in my country. Are you sure the water is okay?"

Busha sounded her usual small laugh and said, "You live in a poor country where it is unsafe to drink water from the tap. This is a rich country that provides potable water everywhere. Now, excuse me. I'm going to our room to take my nightly hot shower."

Alya was quick to speak, "Mariyam hugged me and said a few words in Arabic that I did not understand."

Busha quickly said, "She probably said, 'shuran, tiskah 'ala kheir,' which means 'Thank you and good night.' Now, eat your food. Leave your dirty plate in the sink. Enjoy your pure ma'an. That's Arabic for water."

The quietness of the house enveloped Alya and helped put her deep in thought as she hesitantly ate all the strange food on her plate. Although the food was new to her, she found it tasty and to her liking. She was hungry, so she ate it all. She washed it all down with an enjoyable glass of ma'an.

As she drained the last drop of tap water from her glass, she thought maybe things were not as bad as they seemed. She dug deep into her being to find the force she needed to overcome all obstacles to succeeding. As she scraped the last bit of food from her plate, she told herself, "I got this."

CHAPTER NINE

Home Contact

Alya found Busha fast asleep in their darkened bedroom. Her intention was to take a quick shower, but she was exhausted. Going to bed was a better option. On the nightstand next to her bed was a notebook and ballpoint. Busha had kept her promise. She could now note the Arabic words and phrases she was learning. She was too tired to think about this or anything else. All she wanted at that moment was to lay down and sleep. She crawled under the covers and quickly drifted into a deep slumber.

The next thing she knew Busha was pulling on her big toe which stuck up from beneath her bed covers. Busha said emphatically, "Time to get up. Your two babies are crying."

Busha left the room and an alarmed Alya sprang out of bed and rushed to the bathroom to do her toiletries. She threw on some clothes and exited the room, running down the hall to Hammed and Mariyam's rooms. The day was just dawning and she was surprised that the children were already up. She was more surprised when she found the stately Hadjara holding Hammed, trying to rock him in her arms to quiet him down. Hadjara said, "I know this is only your second day, but you need to be more attentive to my children. Maybe you should sleep in Hammed's room."

An intimidated Alya blushed and said softly with her head bowed, "Yes, ma'am. I'll start sleeping in Hammed's room tonight."

Hadjara handed Hammed to Alya saying, "Take him. I need to go and get ready for my work. Maybe you can carry him to Mariyam's room because she also needs attention. Salaam alaikoum."

Alya knew that Hadjara's final words meant 'peace be upon you.' This greeting was often used by the Muslim people in her own country. She did not know how to keep Hammed and Mariyam quiet and happy. They entered Mariyam's room but the little girl was not there. They stepped out into the hallway and heard a slight grunting sound coming from behind the door at the end of the hall.

Immediately, Alya expected Mariyam to be hiding behind the door to do her nasty business. Therefore, it was not surprising to find the smiling Mariyam behind the door straddling a stinky pile of her excrement on the floor. Rapidly, Alya grabbed Mariyam with her free hand while balancing Hammed in her arms and dashed with her in tow the short distance down the hallway to the children's bathroom. Alya placed Mariyam on the toilet seat and said in English in no uncertain terms, "Sit there and do what you did in the hallway. This is how you should relieve yourself."

Of course, Mariyam did not understand a word that Alya said, but she could tell from the emotional tone of Alya's voice that she was not happy with her. Mariyam hung her head briefly but then tried to cheer up Alya by smiling. Alya could not help but laugh at Mariyam's antics. She asked herself, "What am I going to do with this little girl?"

She went through the same routine with bathing and dressing the children as she did the day before and would do every day of the week going forward. She also had to take the children to the kitchen countertop to feed them bowls of sugary cereal immersed in cold milk from the fridge. Fortunately, the TV broadcast cartoons nonstop and this captivated the attention of the children, leaving Alya some time to clean up Mariyam's mess and do other chores.

Alya was determined to break Mariyam's habit of doing her dirty business behind the hallway door. As she cleaned up her daily dump behind the door, she contemplated ways she could prevent her from doing this nasty act again. She tried to block the door with one of the unused dining room chairs, but Mariyam would just scoot it away and go about her daily dirty business. She tried to catch Mariyam as she sneaked into the hallway and pull her into the bathroom to sit on the toilet, but no matter how long she sat on the toilet, she did not have a bowel movement. No matter what Alya did to break Mariyam's nasty habit, there was no change.

Alya asked Busha about what she should do and was told, "Everything has been tried to get her to change and nothing has worked. I don't know what to tell you."

"What about having the door removed so she no longer can hide behind it?" Alya asked Busha.

Busha chuckled in her usual way and said, "To do that, you'd have to ask the permission of the masters of the house and explain to them why you want to do that. Do you really want to explain what their precious daughter is doing?"

"You know that I would never dare explain that to them, but they should know about the problem I'm dealing with," said Alya.

"They will not know that until they take care of their own children and that may be never," said Busha in a solemn tone.

Alya returned to the living room to watch cartoons with Mariyam and Hammed. She was always ready to attend to their every need. They were spoiled but that was just how things were in this foreign land where all Arab children are spoiled. Alya found her new life confining and deadly monotonous. She knew now how prisoners felt doing the same things every day in the same place while the whole world was calling to her. She longed to be free to do what she wanted, but freedom did not pay the bills. She did not like that her position of servitude did not allow her to have the freedom of her dreams.

Weekends did offer Alya and Busha some respite from their daily routines. They and the two children piled into Hadjara's car early in the morning and went shopping in the congested center of town at the lively open market and the busy modern supermarket. Their eyes followed Hadjara's every move through the dense crowds of people. Alya pushed Hammed in his stroller and held Mariyam's hand tightly. The open market reminded Alya of the marketplaces in her home country. Many of those managing market stalls were from somewhere else. There were many groupings like hers with an Arabic woman in the lead and her dutiful household servants behind them, ready to take whatever was bought. Sometimes Alya thought she spied some other Ethiopian women, accompanying their masters and wanted to greet them in Amharic but remained silent because she thought speaking to her compatriots would be improper. This opportunity to get out of the house was a festive occasion for Alya and Busha.

Hadjara enjoyed what she was doing, but this was a duty that her role as a wife was thrust upon her. Hadjara's freedom was also limited by her duties as a mother and a wife, a school employee, and by her overarching culture. Alya thought, "My master will never be free, but someday I will be." On the other hand, Alya's master would always belong to the wealthy upper class that ruled and lived lives of luxury, having people like her do all the jobs they did not want to do. Alya looked across the crowds of people and could easily see that most of them were not from the UAE. She realized she was in a rich foreign country that depended on the cheap labor provided by foreigners from poor countries.

Alya found that these weekly outings provided an excellent opportunity to learn some Arabic from her madame. Every time Hadjara purchased an item she would say distinctly in Arabic what she was buying. Alya would repeat after her and Hadjara would pleasingly correct her pronunciation.

There was an impressive variety of items available for sale in the supermarket. A wide-eyed Alya asked Hadjara, "Wow. Are all these items produced in the UAE?"

Hadjara laughed and said, "Nonsense. The UAE produces almost nothing. All these items are imported. The only thing that is grown locally are dates."

Alya was puzzled. She wondered where all the money came from to import this vast array of items. She could not help but ask, "How can your country afford to import all this?"

"That's a complicated question. We have some oil but over the years we have become an international financial center and a place for the world to do business. Our ruling families have had the foresight to make our country a peaceful haven that attracts talent from across the world. It's hard to describe but the wise fruits of our leaders are evident."

Hadjara's words were more than Alya could digest. This made her reluctant to ask any more questions. Obviously, she had a lot to learn about her surroundings. She knew for sure that she should never express anything negative about the families which had ruled the emirates for decades. For the best, she stirred her thoughts away from politics or religion.

On pay day, Hadjara would take Alya and Busha on her usual shopping trip, making a special stop at the Western Union office so they could send money home. Hadjara waited patiently in her car with the children. She kept the car motor running so she could run the air conditioning. Although it was early in the morning, it was already hot outside. Alya and Busha wanted to hurry and conclude their business with Western Union so that their madame would not have to wait long, but they were not the only ones wanting to send money home and thus the line to the counter was long and moving slowly. Alya followed Busha and duplicated her every move.

Busha had sent money many times so she was in the system, thus her time at the counter with the agent was brief. This was Alya's first time sending money, so it took her a little longer. She gave her name and the name of the person she wanted to send the money to. She also had to say the country and city this person lived in. Then the teller asked her how much she wanted to send. Alya blurted out, "All of it."

The non-Arab teller sensibly asked, "How much is all?"

"All my monthly salary of two hundred dollars."

The man behind the counter said, "Okay, but it won't be for that amount after we deduct our transfer fee. All is fine. Here's your receipt. You can communicate the number on the receipt and the amount to ease good reception. Any Western Union outlet can pay."

Alya left the Western Union office in a daze as several questions were tormenting her head. She told herself that there was no way that she could get any words to her family which did not have a workable phone. Busha could see that Alya was disturbed and said softly, "Don't worry. Next to the supermarket is a small shop that sells calling cards." Alya tightened her grip on Hammed and Mariyam who were squeezed between her and Busha in the back seat of the car. She was hesitant to admit to Busha that her family did not have a phone but finally she told Busha in barely inaudible voice, "Our home phone is not connected."

Busha saw how distressed Alya had become and said in a soothing tone, "Don't stress yourself. We'll find a way to solve your problem. Maybe the Ethiopian woman who works at the small shop can help you."

Alya's ears perked up when Busha mentioned another Ethiopian woman. She could not wait to meet another Habesha and speak to her in Amharic. Hadjara excused them to go to the shop for a short while and she entered the supermarket with her two children. As soon as Busha went into the adjoining shop, the woman behind the counter knew that she wanted to buy a calling card.

The woman did not see the diminutive Alya trailing Busha. It was only when Alya got on the side of Busha at the counter that the woman instantly recognized another compatriot and let out a torrent of words in Amharic to welcome Alya and introduce herself as "Fanaawit." It was a joyous encounter. They had much they wanted to ask each other, but they did not have the time to do so. They spoke briefly, trying to pack as many as words as possible into a few minutes. Their conversation came to an abrupt close when Busha paid for her card and said, "We have to go. Our madame is waiting for us."

Fanaawit said hurriedly, "Wait a second. I want to give this paper to Alya with my contacts. I'll also want to write down her address in Addis before I forget. Go quickly now before you get in trouble with your madame."

Alya's head was spinning. Her contact with another Ethiopian and speaking with her in their native tongue had completely thrown her off balance. She came down to Earth when Busha admonished her by saying, "You have to exercise more discipline. Always save back enough money in your salary for a calling card. So when our madame gives us permission to use her house phone, you can call home."

"I know that now and by the time I get paid next month I'll know what to do. Also, by that time my family should have their house phone hooked up," Alya said quickly as they entered the supermarket.

After they entered the highly-air-conditioned store, they looked about for their madame and her two children. As they could not find their madame quickly, Alya relayed to Busha, "Fanaawit will give a message to her sister in her next call and ask her to go and see my family with the number and amount of money they can get at their nearest Western Union outlet. Her sister will also tell my family to renew their phone hookup and tell her sister the number so the next time we come here, Fanaawit will give me the number. A bit complicated but all very promising for next month."

Busha could only say, "Sounds good. Let's hope it all works out for you next month. You should give the telephone number of madame's house phone, so your family can call you in case of an emergency. Always keep in mind the difference between local time and the time in your country. There's Madame at the meat counter, so be prepared to get back to work."

Hadjara was the first to speak. "Where have you been? You've been gone too long. Alya please take charge of the children while I see the meats they have for sale."

Alya immediately took ahold of Hammed's stroller and gripped Mariyam's hand. The children were tired and wanted to go home. Hadjara asked Busha in a sharp tone, "What do you think if I buy camel meat. It's on sale at a special price."

Busha did not like camel meat but said, "Good choice. I'll get a shopping cart."

Alya had never eaten camel meat, but she was willing to try everything. After the purchase of a big package of camel meat, Hadjara went to a part of the store that displayed dates and bought several packets of dates as she said, "There are two food items that are always available in our sand-covered emirates … camels and dates. We snack on the latter all the time and we never travel without them."

She did not want to say anything and she was fully occupied with the children but her curiosity got the best of her, so Alya timidly asked, "Excuse me, but I never seen a camel here and I've never seen a camel in my life. Where are your camels?"

Hadjara smiled at this innocent question and said, "Almost every Emirati family has several camels which are kept for them at one of our oasis farms. We have some camels and when we get a break, we'll go see them. Camels are an important part of Emirati tradition. We all love and respect our camels. A good camel is very costly. We only eat the meat of old or disabled camels. The fastest camels are raced. Let's go now and check out of the store and get our car cooled down so nothing spoils."

CHAPTER TEN

One Too Many

THE DAYS PASSED QUICKLY AS they turned into months. Alya got her calling card and her family in Addis got their money and phone hooked up. They talked once a month on the masters' house phone. She had made caring for Hammed and Mariyam routine. Sleeping in Hammed's room helped her do her childcare duties better. She became quite proficient in speaking and understanding the Arabic she needed to know to do her job well.

Everything was going smoothly until Hadjara gave birth to baby Moussa. He was a good baby, but he required constant attention. Hadjara got a lengthy maternity leave from her job and she concentrated on caring for her newborn. Toward the end of her maternity leave she began to show Alya all she would have to do to care properly for Moussa.

The day came when Hadjara said, "Tomorrow I return to work and you'll be in charge of taking care of my baby as well as continuing to care for Hammed and Mariyam. You know all about what this care of my three children entails. You'll need to stay in Hammed's room because I will place Moussa's baby bed and all his care items in that bedroom."

Hadjara spoke to Alya in Arabic, acknowledging her growing proficiency in their language. Alya appreciated Hadjara speaking to her in Arabic. She used these occasions to learn more Arabic and strengthen her ability to speak in this language. Hadjara was quite impressed by how quickly Alya had learned basic Arabic.

Alya was surprised by her aptitude to learn Arabic. Speaking Arabic was easy for her, but she found writing it a huge challenge. Like her own Amharic language, the writing of Arabic was in a different script and they read from right to left instead of vice versa. In Arabic, Alya told Hadjara not to worry that she would take good care of Moussa and her two other kids. Hadjara thanked her and gave her a piece of paper with her work phone number and her home number, telling her not to hesitate to call her at work if there was an emergency. Alya said, "Shouldn't I have your husband's work number too?"

Hadjara replied tersely, "You don't contact a man about a woman's business. I only contact my husband at work if there is a life and death emergency, and I ask his father to make the contact. We must never contact my husband at work."

Alya replied politely, "I understand."

She did wonder why she had not seen Ibrahim since her arrival several months ago. He had to work nights but his absence was just too much. She thought that he must have another woman. Yet, he had given Hadjara three children so they must find some time together. Anyway this was none of her business. It did not have any bearing on how well she did her job.

Hadjara left the next day for work and Alya immediately started dealing with the care of a two-month-old baby and two toddler children. She found that taking care of the baby fully occupied her and she had much less time than she formerly did to care for Hammed and Mariyam and keep a watchful eye over them. The baby kept her busy night and day. She tried to get Busha to help her at times, but Busha made it clear that she did not sign up for the care of children.

Moussa got Alya's priority attention, but Hammed and Mariyam needed their usual care. There were many times that Alya felt pulled in three directions at once. She had to constantly change and dispose of Moussa diapers and prepare his formula for feeding at specified times. Moussa alone took all her time and kept her awake at night. It was only when baby Moussa slept that she could give her full attention to Hammed and Mariyam.

She became sleep deprived and underweight. There were times she almost went mad. Moussa and Hammed were crying for attention and Mariyam was still defecating behind the hallway door. Sometimes Alya just did not know where to turn. In these frequent moments of ultra-stress, she shed tears and was in a constant panic. Caring for three young children properly was more than she could manage.

Busha could see that Alya was mentally and physically in a downward spiral, but she minded her own business and stayed removed, providing no solace to Alya. Busha knew that it was not possible to care properly for three small children and it was only a matter of time before Alya reached the breaking point. Busha also believed their madame should see that Alya had been assigned something akin to mission impossible.

Alya fell gravely ill. She could no longer stand and put one foot in front of the other. Her emaciated body was too frail to function. She developed a fever and was close to dying. If there was ever a case of working someone to death, it described well Alya's deplorable case. Busha alerted Hadjara about Alya's dreadful state. Hadjara checked on Alya and readily could see that she was not in good condition. She could not believe that the chubby and lively Alya had been so quickly transformed into skin and bones. Hadjara did not want the trouble of her imported house servant dying while in her employ, so she told Alya to rest and

Busha to bring her food. She muttered under her breath, "We've got to make her healthy enough to travel. I will take off work until she is safely on her way."

Hadjara's words were overheard by Busha who groaned internally as she knew her freedom to work as she pleased would end with her madame in the house. She also knew that with Hadjara in charge of caring for her children, she would be sucked into doing childcare duties she did not like. Busha could not say no to her madame, but she hoped she saw the need for someone like Alya.

It took over a month, but they were finally successful in nursing Alya back to health. During this time Alya had been confined to her bedroom and Busha brought food and drink on a tray to her. Once she got her strength back and could speak coherently, she asked Busha, "What are they going to do about me?"

Busha hesitated but finally said, "Well, they don't want you to die here, although like any house servant you are easily expendable and unimportant. I think they are going to give you back your passport and a one-way ticket home."

Alya said, "Then I'm done here and my salary will stop?"

"You're lucky to have your life. You're only alive because they did not want all the hassles caused by having a dead foreign body in their hands. I hope your family appreciates how precarious a servant's life abroad can be. You'll go home as poor as you were before—poor but alive."

Although it was difficult for Alya to speak, she said sadly to Busha, "I'll miss you. You'll always be in my thoughts. I hope my absence is not too hard on you."

Busha said quietly, "Don't waste your breath on me. I'm used to this servant's life. I know my place in the world. If it is not here, it would be somewhere else. I hope you learned some lessons and you find some way to get money for your survival and that of your family."

Hadjara never entered the servants' bedroom but was standing outside the door when Busha exited and said brusquely, "Is she well enough to travel?"

Busha replied, "Yes."

"Good. I'll ask my husband to get her a ticket to Addis Ababa and plan to take her to the airport in Dubai City. The sooner she's gone and on the plane home, the better it will be for all of us. Excuse me. I must return to my children."

The next day Hadjara told Busha to tell Alya to be ready to travel home early tomorrow. Busha nodded in the affirmative and headed to their bedroom to inform Alya of her departure, saying. "Get yourself ready to travel at daybreak tomorrow. Okay?"

"Okay," replied Alya. "I'm packing my few belongings in my suitcase. Do you know if they will be giving me any money?"

"I don't know, but I doubt it. Maybe they'll give you a little money for traveling and an airport taxi when you get there. You'll have to ask Ibrahim who will be driving you to the airport."

"This will be the second time I've seen Ibrahim. The first time was when I arrived. I guess I'll have to appeal to his better nature. When do I say my goodbyes to the children and madame?"

Busha thought for a moment but answered crisply, "I don't think there will be any goodbyes. They just want you to leave so they'll be rid of the problem you represent for them."

Alya was clearly disturbed by Busha's words and said in a distressed manner, "After all the months I've spent in their house serving them and bonding with their children, they just discard me like undesirable baggage?"

"Yes. For them, you are dead. For them, you and I are nothing. That is the way things are and neither of us can change them. Just get yourself ready to leave early tomorrow. There will be no goodbyes. Get used to it or never try to be a servant again."

Alya could not resist saying, "I'm a slave to no one."

Busha laughed and said whimsically, "But you're a slave to the money the masters pay you and you're at their mercy because they control you by keeping your passport. Those are realities you must recognize and accept."

There was no use in continuing a conversation with Busha. She had been working in the overseas household bondage system so long that she had lost any perspective of a life that did not involve working as a servant. She was used to working for foreigners on a day-to-day basis without any benefits. For her, she would do her servant's job until she was too old and then return to her home country to be cared for by relatives receiving remittances from other family members working abroad. Without the wealthy nations, they would be reduced to bare subsistence and live on the edge of survival.

Alya was thinking that she was not cut out to be household servant but what options did she have? There were no jobs that paid a livable wage in her home country and there were several mouths to feed in her house in Addis. She was uncertain as to what to do. For the time being, she had to concentrate on the present and returning home.

She finished packing her small suitcase and laid on her bed, waiting for Busha to bring her food tray. She was too ashamed to go out and see any members of the family for which she had worked. Her shame stemmed from her failure to do her job. Under these conditions, she could not ask for a letter of reference. It was best that she remain hidden from all household members.

Busha came with a tray of food and said, "When you finished, leave your tray on the floor. I'm not going out again."

After going into the bathroom, Busha went to bed without saying a further word. Alya lay in her bed sobbing. She thought to herself that she came with nothing and is leaving with nothing. She worried about what her family would think. The thought of facing Yeshi haunted her. All her family's hopes had been placed on her and she had failed them. She was particularly sad for her little daughter because she would not have all the things she needed.

There was no sleeping on Alya's last night in Khor Fakkan, although sleep is what she needed before she traveled back to Ethiopia. She tossed and turned as she worried about her exit from the Khor Fakkan house, from the UAE, and her arrival in Addis. Mostly she was deeply tormented by what she would tell her family about her unexpected return home.

It was well before dawn when Alya decided to get up and ready for her departure. She sat on the edge of her bed, waiting for Busha to get up. When Busha sat up in her bed, Alya whispered, "I'm up and ready."

Busha gave her a furtive glance before going into the bathroom to do her toiletries and get dressed. When she was ready to go out of the room, she said, "Follow me with your things and be ready in front to leave as soon as Ibrahim arrives. I know he'll want to drive you to the airport in the cool part of the day."

Alya wrapped her long white Ethiopian shawl around her head and shoulders. She kept her head bowed and walked slowly straight behind Busha. When she went to the front of the house, Ibrahim was just arriving to pick her up. She wondered for a second where Ibrahim was coming from, but that was none of her concern. He, his house, and his family would soon be history for her.

Busha stood watching at the window from inside the house. There was no sign of Hadjara and her children. The only human voice she heard was Ibrahim's saying, "Get in. We must hurry if you're going to make your plane in time."

Alya sat in the same place in the back seat as she did when she came. She had some questions for Ibrahim but was in a subdued behavior mode and told herself that her questions could wait until they were well on their way. Ibrahim drove his fancy car out of town, over the low-lying mountains and into the sands of Dubai. After a couple of hours of not speaking to one another and seeing they were on the outskirts of Dubai City, Alya cleared her throat and said in a low and respectful tone, "Sir, what am I to do without any money?"

Ibrahim waited a few minutes before handing back to Alya her passport and ticket, saying in an irritated fashion, "You'll find in your passport two one-hundred-dollar bills."

Alya studied her passport with its UAE visa and ticket. She tucked away the two bills deep inside of the interior of the left bra cup. She did not have to say anything, but automatically she said, "Shukran."

They passed through the airport entrance when Ibrahim pointed excitedly to the northwest horizon and said loudly in Arabic, "Esifat ramalia."

Alya did not know what he was saying, but his excitement was contagious. Ibrahim glanced at Alya and saw the puzzled look on her face and said more loudly as he pointed to the horizon, "Haboob!"

As Alya scanned the huge mounting sandstorm on the horizon, saying clearly in Arabic, "Tafah" (meaning in English, "I understand").

The wind was speeding up and the scary haboob was quickly moving their way. It towered above their view of the distant mountains and blocked out the sunlight. As the haboob moved toward them it became increasingly darker. They arrived at the arrivals' gate of the airport terminal and Ibrahim said forcefully, "Get out quickly. I want to speed away so the haboob stays behind me. Go now."

Alya got out of the car and did not look back. She hustled into the terminal and took shelter along with the other passengers. The terminal was shut and no business could be conducted until the dust storm had passed. When the blowing dust and sand had subsided, swarms of workers began sweeping and scooping up the dirt and sand left by the storm. Evidently, this climatic event was frequent in this sandy part of the world.

All Alya could think of was checking in, getting her boarding pass, going through immigration and security officials so she could go to her designated gate, and wait for her plane back home. She did not want to go home but she had no other choice. Her failure to make a go of it in the UAE made her feel hollow inside. Certainly, she had not lived up to her dreams and to her family's high expectations. She had fallen down and was not sure she could get up again.

CHAPTER ELEVEN

No Where to Turn

IT WAS A SMOOTH LANDING at the new Bole International Airport in Addis Ababa. Alya was pleased to be back in her home country but even the wonders of the new airport terminal could not free her from the dark depression that enveloped her. She felt like her heavy feet were anchored to the floor. She was in a daze and feared going home to face the harsh judgement of her family, especially Yeshi.

Her trauma clouded her thoughts. She could not think straight and went through the airport formalities in a somnolent state. Rain was falling softly when she exited the terminal. A man immediately accosted her, asking energetically, "Need a taxi?

Alya needed a taxi, but she only had two hundred-dollar bills. She did an about face and re-entered the terminal to look for a money exchange bureau so she could trade one of her one-hundred-dollar bills for the local currency, birr. She slid her hundred-dollar bill under the teller's window with her passport. The teller quickly counted the birr equivalent and shoved the stack of money through the slot under the glass window with Alya's passport. This pile of birr represented more birr than Alya had ever seen. She thought, "At least I have something to give to my family."

The taximan was waiting for her when she exited the airport terminal with her small suitcase. The taximan grabbed her suitcase and said in pure Amharic, "My car is close by in the parking lot. Where do you want to go?

Alya hesitated to respond to his question but finally replied with the name of her neighborhood church, "Saint Kirkos." She needed to pray in the church before going home. Only through prayer could she get the strength needed to face her family. Her fragile being would shatter under the scrutiny of her family which would be shocked by her unexpected arrival. She did not have the courage to face her family without God at her side.

After about a forty-five-minute drive, they arrived at Kirkos church. The taxi driver was not perplexed by her destination. It was not unusual for an orthodox Ethiopian passenger to go to church before going home.

It was raining more heavily now. Alya settled the taxi fare and rushed out of the car to enter the church, being careful to remove her shoes before entering the holy sanctum, taking her suitcase with her. She automatically found a place among the throngs of women prostrated on the right side of the interior of the church. Her shawl fully covered her head and body as she beseeched the holy trinity and Virgin Mariyam to give her the ability to explain to her family the reasons for her early return.

Others in the church and the priest observed her lengthy stay in this holy place and assumed she was paying penance for a sinful transgression of high importance. They let her be, but they wondered how long she could continue without consuming any food or water or going to the restroom. Although her case was extreme, the priest let her be, but he was prepared to intervene if absolutely necessary.

Alya remained in church the entire day. She had lost physical strength, but she had gained spiritual strength. Her face was covered when she left the church at sundown and weakly walked the few blocks to her home. Nobody recognized her as she sneaked into her housing compound on a dark rainy night and softly knocked on the old wooden door of her home.

Before there was any response from the other side of the door, Alya was on the verge of collapsing. Her physical condition was poor and emotionally she was unprepared to meet her family. She wanted to run away but she had nowhere to go. She was eager to see her family, especially her baby girl, but she was ashamed to appear among them so broken.

After a long wait in the rain, Alya could hear someone fumbling with the inside door lock and then slowly opened the door with a crack to peer out to see who was knocking. In the dim light, Yeshi could make out the form of her dear daughter, but her mind was telling her that could not be because Alya is in Dubai.

Yeshi said, "Go away. Stop bothering us."

Alya could see that her unexpected presence was confusing Yeshi and she threw off her shawl and said in the softest of voices, "Yeshi. It's me, Alya."

Upon hearing these words, Yeshi opened the door widely and shined her flashlight on Alya's face. She readily recognized her daughter, but her mind could not accept that she was no longer in Dubai but on her front doorstep. She asked herself, "Could this really be Alya?"

It took several minutes for Yeshi's shock level to decline sufficiently to allow Alya to enter the house. Once Alya had entered she also confronted her sisters, Belkis and Fana. She wanted to take her baby girl in her arms, but Hiyab fled to the adjoining room saying, "You're not my mother."

Her sisters were spellbound and their tongues were tied. Yeshi was worried by the presence among them of Alya and could not help but say, “How will we live? Our only breadwinner has returned.”

Alya could see that Yeshi was ready to launch a tirade centered on their impoverished condition and how things would get even worse for them now, so she humbly said, “Please. We can discuss all this tomorrow. Please make a place for me to sleep.”

Yeshi immediately directed her two sisters to arrange a place for Alya to sleep. A comfortable pile of blankets and a pillow was made on the floor and Alya plopped down without changing her clothes and fell fast asleep. They stood above Alya, trying to convince themselves that this was truly Alya—the woman who sent them a money transfer every month. They could not get over the thought, “If this was Alya, who would send us the money every month we need to survive?”

While Alya was in a deep sleep, her presence prevented all of them from sleeping. The next day came and the room was bright with the daylight that filtered through the fissures in the walls of their simple, aged abode. They sat next to the sleeping Alya, staring at her and wondering what happened to cause her to return so abruptly. They leaned toward Alya’s body when it stirred under the covers. In anticipation of Alya’s wakening, they tried to smile to communicate sympathy but deep down they were all worried about from where their next meal would come. Their meal ticket was lying on the floor before them and that was a reality they could not escape. There was nothing but doom and gloom in their forecast for their lives.

Alya opened her eyes to see the faces of all her family members focused on her. She knew they were waiting for an explanation of her situation but her stomach pangs urgently prompted her to say, “Do you have anything for me to eat?”

The unexpected words coming out of Alya’s mouth caused Yeshi to look at Belkis and Fana, and command, "Get her the leftovers from yesterday."

Belkis and Fana went quickly outside to their small kitchen and brought back some food pots and sat them beside the reclined Alya. Belkis said, "Sit up. Here's some cold injera and chiro. We could warm it up, but it will take time to light our charcoal fire."

Before Belkis could finish talking, Alya was sitting up and ravenously eating the food brought her. She had reached the hunger stage that could not afford any delay in getting her famished body some nourishment. Her family said nothing while she ate. Fana set a big tin mug filled with fresh water beside her. Alya nodded her head to express her thanks for the food and water.

Alya finished her food and water, cleared her throat, and said softly, "I fell ill. I could not care for three small children and they sent me home. I was ready to welcome death, but here I am with you. I have no idea what to do about the future."

Her words were like pouring ice cold water on her family members. There was nothing they could say or do to change the reality of Alya's shocking return. Yeshi went to the back room to pray. Belkis and Fana went outside to their communal courtyard with Hiyab in tow. They tried to act in a way that would not alert their neighbors of Alya's return. If they knew of her premature return, they would know that they would face financial difficulties.

One of their neighbors, Tigist, approached the sisters and made the usual Amharic greetings before saying, "You know I returned last week from Lebanon. I thought I saw Alya pass silently by in the night. Is she home?"

Belkis looked at Fana before saying unsteadily, "Yes, she's home but sleeping."

Tigist appreciated this reply and said, "Okay. I'll see her later."

The sisters knew if Tigist knew about Alya's return, everyone in the neighborhood would know. It was only a matter of hours before Alya would be up and around for everyone to see her. They were not prepared for the sudden appearance of Alya in their doorway.

Alya had gotten up, did her toiletries, and dressed. She spoke to Belkis. "I thought I heard the voice of Tigist. Where is she? I want to see her."

Just as Alya finished talking, Tigist stepped out of her adjoining house and said, "Alya is that you? Good to see you."

Alya walked toward Tigist and greeted her warmly before saying cooly, "We need to talk when you have time."

"I have time now."

"Then, come into my house," said Alya nonchalantly.

Yeshi saw them coming and hurriedly rolled up Alya's bedding and carried it to the back room. Alya and Tigist sat beside each other on the small sofa in the sitting room of her small house. They entered into an animated conversation that sounded like morning birds chirping in the trees. Tigist told all about her time in Beirut and her precarious departure from Lebanon. Alya pretended as if all went well in Dubai and her contract came to an end.

Tigist was intrigued by Alya's time in Dubai and encouraged her to return to the UAE as there were many jobs for foreigners there. She said, "I know an Ethiopian woman whose name is Samrawit who has had a house in Dubai for many years and she knows all about the job market in Dubai. We should go see if she is here."

Alya replied, "I'm ready to go and see her as soon as you can assure me she is at her Addis house and ready to receive us. Another job in Dubai is what I urgently need. I also need to fully recover my health."

"Good. I will tell you today if she can see us. She's a distant family member, so she'll see us if she is here."

Tigist left and Yeshi stepped into the room. Alya gave a serious look at her grandmother and rushed to say, "As your just heard, Tigist and I are going to see a woman about jobs in Dubai. I hope to return to a new and different job in Dubai. Now that I've been there I've a better idea of what to do. Let's try to enjoy our time together."

Alya's words made Yeshi change gears and say in the happiest voice she could muster, "Yes, let's celebrate your return. We need to buy some food, coffee, and charcoal. I don't have any money. Do you?"

Alya dug into her bulging bra and pulled out a wad of Birr and handed it to a surprised Yeshi, saying, "Is this enough?"

Yeshi snatched quicky the money offered her, grinned, and said, "Thank you. That'll do. I'll send one of your sisters to our local market."

As quickly as Yeshi went out of the front door, she came back to say, "Tigist is here to see you."

Tigist came in as Yeshi went out again and said breathlessly, "We're in luck. Samrawit is here and ready to see us at any time. When can you go?"

"I can go now. Can you?"

"Yes, let's go now. Bring your passport with you just in case she asks for it," suggested Tigist.

"I hope we can walk there. How did you find out so quickly about her being in Addis?"

"I sent a boy in our house to go check for us and he ran back to tell me about her availability."

While they walked quickly to Samrawit's house, they discussed the points they wanted to raise with her. Alya summed up her thoughts by stating simply, "All I want to know is if she can find me a job in Dubai."

They passed through the entrance to Samrawit's cozy cottage to find her sitting on a cushion-laden sofa under the shade of eucalyptus trees. After the traditional greetings and paying the older Samrawit their respects, she invited them to sit down by saying, "Please join me by sitting in these comfortable armchairs."

Alya and Tigist were impressed by the surroundings of this obviously well-off woman. Their envious views of Samrawit's life were further augmented when a servant girl sat small coffee cups on the side tables adjoining their chairs, asking politely, "Do you want sugar and milk in your coffee?"

Their answers were brief as their soaring feelings cut short their words. They had never before been served coffee outside of their own homes. With the Ethiopian Arabic coffee coming, they knew that they were off to a good start with Samrawit."

After their coffee was served and drunk, Samrawit said in an even tone, "Thank you for coming. As you know, I also have had a house in Dubai for many years. Everything you see here has been bought with the money I made in Dubai. How can I help you?"

Tigist was the first to speak, "Thank you for receiving us on such short notice. Briefly, we're both seeking jobs and we thought you may be able to help us get some work in Dubai."

Samrawit smiled and said, "There are plenty of jobs for my Ethiopian sisters in Dubai. When can you go?"

It was Alya's turn to talk and said, "I think I speak for both of us when I say as soon as you can find us work."

"Let me see your passports," said Samrawit in a business-like tone.

They handed Samrawit their passports for her careful scrutiny before saying, "I see that Alya has a valid UAE visa so she can go to Dubai at any time. Tigist's case is more complicated because she will have to get a visa on arrival. That will take some time to arrange, but it is doable. I will make a call to my representative in Dubai and give him all the information. Check back with me in three days."

Alya and Tigist left Samrawit's house energized by the promising prospects of finding work in Dubai. Alya felt uplifted and could not wait to get home and tell her family that she would be returning to Dubai to work in a new job. She had been feeling at rock bottom yesterday and today she was on top of the world. She would take any job in Dubai that paid a livable wage and did not involve caring for small children.

CHAPTER TWELVE

Buna Tetu (Drink Coffee)

THE NEIGHBORS HEARD LAUGHTER. IT was emanating from Alya's cramped Addis house. She and her family were enjoying a sumptuous Ethiopian meal followed by a traditional coffee ceremony—the highest form of Ethiopian hospitality. They were in an unusual state of ecstasy.

They were waving into their faces the smoke emitted by the roasted coffee beans that Belkis was parading in front of all of them in a long-handled flat metal pan. Then she proceeded to make coffee at her Ethiopian decorated foot-high, white settee table on a green woven mat. The fragrance of freshly cut grass and the petals of small yellow ade ababa flowers spread evenly on the mat permeated the air. Belkis sat on a low stool behind the settee where all the small China cups were placed.

They were all dressed in traditional ankle-length white cotton dresses with colorful embroidery around the edges of their garments. Belkis ground the coffee beans with a pestle (mukecha) and mortar (zenezene) and put them into her handmade clay coffee pot (jebena). All the items used in the coffee ceremony had been handed down to Yeshi by previous generations on her side of the family. Yeshi was proud to see a coffee ceremony conducted in accordance with her heritage and country's ancient traditions.

Belkis carefully balanced her old clay pottery coffee pot on her charcoal stove (metacha). When the coffee was hot and fully brewed, she removed the straw stopper on the top of the pot and poured it slowly from a foot in the air (so the dregs would stay in the pot) into small white porcelain, handle less coffee cups (cine) for serving to each family member. For this truly special event, she also served small plates of popcorn and included in her boiling coffee a local herb (t'ena adam). The adding of this spice increased the intoxicating mixed aroma of the coffee fumes and the wafts of incense. Belkis was a young woman and the best at doing a coffee ceremony which she had elevated to an art form.

Whiffs of the smoky coffee beans and the burning of sandalwood incense in its own small burner (etan manchesha) transformed their spirits. It had been a long time since they had gathered to participate as a family to be uplifted by what has been an important central part of Ethiopian cultural life for over ten centuries. They were reminded that Ethiopia was the birthplace of coffee and it was religious Orthodox monks who started this key sacred ritual.

They truly enjoyed the bitterness, thickness, and potency of the coffee that they were encouraged to be fully blessed by drinking three small cups. The first cup was the strongest and was called "abol." The second cup was weaker and was called "tona." The drinking of a third cup was a true blessing and was exactly called that in Amharic, "baraka." The drinking of these three cups truly blessed them and reconnected them in a way that nothing else could. The ingrained spiritual qualities of the Ethiopian coffee ceremony cannot be overestimated.

They wanted to add sugar and milk to their cups of coffee but refrained from doing so in order to maximize the ceremony's spiritual properties. They were all teary-eyed, saying repeatedly, "Buna dabo naw" (coffee is our bread). The entire coffee ceremony took a couple of hours and was filled with a lively conversation about their lives and Alya's promising new job prospects in Dubai. Little Hiyab joined in the gaiety of the moment by doing a little jig which caused much laughter among the happy group. It was as if they had a newfound meaning of what their entirely female family meant.

They were celebrating the news that Alya received earlier in the day about a new job in Dubai that Samrawit had arranged for her. She was to travel back to Dubai city with her at the end of the week. Alya was excited by her return to Dubai and her family was happy because she would again be able to send them the money transfers on which their survival depended.

When they had finished their coffee ceremony, Alya went to inquire about Tigist in a neighboring compound. She found Tigist sitting peacefully alone on a low bench placed in front of her house. Tigist asked Alya to sit down beside her. When Alya snuggled up against Tigist, she asked, "What's the latest on your UAE visa?"

Tigist replied, "Samrawit took my passport and said she'll get my visa when you go to Dubai and when she has it, she'll come back to Addis to get me."

Alya interjected, "You can count on Samrawit to act as fast as she can. I hope to see you in Dubai when you get there."

Tigist was curious and asked, "What kind of job did Samrawit get for you?

"She says it is housekeeper job with good Arab family on the outskirts of Dubai City. I'll take any job as long as I don't have to care for baby children."

Tigist laughed at Alya's words and said, "I'll take any job that pays me well, period."

It was Alya's turn to laugh. Their discussion continued with small talk until the sun had ducked down behind their adjoining neighbor's house. Alya returned to her house softly humming a religious tune that helped reinforce her spirit and prepare her for the return trip to Dubai. She would be ready to go when Samrawit said.

The days passed quickly and then the day came when a young boy came to Alya's house and said, "In one hour, Samrawit will come in a taxi that will take you to the airport."

As the boy ran away, Alya rushed to check her baggage again, making sure she had not forgotten anything, and to say her final goodbyes to her family and neighbors. In particular, she took her baby daughter in her arms and smothered her in kisses. Hiyab squirmed and resisted all the affection Alya was showering on her. It was clear that whether Alya stayed or traveled made no difference to Hiyab. She tried to remind her daughter that her name was from the ancient religious Ge'ez language and meant "Gift of God," and she was just that to Alya.

Her family stood waving as Alya got into the taxi and sat next to Samrawit who said, "Your family will get used to your absence and become accustomed to you working in Dubai. There are millions of Ethiopians working abroad who are sending money back to their families. A really poor household is one that has does not receive money from a relative working abroad."

Samrawit was quiet for the rest of the airport and Alya was afraid to say anything. When they arrived at the departure gate, they got out of the taxi and Samrawit said, "Follow me. Once people know you are with me, you'll not be hassled."

Samrawit took care of everything and before Alya knew it, she was sitting inside the airport at their gate, waiting for their flight to Dubai. Alya learned to put herself under Samrawit's wing and not to talk unless spoken to. It was only when they had boarded the plane and were comfortably sitting in their assigned seats that Samrawit said, "I suggest sleeping on the flight because you will go right to work when you arrive."

Alya could only say in a hushed voice, "Thank you for all you are doing for me. The last thing I want to do is let you down."

Oddly, Samrawit chuckled and said softly, "The main thing is not to let yourself and your family down. I have every confidence that you will do a good job. Otherwise, you would not be sitting next to me."

With those words, Samrawit closed her eyes. Alya followed suit and to her surprise slept until their arrival was announced over the PA system and the lights were turned on inside their plane's cabin. Samrawit said, "Let's get out and go to the restroom before the plane lands." The passenger in the aisle seat was already gone so they passed easily into the aisle and got in the line to the small plane restroom. The flight path of their plane was smooth. The fasten seatbelt signal was still off. They hoped to finish relieving themselves in the bathroom and return to their seat and buckle their seatbelts before the signal was illuminated. All worked in their favor and they were thankful when their plane touched down gently on the runway and was coasting to its assigned docking tunnel in the Dubai Airport.

Samrawit used this time to explain to Alya how things should work, "I've done this countless times so I know what to expect. Stay close to me and all should go quickly without a hitch. I frequently make this trip, so I'm well known. When we get through the airport formalities, my man should be waiting for me with your new employer. If not, you can stay with me until things are straightened out."

Alya swallowed deeply, even though she had the utmost trust in Samrawit. She was impressed that Samrawit spoke to her in Amharic and greeted the many officials working in the airport in fluent Arabic. She knew enough Arabic to know that Samrawit was saying she was her daughter. That falsehood did not bother Alya in the least. In fact, she was proud to be considered Samrawit's daughter.

They entered the departure hall and at the baggage collection area Samrawit said, "There's my guy. He's not alone, so the man with him must be your boss."

Samrawit made the introductions, presenting Alya to an imposing Arab man dressed as expected in the traditional white robes of his country, saying, "This is Alya, your new housekeeper. Here's her passport for safe keeping. I'm sure you have paid my fee to my representative. I'm more than sure she'll give you full satisfaction. We'll be going now." Before Samrawit departed with her guy, she turned to Alya and said, "Goodbye. You're on your own now. I'm sure you'll do well."

Alya wanted to hug Samrawit and tell her how much she appreciated all her help, but this was no place for hugs or expressing any sort of sentiment. She contented herself by saying with heartfelt sincerity in Amharic, "Thank you." She then turned to her new Arab boss who said, "Don't be afraid. Bring your bag and then we can go in my car to our house. By the way, my name is Yaqub, but you can call me in its English equivalent, Jacob."

Alya said "Thank you" in Arabic so Yaqub would know that she spoke some Arabic as well as English and her native tongue, Amharic.

She rushed to remove her small suitcase from the conveyor belt and then followed Yaqub to the parking lot. She tried to act like she was used to the oppressive heat. It was stifling hot inside of Yaqub's car in spite of the reflecting sunscreen he had placed on the front windshield, prompting him to say, "Before you take your place in the backseat, wait a few minutes for the car air conditioner to cool things inside down a bit."

Alya was perspiring when she slid into the back seat of Yaqub's car. The air conditioner was going full blast, but Alya's body was still too hot. Her eyes were glued to her car window and she spied many roadside shops. In the distance, she could see the tops of modern skyscrapers of the glamorous center of Dubai City and beyond she spotted the glistening sea.

The drive to Yaqub's classy suburban family home was short, lasting about fifteen minutes. Yaqub's wife and two teenage sons were waiting for them behind the glass front wall. As soon as they entered the house, Yaqub graciously introduced his wife and sons, "This is my wife, Halimah, and my two sons, Yusuf and Benyamin. I have to go to work. Halimah will show you your room and describe your work tasks."

Halimah was more beautiful than Alya's previous madame. The wearing of the latest Parisian fashion in her house put her in a different class. They had the same long black shiny hair but Halimah's elegant way of walking set her apart. Also her height and slim body distinguished her. She diplomatically showed Alya her tiny but tidy bedroom and shower stall in the back corner of the house. Alya was happy with her room because she would not be sharing it with anyone else. Timidly, she asked Halimah, "Do you have other servants besides me?"

Halimah replied in a velvety voice, "Only one. Our Sri Lankan cook, Pamu. He's in charge of our kitchen. He does all the cooking and is responsible for washing the dishes and keeping the kitchen clean."

Alya was glad to see that somebody else was responsible for the cooking. She was hesitant to speak but said, "Please. What are my duties?"

Halimah was quick to say, "Why my dear, you have the rest of the house to deal with. Among your major duties are keeping the rest of the house clean, washing and ironing our dirty clothes, and making our beds. You're our housekeeper. Of course, our two teenage boys, ages thirteen and fifteen, will need your help from time to time. Now, let me show you around our house."

They briefly visited every room of the five-bedroom luxury house. Halimah pointed out in each room those items which would require

Alya's special attention. They went out on the back veranda and Halimah explained that the neighboring house was where her husband's parents lived and that is why there was no fence between them. She also said, "I don't work outside the house, so when I'm not here, I'm at their house. You don't need to go there unless you are asked to do so."

Alya observed that their small yard wrapped around the house and was covered with sand. Halimah saw Alya looking at the yard and volunteered, "Don't worry about our yard. When it's dirty, we call a service to clean it."

No small children to take care of was a core recipe for a job that Alya could easily and happily do. Only one thing bothered her—how would she send money to her family in Ethiopia? After all, that is why she had gone abroad to work. This point so occupied her mind that she defied protocol by asking Halimah gently, "When can I go to town to transfer money to my family in Ethiopia?"

Halimah smiled in an effort to put Alya at ease and said sweetly, "Don't worry about that my dear. We can go to town in my car any time you get a break. But that will probably not be until we pay you at the end of the month."

Alya in a barely audible voice said, "Sorry to ask such a question." But she did wonder to herself how much they would pay her each month.

"That's not a problem. We want you to be at ease when you start working tomorrow. Now, you should go to your room, unpack, and rest. Pamu will bring your dinner on a tray to your room. You'll find him very efficient but as quiet as a stone. Can you find your way back to your room? I'm going to my in-laws house now. Be thinking of any more questions you have so you can ask them of me the next time we are together."

Alya thanked Halimah in Arabic and this caused Halimah to smile and say, "How sweet. You speak some words in our language."

Halimah crossed to the other house on the concrete stepping-stone passageway. Alya turned to go back into the house to go to her bedroom but found her way blocked by Yusuf and Benyamin who were eyeing Alya from top to bottom. Irritated by their gawking at her she said firmly in Arabic, "Excuse me."

After hearing Alya's words, they parted and waved her through the space between them to the house door. Alya noted the smirks on their faces as she passed by them and thought, "Those sons of the Biblical Jacob will be a problem for me. Haram on the thoughts they have about me in their heads."

CHAPTER THIRTEEN

Dubai Redux

THE LIGHT KNOCK ON ALYA's bedroom door aroused her from a deep sleep. At first, she had difficulty orienting herself to her new surroundings. Then a sudden deep fear struck her like a thunder bolt. She was afraid the sound of the knock on her door was made by Yusuf and Benjamin. Their overactive teenage male hormones were urgently seeking her sexual services. For them, a foreign young house maid was free game.

"Food," was the single word said by the person knocking on her door.

This word was received by Alya with great relief. She now understood it was Pamu who knocked on her door, leaving a tray of food outside her door on the hallway floor. She opened the door to retrieve her food tray and set it at the foot of her bed. Her hunger urged her to eat while standing. When there was nothing left to drink or eat, she placed the tray where she had found it.

In spite of her hunger, she could not digest the tasty food well. She did not know why this was so. It finally dawned on her that eating alone was causing he some indigestion. Hers was a communal life in Ethiopia and there were always family members and friends assembled for a meal. In her home country, nobody ate alone. She felt like she was being punished for eating alone but accepted her condemnation to this way of life in order to make money.

It was time to get to work. She wanted to show Halimah she was busy working. Everything needed dusting and the floors needed sweeping. Her job was to clean the house, but she also had other tasks to do. She asked herself, "Where's all the supplies I need to do my job?"

The only person she could find at this early morning hour was Pamu. She carried her food tray back to him and said cordially, "Good morning. Thank you for the food. Where do I find what I need to do my job?"

The silent Pamu pointed to a nearby door. Alya immediately walked to the door, opened it, and saw more than she needed. As she exited the kitchen, she saw appliances she did not know existed. This observation made her glad she did not have Pamu's job. At least half the items in the kitchen, she did not know how to operate. Although she was impressed by all the electrical appliances in the kitchen, she thought, "Even if we had electricity back home, we could never afford these appliances." From the utility closet, she took familiar items—dust cloths and pan, and broom. She looked at all that was available in the closet. There was one particularly large item she had never seen before. This item was a vacuum cleaner that she would learn how to use when she was out of eyeshot of anyone else.

Alya could see that Pamu was setting the breakfast table for four people. She assumed that the table setting was for the resident Arab family and that Pamu had already had his breakfast. She was about to start cleaning in an unoccupied part of the house when Halimah came rushing down the hallway from her bedroom, quickly spouting out in Arabic, "Sabah al-kheir."

Nodding her head like a statue, Alya froze because she did not know the proper response in Arabic. She assumed Halimah was saying "Good morning" in Arabic and was ill at ease because she was at a loss to find the common response. She should know this. In passing, Halimah noticed the downcast look on Alya's face and said, "I said in Arabic 'Good morning.' You should say, 'sabah al-noor, which I think in English means 'morning of light.'" Halimah took a few more hurried steps and abruptly turned to say to Alya, "When you finish cleaning the rooms, wash and dry the bed clothes. We want all clean and fresh when we sleep tonight. Now, I must rush for breakfast and then take my two sons to school."

After hearing Halimah, Alya began cleaning a house that was much larger and endowed with a grandeur that dwarfed any place she had known previously. She proceeded with cleaning from top-to-bottom the house's many rooms, treating every item with the utmost care and reverence. In the bucket, she carried with her were several cleaning products and rags. Her main goal on her first day at work was to make an effort which satisfied Halimah. When she heard the clatter of plates and the front door close, she knew that the boys had left for school with their mother and, therefore, she breathed a sigh of relief. She could now do this job fully as she did not have to deal with the unwanted signals from Yusuf and Benjamin. Her main approach was to avoid them as much as she could. With their unwanted looks in mind, she started covering her head to demonstrate her religious devoutness. She thought by doing this she would discourage them from attempting to do anything more serious.

When the boys were home and their mother was absent, she would leave any work she had and confine herself to her room, locking the door behind her. Or, if her room were too far away, she would hide in their small sandy yard in the oppressive heat. She almost preferred caring for two small children to dealing with two teenage boys. Her prayers were unceasing about keeping the boys at a distance. She knew she had little recourse if they forced themselves on her. Of course, she would fight them and yell at the top of her voice, "Haram." On the other hand, she was acutely aware that her true value as a human being was zero in the Arab society in which she lived. The head of the family kept her passport so she was at the mercy of his whims and whatever the boys might do to her, he would always take the side of his family members. She was dispensable and easily discarded, and no mercy was shown to foreigners when they were pitted against an Arab native. Any fight on her part would be a losing battle and she could lose her life and be forgotten forever as she was buried in the shifting sands of the vast desert.

Alya thought about all these things but behaved in a way that would ideally prevent them from ever happening. Her interests were focused on doing her job and getting paid at the end of the month, so she could do a money transfer to her family in Addis. Doing her job day after day was a sacrifice and she wondered how long she could keep doing the same thing all alone every day. She asked herself, "Is this what I'm condemned to do the rest of my life?"

No doubt about it. She was like a slave without any rights. Her death in this country would not be reported and life would go on. The host family would complain that their household chores were not done or they had to take the unusual step of doing their home chores themselves. Every household in the UAE needed foreign servants from poorer countries.

Alya had no choice but to persevere. She had to remind herself that she needed to stay healthy, out of trouble and do a good job. There was no room for any complaining. After all, she had plenty to eat, her own bedroom and she was paid on time and given enough freedom once a month to send a monthly money transfer to her family in Ethiopia. Right now she was worried about correctly operating the upright vacuum cleaner. She had rolled the cleaner onto the thick carpet covering the living room floor but no matter how many times she moved back and forth the off-on switch, it would not work. Pamu heard the clicking sound of the switch and stepped out of the kitchen to see what was happening. He immediately saw the problem and walked forthrightly up to Alya and the cleaner. He grabbed the cleaner's electrical cord and plugged it into the nearest wall socket.

The cleaner immediately sprang to life and a happy Alya began awkwardly moving the cleaning machine over the carpet. When Pamu turned to go into the kitchen, he saw out of the corner of his eyes that Alya was struggling to move the cleaner on the carpet. He pivoted immediately and walked rapidly back to Alya and flipped the siding switch on the cleaner to unlock its handle so it could easily be pushed back and forth across the surface of the carpet.

Pamu did all his helpful interventions with the vacuum cleaner without saying a word or making any facial expressions. Each time he intervened, Alya timidly said a heartfelt, "Thank you."

While she smoothly sucked up with the vacuum cleaner any filth on the carpet, Alya could not help but think about Pamu. She thought, "Maybe he can't speak. For certain, he knows more than me. Maybe in time we can be friends. He knows a lot and can be of help to me."

She was able to turn off the vacuum cleaner, unplug it and wrap the cord so it hung neatly on the side of the handle which was locked into its upright position. She rolled the cleaner to its storage place in the utility closet. The clear plastic debris compartment was full and needed to be emptied into the trash bin but Alya said to herself, "I'll return later to study more this modern cleaning machine before fiddling with it more."

It was getting late and Alya had more house cleaning tasks to complete. She still had to clean the bathrooms and the bedrooms. Her work pace was feverous, but she never seemed to finish every task as quickly as she wanted. When she saw the beds with their jumble of covers, she was reminded that Halimah had instructed her to wash and dry all the bedclothes.

She immediately stopped what she was doing and stripped all the beds of their sheets and pillowcases, placing them in a clothes hamper and then carried them to the laundry room where the washing machine and dryer were located. She sat the fully loaded hamper down with a soft thud and began to sob because she had never operated such machines. Yet, she had to operate them to do her job.

She was too ashamed to ask Pamu for help. In her panic, she searched in the wall cupboards above the machines and found instruction manuals. She sat on the floor and read their pertinent parts. With great trepidation, she stood up and loaded the washer with all the bedclothes she thought were safe to load. Following the written instructions, she carefully fetched the box of laundry detergent from the cupboard and poured the designated amount into the measuring cup and then spread it over the bedclothes in the washer.

The moment of truth was nearing as she closed the washer lid and pushed the start button. The swishing sound of the washer scared her, but she was determined to show that she could machine wash clothes. There were other settings on the washer, but Alya was reluctant to touch them, thinking that whoever set them before knew what they were doing. The washer seemed to be working properly, but Alya did not want to leave while the machine was operating. On the other hand, she was concerned that watching all the cycles of the washing machine would identify her as an amateur, so after a few spins of the washer, she left the laundry room for a while to finish cleaning the bathrooms.

The laundry room was silent when Alya returned. The washing of the first load of bedclothes was done and she had to transfer these damp clothes to the adjoining dryer. Doing this and starting the dryer was easier than she thought. She glowed with pride as the dryer started making its muffled rounds. Her initial mastery of the laundry room elevated her spirits. And she was pleased when the bedclothes were dry and folded. She delighted at making the beds neat with bedclothes she had washed and dried.

After a few months on the job, Alya became accustomed to her housemaid job. She missed her Ethiopian family very much, but she reminded herself daily that she was doing this for them. Every payday Halimah took them to an upscale shopping center where she and Pamu could send a money transfer and shop for anything they needed and could afford. They would later join Halimah in a fancy nearby supermarket and Pamu would dutifully follow behind her with a shopping cart to collect all she would buy and all that he indicated he needed for his home kitchen.

Alya tarried at a kiosk that was selling an item she had not seen before. She was entranced as the vendor demonstrated its use. It was hard to believe that such a small item could operate like a telephone. As soon as the vendor finished his marketing spiel, Alya rapidly asked, "Can I call home to Ethiopia with that?"

The vendor was quick to answer, "You can call anywhere in the world with this cell phone as long as you have phone credits."

That did it for Alya. She fished out of her small purse for the last of her money to buy a cheap cell phone and a calling card. The vendor took her money and handed her the phone and card. Alya immediately looked both ways as she stuffed the phone into her purse. She knew instinctively that her bosses should never know that she had a way to communicate with the outside world.

Alya thanked the vendor and was starting to leave when he asked, "Where are you from?"

"Ethiopia," responded Alya before asking in a like manner, "Where you from?"

The vendor replied. "India. Everybody in the UAE is from some other country. Emiratis are a small minority of the population in the UAE. There are many more people from my home country than there are Emiratis. Not so many from your country, but there are thousands of people from your country spread across the seven tribal emirates that make up the UAE."

The Indian vendor was prepared to say more, but he was interrupted by Alya who said, "Sorry, I have to go now, and join my madame."

"I understand," said the vendor.

Alya rushed to look for Halima and Pamu in the vastness of the modern supermarket. She spied them at the end of one aisle of shelves packed with goods from all over the world. As she approached them, she tried to rein in her giddiness over her new purchase so they would not notice any change in her behavior and start asking her nosy questions. She acted as if nothing had changed and fell silently in line behind Pamu.

They drove back to their house on the outskirts of Dubai city. Pamu and Alya rapidly carried all the purchases into the house, hurrying to get all items out of the blazing sun and into the coolness of the house. Pamu quickly placed all those items needing refrigeration into the fridge and the frozen items into the freezer.

Internally, Alya was dying to go to her room so she could be alone to secretly try out her new cell phone by calling home. Once in her room behind a locked door, she charged her cell phone as she had been instructed. Her fingers trembled as she pressed the buttons to put in her Addis home number. She thought they would not recognize her incoming number so they would not answer their phone. But like a miracle Alya, was hearing Yeshi's voice in Amharic. She was so excited that she almost dropped her cell phone when she said, "Yeshi, it's me, Alya. I'm talking on my new cell phone."

Hearing Alya's voice made Yeshi worry that she had again lost her job in Dubai and she said, "Where are you?"

"I'm here in my workhouse. All is fine. I just wanted to see if my new phone worked. I have to go now. Bye."

The line went dead. Alya looked about her room to see where she could hide her phone so no one would ever know she had her own phone. She felt guilty for doing this clandestinely, but she knew she would be in trouble with her bosses if they found out about her ability to talk anytime with outsiders. Such an act would erode their power over her and would not be tolerated. If found out, they would confiscate her phone and she would no longer be trusted as a loyal servant. The stakes were high, but for Alya, having her own phone was worth the risk.

CHAPTER FOURTEEN

Camels Rule

The loud voices woke Alya early in the morning. She rose from her bed and pressed her ear against the inside of her bedroom door. Her efforts to make out what was being said were thwarted by a heated argument being spoken so rapidly in Arabic that she could not catch a word. By the sound of the two voices, she knew that Yaqub and Halimah were in the living room having a rare verbal disagreement.

There was a sudden spell of silence followed by Halimah saying frantically at the other side of Alya's bedroom door, "Get ready to go. Yaqub insists we go to his camel camp for a few days and participate in the annual Al Dhafra Festival in Abu Dhabi."

Alya was flabbergasted. She did not understand anything Halimah said except that she had to go with her, so she dutifully replied, "Yes, ma'am. I'll get ready to go as fast as I can."

Halimah said through Alya's bedroom door, "Good. I'll need your help and company. I'll explain more later. I have to go and get ready and tell the boys to get ready to join their father in his car."

These words told Alya that the whole family was going. This meant that it was indeed important. She assumed Pamu would be left behind to care for the house. Her toiletries were done at top speed. She threw a few things in a bag and made her bed before flying out the door and through the house to the cars parked in front.

Yaqub was standing beside one of the two big U.S.-made double-cabin, four-wheel drive pick-ups. He was dressed in his usual white gown, but he had changed his head dress to a red and white checkered keffiyeh square cotton scarf held in place by a black agal round band. Besides being fashionable, this scarf provided some protection from the fierce sun and the frequent swirls of dust and sand. His big belly gave his ample gown a midriff bulge. His most distinguishing feature was a smart curly moustache on his unshaven face. He had an infectious smile and his words glided smoothly through his pearly white teeth. His personage fit in well with the fresh early morning breeze. But his words at this moment contradicted this peaceful image. His puzzling loud shouts pleaded, "Hurry, my babies are crying for me."

Alya stood confused in front of him. He took little notice of her before saying, "Go get in the other truck that my father will drive. Halimah will go with you. I'll take my two boys and try to talk some sense to them on the long drive."

The doors to the second pick-up were wide open to allow some airing in the fresh early morning ambience. The sun was just starting to peek over the eastern horizon. It was evident that Yaqub was in a hurry to get on the road and thus he was not happy that Halimah and his two boys were taking so long.

His father did arrive and apologized for being late. He climbed into the second car and sat behind the wheel. This gray-haired elderly gentlemen was dressed in the same clothing that Yaqub wore. His nicely trimmed white beard made him stand out. He motioned to Alya to sit behind him in the passenger row. She did as he wanted. They all waited for Halimah and the boys so they could depart.

They did not have to wait long. Halimah and her two teenage sons came running out of the house. The boys got into their father's pickup and Halimah rushed to find a place next to Alya. Yaqub gunned his pick-up and spun it around to speed ahead on the smooth blacktop. His father lost no time in following him. Both father and son were happy to speed along to their destination in their imported automotive beasts. They had full tanks of gas and wanted to get the most out of their shiny pick-ups.

Alya was tense. She did not know where they were going or why. Halimah saw the puzzled look on Alya's face and said in a soothing voice, "Don't worry. We're just going to see Yaqub's camels and participate in the annual camel festival. All Emiratis will be there with their thousands of camels. Yaqub will be entering three of his prized camels in a beauty contest."

Halimah's words raised more questions in Alya's head than they answered. She was reluctant to say anything but finally mumbled, "I guess when Mister Yaqub spoke of his babies he was talking about his camels."

"Correct. He has thirty-five camels and he loves them more than his children. He certainly spends more time with them. All our wealth is invested in his camels which are a big status symbol for our family. You need to understand how camels are central to Emirati Bedouin culture and traditions. Before we were rich, we were dependent upon camels and at heart every Emirati associates a good life with the lives of camels. In spite of all the glitter of our modern urban cities, we recognize our links with the desert and our camels. For example, Yaqub is only truly at peace when he's with his camels."

Halimah's generous explanation helped Alya understand better the underpinnings of their trip into the sandy desert which she was seeing had many high dunes. But she still had some questions. She asked, "Then why were you arguing?"

"Yaqub was insisting that our sons go with him and they didn't want to go. He contended that in all due respect for our culture and traditions and the high status of our family it was necessary for them to go. He could not accept that the young generation did not want anything to do with camels. I'm sure he's talking now to them about the importance of camels to Emiratis."

Alya wanted to keep quiet but she had to ask, "Where are we going?"

"To his camel camp which is located along the huge Liwa Oasis. He has a house there and several camel caretakers. We'll spend the night there and early in the morning we'll hook up a trailer to carry his three best camels. It'll take up to three hours of travel through the desert to get there. The best thing about the oasis for me is its large number of date palms, so we can eat all the dates we want."

Alya looked out her window only to see a desolate desert as far as the eye could see. She wondered how people who originated in this large mass of sand could be wealthy patrons today. She was awe-struck by the towering height of a number of the sand dunes and feared the breakdown of their vehicle in this hot empty space, far from any help.

Halimah broke the silence by saying, "When we go to Al Dhafra festival, we'll be on the edge of our biggest desert, Rub' All Khali, which is surrounded by tall sand dunes. At the core of the festival are the mazayna—camel beauty contests. Only purebred camels from the best camel lineages participate. The number of camels entered is in the thousands. Hopefully, Yaqub will win one of the top prizes with his three high pedigree camels. These prizes are worth thousands of dollars. Any camel winning a top prize can be sold for over a million dollars. Camels are not only a fundamental part of our cultural heritage but are big business."

The drive across the desert went on. The pick-up's air conditioning was going full blast but the temperature was rising. Outside heat waves were shimmering off the surface of the smooth asphalt highway. After a long drive in the emptiness of the vast desolation of the desert, they neared a small town. Alya was surprised to spy something that looked like a soccer stadium and asked, "What is that?"

Halimah laughed quietly and said, "That my dear is one of many camel racing tracks that we have in every UAE town. Camel racing is a national sport and sponsored by our sheiks. Winning a camel race also has its lucrative rewards. We'll have to go to a race someday. Now, we're getting close the Liwa Oasis."

Alya's eyes were riveted on the lush green vegetation that appeared magically in the middle of reddish sand dunes. She was surprised to also see many foreigners hiking around the oasis. Halimah could see that Alya was seeing the outsiders and said, "Yes, we get many tourists. They visit our oases and attend our camel races and beauty contests. It's big business catering to their needs."

Deep under the shade of date palms and near the edge of the water the pick-ups came to a sudden halt. Several men rushed to open the pick-up doors and greet the occupants, particularly Yaqub. The head of the group gave his updated verbal report on the health of the camels. Yaqub grunted his acknowledgement of his report as he descended rapidly from the pick-up to a spot where he could greet his camels and all his camels could see him. He told the lead man, "Tell my wife and sons to stay put while I greet my camels."

Each of his thirty-five camels came up to him and he patted each camel on the head and said sweetly the camel's name which was according to the year of its birth. The name of a camel would change with each of its birthdates. There were different names for female and male camels. Alya could not only see that Yaqub loved his camels but the camels also loved him. She thought, "If I lived to be a hundred, I could never love such a weird animal."

In general, Alya could not believe what she was seeing. She was spellbound to see each camel approach Yaqub like a pet animal and he knew the names of each camel. When he hugged some of the camels to show them special affection, it dawned on Alya that the strange smell she sensed when she washed Yaqub's clothes was the scent of his camels. It was an odd smell she could never forget.

After Yaqub had finished greeting his camels, Halimah said, "Let's get out and look around."

They walked through a forest of old date palm trees to the edge of the oasis water. Halimah did not want to admit it, but the place brought her much internal peace and relieved all the stress of town-living. The traditional harmony of the oasis setting settled in every pore of her being. She stayed silent to express her reverence for this place and all the ancestors who had come before her and camped out in this place of salvation.

Halimah showed Alya the path to the house and when they arrived at the front door, she said, "We'll not go in unless invited to do so by my husband. The space in the house is usually reserved for men, but nobody sleeps in the house. It's too hot. The men sleep in the open big Bedouin tent next to the house. Let me show you the tent."

A short distance from the house, amidst a grove of shady date palms, was a spacious tent erected in the old ancestral style. They spent a few minutes to gander into the tent with is flaps wide open. It was decorated with many traditional items and swords and knives owned by previous generations. On the floor, were colorful dyed carpets of handwoven camel hair. Halimah was careful to note for Alya, "The men will sleep on the camel wool carpets. In the olden days, our ancestors depended on every product of the camel—its hair, its meat and milk, and even camel urine was valued a medicine. A family without camels was unheard of, but a family without camels would indeed be a poor one. Before, there could be no human life in the desert without camels."

The key importance of camels to Emirati life was sinking into Alya's tired brain, but there was one thing that troubled her, so she asked, "If the men sleep in the tent, where do we sleep?"

This question made Halimah laugh and she replied, "In the pick-up. Don't worry too much. It will be too hot to sleep and we'll get up before dawn to load the camels. Now, let's return to where the pick-ups are parked."

This was a strange world for Alya—one that she had never experienced before. She was concerned that she could not survive the heat. And she was hungry and thirsty. She was glad to see the foreign camel caretakers preparing a place with carpets on the sandy ground near the pick-ups. It looked like some sort of picnic in the making.

A small pit had been dug for a hot-stone pebble fire next to one carpet for the boiling of traditional strong Arabic coffee. This centuries-old coffee custom was familiar to Alya as their coffee ceremony pre-dated the one practiced in the UAE. Moreover, the Arabic coffee used in the UAE originated in Ethiopia.

Alya asked Halimah, "Who will serve the coffee? I can do that."

"No, my dear. It's a little different than a similar serving of coffee in your country. I'm sure Yaqub has trained one of his Bangladeshi workers to prepare and serve coffee as required here. We call coffee 'gawah.' This is an opportunity for you to learn more of our customs and language." Halimah continued by saying, "The place arranged for sitting down to drink coffee and eat dates and nuts is called 'majlis.' The long-spouted clay jug used to boil the coffee is called 'dallah.' Our coffee always includes cardamon and saffron spices."

Alya was struck by the similarities of preparing and serving coffee with the customs of her own country. The 'dallah' was not unlike the 'jabena' they used back home. The main difference was that a man served the coffee. Evidently, the man had been shown all the etiquette involved with serving coffee. He served first Yaqub's father. Each of the handle less small cups was filled with steaming black coffee one-fourth the way from the top of the cup. Alya learned that no more than three cups of coffee should be served to anyone. This fact also agreed with the coffee-drinking practices in her own country.

Plates full of dates were passed around to eat. Alya found the sweet dates to be delicious. She and Halimah were comfortable sitting on the carpet behind the men. All the time she tried to avoid the glances of the two boys. Looking at them disgusted her and all she could think about was how nasty they were. In particular, every time she washed their scummy bed sheets she was reminded of their overactive teenage boy hormones.

The sun was going down, providing some relief from the intense heat and signaled to Halimah that they should withdraw so she could do her nightly Islamic prayers. She was followed by Alya as she returned to the pick-up to fetch her prayer rug and necklace of beads. Halimah said to Alya, "Come with me and see how we pray. It's important that you learn about our religion."

Alya followed Halimah into a dense grove of date palms and was obliged by nature to ask, "May I relieve myself?"

"Of course, go behind a palm tree to do your business. I will find my own tree and do the same. We'll meet back in this spot in five minutes."

They rejoined and Halimah found a spot to roll out her prayer rug so she would be facing East. She said to Alya, "Watch me. Imitate me if you want. Later, if you have any questions, ask me."

Alya withdrew a short distance from Halimah, watching her pray out of the corner of her eyes. She concentrated on her own prayers, beseeching her Chistian God, Jesus, and the Saints, particularly Mariyam,

Earthly mother of Jesus the son of God. This was her orthodox religion and she was deeply content with this earlier revelation. But she wanted to learn as much as she could about the local culture and history and that meant learning about their Islamic faith. But, for the moment, she was praying to the God she had known all her life for good health and for an increased understanding of the new world in which she found herself.

CHAPTER FIFTEEN

A Good But Sad Start

SLEEPING PRACTICALLY IN AN UPRIGHT position in one's clothes in a pick-up parked on the edge of a hot desert meant not getting much nocturnal rest. Any sleep came in stops and starts when bodily exhaustion overcame discomfort. Even though they were on their way well before sunrise, the night seemed unbearably long. Alya could not help but want to return to the comfortable comforts of her own bed. Maybe it was the eerie glow that filtered through the date palm branches made by the random low voltage electric lights that had been fixed about the camel camp that prevented Alya from getting much sleep. She was surprised that electrical power illuminated without fail the oasis and all its many dwellings. Her Addis home rarely had electricity and when it did it was expensive. At home, they mainly got by at night with cheap candles and kerosene lamps.

Before Alya was fully awake, Halimah was already doing her morning prayers on the ground beside the pick-up. She watched out of the corner of her eyes as she bowed and stood, doing the requisite number of rak'as of the dawn prayer. Each time she bowed down she touched her head to the ground, confirming her devoutness by deepening the brown spot in the middle of her forehead. Halimah was a devout Muslim and she carried her prayer rug with her wherever she went so she could do her five Islamic prayers (salat) each day.

Halimah also carried purified water with her for the ritual ablutions her faith required before each prayer. This holy water was kept separate from their ample supply of plastic bottles filled with cool drinking water that were kept in an ice chest on the floor of the pick-up. Obviously, the camp workers had prepared these chests in advance. They had raided the large refrigerator in the camp kitchen building that had been constructed next to the main house. They packed the chests with ice cubes and bottles of water before placing them in the pick-ups.

As soon as Halimah finished her prayer, pick-up doors slammed shut and their motors roared as they sped north to Madinat Zayed, following the asphalt highway that skirted the endless desert on the west that stretched into Saudi Arabia's empty quarter. Madinat Zayed was a small town representing the region of Al Gharbia of Abu Dhabi, one of the seven Emirates of the UAE. This region was composed entirely of desert.

Alya did not know any of this. The radical contrast with her home country was stark. Whereas she grew up in verdant high mountains of Addis Ababa, there was nothing around her except sandy desert. The landscape was not flat but interrupted by high sand dunes. The dim light of the dawning sun confirmed to her that she was lost in a sandy bleakness.

Although blurry eyed as they headed toward the annual Al Dhafara Festival with Yaqub's three show camels, her sandy surroundings prompted Alya to ask Halimah, "If you have nothing but sand, why is your country richer than mine which is covered with greenery?"

Halimah laughed and said simply, "Under this sand, large pools of oil exist. The sale of that oil helped us become an important financial center. Of course, all this was only possible under the wise guidance of our Sheiks."

There it was again— Halimah's use of the word, "sheik." Alya did not understand, so she asked Halimah, "Excuse me, but what's a sheik?"

Halimah did not want to laugh over Alya's ignorance, but she laughed at length before saying, "The Sheiks are our hereditary leaders. Each of our seven emirates has a main tribe of Bedouins and each tribe has a dominant royal family. For example, we're in the Abu Dhabi emirate and the leading tribe historically is the Bani Yas, therefore the Sheik is chosen from the royal family of this tribe. Abu Dhabi is the most populous of the emirates and the leader of Bani Yas tribe is the UAE president. Usually the sheik is the son of the former sheik. Complicated for an outsider but for us this is normal."

Alya's head was aching from an overdose of information. Her simple question had generated a lengthy and involved reply from Halimah that she did not expect. She decided to confine any of her questions to the events of the moment, so she asked, "How long before we reach the camel festival site?"

"It's about an hour's drive more but we are going slow because of the trailer carrying Yaqub's prize camels. We should arrive as the sun comes up. The festival lasts many days and activities are done in the cool mornings. Yaqub is going today because he is scheduled to show his three camels to the beauty contest judges."

Alya was progressively learning more about the UAE and its people but nothing prepared her for the sight of the approaching lieu of the annual camel festival. She could not believe her eyes. There was a huge jumble of people, cars, trucks, trailers, animals and tents. She was impressed by the large number of foreign tourists who had traveled to the middle of the expansive desert to witness part of the festival. No visitor could see it all by staying the many days it took from beginning to end.

It appeared that all Emiratis were there to celebrate their cultural heritage. Many of them possessed animals to show off. Principal among these animals were thousands of camels, some of them for speed racing and others to compete with Yaqub's camels in beauty pageants. The were also Arabian horses and saluki dogs that would compete in their respective races. There were also popular falcon races.

Every aspect of Emirati traditions were covered. The aroma emanating from the coffee and food stalls erected enticed Halimah and Alya to go on their own to visit the many souks. As they thread their way through the crowds, out of curiosity, Alya asked. "Where are your sons?'

"They are with their father. He wants them to observe all that he does with his beauties so some day they will be able to do the same and maintain the reputation of our family."

They wound their way through the open air, makeshift labyrinth marketplace, stopping at dozens of shops so Halimah could look at the many items for sale. She examined gold jewelry, hand-woven carpets, and expensive embroidered cloth and cushions. She spent a lot of time in shops devoted to aromatic spices. As the day progressed, she said to Alya, "We must hurry so we can be there when Yaqub finishes showing his three camels. We want to avoid the blistering heat of the midday sun."

They returned to their pickup to find it empty and locked. They sat down on the sandy ground on the shady side of the pickup, but the sun was rising quickly to its zenith. Both of them wished for a quick return of Yaqub's father, not only because he would open and start the pickup so that its air conditioner would cool its interior, but to see if he had heard from anyone any good news about the score given Yaqub's camels by the judges.

Halimah was afraid that the increasing velocity of the wind would make all their lives miserable by producing a sandstorm. Her worry was dissipated by the sudden return of Yaqub's father who rapidly opened the driver's side of the pick-up, started the engine and turned on the air-conditioner. He then waved to Halimah and Alya to get in the pick-up.

As soon as they were seated and their doors closed, the pick-up was driven slowly to where the other pick-up and its trailer were parked. They could see Yaqub and the two boys were seated in their pick-up and ready to go. It was assumed the three camels had already been loaded into the trailer with one of their caretakers. As soon as Yaqub saw them coming, he turned his pick-up and started heading toward the main highway leading to Liwa Oasis and his camel camp. This signaled that the showing of his camels was over.

Silently, Yaqub's father followed his son's pick-up. They were returning to their oasis camel camp. Halimah wanted to ask Yaqub's father about the showing at the camel beauty contest, but she thought it best that he volunteer this information. Yaqub's father was tight-lipped during the return journey. He thought it was best for Yaqub to say what he wanted known about the judges verdicts on his three camels. The suspense weighed heavily on Halimah and Alya, but they could do nothing until words on this subject came out of Yaqub's mouth.

They arrived at the camel camp without fanfare. The camel caretakers dutifully unloaded the three camels and led them to eat and drink. Halimah and Alya were invited into the air-conditioned oasis house to rest and prepare for tomorrow's long drive home. Halimah thought that Yaqub would announce the results of his camels' entry into the beauty contest, but all Yaqub did was take a nap on one of his camel hair rugs. It was evident that either his camels were graded poorly by the judges or were rated prize-worthy.

After they had all rested in the air-conditioned house they withdrew to the nearby maljis seating place in the evening shade of the thick palm tree grove. Coffee had already been prepared by one of the caretakers and big plates of dates were set out on the mat. They all sat in their same places, waiting for the tiny cups of strong coffee and heaping plates of delicious juicy sweet dates to be passed around. Everyone thought there was no better time for Yaqub to announce the judges' decisions on his camels.

Silence blanketed the group. All eyes were focused on Yaqub who was acutely aware of the stares and the expectation for him to talk. After first cups of coffee had been drunk, Yaqub cleared his throat and said in a solemn fashion, "This is a sad day for our family. The judges did not consider that our camels should be ranked. I'm sure we'll have better luck next year. We'll start preparing now for next year's festival."

Yaqub's sobering words put the group in a somber mood. Alya struggled to decipher Yaqub's Arabic words, but she could see by the faces made by his family members that what he said was not good. She saw this was not a subject to delve into more deeply. But she was not only disturbed by how their spirits were doused by Yaqub's sober words, the furtive glances directed at her by the two teenage boys also troubled her.

In spite of the heat, these glances sent a chill up her spine and she was afraid they would try something before they left for home in the outskirts of Dubai City early the next morning. She made a mental note to close and lock the pick-up door no matter how hot and uncomfortable it was on this last night in the camel camp. She swore softly to herself that she would not allow these boys to upset her job by taking advantage of her in any way. If needed, she would discuss her concerns with Halimah.

The night in the pick-up passed quickly in spite of the flimsy efforts of the boys to get to Alya who always kept one eye open and was ready to fight off any attacker. She was glad when morning coffee was over and they boarded the pick-ups for the return trip back to their house in the Dubai Emirate. Halimah and Alya slept most of the way back home, trusting Yaqub's father to transport them home safely.

They arrived exhausted. Everyone went straight to their rooms to sleep. Once all had gone and she greeted Pamu, Alya followed suit and went to her room to take a hot shower and get fully rested in her bed so she could rise early the next morning and do her job. She was snuggled comfortably under her bed covers when there was a soft knock on her door. At first, she thought it was Pamu leaving a food tray, but after several knocks she heard the unmistakable voice of Yusuf, calling her name. Her hands trembled involuntarily and her heartbeat sped up while she tried to remain stone silent.

Alya wanted Yusuf to go away and never bother her again. She pretended to be asleep and not hearing his knocking on the door. Then, he knocked more loudly again. She could sense the urgency of his knock and tried to assuage her fears of being sexually attacked by the fact that the door was locked. Thus, he could not get into her bedroom.

There on the nightstand next to her bed was the bedroom door key. The more she looked at the key, the more doubts arose in her frightened mind that she had indeed locked the door to her bedroom. She tried to remember locking the door but could not recall inserting the key in the door keyhole and turning it twice to assure it was bolt locked. Her faulty memory about locking the door caused her to quietly get up, grab the key and scurry to the door and insert the key so she could assure herself that it was indeed locked. She found the door was fully locked and she breathed a sigh of relief that something done routinely could often not be clearly remembered. But she knew that the locking sound would alert Yusuf of her presence. She had no choice but to yell through the door, "Go away now. Otherwise I will tell your parents. I will scream if you don't go away now. What you want is haram and you know it."

Alya stood for a long time at her bedroom door. She thought she heard Yusuf retreat and run back to his bedroom. As she heard no more knocking, she was satisfied that her verbal threats had worked this time. But she worried about the next time Yusuf or his younger brother, Benjamin, would try to enter her bedroom. Her concerns about being sexually assaulted by them were growing bigger and stronger. She was unsure of what she should do about the problem they posed.

Then she remembered that she had a cellphone that allowed her to call home and ask her grandmother for advice. She retrieved her cellphone from its hiding place and hooked up its charging cord to an electrical outlet. She sat on the floor beside the outlet determined to talk with Yeshi. Even though it would be in the middle of the night back in her Addis home, she considered this an emergency and she had to talk with Yeshi no matter what.

Alya nervously pressed the buttons on the cellphone that would connect with her Addis home. The phone rang on the other end incessantly but nobody answered. She called several times more, telling herself they were sleeping and had to wake up. The fourth time she called there was a feeble answer. It was the voice of Yeshi. Alya blurted out, "Yeshi, is that you. I'm in trouble. I need to talk with you."

Yeshi was shocked by Alya's unexpected news about her trouble. Alya explained her undesirable situation. Yeshi did not know what advice to give her sole breadwinner. She said, "Do all you can to avoid those boys and keep doing a good job. We're depending on you to do whatever it takes to maintain you job. We'll pray for you so you can overcome the menace posed by these two boys. I understand how hard it is for you, but we're counting on you to overcome any obstacle. Please get some rest so you can carry on as before. Good night. We love you."

The connection went dead. Again Alya found herself alone in the dark in a foreign country with a people and culture vastly different than her home country and all she had known growing up in Ethiopia. Her grandmother's words helped her redouble her efforts to adapt to the job and her new surroundings. She tried to convince herself that this was a good job in spite of the wayward tendencies of Yusuf and Benyamin. She would do her utmost to avoid and discourage them at all costs. Their presence in the house made doing her job harder, but she was determined to do a job which satisfied Halimah. She had to succeed, boys or no boys.

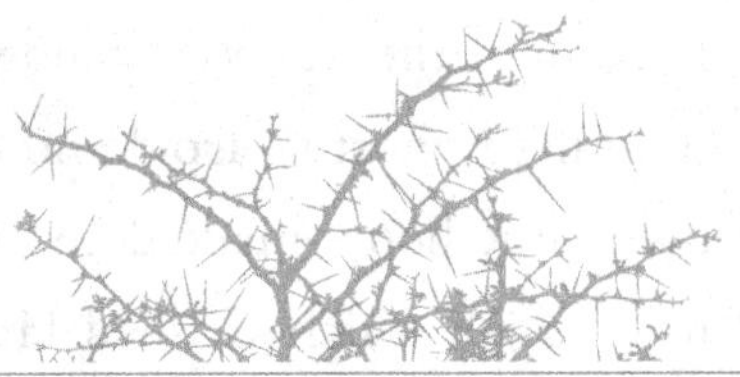

CHAPTER SIXTEEN

Thrown Off Track

PRIORITY WAS GIVEN BY ALYA to do as perfectly as possible her household tasks. She was doing her best to satisfy her bosses who never complained about her work. In doing so, she had become a reliable member of the family. When Halimah complemented her on any task she had performed, she was on cloud nine. Halimah was not only happy with her work, but she was also pleased with the progress she was making in learning Arabic and her growing knowledge of their Islamic religious faith.

All was going fine for Alya except the augmented pressure placed on her by Yusuf and Benyamin. These two boys had become more aggressive in their pursuit of Alya. She did all she could to avoid and discourage them, but they never ceased in their efforts to corner Alya so they could satisfy their sexual urges. For them, Alya was free game and they fixated on her as their supreme sexual symbol. They had become obsessed with Alya and believed that part of her servant's job was to allow them to have sex with her.

Alya's approach was to have no contact with Yusuf and Benyamin.

When they were home, she would lock herself in her bedroom or go to a distant part of the house that they never frequented. If she passed them at all, she told them in Arabic that what they were doing was counter to their Islamic faith. She did everything possible to develop a close bond with Halimah in order to make them afraid of violating her.

The boys were bigger than Alya and she knew if they tried to pin her down, she could not fight them off her. The job was going fine. Her relationship with Halimah was strongly cemented and she had her utmost trust. But she could not bring herself to tell Halimah about the problem her sons posed for her. It was too sensitive of a subject and she was afraid that talking about it with her would make her dicey situation worse.

Somehow Alya continued to dodge the boys and do her work to the satisfaction of her employers who were pleased with her and her work. At the end of her first year, they made the exceptional gesture of buying her a roundtrip ticket so she could go home to see her family in Addis Ababa. She could not believe the magnanimity of Halimah's vacation gift and tears streamed down her cheeks when Halimah handed her a ticket and her passport. She knew this was an unheard-of demonstration of trust. She openly cried when Halimah said, "Don't cry. You are like a sister to me. We highly appreciate your work and don't want to lose you. You are a part of our family and you deserve a break."

Alya wiped away her tears and said, "Thank you so much. Your words mean a lot to me. Please excuse me now as I want to go to my room to compose myself."

Halimah was quick to rejoin, "I thought you would want to go to your room to pack because we have booked you on a flight that leaves tomorrow afternoon. Study your ticket so you know your departure and return dates well. Of course, I'll take you to the airport in plenty of time to board your flight."

Hearing these words from Halimah prompted a rise in Alya's

excitement level. She had not been this happy in a long time. Getting far away from the clutches of the two boys by going home for two weeks was like a dream come true. Halimah did not know about Alya's problem with her sons. She also did not know the main reason she wanted to rush to her room was to use her hidden cellphone to call home. Alya could not wait to inform her family of the wonderful surprise of a two-week vacation with them.

Alya charged her phone and immediately called home. Yeshi answered quickly after the first two rings. Breathlessly, Alya joyfully said, "I'm coming home. I'll be there the day after tomorrow."

A confused Yeshi was scared that Alya had lost her job and said, "Why are you coming home? You didn't lose your job again?"

"No. All is good. My bosses liked my work so much that they gave me a ticket and my passport and told me to go home to visit my family for two weeks. Isn't this good news?"

Yeshi tried to digest Alya's words in spite of her shock. She sensed the high excitement communicated by Alya's happy voice but all she could say was, "I don't believe you but if you have to come home, we'll receive you with open arms."

"Okay. See you the day after tomorrow. I'm looking forward to my two weeks at home. I can tell all to you better when I'm there. Goodbye for now."

Alya sprang up quickly from her usual sitting position on the tiled floor and unplugged her cellphone from the only wall electrical outlet in her room. She hid her phone in a place deep in her closet that was only known to her. She then withdrew her small suitcase from the same closet and began to place the clothes she wanted to take with her on her home vacation. She was excited and began to sing an Amharic song. Her singing was not only to express her gaiety but to steady her nerves. With her suitcase packed, she wondered what more she had to do to get ready for her departure tomorrow.

Alya examined closely her ticket and passport several times. This repeated process served to convince her that all was in order and it was true that she was actually going home for a visit with her family. Her passport had a visa for Dubai stamped in it that was valid for four more years. Her confirmed Dubai-Addis Ababa roundtrip ticket was accurate and in hand. Alya wanted to shout out the glorious news of her trip so the whole world would know of her unbelievable good luck.

This moment of celebration was interrupted by a single knock on the door. Alya associated this knock with Pamu, but she was afraid that the boys were playing a trick so they could get to her inside her bedroom. Hesitantly, she approached her side of the door and cupped her right ear against the door to listen better. She then heard Pamu's voice saying. "I brought you a tray of food, but I also want to say a few words to you."

As it was highly uncharacteristic of Pamu to say anything, Alya was still afraid the boys were playing a trick on her to gain access to her bedroom. Then Pamu's voice was heard again, saying. "I'm alone. I wanted to say goodbye. I know you are leaving tomorrow and that you will not be back."

Alya was surprised that Pamu had waited until now to talk and by his belief that she would not return. She had sufficient confidence that Pamu was alone, so she unlocked and opened the door a crack. As soon as she did that, the normally speechless Pamu said quickly, "I see your problem and believe you should not come back to this house to avoid this problem from becoming worse. I can't risk my job by becoming involved. I wish you well. You've been a good house worker. Bye."

Pamu left as surreptitiously as he had come. He did not want to be seen talking to Alya. The food was retrieved and the bedroom door was immediately closed and locked. Alya was trying to interpret in her mind

Pamu's words, which were more than she had heard from him in a year. She was impressed that he had known about her problem with her two teenage male predators and she understood why he could not become involved. The potential for scandal and much trouble were too great.

She did not understand his telling her not to come back to this house. What choice did she have but to return to her job in this house? After all, she had to keep her job so she could continue to support her family and, especially, her little daughter in Addis. Not having a paying job was in no way acceptable to her. Pamu's words tormented Alya. His words and the excitement of her departure prevented her from sleeping. She passed the time by praying in front of a small painting she always carried with her of Mariyam, the virgin mother of Jesus Christ. As she prostrated herself in front of the image of Mariyam, she tried to rid her mind of Pamu's words about not coming back to this house.

Alya laid on top of her bed all night long with the electric lights on. She was fearful that the two teenage demons would try to break into her room. Her fears stemmed from the fact that they knew this was her last night before going on a two-week vacation. She was ready for anything and she was prepared to suffer death before she would give into the sexual desires of Yusuf and Benyamin.

It was early morning and there was a slight tap on her door. She smiled when she heard through the door a single word, "Food."

Pamu was dependable and efficient in doing his job. It was ingrained in him a servant's duty and he did his cooking duties without fail. This duty included not doing anything to jeopardize his job and his ability to remit money to his family in Sri Lanka. Alya wished she were a man and could be like Pamu. Her basic tendencies made her an unlikely candidate to play a servant's role forever.

Alya did her toiletries and dressed in her housemaid uniform that Halimah had graciously purchased for her. She left her bedroom and began tidying the house. Halimah appeared and seeing her busy at work said cheerfully, "My dear Alya, you should be resting for your long flight home this afternoon and evening. Please take this time to rest. Make sure you're ready to leave at one p.m. I'll drive you to the airport."

Alya did not know what to say so she just said, "Thank you. I'll be ready to go at one."

The clatter of plates in the kitchen told Alya that Pamu was there. After Halimah left the premises, she wanted to go to the kitchen to talk with Pamu but on second thought she knew he would not say anything, so she did not go see him and went to her boring room to while away the time until she left. She needed a timepiece so she would know when one p.m. would occur in local time. Thus, she retrieved her cellphone which gave her the time and she did not want to forget to take it with her. She did not want her bosses to find it, but she wanted to show it off to her family in Addis.

Halimah started her car before one p.m. to let the air-conditioner circulate cool air. Although the roof of their carport reflected the sun's rays, it was hot enough outside to fry an egg on the pavement. Alya saw Halimah in her luxury car and rushed to throw her suitcase in the back seat and take a seat next to Halimah in the front seat. In her usual fashion, Halimah zoomed off at top speed, saying, "I love to drive fast my car."

After saying those few words, Halimah was silent as she concentrated on her speedy driving. Alya clutched her seat and made sure her seatbelt was fastened. Halimah's fast driving habit scared Alya. Before she knew it, Halimah screeched to a stop in front the departure terminal and turning to look at Alya, said "Here you are. You can get out now. Have a good vacation. See you in two weeks. Here, take this. Safe travels."

Alya stood alone on the sizzling sidewalk, waving to Halimah as she sped off. Halimah's generosity always amazed Alya. The two hundred

U.S. dollar bills she had handed her were equal to a month's salary. She turned to enter the terminal and was happy that the officials at the entrance handed her passport and ticket back to her without comment. There were no problems with checking in and passing through the formalities.

As she passed by the many shops, she said to herself, I should buy some souvenirs for my family. She went into a shop and bought a small stuffed camel to give to her little daughter. She went into another shop and bought bracelets made of beads of different colors. Her most expensive gift in the same shop was a silver necklace for Yeshi. She had spent some money, but she knew she could not go home empty handed.

Alya grabbed her plastic bags with her gifts and got in line to board her flight. She found her window seat on the plane and acted as if she had flown on planes many times. After casual greetings to her seat mates and the plane took off, she decided to try to sleep so she would be wide awake to meet her family and spend the day talking with them to describe in some detail her existence in Dubai.

To her surprise, she fell into a deep sleep and did not wake up until it was announced over the plane's PA system its approach to Addis Ababa. She deboarded the plane and walked briskly to the baggage claim area to retrieve her small suitcase. With nothing of great value to declare, she walked through customs with an air of superiority. Her heart sang by hearing everyone speak in Amharic. It was good to be back in her home country. She secretly wished she could find a good paying job in her own country so she would not have to go abroad again.

Many taxis were in front of the airport. All of them were in search of fares and were hawking their services loudly. Alya did not know which taxi to pick. There was one taxi driver not saying anything, so Alya had doubts about choosing him but she picked him up anyway. Once she and her suitcase were in the taxi, Alya explained to the taximan where she wanted to go.

It was a bright sunny day and Alya was enjoying immensely being in familiar surroundings. In particular, she enjoyed the freshness of the temperature of Addis. It never got this cool in Dubai. The agreeable weather made her wish that she never had to return to Dubai. Although she rebelled against the idea, she realized deep down that her destiny as a house servant was in Dubai if she wanted her family to survive. She hated being in the prison of the poor and not having the money to be free to do what she wanted.

The taxi stopped in front of her housing compound. All eyes along the road were fixated on the taxi to see who would get out of it. These eyes mostly belonged to friends and neighbors. When they saw Alya get out of the taxi, they immediately wondered what had happened to her job in Dubai. They realized her work in Dubai was a vital lifeline for her family. There was a mass sigh of relief when they saw that Alya had a big smile on her face. This sparkling smile told them that all was well and she was only visiting for a brief while before returning to work abroad. Alya was eager to hug her family members. She paid the taximan with some dollars she had received as change in the shops in the Dubai Airport, grabbed her suitcase and ducked into her ramshackle housing compound.

She immediately took her little girl in her arms and lifted her high into the air before hugging her close to her body. Her little girl, Hiyab, did not know Alya was her mother, and squealed and squirmed to be released from the grip of this strange woman. Her two younger teenage sisters, Belkis and Fana, gave her a hug and welcomed her home. Yeshi stood at some distance away like a granite statue when Alya walked up to her and kissed her softly on the cheek. Yeshi tried to hide the tears in her eyes and roughly said, "I'm sorry, but you've to go back soon. Our lives depend upon you working."

"Don't worry. I'm going back. I was given this short vacation in honor of my good work and the trust my Arab employer has for me. All is well and going better than expected, Alya said to Yeshi, but she knew that for her money talked louder than words.

It was what Alya did not say that was perhaps more important. She did not say a word about her encounters with Yusuf and Benyamin, and about Pamu's warning not to come back. She would keep these sad realities hidden from her family. She did not want them to know the whole truth. She would have to deal with that herself.

CHAPTER SEVENTEEN

The Best Way Forward

YESHI SMILED UPON SEEING ALYA'S return ticket and her valid visa. Alya had to laugh because she had never seen Yeshi smile before. She could not resist hugging Yeshi and whispering in her ear, "You can always count on me. I'll never let you down."

Tears came to Yeshi's eyes which were like twinkling stars set in a wrinkled face. But then in an instant she was standing up and clapping her hands to get everyone's attention and yelling, "Come on everyone. Let's celebrate Alya's return before she leaves us again." Yeshi's teary eyes were transformed into sparkling jewels and she went about barking orders to Alya's sisters to get everything ready for an Ethiopian feast. This meant making lots of injera and an assortment of spicy sauces. Of course, this would include a traditional coffee ceremony and the burning of incense. All these things had to be procured and that took more money from Alya as she was the only one whom they could turn to for money.

Their compound neighbors quickly learned of what was going on and contributed several bottles of honey wine. While Alya was handing out money to her two sisters, she saw how worn and ragged their sitting room couch had become. The ugly status of the couch caused her to make a snap decision to replace it with a new one so they could celebrate in style. She immediately corralled Fana and said, "Take me to where they sell new furniture. We have to buy a new couch before the celebration starts."

When Fana said she was ready to go, Alya hollered to Yeshi, "We're going out. We'll be back in an hour or so."

While greeting their neighbors, Alya and Fana exited their housing compound to hail a passing taxi. Alya instructed the taximan to take them to the place where they made furniture along the roadside. Within ten minutes, they had arrived at the place and after dispatching their taxi, they meandered among the rows of furniture. They looked for a well-made, colorful couch that would fit nicely along the wall in their sitting room. There were many to choose from but Fana had made up her mind and said gleefully, "This is the one."

Alya said, "Are you sure this will be acceptable to the rest of the family?"

"Of course, they'll love it."

Alya told herself that she should know what she is talking about because she would be one of the family members sitting on the couch. Alya signaled to the guy overseeing the display of locally made furniture and said simply, "We'll take this one. How much?"

After some bargaining, they agreed on a final price for the couch and the cost of its transport to their house. As soon as Alya handed some of her dollars over to the man, a couple of young guys showed up to load the couch onto a nearby beat-up old pickup. These same guys helped Alya and Fana to sit alongside the couch in the bed of the aged pickup. Their job was to hold the couch in place as they rattled along, often falling into potholes, over a bumpy road pocked with deep holes.

They arrived in front of their compound entrance and came to an abrupt stop after Alya signaled to the driver that this was her house. People from the neighborhood gathered around to ogle at the new couch and to offer their services to carry it to the front door of her house inside the compound. All along the way people applauded inside and outside the compound in support of the acquisition of a new couch. This was evidence of the work sacrifices abroad of Alya paying off. They all envied her and the money she made.

The couch was set down outside Alya's front door and she thanked everyone, especially those who had carried the couch. Yeshi appeared on the doorstep and declared, "Such a blessing for our humble house."

Alya asked respectfully for Yeshi to step outside while she and her sisters moved the old couch so they could carry in the new couch. They moved the old couch aside, showing a large amount of filth that had accumulated beneath and behind it. Yeshi immediately set about sweeping and dusting the place where the old couch had been. When they finished cleaning the spot where the old couch had been located, Belkis said, "Okay. All clean. Now let's carry in the new couch and haul the old one out."

Alya's heard Belkis' word but her eyes were focused on an envelope lying against the wall where the old couch had been. It was obvious that the dusty envelope had been there many years. She called Yeshi to come and see and said to her, "What is that?"

Yeshi stared at the envelope for a couple of minutes, trying to collect her thoughts, before saying in disbelief, "I thought that envelope had been lost for all time years ago."

Alya eagerly said, "What's in it?"

"The last time I saw it, it contained old black-and-white photographs of my deceased husband and your murdered father. Bring me the envelope and we'll see together what it contains."

Alya fetched the old envelope and gave it to Yeshi, saying, "Wait until we get the new couch in place and we'll sit on it as we open the envelope and view its contents."

Yeshi withdrew to the far side of their small sitting room while Alya and her two sisters lifted the new couch and placed it where the old couch had been. They then proceeded to take the old couch outside and placed it under the eaves of their house so it could be used as an outdoor sitting place. They did this happily because there was some prestige attached to having such an outdoor sitting place.

Yeshi stared at the new couch. That she had such a beautiful couch in her sitting room was beyond her wildest imagination. Among her first thoughts was that it was too pretty to sit on. Alya and her sisters knew they could not sit on the couch until Yeshi did. Alya turned to Yeshi and said, "Please sit down on your couch. I'll sit down beside you and we'll look at the envelope's contents together."

Reluctantly, Yeshi stepped forward to the couch and sat down. Alya said, "Now, I'll sit down with you on your new couch."

When Alya and Yeshi were comfortably seated, they laughed together in recognition of adding a new piece of furniture to their sitting room after so many years of having the same old furniture. This was indeed a special occasion that merited their celebration. Afterall, it was not every day you enjoyed a new couch in your house. It was a reminder of the necessity of Alya's work and a brighter future ahead for her family.

The photos in the envelope were taken long before Alya was born. Among the old photos were snaps of Yeshi when she was a young woman and of her handsome husband before he was killed in the war against the Italian occupation. There was also a photo of Alya's father who had been put to death many years ago by Ethiopia's military communist dictator. Upon seeing these photos, it was hard for them to retain their tears. They were sad not only for the dearly departed but for the better days they enjoyed decades ago.

Alya spread some of her money around and preparations for a feast were in a fast forward motion. She surprised her family members with the gifts she had bought for them in Dubai Airport. Little Hiyab liked the feeling of her little stuffed camel, but she did not know what a camel was and called it in Amharic an Arab horse. No matter how small and cheap Alya's gifts were, they could only express high appreciation of these unexpected souvenirs. They had no choice but to cherish them forever.

There was much gaiety as they ate, drank, sang and talked nonstop to one another. Then they prayed and talked again. Ethiopian music was broadcast from a small battery-operated radio. A foreign onlooker might think Yeshi's house was full of birds chirping away in a happy chorus. It was a time to forget your troubles in life and enjoy fully the moment. Their neighbors joined in the festivities and contributed additional incense and other food items to make this truly a community event. It was a couple of hours before the coffee ceremony started. Given the size of the group, a neighbor added another coffee stand with cups and a burning charcoal holder for another jabena coffee pot. It was a joyous time that will not be soon forgotten. It was not lost on anyone that this happy time was made possible by Alya's work abroad.

For Alya, she wished this time could last forever. She wished that Tigist could be here now, but her family said she had also gone to Dubai. Alya tried not to think of the dark side of her employment in Dubai but pounding in her head was the daunting question, "What'll I do about the boys?"

She decided to tell the truth to Samrawit and ask her what she should do. Pamu's warning had scared her more than she wanted to admit. Samrawit was the only one she could think of who had the experience in Dubai to advise her on what action she should take. Alya promised herself that beginning tomorrow she would seek out the wise counsel of Samrawit. She was prepared to do anything Samrawit recommended, but she had to be engaged in a good paying job.

Early the next morning she walked to Samrawit's house. She announced her intentions to a man guarding the front gate and he said, "Samrawit is not here. Come tomorrow at the same time to see if she has returned. Tell me your name so I can tell her who wants to see her?"

"Tell her Alya is here on vacation from her job in Dubai and she wanted to greet her and ask her something."

After saying these words to the door guard, Alya slowly walked back through the misty, sunless weather to her neighborhood. She found all her family members sitting bunched up on the new couch. As soon as she entered their sitting room, they all thanked her for her gifts, especially the gift of a new couch. Each of them told her how thankful they were for the money she sent to them each month. Even baby Hiyab kept repeating in a nonsensical fashion the word in Amharic for thank you. Their words underscored the critical importance of her keeping her job in Dubai no matter what.

Alya spent the day with her family. Each chatted about everyday events of the past year. Alya gave more details on her year of living and working in Dubai. She tried to tell them as much as she could about her experiences in Dubai, knowing fully there were many things they could not grasp as they were beyond their known world. In telling about her Dubai adventures, she also realized that there was much she did not know about the UAE and its people.

The next day Alya walked to Samrawit's house again. This time the front gate was open and the same gate guard told her. "Go in. She is expecting you. You'll find her seated in the courtyard garden."

Alya stepped inside Samrawit's lovely home and followed the walking stones to where Samrawit was sitting on the cushions piled atop her comfortable lounge chair. Samrawit smiled and welcomed Alya, asking her to sit in the chair next to hers. They sat quietly while a woman served them coffee. After hot coffee was served, Samrawit said, "Tell me all about it. I want to know everything important. I'll not assume anything.

I've learned after all my years in Dubai to not expect exciting news, but you've been gone a year so I assume all is going well."

At first, Alya did not know what to say in spite of Samrawit's efforts to put her at ease. Slowly, Alya said, "Overall, my experiences working as a housemaid were positive. The fact that I'm here on vacation tells you that my bosses have been exceptionally good to me. They are expecting me to return for another year of work in their house."

Samrawit could see that Alya was nervous and interrupted by saying, "Sounds too good to be true, but I don't think you came to see me to talk about your rosy experience in Dubai. Sure, you've done well, but there must be some problem."

After hearing Samrawit's forceful words, Alya paused for several minutes and cleared her throat before saying, "Yes, there is a problem and I'm not sure about how I should describe it to you. It's not an easy subject to address."

Samrawit could see that Alya needed to talk with her but was stressed by the subject she had to discuss, understanding that she should make every effort to put Alya at ease by saying, "Please settle down and tell me all you are not telling me, no matter how shameful it may be. Rest assured that what you tell me will stay between us two."

By this time, tears were flowing down the golden-brown cheeks of Alya even though she was trying not to get too emotional and tell Samrawit in all confidence what the problem was with her job. When her nerves were steadied, she wiped away her tears with a tissue from a box that Samrawit had provided and blurted out, "My boss has two teenage sons who will not leave me alone. I fear what they will do to me when I return. I've done everything to avoid and discourage them, but their relentless pursuit of me has persisted and grown."

"Stop right there. No need to say more. I understand," Samrawit interjected.

"But what should I do? If I return to that house, I'm doomed by the presence of those two boys," said a clearly strained Alya.

Samrawit thought for a moment and said, "You have your return ticket and passport with a valid UAE visa. Right?"

"Yes, but what does that have to do with my problem?" Alya replied in a quizzical tone.

Samrawit with an air of superiority responded, "Everything. Listen well to me and do as I say. You can't return to the same house unless you are willing to give into the passions of the two boys and suffer the worst consequences."

While Samrawit paused, a shocked Alya said, "You got my attention. I'll do as you say."

"Go to the Ethiopian Airline office to change your departure date to two days earlier. I will meet you at the airport and take you to my place in Dubai City. There are plenty of jobs in town and I'll find one for you. I'm sorry for your old job and the impact your absence will have on the occupants of your UAE house, but they'll get over it and think you decided not to return. If they want, I can find them somebody else to work in their house."

The idea of not returning to the same house in Dubai greatly disturbed Alya. By not returning she had betrayed Halimah and the trust she had in her. She was sad for this reason, but she so dreaded dealing with the two boys again that with much remorse she accepted Samrawit's unfathomable solution to her woes. She simply said to Samrawit, "I will go and change my ticket right after leaving your house and come back here to inform you of the new dates of my arrival. Thank you. I hope all this works out to be the best course of action. I'm going now."

"Yes, my dear go now and do as you said. I'll be waiting to learn your new arrival information. Please don't worry. This is the best way forward."

CHAPTER EIGHTEEN

Freelancing in Dubai

It was an unforgivable crime to change her ticket as instructed by Samrawit, but she had no other choice. Alya knew she was in between a rock and a hard place. She no longer felt good about herself, but what could she do otherwise? As long as she made money for the support of her family, nothing else mattered. She was trapped in a prison made of money that was not of her own making but it was the way for much of the world.

Terrifying thoughts ran through her mind as she waited for the Ethiopian Airlines agent to change her ticket. In her head, there were images of Halimah waiting for her in the Dubai Airport arrival terminal. She wondered what she would do when she became aware that her faithful Alya was a "no show." Would Halimah think she missed her plane or had decided to stay in Ethiopia? Alya felt deeply guilty for the deceitful trouble she was causing Halimah and asked herself how she could do such a bad thing to a woman who had been so good to her. After all, this was the woman who had surprised her by buying her a round-trip ticket and giving her two weeks of vacation. There was no getting around the fact that Alya had betrayed Halimah's trust in her. She would never be able to forgive herself for this dreadful act which had transformed her into a different and less kind person. She could not believe she could become so self-serving. The young woman she saw looking back at her in the mirror was not her.

Alya had decided that the guilt for her treacherous act was better than being sexually assaulted by two teenage boys. For her, death would be better than such an assault and she would not be good for anyone if she were dead. Much better to take her chances as a freelance worker under the auspices of Samrawit in Dubai City. In this case, she placed her full trust in Samrawit to determine the best course of action for her.

With her airline reservation changed to an earlier date, Alya put her revised ticket between the pages in her passport and stuffed them both carefully into her small black purse. She trudged the many blocks to her neighborhood and entered her housing compound. Yeshi was standing on her front step waiting for her and asked, "Where have you been?"

"I went to see Samrawit and our meeting lasted longer than I expected. All is well."

Alya said these words, but she knew she was doing something she had never done before—she was telling a lie. Previously, she had always accounted fully to Yeshi for her time away from her house. Now, she found herself hiding from Yeshi all the truth. Certainly, she did not want to tell her that she was changing jobs and betraying her generous employer. She avoided this subject because she did not want anyone in her family to know what she was doing and why. All Yeshi really cared about was her monthly remittance. Alya asked herself, "Does anybody really care about me and all my sacrifices?"

Yeshi was no dummy. Her woman's intuition was on full alert. She sensed that there was something Alya was not telling her, but she also sensed she could not push her to reveal the full truth about her situation.

They went to their front door which opened onto their small sitting room and sat silently on their new couch. Alya held Yeshi's hand and said, "Next week I leave to go back to Dubai. Please let me know of anything I can do to help you and my family before I go."

Yeshi softly replied, "All we want is to be with you as much as we can. There is one thing I would like and that is for you to go to church with me. We must pray to God and the saints to lead and support you while you are in Dubai."

"Of course, we must pray unceasingly for the year or more that I'll be away from you in an Arab world. I will call you often on my cell phone but that is no substitute for praying in our own Orthodox Christian church where I was baptized when I was a tiny baby."

When Alya was finished talking, Yeshi said, "Yes, we should go to our church now and pray for your safety and the strength you'll need to work far away from home in a foreign country."

Yeshi got up and went to the adjoining room to fetch two netela scarves so that she and Alya could cover their heads before entering the church. They walked the several blocks to their neighborhood church, greeting people along the way. This would be the first time Alya had entered church as a sinner. She had hidden the truth from her family and betrayed Halimah. No amount of praying could erase these unholy deeds.

Alya entered the church and crossed herself as she faced the altar. She half expected to be struck by God's holy fury for her sin. She followed Yeshi to their usual place in the cavernous and dimly lit church to prostrate themselves in prayer. Alya asked for forgiveness for what she had done, hoping God would understand that she could not return to her old job because of the potential aggression of two teenage boys.

The peace she felt in her soul made her think that God understood her problems and supported her in what she was doing. She knew she could never tell her family the truth about her situation, but with God on her side she was on solid ground for pursuing her dream of working abroad. She believed nothing could stop her if God were on her side. All she wanted was an unfettered chance to prove herself.

They stayed in God's house for several hours. When they came out of the church the sun was setting and the atmosphere was clouded by a light drizzle. They walked home in silence. Neither of them wanted to break the spiritual bond that had enveloped them in the church. This bond would be broken soon enough by the clamor of their housing compound and the nosy questions of their family and neighbors.

Alya entered the house and went straight to the adjoining room to arrange a sleeping pallet for herself. She could not wait to bed down and close her eyes so she could think through the events of the day. Her guilt over changing her ticket had been squelched by her time in the church, but fragments of it were still alive within her. Her remaining guilt surged within her until its grip obliged her to shed tears. She felt as if the evil she had done was enough for her to fall down and make it so the good Lord could not help her rise again.

As her tears rolled down her cheeks, Alya again asked God to forgive her of the wrong she had done. She could not shake letting down Halimah in such an alarming manner. Her grief over this trickery made it tough for her to forge ahead with a straight face. She was troubled by the fact that she was not the same good person. Maybe this was part of what growing up was like, but she did not like the bitter taste it left in her mouth.

In front of her family and friends, it was hard to hide her guilt. On the surface, she pretended to be her old self, but deep down her entire being had been transformed into a person she did not like or want to be. It was no easy task to present herself as the same caring person and harbor at the same time her new less-caring self. It disturbed her greatly to now know she was capable of sinning.

Alya tried to convince herself that her sin was not serious because Halimah was not of the same religious faith. Halimah was an Arab and a devoted Muslim. Halimah's Islamic religion was different from her Christian religion. Certainly, a sin by a Christian against a Muslim is not as serious as sinning against another Christian. She asked herself, "How could a Christian be guilty of committing a sin against someone who believes in a later revelation and who has not accepted Jesus as their Savior?"

The days whipped by and before Alya and her family knew it, she was headed to the Addis airport to catch a flight to Dubai to do a job unknown to her. She passed through the formalities and boarded the plane just like she had done before. In some ways, this time she was a free woman with a ticket and a UAE visa. As short-lived as this freedom was, she missed the role of a servant beholden to a master. She did not care about freedom. She did care about being in a secure environment that permitted her to make money. It was all about prosperity for her and her family.

The daily overnight flight to Dubai was on schedule and any turbulence was avoided. Alya knew the airport arrival drill. She had no problems with immigration officials and claimed her tattered suitcase. She did not know what to expect in the waiting lounge. She was not sure if Samrawit would meet her or if she would send someone else to meet her and transport her to her place in Dubai City.

Alya had been in the arrival's terminal for over thirty minutes and she could not identify anyone in the crowd who was there for her. She slowly walked in front of a multinational crowd of people waiting eagerly for passengers to deboard so they could escort them to their destinations. She could see from the people arriving that most of them were migrants like her who the UAE depended upon. The babble of the many languages spoken by the waiting crowd reminded her that she was indeed far from home.

Suddenly, there was a small tap from behind on her shoulder. At first, Alya panicked but a few mellow words in Amharic settled her down quickly. She turned around rapidly to see that a tall, brown Habesha man had said the words. The man said, “Are you Alya? Samrawit sent me to meet you and take you to her.”

“Yes, I’m Alya. Please take me to Samrawit.”

They sped off in the car driven by the Habesha man toward the glittering oceanside city of Dubai. The buildings in the city center were the tallest Alya had ever seen. They stopped in front of one of the buildings and the Habesha man instructed Alya to get out, enter the building and take the lift to the sixth floor where she would find Samrawit in apartment 604.

Alya thanked her driver and proceeded to walk through the glass revolving door into the tall building. She tried to act as if she had done all this before but that was a ruse to hide how terribly daunted she was by this new experience. She had never seen revolving doors before and been in such a tall building. Moreover, she had never before taken a lift.

The lift doors were a prominent feature in the lobby. Looking right and left, Alya decided to join a group of people waiting in front of stainless-steel sliding doors. The doors opened to let a stream of people out into the lobby. When all these people were well on their way, Alya followed the people she was inter-mixed with into the mechanical stainless-steel cubicle. She tried to hide her fear over this first experience on a lift.

The tight-fitting group in the lift caused Alya to feel feint. There was a man standing near buttons with numbers on a wall panel. He called out to find out which floor each person was going to. Alya managed to say, "Six," although somebody had already said that number.

Once out of the lift and on the sixth floor, Alya saw that there were numbers on each of the doors. She found a door with the number 604 on it and knocked timidly. As soon as she knocked, the door was opened widely and she saw a welcoming sight. There was Samrawit in Ethiopian dress saying repeatedly, "My baby has made it. Come in and make yourself at home."

Alya was overjoyed to see Samrawit again and entered into the spacious apartment which was decorated with items from Ethiopia. It was obvious that Samrawit was happy to see Alya whom she beseeched to feel free to look around and to be at ease. Alya looked at the city and the glistening coastline out the apartment's big picture windows. She had never been so high up and marveled at how little the people and cars looked on the street below.

All was so pleasant for Alya that she decided at that moment what she wanted to do with her life. She aspired to be like Samrawit and operate employment services for the plethora of foreign workers in the UAE. It was like Samrawit was reading her mind when she said, "Sit down with me. If you are not too tired from your trip, we need to talk."

They sat comfortably side by side on a soft well-upholstered sofa and Samrawit expressed in the purest and most affectionate Amharic, "I'm so glad you are here. You know I've been doing this job for over twenty years. I'm looking for a person to replace me. You might be that person. What do you think?" Alya was surprised and caught off guard by Samrawit's words. She did not know what to say. Her hesitation in speaking caused Samrawit to say, "Surely, you've got something to say."

After a couple of false starts and clearing her throat, Alya looked at the floor and bashfully said, "I'm honored by your words. Evidently, you see something in me that I don't see in myself. I would love to be the person to do the job you have been doing for so many years. Of course, I would expect you to always be there to guide and teach me all you know."

Samrawit spoke without hesitancy, "I'm just expressing an idea I had. First, you must prove yourself to me by doing well in the first job I've lined up for you. There is a Lebanese couple living nearby who have been desperately seeking a domestic servant for several months. They have paid my finder's fee and you are exactly the kind of servant they are looking for. They are Maronite Christians and they want a good Christian woman to work for them. Not the same as our Tewahedo Orthodox church, but they also follow the path of Jesus."

"Sounds good. When do I start working for them?"

Samrawit was quick to answer, "They are coming here early tomorrow morning to see you and if they like what they see, you'll leave with them to start your new job."

Alya did not know that a job had been already arranged for her but she said, "That's fine with me. I count on you to give me any feedback on my work at the new job you deem necessary."

Samrawit smiled and embraced Alya to demonstrate her satisfaction, then she said, "Let me show you your room. I'm sure you're tired after such a long flight from our homeland."

The sleeping room was small but it was all hers. She could not complain. There was all she needed. Certainly, there was more in her room than she was accustomed to back home. Alya could not ask for better. She could not fall down under Samrawit's watchful eyes. She felt that she was being given a new start in life which would not let her fall down again.

CHAPTER NINETEEN

High Promises

Her bedroom was so nice and the bed so comfortable that Alya did not want to get up. The first rays of a new day were illuminating the thin lace curtains on her window. Suddenly the memory of where she was and what this day represented for her caused her to jump out of bed and begin getting herself ready to see her new bosses. She thanked God for Samrawit and the work opportunity she had provided her. Her excitement over beginning a new life was in high gear.

Alya rapidly did her morning toiletries and made herself presentable. She dressed modestly and prepared herself mentally to meet and impress favorably the Lebanese couple for whom she would be working. Most of all, she did not want to let Samrawit down. She quietly exited her bedroom to find a table that had already been set with a sumptuous breakfast. Samrawit was seated at the table drinking a cup of black coffee. She offered a smiling face to Alya and said in her pure Amharic dialect, "Good morning. I hope you had a restful night. Please come and join me for breakfast. Your new bosses should be arriving soon."

There were many chairs around the table. Alya did not know which one to sit on until Samrawit said, "Please sit next to me so we can talk."

Alya scurried to sit in a chair next to Samrawit who startled her by clapping her hands. A teenage Habesha woman came out of the kitchen with a plate piled high with food. She placed it on the table in front of Alya. After delivering the food, the young woman disappeared into the kitchen. Alya could not help but ask, "Who's that?"

Samrawit was quick to answer, "That's my youngest daughter, Lidiya. I have four children—two girls and two boys. All except Lidiya are in Ethiopia. Lidiya is my helper, but she does not have the mind for my business. That's why I'm counting on you to continue my work after I've retired."

The food was delicious. Alya told herself that she had never had it so good and all this was thanks to Samrawit. She looked at Samrawit and was about to speak when Samrawit said, "This should be an easy job for you. They're a young couple and they do not have any children yet. They are trying to start a new business so they leave their apartment all day. They want someone they can trust to live in their apartment and take care of it for them."

Alya was about to react to these words when there was a knock on the front door. Samrawit said, "That must be them. Get up and be ready to receive them after I open the door. This is the time to put your best foot forward."

Samrawit opened the door and welcomed her Lebanese clients, inviting them into her apartment's sitting room. She introduced Alya who was quietly standing on the side of the room. The Lebanese couple's eyes examined Alya from head to toe. Alya kept her head slightly bowed until Samrawit said, "Please sit down. Alya, come and join us."

When Alya was seated on Samrawit's side across from the Lebanese couple who were comfortably seated in a soft three-person sofa, Samrawit continued by saying politely, "As for introductions, I present you Alya."

Quickly the Lebanese man said in good but accented English, "My name is Elias and my wife's name is Lena. Sorry for being in such a hurry, but we are late for work."

Samrawit interrupted Elias by saying, "Forgive me for my bad manners. Would you like to drink some coffee or tea?"

"Thank you, but as I said we have no time now. Is this the girl you had in mind for us?"

"Yes, this is Alya and she is exactly what you want. She is ready to go to work immediately for you. If there is any problem, you can always contact me."

It was time for Lena to chime in by saying simply in her honey-dew voice, "Good. When can she start?"

Samrawit gave Alya an inquiring glance, obliging Alya to say, "Any time from now."

Lena said again, "Good. Get your things and let's go. We live in the same building on a different floor."

Alya excused herself to go to her room and close her suitcase. She returned in less than five minutes with her suitcase in hand and said to the group, "I'm ready to go."

Elias and Lena stood up and thanked Samrawit and Elias added, "If we have any problems with Alya, we'll let you know. If you don't hear anything from us, that means we're satisfied with her and her work. Sorry again to be in such a rush, but we do have to open our shop. Come Alya … let's go."

Samrawit opened the door and bid farewell to the Lebanese couple and hugged Alya as she said, "I'm sure you'll do well."

Alya followed the Lebanese couple down the hallway to the lift. She noticed the couple were speaking to each other in a language she did not know. Later she learned they were speaking French to each other. Their main reason for speaking in that language was so nobody could eavesdrop. Of course, they were also fluent in Arabic and English.

They entered the lift and descended two floors. Their apartment was near the lift so they did not have far to walk. Elias used a key to open the apartment door and said to Alya, "Voila, your new home. I will show you your bedroom and then we must rush to open our shop. You can then take your time to get to know our place better."

Already Alya noticed the apartment was similar to Samrawit's but less well decorated and sparsely furnished. As Elias and Lena were leaving, Lena spoke, "We depend on you to do all the upkeep the apartment needs, as well as all the washing and ironing. You'll see what needs to be done. We'll talk more when we get home tonight. Bye."

They shut the door softly. Alya found herself standing in the middle of the living room floor in a strange place far different from what she was accustomed to. It was eerily quiet. Alya looked around herself, trying to figure out where she would start working. She decided that her first task would be a thorough cleaning and dusting of the entire apartment. Doing this would allow her to see what else needed to be done.

Before diving into this routine task, she would plug her cellphone in her bedroom to charge so she could call Yeshi. She could not decide if she should hide her cellphone or openly allow her new Lebanese bosses to know she had a phone. She decided that it was all right to have a phone as long as she continued to have control over her passport.

She immediately called Yeshi and informed her that she had arrived safely and was busy at work. She did not tell her that she had a new job with different people and that she was working as a free agent. It was quick conversation whereby each assured the other that all was okay in their respective lives.

Alya found a utility closet next to the kitchen which contained all she needed to do a thorough, top-to-bottom cleaning of the apartment. She also found the laundry room with a dryer and washer. She was proud that she knew how to operate each machine and used them to wash and dry the bedclothes and all that she found in the dirty clothes hamper. She also washed and dried the towels she found hanging in the bathrooms. Her goal was to have the apartment well-organized and spic-and-span before her bosses came home.

She finished her tasks a few hours before her new bosses came home. The fridge and kitchen cupboards were full of food, but she forced herself to suppress her hunger because she did not know if she was allowed to eat their food. She did make sure all the dishes, silverware, pots, and pans were clean and stored in their places. It was with great satisfaction that she perceived her new world as being clean and orderly.

Looking out the front window into the street was a learning experience for Alya. She watched the comings and goings of the cars and people. As her interest in being a part of the scene she observed below grew, she reminded herself that her previous employer could not know of her whereabouts. She feared their reaction if they learned she had hoodwinked them and returned on her own to Dubai to work.

After an hour of studying the continuous activity in the street below, Alya walked around the apartment to see if there was anything remaining for her to do. Not finding any more work to do, she sat down on a cushioned chair in front of what she assumed was a television set. She spotted on the coffee table what she thought was the TV control. Casually, she picked up the control and push the power button. To her amazement, the TV sprang to life, displaying on its large color screen animated cartoons. Immediately, she was captivated by the images.

Alya was so entranced and sucked in by the unending stream of cartoon characters that she did not hear the front door open and close. It was only when Lena hovered above her and loudly cleared her throat that she was able to rejoin reality. Alya scrambled to find the control to turn the power off when Lena laughed and said, "Please don't disturb yourself. It's good to see you're making yourself at home. Excuse us for a few minutes as we change into our house clothes."

The TV was turned off and Alya stood in her dutiful pose at the entrance of the kitchen. She was not sure of what she was supposed to do. She waited for Lena to reappear before doing anything. Lena came walking quickly toward her and said, "Come, let's fix some dinner."

Alya tailed Lena into the kitchen and stood at her side ready to do any task she asked of her. This gave a chance for Alya to observe Lena up close. Her skin was almost white but she would qualify as a white *farenji* (foreigner) back home. Alya admired her long black hair that fell almost to her waistline and told herself, "I'll let my hair grow as long as Lena's."

Lena told Alya, "Why don't you set the table while I prepare dinner?"

Alya turned immediately and marched into the adjoining dining room. The table was already covered with a cloth. Alya retrieved plates and glasses from one cupboard, and utensils from another cupboard drawer. Paper napkins were already in a holder on the table. When Alya had arranged the table the best she knew how, she returned to the kitchen to do Lena's bidding which entailed carrying plates of food and setting them on the table in the dining room.

Lena followed Alya into the dining room and exclaimed. "You have done a wonderful job of setting the table. I don't see anything I would change. I can see that you are learning by doing and that's the way it should be for a few more days. I realize these surroundings are new for you, but I've every confidence that you will become a member of our small family. You are near my age, so we should be like sisters. Now, let me call Elias to dine."

All this time Elias had been sitting in the living room watching the news in Arabic on TV. He was particularly concerned with seeing any news of his country which was plagued with political infighting and violence. Lena called, "Elias, it's time to eat. Please come and join us."

After saying these words, Lena returned to the dining room and told Alya, "Elias is coming. Let him sit first and then we can sit down."

Alya was a bit confused. She did not expect to eat at the table with her bosses. She thought she would make a plate and retire to some obscure corner to eat her food. At the same time, she was obligated to do what Lena asked of her, so she joined them at the dinner table.

As soon as Alya sat down, Elias and Lena crossed themselves and said a brief prayer thanking God for the food and their day. Alya was pleased to see them do this and crossed herself to indicate to them that she was a Christian too. Lena was the first to speak and said, "My husband and I are delighted to have someone who can take care of our apartment while we concentrate on building our business. Our glasses only contain water, but let's toast the arrival of Alya."

They all raised their glasses and clinked them together. Alya was impressed by the warm welcome and the idea that she would become an integral part of the lives of this young couple. Tears swelled up in her eyes. She was so happy. All the words she had in mind to say were buried deeply within her. She did manage to say much less than she wanted. "Thank you for this wonderful opportunity. I will do my best to make sure you're satisfied with my presence."

From that point on, Lena led an animated conversation aimed at informing Alya all she needed to know about them and their business. Alya could see that Lena was intelligent and more outgoing than Elias. Alya faced Elias and Lena at the table. This position gave her an ample opportunity to get to know them better. With all the information Lena freely conveyed in a non-stop fashion, she actually learned more about them and their business than she needed to know.

Alya got the impression that besides being their housemaid, they genuinely wanted her to be part of their family. She could not believe her good luck. She had a relatively easy job and the support of a friendly couple, and they paid her more than her previous job. Overall her situation was too good to be true.

They finished eating and Elias retired to the TV room. Lena began to take the dirty dishes to the kitchen to be washed, but Alya promptly and politely told her, "Please, ma'am. This is my job. I'll clean the table and wash and dry the dishes."

Lena smiled and said, "Of course, you're right. I've got to get used to the idea that you're here now. But please don't hesitate to call on me if you need any help or want advice on anything."

Alya stood at the kitchen sink washing the dishes, thanking God silently for her good luck to have such a job with such gracious bosses. She believed God was blessing her and she had to behave in a way that merited His blessing. When she had finished her nightly chores, she excused herself to go to her room so she could pray to God, Jesus, and Mariyam in her usual fashion.

As Alya was finishing her work in the kitchen, she felt a stabbing pain in her lower abdomen. She had never experienced this kind of pain before but as it passed as quickly as it started, she paid no mind and wrote it off as a passing gas pain. She was certainly not letting such a simple pain get in the way of her enjoying this wonderful work opportunity.

CHAPTER TWENTY

Falling Again

NO DOUBT ABOUT IT. THIS had to be her dream job. The work was easy for her and she had been accepted as part of the family. She was free to do as she pleased in her spare time. Her bosses were happy and she was exceedingly happy. Nothing could stop Alya from continuing on her successful track of providing her family in Ethiopia with the means they needed to survive and thrive.

Unexpected obstacles frustrated her successful path. After a few months of enjoying working for Elias and Lena, she was shocked to learn that this industrious couple was obliged to leave the UAE. Evidently, local authorities were in connivance with their business competitors, forcing them to consider seriously their options. Moreover key family members in Lebanon were seriously ill and clamoring for their return.

Elias and Lena did not want to leave. Their electronics shop was just turning a profit. They knew their success caused jealousy with competing shops; thus they blamed them for the innumerable inspections by UAE agents. Normally, they would bribe UAE officials, but they could see that the odds were stacked against them since they were in a weak position to out-bribe their competitors. All things considered, they decided to call it quits and return home. They told themselves that it was better to suffer the consequences of being home in an unruly country than being outsiders in a foreign country.

Alya was shocked when Lena told her of their decision to return to Lebanon in two weeks. Elias and Lena had sold their business to a well-connected Bangladeshi competitor and were beginning to sell their household belongings. Alya did not know what to do. Her main concern was her livelihood. She called Yeshi on her cell phone to inform her of what was going on and ask her for advice. After hearing about Alya's predicament, Yeshi was quick to answer, "Find as quick as you can another job."

The only recourse for Alya was to see Samrawit and tell her what was going on. It took several trips to Samrawit's apartment before Alya found her at home. "Come on in. I know all about your problem. Don't worry, I've already found you another job," said Samrawit firmly and without hesitation.

"Thank you. Your words are like music to my ears and do much to settle my panicky nerves," said a much-relieved Alya.

"Lydia, we have another Habesha woman. Make us cups of hot tea," hollered Samrawit in direction of the kitchen and she pointed to a place on the sofa for Alya to sit beside her. After they were seated, Samrawit broke into a long monologue about Alya's new job, saying in part, "The new job I've for you is with an Egyptian family. Another industrious couple but they have two young daughters about six and eight years old. I'm sure you will serve them and fit in well. Incidentally, they are Coptic Christians, so their religion is almost the same as we practice in our orthodox church."

Alya breathed a sigh of relief and with joy growing in her heart said in her best Amharic, "Thank you so much. Sorry for being such a bother. I would be dead without you. I can't thank you enough."

"Don't give my aid a second thought. You are like a daughter to me and whether you know it or not, I've got my eyes on you as my possible successor. We need to do everything possible to maintain and increase the UAE's reputation as a good place for Ethiopians to gain employment."

"Obviously, you have expectations of me that I don't have for myself. Time will tell, but I'm honored by the plans you have for me," said calmly Alya.

Lydia set the tea tray gently down on the coffee table facing them and Samrawit poured tea into their cups. After the tea had cooled sufficiently they sipped it in silence. Samrawit eyed her protege with a steely gaze and broke their silence by saying, "You don't look well. How's your health?"

Alya took her time, trying to decide what to tell about her physical well-being to Samrawit. After a few minutes, Alya said quietly, "I don't feel well. My stomach cramps keep getting worse. Sometimes I feel feverish and take a couple of aspirins. I don't know what is wrong with me. I never had this ailment before."

After hearing Alya's sad expression of her health complaints, Samrawit tried to put her at ease by saying, "Don't worry. This condition will pass. But to be on the safe side, we'll have a local physician check you out when your Lebanese bosses leave and before you start work for the Egyptians. Okay?"

"Yes, that would be ideal. I think that in a few days my Lebanese bosses should be on their way. I'll probably need a place to stay for a couple of nights because they are selling everything in the apartment."

"No worries. This is your home anytime you need it. Just come. Consider yourself a part of our family," said sincerely Samrawit.

They both sipped the last drops of tea from their cups when Alya said, "I must bid you farewell as I have to return to my Lebanese apartment to see what's going on and assist them in any way I can."

Samrawit nodded her understanding and they both stood. After an affectionate embrace, Samrawit opened the front door and Alya said softly, "Thank you again for everything. See you soon. Goodbye."

Alya hustled to return to her apartment. She was surprised when she opened the door to find it emptied of all its furniture. She went straight to her bedroom to see if her bed was still there. She could not believe her eyes when she entered her bedroom to find her bed, side tables and chair absent. The only things remaining in her bedroom were her few clothes hanging in the closet and her old suitcase. She turned immediately, returned to the living room, and called, "Lena."

Nobody answered her call so she sat on the floor and waited for her bosses to appear. Her wait for them lasted for what she thought was an eternity. At last they opened the apartment door and spotted Alya sitting on the floor. Lena was the first to speak "You poor girl. Sorry to make you wait so long. A guy came and paid us a handsome sum for everything. We agreed and he and his workers hauled it all away. We went to Samrawit's to tell you but you were not there."

Although in a state of shock over the abruptness of the change, Alya managed to say, "No problem. I understand. Too good of a deal to pass up. Where will we sleep?"

"As soon as the deal was struck and the furniture and other items were removed, we went straight to our travel agent's office to book a flight home. Then, we went to Samrawit's to tell you what had happened and that we would not be sleeping in this apartment tonight. We have reserved a hotel room for the night. We thought you could stay with Samrawit."

Alya was speechless. Too much was happening too quickly. She finally mumbled, "Give me a few minutes to pack my things in my suitcase."

As Alya dashed to her room, Elias and Lena stood quietly and debated softly how much money they should give as severance pay to Alya. They settled on the sum of $300. Lena placed three one-hundred-dollar bills in a white business envelope. Alya returned at top speed and blurted out, "Ready."

A teary-eyed Lena faced Alya and said with a sad voice, "I wish we could stay together as before, but life is full of breakups and we have to move on. I wish you all possible success in whatever you end up doing."

She then embraced lovingly Alya and handed her the envelope saying, "This is a little something to tide you over. I wish we could do more for you."

Lena's tears brought tears to Alya's eyes, making it difficult for her to say, "Thank you. I wish you well too. I'll never forget you."

All this time, Elias stood stoically as a respectful Lebanese man should but internally he was crying. For him, his situation was too sad for words. It was too sad in this instant and only sadness awaited them in Lebanon. He was weighed down by sadness. And, if the truth be known, he did not like leaving the UAE in this way and was afraid of what awaited him in Lebanon. Elias shook Alya's hand and said, "Thank you for your services. Best of luck. He then turned to lead the way out of their apartment and headed for the elevator. They had already transported their bags to their hotel. Alya waited for them to board the lift and waved goodbye to them. Her heart sank as she knew she would never see them again.

Alya waited for the same lift to take her up to Samrawit's floor. She knocked lightly on Samrawit's apartment door and it was immediately flung open by Samrawit who said, "I was expecting you. Come in and make yourself at home. You are always welcome here. The Lebanese couple alerted me to expect you. Go right to your bedroom and wash up for a dinner of injera."

While they were feasting and drinking coffee, enjoying an Ethiopian ambience, suddenly amid the gaiety of the moment, Alya doubled up in pain. The sharpness of her stomach pains were worse than she had ever experienced. She fell to the floor in a fetal position with her hands clutching firmly her stomach. Samrawit was alarmed and said, "It's urgent that we get you medical care now."

Alya's pain subsided to the point that she lifted her head and said, "Yes, let's go to see a doctor now."

Samrawit helped to raise Alya from the floor and yelled to Lydia, "We're going down to the ground floor to see Dr. Hassan."

Arm-in-arm they walked slowly together to the lift. Alya was feeling better but she agreed with Samrawit that getting checked by the doctor was a good idea. On the ground floor, Samrawit guided Alya to the doctor's small office and had her sit down in the waiting room. She informed the receptionist that her friend was sick and needed to be examined quickly by Dr. Hassan.

They waited for their turn to see the doctor. Their turn came after waiting for a half-hour. Alya entered the doctor's office alone. His assistant took all her vital signs and told the doctor, "Normal range." The assistant exited and the doctor asked her, "Please sit here while I listen to you heart. Breathe deeply."

Dr. Hassan pressed on her abdomen and looked closely at her. After completing his examination, he said gently, "I find you to be healthy. I detect nothing that puts you in great pain. I need stool and urine samples to determine if your intestinal stress is caused by any bacteria."

"How can I provide you with stool and urine samples," asked Alya.

Dr. Hassan replied, "That's simple. The analysis of these samples in our lab is part of our routine. My assistant will give you containers for these samples and instruct you on how to collect them and deposit them here. If there is anything wrong, an analysis of these samples will inform us as to the best course of treatment. Goodbye for now. Don't worry about a thing."

With the kind words of Dr. Hassan, Alya felt better already. His assistant in his outer office handed her the sample kits in a small brown bag with written instructions of how to collect the sample and the best time to do each. She also said, "You can pay at the cashiers window located on the other side of our outer office."

Alya had no idea of how much this initial medical examination would cost but she had all her money with her. But still she could not believe it when the cashier said, "That'll be one-hundred dollars."

That amount was more than Alya had in mind. She calmly paid but was worried she would not have enough money to send to Yeshi. The medical check-up was necessary, but Alya was hopeful that she was done with doctors for a long time. She rushed back to Samrawit's apartment to find her door open. Evidently, there were visitors because she could hear many people talking from inside.

Alya entered timidly and as soon as Samrawit noticed her, she swept Alya up and paraded her a few steps to a couple who were standing with two children in the middle of Samrawit's sitting room and said forthrightly, "I'm pleased to present to you your new maid, Alya." The family of four studied her briefly from head-to-toe and the tall man said, "Very pleased to meet you. My name is Nicolas and next to me is my wife, Sarah. We are here with our two daughters. Maria is the oldest at six years and Mariyam is the youngest at four years. We all look forward to you joining our family."

There was a long pause as they waited for some words from Alya. It was only after a little nudging that Alya softly said, "Pleased to meet you. I'm sure we'll get along fine."

Nicolas was quick to interject, "When can you start? We need someone so we can both work in our store."

Alya smiled and said, "I'm ready to start as soon as I drop off these medical samples tomorrow morning. Maybe I stay here one more night and come to your place early tomorrow."

Nicolas quickly said, "That works for us." The entire Nicolas family extended their hands to shake the right hand of Alya. The children did not want to let go of Alya, trying to express their eagerness for Alya to join them. Nicolas said, "We are pleased for another Orthodox Christian to be part of our family. We look forward to praying with you. We must go now. I'm sure Samrawit can tell you how to get to our place. It's in the next building. See you tomorrow morning."

Alya said goodbye and closed the door behind them. She then turned to Samrawit and said, "That's that. I wonder why they gave their daughters almost the same name."

Samrawit laughed and said jovially, "They didn't want them to be jealous about their names and wanted to treat them the same."

A sharp intestinal pain was building up in Alya's lower abdomen and she could only blurt out, "Excuse me. I have to go to my room."

After a while, Alya's innards calmed down and she joined Samrawit in the sitting room. The usual tea setting was waiting for her. Samrawit was the first to talk, "Are you okay?"

"I think so. The doctor examined me and found nothing wrong. Early tomorrow I will drop off some samples for lab analysis. I don't think there's anything to worry about."

"It's good you are doing a medical checkup before you start your new job with the Egyptian Coptic family. I sincerely hope there is nothing wrong with you. I can see that your stomach pains are more frequent. The only time I've seen such symptoms before was with a person that had been secretly given a poison."

Alya gulped when Samrawit said the word "poison." She stopped her thought processes and dwelled upon this word. She broke through the spell that this word had driven her into to say, "Please excuse me. I'm feeling tired and I got to figure out this medical sample business. Also, I got to get ready to start my new job tomorrow."

After she shut her room bedroom door, Alya's fear of having been poisoned surged. She was genuinely scared that she had been poisoned. But who would poison her and how would they do it? She could not think of any person who held a grudge against her to the extent they would poison her. There was only one person, Halimah, who she let down, but she did not think Halimah knew where she was and she thought Halimah would never do such a terrible thing.

These maddening thoughts had to be put aside. If there was anything amiss, the lab analyses would find it. She tried to convince herself that she had not been poisoned and the lab results would indicate the reasons for her growing abdominal pains.

CHAPTER TWENTY-ONE

Working Sick

THERE WAS NO TIME TO reflect. It was about getting up early and rushing to drop off her medical samples and getting as fast as possible to her new job with her new Egyptian family. She skipped the sumptuous breakfast placed on the dining table for her, saying she was in a hurry to get to her new bosses' apartment. Her hunger gnawed at her stomach, but she did not like the idea of food being prepared just for her consumption. It was not that she suspected Samrawit or Lydia of trying to poison her, but to be completely on the safe side, she changed her usual consumption patterns to see if there was any impact on her painful ailment. The door to the medical clinic was open when she arrived. She quickly dropped off her samples at the receptionist desk. The young woman sitting at this desk said in a perfunctory matter, "Thank you. Come back tomorrow at the same time to get your results and pay."

Alya nodded in acknowledgement of these routine words and briskly walked out the door with her cheap old suitcase in hand. Once out in the heat on the bustling street of the fascinating big modern city of Dubai, she took a moment to get her bearings and then headed toward the building she thought her new Egyptian family was lodged. She entered the building timidly and wanted to ask one of the persons in the lobby for directions to where an Egyptian family lived, but she was discouraged from doing so because of the multiple nationalities she could see sitting in the large lobby. She tried to act as being familiar with the place, but her first-time appearance and her old suitcase tagged her as a newcomer. Most of the people in the lobby could care less if she were new or old. Many of them were jaded by all the comings and goings they had seen in Dubai. Alya was only one of tens of thousands of foreign workers in Dubai. Although Alya could have easily walked up the stairs to the second floor, she chose to take the lift. She did this because she was fascinated by lifts and she wanted to show all those who cared that she was not a newcomer. When the shiny metal doors of the lift opened, she entered without hesitation and promptly pressed the circular button with the number 2.

It was a short ride to the second floor in this fancy eight-story apartment building. Alya stepped out of the sliding lift doors as soon as they opened. She was looking for apartment 204 which she could see was located close to the lift. She knocked lightly on the door and was happy to see it immediately open. There in front of her was standing the lovely Sarah who yelled loudly, "Come quickly. Alya is here."

"Then she said softly, "Dear Alya, please come into your new home. We are so happy that you are here. Please come in my sister."

Alya was overwhelmed with the warmness of her welcome. She came in just as the two young girls, Maria and Mariyam, were scampering forward as they laughed gleefully. It was obvious that they were overjoyed to have Alya among them. Maria took her suitcase and Mariyam took Alya's hand while Maria said, "Come and see our room."

Just as the girls were going to tow Alya to their room, Nicolas appeared at a quick step and stopped in front of Alya to say, "Welcome to our home. We're glad that you are here. Please make yourself at home."

While the two girls pulled her in the direction of their room, she said "Thank you. I'm happy to be here."

The girls were excited by the presence of Alya. They were looking forward to playing with her. They could sense that Alya had a deep reservoir of affection for children. It was something like mutual love at first sight.

They entered their room and at once closed the door. Maria began immediately to show her all their toys. When Maria showed Alya where she would place her clothes, she commented, "Wait a minute. Shouldn't I put my clothes in my room?"

Maria replied, "This is your room. You're going to stay in our room with us. Isn't that grand?"

"Where will I sleep?"

"In between us in our bed. We are looking forward to sleeping with you. It'll be nice for us to be so close. You'll be like a second mother to us."

Alya had no choice but to make the best of her situation and adapt to the desires of Maria and Mariyam. So, she put on a happy face and put her arms around the two girls and said, "Don't worry. I'm here with you and for you."

This was a time of mutual hugs and teary eyes. Already, Alya felt an emotional bond with the girls. She was confident that she would do everything in her power to protect and care for them. She was concerned about having an intestinal attack and how she would conceal her pain from the girls if she were living with them day and night. This concern prompted her to ask, "Where is our bathroom?"

"Oh, let me show you," said Maria. She then opened widely the bedroom door and she and Miriyam ran down the hall, stood pointing at a door, and said while giggling, "Here it is."

Alya was happy to see the bathroom. She saw this as not only a place to bathe herself and the two children, but as a safe refuge for her if she wanted to be alone. In particular, she saw this as a place to go to when and if she had her deep intestinal pains. The good feelings she was enjoying right now made it seem improbable there would be any reoccurrence of her pain. It was with great anticipation she looked forward to getting negative lab results tomorrow morning. That would give her peace of mind and relieve her of anxiety. Right now, Alya had to deal with Maria and Mariyam. They were squealing to show her the rest of the apartment. They visited every room. Alya was wondering if she could care for two children and at the same time, clean the apartment, wash, and iron everyone's clothes.

Sarah caught up with them and said, "I see my babies have already shown you our place. I hope all is okay. If you have any questions, don't hesitate to ask me. I also see that you've already made good friends with my two babies. I'm going to the kitchen now to fix us something to eat."

Obediently, Alya immediately said, "I will assist you."

"No, thank you. You watch over the girls so I don't have to worry about them."

Maria insisted that they go to their bedroom to play with their dolls. Alya allowed the energetic Maria to rule, so they went to their room to play in a nonsensical manner with her baby dolls. Alya sat on the floor of their bedroom with her legs crossed and played gayly in an animated fashion. She was ready to play along as she considered this part of her childcare duties. It was easy for her to adopt a pleasing demeanor and they all laughed in a childish way.

They were having good fun when Alya felt a strange feeling in her abdomen. The sensation grew rapidly and turned into pain. She became dizzy and could not keep her hands off her stomach. When she began to perspire, and before the girls would notice she was suffering, she abruptly excused herself by saying, "Excuse me. I need to go the bathroom."

The crescendo of her intestinal pain reached new heights. The cramping sensation she felt was like being stabbed in the stomach by a sharp knife. She excused herself and staggered to the bathroom. She struggled to lock the door from the inside and collapsed to the floor. While she was laying on the floor in a fetal position, tears flowed amply from her eyes. The pain was so excruciating she was about to pass out. She thought she was about to die. Yellow bile started leaking from her mouth. Then came an unstoppable upsurge of nasty, burning intestinal fluids. She crawled desperately over to the toilet and vomited fiercely in repeated episodes. It was like her stomach was emptying itself of unwanted acids. She saw small bits of an unknown material floating in the water at the bottom of the toilet bowl.

Once she had finished throwing up, she was too exhausted to scream and make known to the world the deathly pain she had suffered. When the pain subsided, she realized she must be quiet so nobody would know about her worsening ailment. Already she thought she would draw attention to herself because she had been gone too long. The girls must be concerned.

Her weakened body refused to stand up as she wanted. She flushed the toilet and splashed a trickle of cold water from the sink faucet on her face. The remaining droplets on her face were wiped away by her shawl. She mouthed a brief prayer, pleading with God, Jesus and all the saints to cure her of any serious sickness. Then she took a few deep breaths and opened the bathroom door as if nothing serious had happened.

Alya quietly entered the girls' bedroom and acted kindly as if nothing was amiss. The girls were busy playing with their dolls and did not take undue notice of Alya, who was calmly composed as she arranged her things in their closet. She told herself she must call Yeshi as soon as possible to confide in her and ask for her counsel as to what she should do.

Just as Alya was about to sit down with the girls, Sarah opened their bedroom door and exclaimed with a big smile on her face, "Come and get it before the flies eat it all."

They were all seated politely at the dining table. Sarah bowed her head and asked that God bless their food, thanking Him for Alya and her presence with them. She then dished out heaps of a sumptuous vegetarian casserole to her two daughters. She passed the serving plate to Alya and said, "Please take all the food you want. Don't worry about me. I'm not hungry and I'll wait for my husband to return from work and eat with him."

Alya was famished and she took a healthy portion of the casserole, but she discovered that her gastric problem prevented her from eating her fill. She was embarrassed because she only ate a small part of the food she had put on her plate. Sarah looked at how little food Alya had consumed and said, "I guess you're tired and a bit nervous eating with us for the first time. No worries. This food will keep well until tomorrow. Maybe you should lie down. I can watch the girls if you want to take a nap."

Alya certainly did not want to reveal anything about her sickness and said in an offhand manner, "Sorry. I feel hungry, but I can't eat as much as I would like. I like your food very much. It's so tasty. Maybe I'll go rest. I can eat leftovers tomorrow."

Caressing the two girls on their heads, Alya withdrew to their bedroom. Something was wrong with her and she did not know how much longer she could conceal her illness. This break was a good time to retrieve her cellphone and call Yeshi. She dug her phone out of her suitcase and went to the bathroom and sat on top of the closed toilet seat. She quickly called to her Addis home and waited impatiently for Yeshi to answer. The phone rang incessantly. After several tries, Yeshi finally answered and offered her excuses for taking so long to answer, "Is this my dear working girl? Sorry to take so long, but I was bathing."

"Yeshi, I'm sick."

"Don't worry my dear. Your sickness will pass and you'll be okay."

"Yeshi, I mean I'm really sick and in deathly pain."

Yeshi did not want to hear what Alya was saying. Her dependence on Alya as their sole breadwinner blocked her brain so she could not accept that anything that would cause Alya to stop working because that would mean no money for her and her family. Their dependence on Alya was total. Anything that interfered with her work and raised the specter of possibly not getting paid could not be entertained.

Alya repeated over and over to Yeshi that she was not well, but Yeshi did not want to hear of anything that could be interpreted as upsetting her receipt of a monthly remittance from Alya. All Yeshi could say was, "My dear girl, your sickness will pass, and you'll feel just as good as you did before. You're strong and healthy, and you will stay that way for years to come."

There was no sense in trying to contradict Yeshi, so Alya abruptly ended their phone conversation by saying, "I'm sick. Nobody cares. I'm going to see the doctor again tomorrow. Goodbye."

Yeshi kept talking, "It's nothing. Even if it is, the doctor will find the cause and treat you. Please, whatever you do, don't spend too much money on the doctor. You know what I mean."

Alya knew what Yeshi had to say and did not want to listen to her. Of course, she wanted to get cured and keep working so she could send money home, but at the same time, she was scared by her unknown sickness and the pain it was causing her body. She had never been sick like this before, and she wanted the doctor to make her sickness go away.

She could not do her work as well as she could with all the worries about her illness weighing her down. It was difficult to function as if nothing was the matter when there was something seriously the matter with her. But she composed herself and tried to entertain Maria and Mariyam when they skipped joyfully into their bedroom. They played together until Maria announced, "It's not light outside anymore so we should go to bed."

Alya was caught off guard, but said calmly, "Shouldn't you take baths first and brush your teeth?"

As usual, the boisterous Maria spoke for both girls by saying in some Arabic and completing her phrase in English, 'Bialtabe,' or, "let's get our pajamas and go to the bathroom." Let's finish quickly so we are in bed before mom comes to check on us."

The girls were not shy at all. They undressed and sat in the bathtub while Alya washed with a soapy washcloth their entire bodies. She was reminded of washing her own daughter back home. Without saying a word, both girls stood up while Alya sprayed water on them from the showerhead. They turned their erect bodies so they were thoroughly rinsed. Mariyam followed every move Maria made.

Alya used big soft light blue towels to dry them off from their toes to the tips of heads, drying their long curly hair the best she could. They opened the bathroom door and ran down the hall to their bedroom, flinging their towels to the floor and jumping wildly on their big bed. Alya caught up with them and after she closed the bedroom door behind her, she proceeded to help them cover their naked bodies with their pajamas. They crawled under the covers and Maria asked, "Are you coming to bed? We're saving a place for you between us. Are you going to read us a story?"

"Let me hang these towels to dry and put your dirty clothes in the hamper. I'll join you in a few minutes."

Alya picked up the towels, fetched her sleeping gown and went to the bathroom to change and do her nightly toiletries. She really liked the girls and how things were going with her new job. It was an agreeable situation that did not deserve being upset by her illness. Her lab results had to tell her what she had and Doctor Hassan had to be prepared to prescribe her the medicine that would cure her.

She rushed back to the bedroom to find both girls fast asleep. It was awkward to slither between them and snuggle under the covers by them. She got into bed and looked tenderly at the two girls sleeping on either side of her. Although this arrangement was uncomfortable for her, she told herself that she could do this.

Before she could close her eyes and try to sleep, she noticed that she had forgotten to turn off the ceiling light. She was trying to figure out how she could get out of bed to turn off the light, when Sarah quietly opened the door and thinking all were asleep she reached the short distance to the wall switch next to the door and smiling she said softly, "Good night. Sweet dreams."

CHAPTER TWENTY-TWO

Survival at Stake

ALL WAS QUIET WHILE ALYA tiptoed out of the dark apartment. She knew what she was doing was wrong, but she hoped to be back before anyone asleep would know she was gone and nobody would be aware of her medical lab visit. She opened and closed the front door softly, scampering down the hall to the lift. Only one thought hammered in her head, "Get my medical lab results and find out what is wrong with me."

She was standing in front of Dr. Hassan's medical lab long before it was open. Being first in line meant she would be the first to receive her results. The wait to find out what was the matter with her was much longer than she expected. She worried about getting back to work before her Egyptian family awoke and found that she was not there. But she worried more about her sickness and getting to the bottom of what ailed her.

Her long wait ended when the receptionist arrived and opened the door. She followed closely behind the receptionist who turned on the lights and sat down at her desk. After she turned on her desktop computer and printed off a paper, she turned and looked straight into Alya's face as she handed her the paper and said dryly, "Here are you results."

The receptionist handed Alya the paper for her to read. Once she had read the paper, Alya looked at the receptionist and said in an irritable tone, “This can’t be. It says all my tests were negative. That can’t be. I’m really sick.”

The receptionist tried to calm Alya down and said, “Do you want to do the lab tests again?”

“No, that’ll cost me more money. Can I have a couple of minutes with Dr. Hassan to explain my recent symptoms?”

“He’s not here yet, but as soon as he arrives I’ll tell him you are waiting to see him.”

Alya took a seat in the waiting room near the door to Dr. Hassan’s office. She wanted him to see her as soon as he arrived. She knew she had to get her exchange with Dr. Hassan done quickly so she could return to work.

She did not have to wait long. Dr. Hassan arrived and walked briskly toward his office. He passed the receptionist who told him softly that one of his patient’s was waiting for him. Alya was standing in front of his office door and said to him when he was close to her, “I need to see you now. It’s urgent.”

“Okay. Come in. Please be brief. I’ve appointments.”

After the door of Dr. Hassan’s office was closed, Alya let loose with a stream of words, waving her lab results, she was vehement in her emphatic words, “These negative results can’t be right. I’m sick and I need to be cured.”

Dr. Hassan could see that Alya was stressed and he tried to cool her down. He asked her to describe her symptoms. Alya rapidly described to him the most recent episode of her sickness. He responded to his distressed patient by saying, “We need to do more tests to get to know what is causing your ailment. I’ll schedule you for an endoscopy with Dr. Batra as soon as possible.”

Alya immediately asked, "What's an endoscopy?'

Dr. Hassan tried to describe an endoscopy the best he could, "It's a nonsurgical procedure. For an upper endoscopy, you will be given a mild sedation. A wire-like flexible tube connected to a light and a miniature video camera will be passed through your mouth and throat to examine by a color TV monitor your esophagus, stomach and the upper part of you small intestine. Still pictures will be taken of anything abnormal. All will take place in the operation room. Dr. Batra is a certified gastroenterologist and he's better able than me in describing endoscopies."

"I assume this will cost money"

"Yes, the procedure is expensive and you must pay 50 percent upfront."

"Okay. Go ahead. I'll have to borrow most of the money. Hopefully, the results of this exam will tell me what is wrong with me. Please go ahead and schedule me. I will be back at this same time tomorrow to know the time of my appointment with Dr. Batra."

"No problem. We'll try to schedule you as soon as possible. Dr. Batra works in the same building, so it will be easy for you to access his clinic. By the way, you should know that if Dr. Batra does not find anything abnormal in doing this examination, he'll probably recommend doing an endoscopy of your lower digestive tract."

"I can see that'll cost more money, but can you tell me what that involves?"

"It is basically the same as the upper endoscopy, but in this instance the tube is inserted into your rectum and your large intestine is examined. This procedure is often called a colonoscopy. You'll be administered an anesthetic."

This was an overload of information for Alya and she said, "Okay, I hope the first examination tells us what is wrong with me and I can be treated so I won't suffer again my serious symptoms. I must go now.

Thank you for receiving me. I'll check in with the receptionist first thing tomorrow to see when my appointment is with Dr. Batra."

As Alya said goodbye to the receptionist, she asked, "How much does an endoscopy with Dr. Batra cost?"

"At least a thousand dirhams, or around $300, if you don't have insurance."

Alya silently winced. She asked herself, "How can I get that amount of money?"

There was no time to think now because she had to rush back to her workstation at her Egyptian family's apartment. Her idea was to enter the apartment without being perceived, but this idea was quickly demolished by the fact that she did not have a key to the apartment door. She was obliged to knock softly.

After her first gentle knock, the door was flung wide open to reveal a worried Sarah, who said, "Alya. We're worried to death. Where have you been?"

The frightened Alya bowed her head and said obediently, "Please excuse me madame. I had an early medical appointment and I expected to return before anyone was up. I want to tell you more, but please excuse me now while I go tend to the girls."

"Yes, we'll talk later. Maria and Mariyam are waiting for you."

Alya said to Sarah in a soft, subservient manner, "See you later," as she dashed off to join the girls in their bedroom.

The girls expressed their glee over Alya's return by jumping up and down and hugging her tightly. Their love for Alya seemed to have no bounds. Tears swelled up in Alya's eyes as she kissed them on their cheeks to manifest her deep affection for the two girls. She did not know why she had such profound feelings for them, but she rejoiced, nonetheless.

As was their custom, Alya bathed and clothed the girls. Sarah called them for breakfast. Alya tried to act normally and enjoy their company, but she could not bring herself to eat. She was afraid that eating would set off her excruciating abdominal pains. She played with her food, nibbling around the edges. Her actions prompted Sarah to say, "Eat. You must eat to stay healthy and maintain your weight."

Alya wanted to obey Sarah, so she placed a fully loaded fork of food into her mouth. She almost choked, but with great difficulty she chewed well and swallowed her food. When this mouthful entered her stomach, she began to feel dizzy. Then she broke out into a sweat. She could not endure the harsh pain that was surging in her innards. The only choice she had was to excuse herself and rush to the bathroom.

Sarah and her two daughters were alarmed and dumbfounded by Alya's sudden departure from the table. Their shock stunned them into silence. Nobody could continue eating. After a few minutes, Sarah asked, "Please be good girls and go to your room. I will look after Alya."

Alya had finished emptying her bowels in the toilet and was laying on the bathroom floor, trying to recover from this vicious bout of vomiting up her guts, when there was a soft knock on the door followed by the sympathetic voice of Sarah, "Anything I can do to help you?"

The sound of Sarah's voice told Alya that she had to explain her odd actions and she said, "Please give me a moment to compose myself?"

It took more than a few minutes for Alya to stand up, and after she washed her face and gargled water from the faucet, she straightened her clothes and opened the door to confront Sarah with bowed head. Sarah in a consoling tone said, "My dear, let's go sit down in the living room and talk."

They slowly walked to a cushy sofa. Sarah demonstrated her concern for Alya by putting her right arm over her shoulders. They sat for a while, eyeing each other, neither knowing quite what to say. Alya was the first to speak, saying only, "I'm sick."

"Obviously."

“I’m sorry. I didn’t tell you when I was hired because I thought I was going to get a treatment that would make my ailment go away, but instead, my sickness got worse.”

“That’s understandable my dear. Please relax and tell me what you’re doing to rid yourself of this illness.”

Alya explained to Sarah all she had done to bring her ailment under control so she could continue to function as a faithful and dependable household servant. She finished by saying, “I like the work I’m doing for you and my main objective is to be cured and continue working for you. I can’t imagine doing anything else.”

“That’s what we want too. We want to help you get better. What can we do to help?”

Happiness surged in Alya’s heart. She was lost for words. She did not expect to hear her madame express such kind words. There was no doubt in her mind that Sarah possessed a good and generous heart. Sarah’s words encouraged Alya to describe her visits to Dr. Hassan’s clinic and her medical pursuit of a cure.

Alya also told Sarah about the financial cost of her ordeal and how she would have to borrow the money to pay for the endoscopy exam. Sarah promptly interrupted by saying, “Don’t worry about the cost. We’ll advance you all the money you need to get through this.”

Her words brought tears to Alya’s eyes. She could not refrain from embracing Sarah. After an emotional few minutes, Alya released Sarah and stood up and said with all sincereness, “Thank you from the bottom of my heart. I’ll never forget what you have done for me. Hopefully, the endoscopy will give us the answers. I’ll go to see the girls now and attend to my other duties.”

Sarah looked at the standing Alya and said, “My dear, you’re getting too skinny. You must eat and keep your food down.”

Alya uttered before she walked off in the direction of the girls' room, "I'll do my best."

Alya busied herself with the girls and her household chores, but her mind dwelled on learning first thing tomorrow when her endoscopy appointment with Dr. Batra would be. She sat at the table to eat dinner with her Egyptian family, although she knew very well that swallowing any food would lead to a painful abdominal cramps. She sat at the table with the family and noticed that Nicholas was staring directly at her, watching her every move. His riveting eyes made her feel uncomfortably nervous. She assumed that Sarah had told him about her condition and therefore it was important he had no qualms about keeping her as a house servant. It appeared that Sarah and the girls had persuaded him to help Alya with her medical bills and to get through her medical ordeal.

Nicholas finally spoke up by saying, "Alya, Sarah has told me all about your medical condition. I want to assure you that we've agreed to support you so that you get better and stay with us for a long time. You are a key member of this family, and we don't want to lose you."

Alya breathed a deep sigh of relief upon hearing Nicholas' words. She felt like crying but out of the highest respect for him, she controlled her emotions and lifted her head to say, "Thank you. Your words mean a lot to me. I can't thank you enough."

"Now, eat and be healthy," loudly said Nicholas.

Tears filled Alya's eyes. She wanted to eat all the food on her plate, but she could not. Sarah noticed Alya's discomfiture and said, "My dear. If you can't eat, don't. The important thing is that you do what your doctor recommends so you can get better."

Alya wanted to stay until all the others at the table had finished their meal and to help Sarah with the dishes, but instead she found herself obliged to ask to be excused. She felt like her stomach was revolted by even to the smell of food. She was afraid to regurgitate bile at the dinner table. Off she went in a hurry to the bathroom, locking the door tightly behind her. She felt hot and dizzy as she rapidly kneeled in front of the toilet and experienced successive bouts of dry heaves.

The central thoughts dominating her mind were: "What's wrong with me? This can't be happening to me."

She was exhausted by her ordeal in the bathroom. She washed her mouth out at the bathroom sink and gazed at herself in the mirror. It was difficult for her to believe the reflection in the mirror was her face. The person in the mirror looking back at her was not the person she remembered herself to be. At that moment, she really feared how fast her health was deteriorating.

She unlocked the bathroom door and staggered down the hall to her and the girls' bedroom. The bedroom door was wide open. She expected to see the girls, but they were not there, and it was eerily quiet. This was good time to call Yeshi, but she decided not to do so because she knew Yeshi would not show any sympathy for her health condition. Instead, she collapsed on the bed in a weakened state and fell fast asleep.

It was early in the morning before Alya woke up. At first, she did not know where she was. Somehow, she was in the bed fully clothed in between the two girls who she observed out of the corners of her eyes and they appeared to be in a deep sleep. She carefully extricated herself from her middle position in bed and gently opened the door to go to the bathroom.

Once in the well-lit bathroom she straightened her clothes, washed her face and rinsed out her mouth. Her intention was to make herself presentable and ready to go to Dr. Hassan's office. When she had finished doing her toiletries, she walked softly through the dark apartment to the living room. It was still dark outside, so she sat quietly and waited for the sun to rise.

When it was light enough outside, Alya sneaked out the apartment door and went to Dr. Hassan's office as quietly as possible. It was still early, but Alya wanted to be the first in line and learn as rapidly as possible when her appointment was with Dr. Batra. For her, this was a matter of life and death. If she were too sick to work, her family in Addis Ababa would become destitute. Her survival and that of her Ethiopia family were at stake.

CHAPTER TWENTY-THREE

Life After Death

"Good that you're here early," said Dr. Hassan's fellow Bangladeshi who worked as his receptionist. "Wait until I unlock the door and retrieve your file."

Alya stood in front of the receptionist's small desk, waiting patiently for her to find her file and finish what she was telling her. She was stunned when the receptionist told her, "I hope you are ready to see Dr. Batra today because we're able to arrange with his office for you to do your endoscopy first thing this morning. Okay?"

This was much faster than Alya expected, but she was excited that her medical procedure could be done so quickly. She knew her delay would worry Sarah, but she knew where she was and, thus, she could imagine what she was doing. She wanted to borrow the receptionist's phone to call Sarah, but she had forgotten the scrap of paper on which she had written down her number. Without hesitation, she replied, "Okay. Just explain to me where to go. I'm glad you are treating my case with the urgency it deserves."

The receptionist lost no time replying to Alya, "Here, take your file.

Inside is an order from Dr. Hassan for your procedure. Take the lift to the second floor. You'll find Dr. Batra's office behind the second door on the right. He will communicate the results to Dr. Hassan and you should be able to see them this afternoon."

This was all happening so fast. Alya was pleasantly pleased by the speed at which she would get her results and thus get to the bottom of what was wrong with her. She had brought all the money she possessed to pay upfront Dr. Batra's office the fifty percent required. She worried that she would have to get an advance from Sarah to pay for the remainder.

Dr. Batra's office was easy to find. Its simple layout was the same as Dr. Hassan's office. The receptionist appeared as a twin of the one she had just left. Their India-like dress was the same. She handed her file to the receptionist who said in stilted English in a mechanical tone, "Very good. Please pay me your down payment and then I'll call my colleague who will prepare you for the procedure in the next room."

Alya carefully counted out her money. The receptionist scooped up the money and said with a smile on her face, "Please take a seat while I inform my colleague of your arrival."

Soon, another foreign-looking woman came out of another room and said, "The doctor is ready to receive you now."

Alya stepped into the examination room and met the mild-mannered, bespectacled Dr. Batra who instructed her, "Please step behind the partition and remove your upper garments and put on the hospital gown you will find there on a chair. As soon as you change and my assistant arrives, we'll start the procedure. It should not take long. We'll give you a mild sedative, so you'll not feel any discomfort. Any questions?"

"No," said Alya as she stepped behind the partition to undress and put on the unwieldy hospital gown. After she had tied the neck strings of her gown, she stepped out from behind the partition to find the same woman she thought was the receptionist.

Dr. Batra noticed her querying look and said, “This is my assistant. Please sit on the patient exam table and lay on your left side so I can administer an upper endoscopy. My assistant will give you a pill which will make what I do painless. I’m sure Dr. Hassan explained to you that I’m going to run a tube down your throat so I can examine on this TV monitor your esophagus, stomach and the upper part of your small intestine. I will inform you of the results and send a report to Dr. Hassan. Okay? Now you can swallow the pill with a small cup of water and we’ll wait for a few minutes before we begin the procedure.”

The bedside manner of Dr. Batra was superb and helped make Alya rely on him. She swallowed the big pill and felt no effects. After a few minutes, Dr. Batra said, “Let’s begin. We’ll be monitoring your vital signs. If you feel any pain, raise your right hand. Just relax and open your mouth wide so I can insert the thin flexible tube and start the procedure. Good, let’s begin.”

Alya felt a slight discomfort as Dr. Batra carefully slid the tube through her mouth and down her throat. She concentrated on being still so Dr. Batra could perform the procedure fully and easily. In a short time, she was surprised to feel Dr. Batra pulling the tube out. She watched him as he removed his latex gloves and looked to see if Alya was alert and said to her, “Get dressed and I’ll tell you my findings.”

Alya stepped off the patient’s table and quickly went behind the partition to remove her hospital gown and put on her bra and blouse. She stepped out in front of the partition and found Dr. Batra all alone, “Thank you for hurrying your dressing. I’m afraid I don’t have much to tell you. As far as I can tell, your upper digestive track appears normal.”

“What? That can’t be. My symptoms are serious. There is something very wrong with my insides. What can I do?”

Dr. Batra replied, “I understand your reaction. We have no recourse but to do an examination of the lower digestive tract.”

"What's that involve and when can you do it? As you can see, I'm eager to know what's wrong me and get treated."

"I can do it tomorrow at the same time if you have the money to pay for the rest of this upper endoscopy and the fifty percent down payment for the lower endoscopy procedure."

"This is for me an emergency. Schedule the procedure. I will borrow the money and pay you what you require this afternoon. By the way, how is a lower endoscopy performed?"

"Do not consume anything after midnight."

"That's easy. What else?"

"This is a more serious procedure and is done in my operation room. An anesthesiologist will administer intravenously an anesthesia that will put you asleep. I will then insert a fine plastic hollow tube into your rectum and view on my TV monitor the interior of your colon and lower small intestine. If there is anything wrong, I'll see it."

"Sounds like a nasty procedure, but in my case it's necessary."

"Don't worry. You'll be fast asleep and won't feel a thing."

"I assume this procedure costs the same as the one that was just done to me."

"No. This procedure is more costly. The amount charged is $500.

Alya gasped. She did not have any money and would have to try to borrow this hefty sum of money and fully pay for the first procedure. Even if they found what was wrong with her and she got cured, it would be a long time before she paid off her debts. She asked herself, "I'm working abroad so I can send money home, but if I pay my debts, I can't send money home. Of course, if I can't work, I can't pay my debts. The only way out of this bad predicament is for me to get cured and work for months."

These thoughts cast Alya into a deep state of depression. She wanted to return to her Egyptian family home and inform Sarah of her medical results, but she really needed to communicate her medical problem to Samrawit. She had worked for years in the UAE and she would know what to advise her. Samrawit is an Ethiopian and they could talk in Amharic. After all, Alya considered Samrawit as her sponsor and counselor. She would do what Samrawit said to do.

As Alya was heading toward the exit of Dr. Batra, she overheard him say something to his assistant in their Bangladeshi language. Immediately after this brief exchange, his assistant turned to her and said, "I expect to see you this afternoon with the money. I'll set aside a laxative for you. See you later."

Sarah would have to wait. Alya had to go to Samrawit's place. She walked briskly with the fear of having an unmerciful attack of her unknown ailment at any time. Her breathing was heavy when she knocked loudly on Samrawit's door. She was pleased when Samrawit opened the door. She was afraid that when she needed her the most she would not be home.

Samrawit tried to act like nothing was wrong, but she was deeply surprised that Alya was rendering her a visit at this time. She was also taken aback by Alya's appearance. Alya was only a shadow of her former self. Samrawit hid her true feelings when she invited Alya into her apartment, "Come in my dear and sit down. I'll bring you some Ethiopian food to eat."

Samrawit turned and headed for the kitchen when Alya said through a veil of tears, "Don't bother. I can't eat."

Samrawit did a quick about face and sat down beside Alya, embracing her. She did her best to comfort an ailing Alya. Several minutes passed before Alya could compose herself to talk coherently in Amharic. The only words she repeated were, "Samrawit, I'm really sick."

In time, Alya explained the nature of her ailment and her visits to the doctor. She hesitantly described to Samrawit her medical exams and said she was broke and her additional medical exam would cost her more. Samrawit patiently listened to Alya and said as sweetly as she could, "Don't worry about the money. You have to do the exams to know what is wrong with you and get the treatment you need."

After a pause, Alya squeaked, "God help me. How can I ever pay back the money I borrowed?"

"My dear, you will not have to pay back anything. I have money collected from the hundreds of people here in the Habesha community. This money is for cases like yours. It's a medical emergency fund that was set up in case anyone in our community needed healthcare that costs beyond their means."

It took a while for Alya to digest Samrawit's much welcomed words. All Alya could say were words of praise to God and all the saints. Teary eyed, she said to Samrawit, "I thank you. My family thanks you. May God bless you eternally. You have come to our rescue."

Upon hearing those words, Samrawit excused herself, went into her bedroom, and came back and handed Alya a wad of dirhams, saying, "This should cover your medical bills. Come and see me if you need more."

Alya stuffed the money in her small purse and was profuse in their native tongue to thank Samrawit. She felt like kissing Samrawit's toes but discarded that thought because she thought she knew that Samrawit would not like that gesture. Instead she stood up and said, "I have to go. I need to pass by Dr. Batra's office and pay what I owe and confirm my appointment. And then I have to rush to my Egyptian family's apartment. Thank you again. I'll keep you informed of my situation."

Samrawit opened door and said, "Please get better fast so you can eat. I want to see some fat on your bones. Bye … until next time."

The hallways and streets were full of people, but Alya did not see them. She was fully absorbed by the need to turn over some of her money to the receptionist at Dr. Batra's office, confirming her lower endoscopy scheduled for early tomorrow. The receptionist was seated behind her desk when Alya arrived and she greeted her by saying, "You back already? You must have the money to pay for your medical procedure."

The receptionist was all business. Alya did not like the compassionless manner in which she treated her. But she also envied the independent way she behaved. Most of all she envied her good health. She did not like being looked upon as an unhealthy person. For a moment, she wished she could trade places with the receptionist but rumblings in her lower abdomen reminded her that she was damaged and of no use to anyone. Her growing pain made her hand the money quickly to the receptionist without counting the many bills, and say, "See you tomorrow morning. I've got to go now."

Alya's stomach pains were growing in intensity and she staggered to the apartment door of her Egyptian family. She saw that Sarah was peering down the hallway, waiting for her. Alya arrived at the spot where Sarah was standing and forced herself to say, "Please excuse me. I have to go to the bathroom now."

The regurgitation pain was excruciating. Alya was afraid she would vomit her guts out before being able to heave her innards in the toilet basin. She barely made it to the bathroom and threw up something that looked like yellow bile. After vomiting and several bouts of dry heaves, she collapsed in a pool of her own sweat on the floor.

Alya was not aware of Sarah standing above her. The urgency of Alya's traumatic state had not allowed her any time to fiddle with closing the bathroom door. Sarah remained silent as she reached to flush the toilet to help rid the room of the stinky smell. By this time, Alya had passed out and was thus in a motionless fetal position on the floor. Sarah did not want to do anything that would disturb the prostrate Alya, but she was eager to talk with her.

Sarah did not want her daughters to see Alya like this and made sure they stayed in their room by walking briskly down the hall to their room and opening their door slightly and saying calmly, "Are you girls having fun? I hope you're ready to show your best behavior for Alya who should be joining you shortly."

Mariyam said, "Don't worry, mama. We'll be right here when Alya arrives."

Sarah gently closed their bedroom door and with a sinking heart she strode toward the bathroom to see how Alya was doing. When she peered through the wide-open door, she was happy to see Alya sitting up with her head resting on her arms propped up by her elevated knees. She had some toilet tissue in her hand to wipe her lips clean of the awful slime she had vomited on the rim of the toilet basin. She raised her head when Sarah arrived and struggled to stand up and utter a few words, "Give me a few minutes to compose myself and then we'll talk."

Sarah was quick to say, "Please don't fret in the least about me or your work. I'm here to help you in any way I can."

Alya heard Sarah's kind words but could not reply. She washed her face and gargled some water streaming out of the sink faucet. Her knees were weak and she did not know if she could walk when she loosened her grip on the edges of the sink cabinet. While she continued to grip the cabinet top, she glanced at Sarah and managed to say, "I'm too sick. I don't think I can walk."

The fearful look in Alya's eyes startled Sarah who was reminded of the wounded sheep she observed in her childhood just before it was to be slaughtered. She got close to Alya and said, "Put your arm over my shoulder and let's go and sit on the sofa in the living room."

They slowly walked in a hobbled fashion to the living room. Alya reluctantly placed her full weight on Sarah. She tried to carry her own light weight but could not find the strength to do so. Alya's head spun and she collapsed on the sofa. She thought that only death could save her from her embarrassing predicament and relieve her of the deep pain she felt.

Sarah was shaken to her core to see a limp and lifeless Alya lying before her. She did not know what to do. Her hand grasped Alya's in the hope of seeing some sign of life. After the passage of around a half-hour, Sarah was pleased to see Alya open her eyes and say in soft starts and stops, "Please don't let me die. Keep me alive so I can make to my doctor's exam tomorrow."

Sarah responded without hesitation, "You'll not die. I'll care for you the best I can and get you to your doctor. Now, you must get some rest. I'll tell the girls to get the bed ready for you. I'm sure they will want to care for you too. We all love you and want you to get better."

Alya formed a little smile and applied a slight pressure on Sarah's hand to acknowledge her words and express her high appreciation for her kindness. She was too sick to think, but she was eternally thankful that she was in the caring hands of Sarah. Maybe she had died but with Sarah at her side there was a glimpse of life after death.

CHAPTER TWENTY-FOUR

Emergency Evacuation

SARAH SPOKE ON HER CELLPHONE with a high sense of urgency, telling her husband, Nicolas, in their Coptic language, "Come home now. I don't know what to do. Alya is deathly sick and has fallen into a coma. Bring a wheelchair with you if you can."

"Don't hang up. I don't understand," said a confused Nicolas.

"Just get home now and you'll see what I'm dealing with," replied Sarah in the same pleading tone of urgency.

There was nothing for Sarah to do but sit quietly by Alya's side. She saw that Alya was still breathing so she was still alive. Sarah noted that Alya's body was hot, prompting her to bring a damp cool wash cloth from the bathroom, fold it, and place it on Alya's forehead."

"Mommy, what's wrong. "We've been waiting for a long time for Alya," Mariyam stumbled through her words in Coptic as she stood across the living room.

Sarah answered by saying, "My darling daughter, Alya is sick and she is resting on the sofa. You can help by arranging your bed so she can go to sleep early."

As Mariyam scampered off, she said, "Okay mama. We'll get the bed ready."

Sarah was making light of Alya illness so that her daughters would not be alarmed. There was some noise at the front door, so Sarah went to the door and opened it. She was happy to see the breathless and perspiring Nicolas with a wheelchair. His first question was, "Where's Alya?"

Sarah replied, "She's sleeping on our sofa. We should let her rest before moving her to the bedroom."

Nicolas observed the worried look on Sarah's face and said, "Shouldn't she be in a hospital? Should I call an ambulance?"

"No," said Sarah emphatically. "We need to get her through the night and take her to the clinic for her medical tests first thing in the morning. To do that, we may have to use the wheelchair you managed to acquire."

Nicolas clearly heard Sarah's words, but he was not sure about his role so he asked gently, "When you go to the clinic in the morning, will you need me to go with you? You know, I have to work."

"I think we can be able to go to the clinic without you. If she can get into the wheelchair, we can make it. My main concern is for the girls because they will be at home alone until we finish with the clinic. What do you think?"

"I'll talk to the girls and ask them for sake of Alya that they have to be on their best behavior. I'm sure they'll be okay. Maybe you'll be back before they get up."

They ate quickly and fixed some food for the girls who went to their bedroom after cleaning their plates, saying, "We'll be in our room waiting for you to bring Alya. Her place in our bed is ready."

Nicolas and Sarah sat quietly in the living room across from where Alya was sleeping on the sofa. They sat as if they were in vigil for a dead person. But they could see that Alya was defying death by breathing shallowly. They were waiting for Alya to stir before asking her if she wanted to go to bed. Suddenly they heard a slight moan coming from Alya. They instantly rose and hovered over Alya. After a few moments they agreeably saw Alya open her eyes a bit and she was trying to talk. She was only able to dribble out a few weak words, "Help me. I don't want to die."

Nicolas hustled to bring the wheelchair near to where Alya was lying down on the sofa and he said tenderly to her, "I have this wheelchair for you. We can use it take you to bed so you can sleep until your appointment tomorrow morning."

Alya lifted the index finger on her right hand to indicate that she heard Nicolas's words. She awkwardly tried to sit up. Sarah and Nicolas immediately tended to Alya, helping her sit up and get seated in the wheelchair. Once seated, Nicolas pushed the wheelchair slowly behind Sarah in the direction of the girls' bedroom.

They entered the bedroom. The girls stopped playing and stood somberly by while the wheelchair was placed beside the bed. They sensed the seriousness of the situation and looked lovingly at Alya and saw the gravity of her illness. Tears started to stream down their cheeks. They wanted to help her, but they knew they were helpless to do so. Their tears turned into cries of fear.

It was upsetting to Sarah to see her girls so distraught and expressed her love for them by saying, "You'll sleep with me tonight. Nicolas can sleep on the sofa. Before we sleep, we'll pray for Alya." Sarah continued to talk to the girls, "Please excuse us while we lift Alya out of the wheelchair so we can place her on the bed. She'll need to rest comfortably until her medical appointment tomorrow morning. Now, go play in the living room."

After the girls left the room, Nicolas said to Sarah, "No problem. She is so small and light that I can put her into bed myself."

Sarah objected by saying, "We have to handle her as we would manage a sick baby. You get on one side of her while I get on the other. We'll lift her gently into bed. We must do this with the utmost delicacy."

Nicolas followed Sarah's every move and together they lifted Alya into bed. Once Alya was in bed, Sarah asked Nicolas to excuse them while she was making Alya comfortable. After Nicolas left the room, Alya moaned her thanks for Sarah's kindnesses. Caringly, Sarah gently removed Alya's clothes and delicately slipped over her head and shoulders her sleeping gown. She stayed at Alya's side and whispered sweetly into her ear, "Rest, my dear. Tomorrow will be a better day for you."

Alya held Sarah's hand for a long while before sliding off into a deep sleep. Sarah kissed her hand and whispered again, "Goodnight my dear. May God keep and bless you."

Sarah placed the wheelchair alongside the bed, within easy reach of Alya. She walked silently toward the door, turning off the ceiling lights, opening and closing the door as quietly as possible. As she left the bedroom, she was overwhelmed by sad emotions and tears filled her eyes. A dreadful thought entered her head, "God forbid. Could this be the last time I see Alya alive?"

Sarah sauntered slowly into living room. She did not feel well. Maybe Alya's pitiful health crisis was making her sick. Certainly, her profound concerns for Alya's wellbeing were dragging her down into heretofore unknown emotional depths. She was not her usual self when she glanced at her husband and said woefully, "I'll take the girls for their baths and then put them in our bed, and then I'll bring your pajamas and a pillow."

Nicolas could see the poor state that Sarah was in and only nodded his head, knowing she could see in his eyes the deep affection he had for her and that he was worried about the profound negative effect

Alya's illness was having on her. He sat down on the sofa to ponder what he could do to shelter his wife from Alya's disastrous medical quagmire.

Sarah returned as promised with the items that would allow him to spend the night comfortably on the sofa. He stood up while Sarah arranged the sofa. When she was done, she embraced her husband and kissed him softly on the cheek before saying, "We need to get some sleep because I'll be getting up before dawn to take Alya to the clinic. Hopefully, the doctor can tell us what's wrong with her and treat her so she can begin the process of restoring herself to good health."

Nicolas did not know what to say in response to his wife's words. He did not want to hurt her feelings in any way. Nor did he want to discourage her in any way. He kept his inner thoughts to himself because he was afraid that revealing those thoughts would douse all the hopes Sarah had for the improvement of Alya's serious health condition. Therefore, Nicolas kept his thoughts to himself.

He was thinking that Alya could not get better, and she would be lucky if she did not die. His family was suffering because of her, and he wanted to rid them of this doleful burden. For him, Alya was damaged beyond repair and should be returned to her own people while she was still breathing. The sooner Alya could be out of their lives the better. For him, as the head of his household, he could not wait until Alya drew her last breath to act.

His love for Sarah caused Nicolas to remain mum and go along with his wife's wishes for caring for Alya, but he was ready to intervene as soon as he saw a safe time to do so. He was deeply troubled, and bottling up his true feelings was also making him ill. It was not sleeping alone on the sofa that kept him awake all night, but the thought of having to deal with a corpse in his apartment in the early morning.

Sarah was up early after trying to get some sleep in a big king-size bed with her daughters. Thoughts of what Alya was going through in the next room kept her from getting even a few winks of sleep. She gave up on sleeping, dressed and did all her toiletries silently in the adjoining bathroom while her two daughters slept soundly. Furtively, she left her bedroom and quietly tiptoed down the hall and opened Alya's bedroom door. She wanted to check on her and see if there was anything she could do to help ease her pain.

In the pre-dawn light, she found Alya lying on her back with her eyes wide open. As she approached her, Alya turned her head toward Sarah and forced her lips to form a little smile. Upon seeing this much welcomed gesture on the part of Alya, Sarah's heart rejoiced, and she said in a whispering tone, "My dear, are you feeling better?"

It took Alya a few minutes to respond by saying in a halting but pleasing fashion, "Yes. Can you take me to the bathroom?"

Sarah replied, "Certainly, let me get the wheelchair tightly against the bed so you can easily slide into it."

Without too much difficulty, Sarah supported Alya as she helped her get out of bed and into the wheelchair. Sarah easily pushed the wheelchair out of the bedroom and down to the bathroom, leaving Alya alone but standing just outside the door in case Alya needed her. She heard that Alya was running water into the sink. She happily assumed Alya was washing her face and told herself, "We're off to a good start. Thank you God."

Alya came out of the bathroom, knowing she had to preserve the little energy she had. She gestured toward the wheelchair. Sarah saw Alya's limp hand movements and helped her get into the wheelchair. She pushed the wheelchair into the living room and bent over to whisper into Alya's ear, "It's too early to go to the clinic. Can you wait here while I tell Nicolas that he can get up and go to our bedroom?"

To answer Sarah's simple question, Alya could only manage raising her right index finger while she continued to hold as tight as she could the handgrips on the wheelchair. She had no energy and even her mind had ceased working. She was physically and mentally a blank. What remained of her body was only a shell of its former being. It was not possible to force her mind to think about anything. She could be already dead and only her remains were sitting in the wheelchair.

Sarah gently poked Nicolas and he immediately sat up and said, "What's going on?

Sarah replied in a loving tone, "I just wanted to tell you that Alya and I are ready to go to the clinic. You can go to our bedroom and to work as soon as you like."

Nicolas stood up, gathered his bed clothing and headed toward his bedroom. He looked straight forward through sleepy eyes, avoiding looking directly at Alya. He did note her out of the corner of his eyes sitting in the wheelchair, but for him she was already dead and needed to be thought of in that way. He no longer recognized her as a living being. For him, she was just a bag of bones.

The best course for Nicolas was to get ready for work as soon as possible. He found it necessary to leave his apartment that harbored death so he could avoid a conflict with his wife whom he deeply loved. He was profoundly upset that the remains of Alya were getting in between him and his beloved family. His mind was taking a turn for the worse and he was becoming a person he did not like. To save himself and avoid an unsavory incident with Sarah, Nicolas rushed out of his apartment. In passing, he gave a small peck of a kiss on Sarah's cheek saying, "Something has come up. I have to go to work."

Sarah nodded her acknowledgement of his words, but she also took good note of his unusual behavior. He did not usually rush to work without eating breakfast and drinking a cup of coffee. And it was not lost on her that he totally neglected Alya.

The time had come when Sarah needed to start pushing Alya's wheelchair toward the clinic which was located few blocks away. She was happy that her daughters were still sleeping soundly. She was also happy that it was the cooler morning and the clinic was nearby. Alya feebly pointed at her wrist to indicate that it was time to go.

It was easy to go down the lift with the wheelchair and to push it along the wide, smooth sidewalks. Before they knew it, they had arrived at the front door of Dr. Batra's clinic. As expected, the door was locked since they had arrived early. Sarah did not care as long as they were first in line so they would be the first to be served. They did not have to wait long. The foreign receptionist arrived to received other foreigners. Sarah remembered that almost everyone in the UAE was from somewhere else.

They were admitted and registered. The receptionist asked for payment. Sarah saw that Alya had left her purse behind and she withdrew money from her own purse to pay. Alya gave her an approving glance to demonstrate her thankfulness for all that she was doing for her.

Dr. Batra and his female assistant were in his operating room. He was quick to observe that Alya was confined to a wheelchair so he allowed Sarah to remain in the room but required that she wear a face mask. He and his assistant helped Alya out of her wheelchair, undress and lay in a hospital gown on the patient's table. No sooner had she laid down than the assistant administered an intravenous dose of an anesthetic.

After a few minutes, Dr. Batra began to run a small tube through Alya's rectum so he could examine on his television monitor her colon. When he had completed the lower endoscopy exam, he turned to Sarah and said, "Nothing."

Sarah could not believe her ears and said in a tone of profound agitation, "What? That can't be. She's almost dead. What's wrong with her?"

Dr. Batra removed his latex gloves and turned fully around to face Sarah and said, "I can see that she's extremely ill. All I can say is that her upper and lower digestive tracks appear to be normal. I don't know what is wrong with her. If you can, I advise to evacuate her to her home country as soon as possible."

In spite of, but perhaps because of her sedation, Alya heard the essential of what Dr. Batra said and made a small noise that sounded like "Samrawit."

CHAPTER TWENTY-FIVE

Nothing More to Do

SARAH'S HAND WAS SHAKING AND she had lost her voice when she called Samrawit on her mobile phone. Samrawit could see who was calling on the screen of her mobile phone so she adjusted her voice to answer in as friendly and respectful way in her English. She stood as she talked into her cellphones, "Sarah, it's a pleasant surprise to hear your voice."

Sarah had no time for pleasantries and cut Samrawit short by saying in an urgent tone, "Are you home? I'm bringing Alya to your place. She is near death. I'm coming with her in a wheelchair."

There was no more time. Samrawit could tell from Sarah's voice that this was an emergency and only managed to get in a couple words edge wise before Sarah switched off her phone. She simply said, "I'm home."

Samrawit knew she had to steel herself and prepare for the trouble coming her way. Her mind was already racing to consider all the options for dealing with Alya. She knew Alya was sick, but she had hoped her medical condition would improve. But now she saw that was wishful thinking and she had to deal with the worst-case scenario. There was only one option—evacuation to Addis Ababa.

Lydia was standing by. She could see the alarming look on Samrawit's face and knew that her mother needed help. As expected, Samrawit barked out instructions, "Call the airlines and say we have a critically ill Ethiopian who must go to Addis on the next available flight. Don't take 'no' for an answer. Tell them she has a passport, visa, and a return ticket. Money is no object if she leaves on the next flight to Addis."

Panic began to overtake Samrawit and Lydia. The latter scurried to the kitchen to call the airlines and the former ducked into her bedroom to check how much money she had in her secret hiding place in clothes hanging in her closet. No matter how much it costs, she did not want Alya to die in her apartment. If Alya was destined to die, it would be at home in Addis with her family.

Lydia stuck her head into the bedroom and said, "I got a seat for Alya on the first flight early tomorrow morning to Addis."

"Okay. Good. Now reserve a car to take us to the airport. Tell them that this is an emergency and try to get our usual Habesha driver. I'm going now to stand just outside the front door for the arrival of Sarah and Alya."

No sooner had Samrawit stepped outside her apartment than she spotted Sarah down the hall pushing as fast as she could a wheelchair with Alya slumped over and her head covered so nobody could see her misery. The out-of-breath Sarah wheeled Alya up to where Samrawit was standing, "Here, take Alya. I wish you and her luck. I've done all I can. I must return home now. When I get a break, I'll bring or send along her few belongings later in the day. You can keep the wheelchair for as long as you need it."

Samrawit was speechless. She had not thought Alya's case was as serious as it is. She was in such a deep state of shock that she could not formulate words to thank Sarah and bid her farewell. Samrawit gave a slight nod of her head to indicate to Sarah that she had heard her, but she was preoccupied by the pitiful sight of Alya. She was in a hurry to do her own examination of Alya.

Alya's wheelchair barely made it through the narrow door of the apartment. Lydia watched in horror as Samrawit uncovered Alya's head. She could not believe this was the same person that she had seen a few weeks ago. The face staring back at her was more like a creepy skull with sunken eyes than the full happy face that had been Alya's only a short time ago.

Samrawit was more concerned about Alya's smell than her looks. There was an awful stench emanating from what remained of Alya's body and it had to be eliminated if she were to get on the plane. She turned to Lydia and said in no uncertain terms, "Run a bath. We must wash Alya from head to toe and put perfume all over her body. Also look for a robe to cover her while we wash and dry her clothes."

Unclothing and washing Alya was almost an insurmountable task. Lydia helped Samrawit unfasten Alya's clothes, but when they got to stripping off all her final layer of clothing, exposing her nudity, Samrawit said, "Thanks for my dear daughter for all your help, but I will take it from here."

As Lydia exited the bathroom, Samrawit thought, "The least I can do is not burn into my daughter's mind the ugliness of what is yet to come."

Alya was in a somnolent state. She was still breathing at a slow, uneven rate, but she had to wake up a bit if Samrawit were to fully undress here and wash off the filth that covered what was left of her body. She gently patted Alya's cheek while saying, "It's Samrawit. I need you to wake up a little so I can unclothe and clean you. I know you are very sick, but I need to clean you so you can travel to Addis early in the morning."

The heavy fog that shrouded Alya's ephemeral existence briefly lifted a bit with the mention of the word, "Addis." Her eyes opened and she used her last ounce of energy to position herself so that Samrawit could fully undress her. Moving her arms and legs hurt her so badly that she thought her last moment in life had arrived. She could not cry out in pain. She was so debilitated that all she could do was to remain involuntarily limp and silent.

The awful odor almost made Samrawit faint. She wanted to hold her nose, but she needed both hands to undress Alya. She struggled to remove Alya's soiled clothes without doing harm to Alya. There was no way to be as gentle as she wanted, but with the utmost effort she was able to remove all of Alya's clothing. She wadded up Alya's dirty clothes, opened the bathroom door and threw them on the floor, yelling, "Lydia come and wash these clothes."

Samrawit did not know how she could wash Alya. For sure, as light as Alya was, there was no way she could remove Alya from the wheelchair. Thus, she made the bold move of wheeling Alya into her walk-in shower. She would let the shower rain down on Alya, washing the wheelchair and her at the same time.

Normally, Alya would shiver from all the cold water falling on her in the shower stall but her weakened body ignored the temperature of the water. She was limp and still while Samrawit washed her boney body, getting soaked in the process. The cleaning of Alya ended when Samrawit turned the shower knob to its off position and wheeled the drenched Alya out of the stall.

At the ready were piles of soft white towels that she heaped on Alya before she used them to dry her quickly and then herself. Samrawit took the robe Lydia had fetched for her and draped it over Alya's emaciated body. After delicately dressing Alya in the cotton pink robe, Samrawit pushed the wheelchair with Alya's inert body to the bedroom. She lifted Alya into her bed and covered her, patting her head and caressing her face. She said softly in an endearing tone, "Rest my dear. If all goes as planned, by this time tomorrow you'll be at home in Addis."

Samrawit stepped quietly out of the bedroom and went to where Lydia was standing in the living room and asked her, "How's all the arrangements for Alya's evacuation going?"

Lydia responded, "All is well. I alerted the leaders of the Habesha community and several of them have called me to express their concern and solidarity with their sister. Alya's clothes are in our dryer. All should be ready when the time comes to dress her."

Samrawit was prepared to react to Lydia's comments, but she was interrupted by a brisk knock at the front door and rushed to see who it was. To her surprise, it was again Sarah who said rapidly, "Here's Alya's suitcase with her things. I have to return fast as I left my daughters alone."

Sarah did an abrupt about-face and raced down the hallway to the lift. Samrawit watched her until she disappeared into the lift. She knew Sarah was fleeing because she cared too much for Alya. Sarah was trying to run away from her cares because she knew that all the care in the world would not diminish in any way the seriousness of Alya's condition.

Samrawit's eyes cast for a moment on Alya's old, scarred cardboard suitcase before she gripped it and carried it into her apartment. This suitcase was in bad shape but in better shape than Alya. She laid it on her sofa and called Lydia to help her rummage through it. They needed to find her passport with a UAE visa and her unused return ticket. They were happy to find these items underneath the few garments she had in her dilapidated suitcase. Lydia was interested in finding any clothes Alya could travel in instead of the ones that were in the dryer. They were both surprised to find in Alya's suitcase a cellphone and its charger. Lydia said to her mother, "I wonder who she was calling."

Samrawit took said, "Let's get the phone charged and find out."

She immediately connected the phone to its charger and plugged it into the nearest electrical wall socket. Samrawit then closed the suitcase and said, "There's no clothing here of use. She'll need to keep the cellphone with her, and we can check-in this laughable excuse for a suitcase in with her at the airport."

Samrawit looked at the cellphone's screen to see if it were charged enough to see who she had been calling. She felt like she was snooping into Alya's private affairs, but her intention was born of necessity. She needed to see if she were calling home and then try to call and tell her family that she was severely ill and coming home.

The phone's screen lit up when Samrawit pressed the icon displaying a telephone. She could see only one number that Alya had called in Addis Ababa. She assumed this number was with her mother at her house in Addis. Lydia was standing by her, peering over her shoulder and said without hesitation, "Call that number."

Without moving, Samrawit assumed that Alya had enough credit on her phone to make at least one call to her home in Addis. She dialed the only number in her phone, and it rang a long time before it was answered, "Alya. Why are you calling at this time? I'm in church. Can you call later?"

Samrawit wasted no time in saying emphatically in Amharic, "Don't hang up. This is not Alya. She is extremely sick and coming home tomorrow."

Yeshi heard a voice that was not Alya's. She was shocked and did not know what to say. She thought for a moment and said, "Who is this? Where's Alya?"

"This is Samrawit. I've arranged for Alya to fly out in the morning. I'll call later to tell you what time her plane arrives and her flight number. Understand?"

Yeshi's head was spinning. She was frozen in place and speechless.

She could not believe what she was hearing and needed more time to digest Samrawit's words. After a long pause, she replied politely, "Thank you."

Samrawit turned to Lydia and said, "Alya's mother was in shock. My words were totally unexpected. I'll call her back later after I have all the flight information and she has had more time to think about what I said." In her mind, Samrawit was going through all the things that must be done to get Alya on her home-bound plane early the next morning. She checked on Alya in bed and saw no change. Alya remained like a dead person who was still barely breathing in a choppy fashion. Samrawit was hoping that Alya could sit up, open her eyes and drink a cup of lemon tea with an extra dose of honey. She wanted to tell her mother that Alya was showing some signs of improvement but that would be too far from the truth.

In the wee hours, they would have to dress Alya and get her ready to go to the airport. Lydia had spoken with airline officials and they were expecting a sick person and not a dead one. Samrawit took from Lydia a piece of paper with the flight number and the plane's arrival time in Addis. With this paper in hand, she called again Yeshi.

This time Yeshi answered her phone as soon as it rang and spoke first, "How's Alya? How's my baby?"

"No change. She's terribly ill and almost unconscious. It'll be a struggle to get her on the plane, but we'll do all possible to get her on the plane early in the morning. We plan to arrive at our airport two hours before the plane departs at 5:40 a.m. The Ethiopian Airlines flight number is 613 and arrives at 8:40 a.m. tomorrow morning your time. Be there at 8 a.m. ready to collect her. She needs a wheelchair. We hope she gets all the care she needs at home. But you must know her health is bad and she may not survive the flight."

"We'll be at the Addis airport with a wheelchair. I can't believe she is so sick that you have to send her home. I don't understand how she got like this. If you want, call me again to see if she has arrived and to be updated on her heath status."

Yeshi hung up her phone with a heavy heart. All her plans for a better life had been shattered. Not only would she not be getting any money from Alya, but she would have to pay for Alya's medical care. She did not know where she could get the money she needed for her and her family to survive. She decided that she needed to inform her daughters at home of Alya's dire condition and get any advice they had to offer.

Samrawit was constantly looking in at Alya. She told Lydia, "I've not been this nervous since you were born."

Lydia could not help but grin at her mother's comment. She hummed a religious tune as she laid out Alya clothes on the sofa. More than anything the tune was for God to make Alya better. In reality, she wanted to do anything that would get her mind off Alya's dreadful case. Samrawit interrupted her train of thought by saying, "I assume we can't eat, but we should try to get some sleep before we wake up early to get Alya ready and take her to the airport."

"I'll lay down, but I doubt if I can sleep. How about you?"

"I'll do the same, but I will lie down next to Alya so I can be of help in case she stirs. Dim the lights and let us go lie down for a while. I'll set my alarm so we can be sure to be up on time. See you soon."

Samrawit dozed off into a light sleep that was interrupted by an unexpected movement by Alya. She turned over to see Alya sitting up in bed. She immediately got out of bed and ran to Alya's side to attend to her. But by the time she got there, Alya had collapsed back into her dormant position. For a moment, she thought her mind was playing tricks on her. She was pleased to think that Alya still had a spark of life but deep down she was certain Alya was ultimately doomed.

Lydia was surprised to see her mother come out of her bedroom.

She could not sleep and was ready to go to the airport. It was early but she said to her mother, "We might as well get Alya dressed and go to the airport, making sure she can get on the plane home."

They both took an item of clothing for Alya. They jointly uncovered her and began the onerous task of dressing a hibernating body. Once they had fully clothed her, they lifted her into the wheelchair and strapped her in place. Samrawit wheeled her into the living room and told Lydia, "Call the driver to let him know that we are ready to go to the airport."

The driver lost little time to get to Samrawit's place. They wheeled Alya to the car and collaborated with the driver to sit her in the back seat between them. They worked to hold Alya in place while the driver sped through the night in the direction of the airport. Although they arrived early at the airport, there was a Habesha man waiting for them with a wheelchair. He helped them carry Alya out of the car and place her in the wheelchair. The man said in Amharic, "Trust me. I've seen these cases before. For me, it's some kind of poisoning. At least she'll die at home. Give me her passport and ticket. Don't worry. I'll take care of everything. You can go now. I know your driver, so you can contact me through him if you want."

Samrawit was troubled by what the man said and was not prepared to relinquish control of Alya. She looked at her daughter and the driver. Lydia had gotten back into the car. She rolled down the back window and said, "Mom, let's go. There's nothing more you can do."

CHAPTER TWENTY-SIX

Seeking a Miracle

Yeshi called Belkis and Fana, "We need to talk. Leave Hiyab with the neighbors."

They knew that anytime Yeshi called them to meet in their modest sitting room it was for a serious talk. It was evening and with candlelight flickering off their faces they sat on the floor with their legs crossed for a long moment before Yeshi opened her mouth and said dolefully, "Alya fell down again, probably for the last time. She's coming home tomorrow morning. If she arrives still alive, she'll be deathly ill."

Belkis and Fana were shocked by Yeshi's words, but they knew that she would not say these things if they were not true. They began to wail but were shushed by Yeshi who said softly, "Be quiet. We don't want the neighbors to know of Alya's woeful condition and the negative consequences her condition has for us. The reason I'm talking to you now is to alert you to her arrival and get your ideas on what we should do."

Belkis spoke immediately, "Our first priority is to restore Alya's health."

Yeshi replied, "Yes, of course. But how if she is almost dead?"

Fana interrupted her sobbing to say softly, "She needs a true miracle to cure her."

These words stopped everyone in their tracks. They thought long and hard on how they could encourage God to miraculously heal Alya. Yeshi was the first to talk in a low voice, "The only place I know where miracles occur is at Mariyam's Entoto Church."

Belkis said simply, "That's it. We'll take her straight from the airport and leave her with the Entoto Church caretakers. Her future is out of our hands and in the Holy hands of God."

While Fana continued to cry, Yeshi told Belkis, "Line up a driver and car to take us to the airport early in the morning to pick up Alya and take her to the Entoto Church. Do it in a way so that our neighbors don't know what is going on. And not a word to Hiyab."

Belkis was surprised that Yeshi used the plural form of the pronoun and asked respectfully, "Do you mean by 'us' both me and Fana?"

Yeshi answered sternly but quietly, "No, both of you stay home and take care of Hiyab. I'll go with Alya and stay with her in Entoto until she dies or is cured."

This was an unusual display of affection by Yeshi, but they understood Alya was not only a young woman she had raised as her daughter but all of them depended upon her. They knew that Yeshi would do everything in her power to keep Alya alive, which was the highest priority for all of them. Belkis took charge and said, "Okay. It's decided. You take care of Alya and we'll take care of Hiyab and our house. We'll pray unceasingly for your well-being and for the restoration of Alya's health. We're committed for as long as it takes. Alya is our lifeline."

Yeshi grabbed a flashlight and dashed into the back of their small house to take all the money she had out of her secret hiding place. She returned with wads of local currency (birrs). She gave a chunk of ragged bills to Belkis and said, "Go out to the street and buy me a basket-full of mixed kolo. We'll munch on these roasted kernels of barley, chickpeas, sunflower seeds, and groundnuts when we get settled in Entoto. Fana, get two blankets that we can take with us. Entoto overlooks Addis so it is much higher and that makes it colder, especially at night."

Fana asked Yeshi, "Have you been to the Mariyam Church in the Entoto mountains north of Addis before?"

"No, but I've heard many stories about it, especially about the holy water that gurgles up from its natural springs. Many people go there to be healed by this sacred water."

"We studied about it in school. It's the oldest orthodox church in Addis. It was built in 1877 by the Emperor Menelik II who founded Addis. He and his wife are buried there."

"It's good you study such things in school. It's truly a holy place."

"Yes, we were also taught that the Emperor planted the first eucalyptus tree that he received from Australia. Today, these trees are abundant in Entoto."

Yeshi sat down and thought of her momentous decision to accompany Alya to Entoto. In a hushed voice, she said, "I must go. Not only will she need my help, but I'll also need all the blessings I can get from the Entoto church and its holy water. I'll need those blessings to get the strength I need to get us through the tough times ahead."

After a pause, she told Fana, "Go look and see if we have a third blanket we can spare? We can use it in Entoto to lay down on."

Belkis returned with the basket of kolo and set it by the pile of worn old blankets. Their sitting room was dimly lit by several flickering candles. Every time they stood up their shadows danced wildly on the cheaply plastered whitewashed walls. Yeshi was in a pensive mood, reflecting on the ordeal that was before her. When she would think of anything, she would address Belkis. She now said, "Get all the empty plastic water bottles that we have in and around our house. We'll need them to collect holy water from the spring, so we can drink our fill of this purifying liquid."

Belkis and Fana knew about bathing naked at sunrise in the holy spring water, but they did not know about drinking the holy water, so Belkis asked, "You drink the water too?"

"Of course, it is in this way that the demons can be fully removed from the inside of your body. You drink as much as you can until the demons of your illness are conquered. You only know you are healed when you spit out an ugly black slime."

Fana asked, "How long will you be away?"

"Until Alya is cured."

"How long is that?"

"I don't know. Much depends on the strength of her faith. It could be from one day until eternity."

These words caused Belkis and Fanis to have frightened looks on their faces. They did not know what to say. The thought of Yeshi and Alya being away in Entoto for a long time scared them. Belkis knew she had to say something and wiping away the tears in her eyes she said haltingly to Yeshi, "We hope and pray you will not be gone too long because we can't live without you."

Yeshi asserted, "We must try to sleep some and get up before dawn so I can go with the taxi to the airport. Fana go get Hiyab. When you come back with her, we'll bed down until the first rays of the sun."

Hiyab returned and made herself comfortable next to Fana, who lay next to Bekis. All three were snuggled up on a ratty comforter spread across the sitting room floor. Yeshi slept on her low bed in the adjoining tiny room. One candle was left burning. The night passed quickly and daylight started to peek timidly over the mountainous eastern horizon. At the first sign of daybreak, Yeshi got up and in an instant she was ready to go.

Yeshi roused the girls in the next room and proceeded outside to wash her face with the water trickling from the rusty standpipe. The girls followed and Belkis volunteered, "I'll make some coffee and warm up yesterday's injera and doro wat sauce."

Yeshi immediately responded, "That's good, but I'll not be eating. From this day on, I'll be fasting and only consume kolo and drink holy water. I must take advantage of this opportunity to purify my soul."

The girls were awed by Yeshi's words and almost wished they would be subjected to the same ordeal. They descended into a state of silent reverence, having a rough idea of what lay ahead for Yeshi and Alya. In the pre-dawn light, they worked silently to make sure Yeshi had everything she needed for her stay in Entoto. Yeshi broke the shroud of silence by saying, "Let's all go into our small sitting room and pray."

Hiyab sensed the seriousness of the situation and was unusually quiet for a child of her age. She was accustomed to family prayer sessions, but she knew that praying now was different. She was the first to prostrate herself and begin praying. While they were praying, the taximan stood respectfully outside their front door. He cleared his throat so they would know it was time for Yeshi to go to the airport.

Yeshi rose and said, "Coming."

Belkis collected the basket of kolo, blankets, and plastic water bottles and placed them in a big cardboard box. They all followed the taxi driver to his car that was parked on the road in front of their humble housing complex. It was early, so nosy neighbors were not up and about.

Yeshi bid farewell to the girls and said, "Pray for me. God willing I'll not be away from you for long."

Yeshi waved goodbye through the back seat window as she held tightly with her right hand the small wooden cross that dangled from a thick black thread tied around her neck. This small cross had also been blessed and given to her by her church priest (abuna). Tears were streaming down her face. She was sorry for herself and family, but she was sorrier for Alya whose poor health was the cause of their profound sorrow.

The drive to the airport in the light rain was slow and uneventful. The sun was up and its bright rays were filtering through the gray rain clouds. The taxicab arrived at the airport arrival gate and let Yeshi out while he found a nearby parking place. There was a man standing at the airport entrance. Yeshi had difficulty finding her voice but asked him, "Where do I go? My daughter is coming from Dubai. She is gravely ill and will need a wheelchair."

The man replied, "Go to the Ethiopian Airlines' counter and they will tell you what to do."

Yeshi entered the vast and busy airport arrival lounge. She looked for a sign indicating the presence of Ethiopian Airlines. Once she found the airline's counter, she politely stood in line, waiting for her turn to talk to an airlines' agent. When her time came to talk to the agent behind the counter, she was told, "Try to sit near where the ill and disabled passengers exit. Your daughter will be taken by wheelchair to your taxi. You'll be given her baggage tag if she has checked any bags. Don't worry. Your daughter is in good hands and will be brought to you as soon as the plane arrives."

Yeshi thanked the young woman who was dressed in a new-looking Ethiopian Airlines uniform. She appreciated her words and said, "Thank you so much for all the information and the expression of your kindness and understanding."

In response, the agent said, "Please. No worries. Your case is not unusual. Ethiopians working abroad often come home in a bad physical or mental condition."

The agent's words reverberated in Yeshi's head as she looked for a lobby chair to sit in that was near the exit the agent had indicated. She began to wish that Alya had never gone to Dubai, but if she had not gone they might be dead. The curse caused by a shortage of jobs at home which paid a livable wage was a cancer in her country. Everyone would prefer to stay at home, but that would mean no money needed for them and their families to survive.

While Yeshi sat, she learned that flight arrival information was broadcast on a TV screen not too distant from her. She watched the screen and as soon as the flight from Dubai had arrived she stood and walked toward the exit. A man told her, "It'll take some time for the flight to turn around and dock. It'll also take time for a member of our crew to maneuver the wheelchair with your daughter to this point. Yes, the desk agent told me that you're waiting to tend to your daughter. You can go sit down. I'll tell you when to come."

"Thank you, but if it's okay, I'll wait here," said Yeshi.

The wait was a long one. It took about an hour before passengers on the Dubai flight started coming out and headed to collect their baggage on the designated conveyor belt. The man standing at the ill-passenger exit asked Yeshi, "Do you know her suitcase? If you do, you can go and collect her suitcase and we'll match her luggage receipt with the tag on her suitcase. You have time to do this before she arrives at this point."

Yeshi left in the direction of the baggage collection area. The man did not tell her that he had heard on his two-way radio that there was a problem in loading a passenger in a coma onto a wheelchair and delivering her to the exit. It was a delicate operation, wrapping an almost dead person in a shawl and strapping her gently into a wheelchair. The airport staff assigned this duty were aware of the gravity of Alya's condition, but her situation was much worse than they had ever experienced. They were eager to turn over this lump of bones and flesh to its owner.

Alya's suitcase was easy to identify. Nobody had such an old and beat-up suitcase. Yeshi grabbed the mostly empty suitcase and walked back to the exit where she expected to see Alya. She found the same man and asked, "Where's my daughter?"

The man pointed at a wheelchair beside him, averting his eyes, and said, "Right here. Anyway, this is what remains of your daughter."

Quickly, Yeshi removed the shawl to see her daughter and only saw a shrunken skeleton with skin. She did not recognize Alya and turned to the man and asked, "Are you sure this is my Alya? There must be some mistake. That bony creature can't be my Alya."

"No mistake. Here are her passport and papers. Now, lead this man to your taxi."

They exited the airport and Yeshi called the taxi driver. When the taxi parked in front of the airport, they lifted Alya with all due care into the back seat of the taxi. Yeshi felt as if she were receiving and transporting the remains of a stranger to Entoto. She prayed to God that she was doing the right thing and not making futilely an ultimate sacrifice.

The taxi driver could not believe they were taking a corpse to Entoto. He accepted that the holy water at Entoto could make miracles, but it could not turn the dead into living human beings. For him, they should be going to a funeral home and the cemetery. It was useless to go to Entoto.

Yeshi was seated in the back seat with the head of Alya's skeleton lying on her lap. She wanted to caress her daughter, but she found the person next to her to be repugnant. Her head was aching as she tried to decide what to do. After a prolonged pause, she softly said to the taxi driver, "Entoto, as planned. I must try to revive Alya at Entoto. Otherwise I could never live with myself. This is our last chance."

CHAPTER TWENTY-SEVEN

Entoto

THE DRIVER EXPERTLY MANEUVERED HIS taxi through the heavy Addis traffic to the north side of the city and then began moving up the Entoto mountain on a narrower and winding blacktop road. The air gradually became cooler as they gained altitude. Also, the number of trees increased until there was a thick forest of eucalyptus trees on either side of the road. Yeshi looked out the car window at the new world enveloping her and meekly asked the driver, "How high is the Entoto mountain?"

The unshaven driver was quick to answer, "I've heard that Entoto is 3,000 meters tall, almost 700 meters higher than Addis. Of course, the Mariyam Church is located at a place lower than the peak."

Yeshi said, "Thanks for the information. I'm glad we brought blankets to wrap in."

The driver could not help but wonder about Yeshi's sanity. In his own mind, he questioned what use there was in wrapping a dead person in a blanket to protect it from the cold. He thought like this, but he knew it was best to refrain from getting involved in Yeshi's deathly dilemma. All he wanted was to be paid and return to the normalcy of Addis.

Suddenly, the taxi came to an abrupt halt. The driver turned his head toward the back seat and said, "The road ends here. You'll have to use the porters to go the rest of the way to the Entoto holy grounds. I'll help you get on your way."

The driver got out of his taxi and began to talk with one of the porters wearing a thick sweater. Yeshi gently laid Alya's head on the back seat of the taxi and joined the driver who said to her, "This man and his comrades have agreed to carry your daughter, your box, and suitcase on a stretcher for a small sum. He says they work for the church and depend on donations."

Yeshi lost no time in responding, "Okay. Let's get started. We've got to carefully remove my daughter from the car, place her on the stretcher, and strap her in so we can go the final couple hundred of meters to the church grounds."

The Entoto man said, "Don't worry. We do this all the time. Our lives are dedicated to the Mariyam Church and cases like yours. Please step back and let us do our job."

Yeshi did as the man requested and watched as the man and his colleagues made the removal of Alya look easy. They quickly laid her fragile body on one of their stretchers. They placed the box and suitcase at one end of the stretcher and strapped Alya tightly in place. At first, Yeshi was afraid they would hurt Alya with the tightness of the straps, but she quickly told herself that Alya was in a state where she could not feel any pain.

The Entoto man said in a raised voice, "Let's get going. I can see that your case is serious. The sooner you can start the treatment the better."

Yeshi turned to pay the driver who said upon receiving payment, "God bless and give you the miracle you seek."

At the same time as the driver was turning around his car to return to the noise and pollution of Addis, the porters took off, going up the trail with Alya in her stretcher. Yeshi followed behind and began silently praying to God for the strength she needed to make it to the grounds of the Mariyam church and deal with challenges that lay ahead of her. The steep path to Mariyam's Church was Yeshi's first test.

After they arrived at the edge of the flat Mariyam Church grounds, the porters placed Alya's stretcher on a level barren place. The head porter said, "Wait here. An elderly woman will come and advise you. We have to go back down now to where you met us."

Yeshi handed some birr to the head porter and said, "Thank you for your service."

No sooner had the porters left than an old woman showed up and said in a rehearsed fashion, "My name is Salem. Looks like you'll be here a while, thus you'll have to rent one of our small wooden sheds to stay in. Come and I will show you the vacant shed. You can leave your relative here. It'll not take more than five minutes to see a shed."

"Let's go and see," Yeshi said without hesitation.

Only a few meters away was a shed that looked more like well-used old wooden outhouse that was ready to collapse. Salem opened the door and said, "I know it's not much, but it is either this tiny shack or sleeping outside. If you want some privacy and protection from the chilly nights, take the shed. It will only cost you a few birrs each week. And if you don't take it, someone else will."

"We'll take it. At least we'll have a roof over our heads. Let's go quickly back to where my sick daughter lies."

As they walked back to check on Alya, Yeshi was awed by the grandeur of the huge and colorful octagonal Saint Mariyam Church. They hovered over the unconscious Alya and Yeshi asked, "How can I get Alya to the shed?"

"Don't worry about that. There are plenty of porters around. I'll go and send some of them to you shortly."

Before Yeshi could give the matter some thought, porters came and with Yeshi in the lead they carried Alya on her stretcher to the nearby shed. They placed Alya on the ground in front of the shed's door. Yeshi said, "Wait while I spread one of our blankets on the floor of the shed before you carry Alya in and lay her down."

The porters dutifully fulfilled the task that Yeshi demanded, just like they had previously done hundreds of times. As the head porter was leaving, he said, "Get some rest. We'll be back before dawn to take you to participate in the holy water ritual."

Yeshi bowed her head and said, "Thank you. By the way, can you tell me how many people are here seeking a cure?"

The head porter grinned and said, "Hundreds."

One of the colleagues of the head porter's barefoot team popped up and contradicted his boss by saying, "Thousands."

The head porter said, "I stand corrected. Anyway, there is a large mass of people. And since the onset of the HIV/AIDS epidemic the number has been growing. We have to go now. Be ready in the dark before the first rays of the sun so we can take you to do your ritual bath conducted by orthodox priests who pour the holy water from the Saint Mariyam spring. There's a candle and matches at the right of the door."

It was still day and the light did not reveal kindly the interior of the shed. It was a poor excuse of a rudimentary wooden structure. It was hard to believe that this is where she would live until Alya got better or died. Tears came to her eyes as she started to feel sorry for herself. This episode of self-pity was abruptly stopped by a loud bang on the side of the shed. Yeshi looked out the front door to see who it was. There was the same woman, Salem, who they had seen before and she said, "Just checking to see if it were your time of the month."

Yeshi was quick to respond, "I'm too old for that and my daughter is more dead than alive. All her bodily functions have ceased to operate. So, you don't have to worry about any impurities on our part."

Salem grumpily assented and went on to the next shed to check the women to make sure none of them were unclean. A woman on her period entering the holy water ritual would nullify the entire cleansing ceremony. She had to make doubly sure there would be no unclean woman mixing in the group, bathing in the holy water administered by the priests.

Yeshi sat on the smooth rock stoop of her shed and looked out across the Mariyam Church grounds. It had taken many years and many people sitting like her to wear thin and smooth two-by-four rock slab at the bottom of the door frame. Her eyes were focused on the imposing old church structure. She wanted to go there to pray, but she was obliged to stay with Alya who had been placed on the blanketed floor in the shed like a lumpy bag of bones. Yeshi told herself, "As long as Alya is still breathing, I'm with her for better or worse."

Next to the church she also spied on the tombs of the former emperor and his wife. She recalled that their final resting place was called "Shera Bet." Silently, she asked God to bless and thank the dearly departed emperor for all that he had achieved in his life, especially the creation of this holy sanctuary. The hope that he had given all the people was irreplaceable. Most impressive to Yeshi were the hundreds of people milling silently about in search of a divine miracle that will cure them or their ailing family members of their ills by casting out the evil demons occupying their bodies. The large number of people reminded her to rise early so she and her daughter could arrive in time for the dawn bathing in the cascades of holy water (tsebel) poured down on them by the priests assigned to Saint Mariyam Church. They did not dare be late for this life-giving act.

She sat for several hours watching the coming and goings of the crowds. Her observations helped her become accustomed to this Godly place. She nibbled on a handful of kobo. This snack was her evening meal. She would wait for the opportunity to fill her plastic bottles with holy spring water.

The surrounding mountains and eucalyptus forest blocked the rays of the sun, causing the night to come swiftly. Yeshi quickly dodged inside her ragtag shed. She found the candle and matches, and lit the candle, allowing the wax to burn and drip from the candle onto an old glass jar lid that somebody had left for that purpose. Once the drippings in the lid were sufficient, she stuck the candle firmly in an upright position in the smidgeon drop of hot wax. Yeshi carefully set the candle in a place inside the shed where it could not be knocked over or catch the shed on fire. She told herself that this was a good time to go into the woods behind the shed to do her personal business. Scurrying outside into the woods told her immediately that she was not the first one to use the open defecation mode to relieve themselves.

There were others in the woods doing the same as Yeshi, so she finished as quickly as possible and rushed back to her shed. Once inside the shed, she closed and latched the door. She laid down next to Alya's hollow shriveled body and pulled over herself the remaining blanket they had brought with them. Her eyes were wide open as she watched the flickering candlelight dance on the walls of the shed, but her mind was full of sorrowful worries.

Any sleep kept evaded her because she worried about getting up in time to get to the bathing ceremonial place. She finally decided that the only way she could be sure of doing everything in a timely manner was not to allow herself to shut her eyes. But sleep finally got the best of her exhausted body and she dozed off unknowingly.

The candle was down to its last flame when outside noises caused

Yeshi to wake with a start. She got up and straightened her clothes and hair before unlatching and throwing open the front door to see what the clamor was all about. In the cool night air, she could see the silhouettes of people streaming toward a spot beneath a bluff on the other side of the church courtyard.

The porters showed up at her front door and asked, "Are you ready?"

At that moment, Yeshi knew where all the people were going and she said to the head porter, "Please come in and carry my daughter. I'm as ready as I'll ever be."

Two of the porters went into the shed to extract the remains of Alya and place them gently on a goat-leather stretcher in front of the shed. The head porter instructed, "Follow us."

Yeshi replied. "Of course. Let me put on my sandals."

The porter's irritated refrain was, "Hurry. Leave your sandals. You won't need them."

Immediately, Yeshi stepped out of her shed barefoot and followed the porters with Alya across the courtyard into a deep ravine. The head porter said, "This is where we leave you. When dawn breaks, the priests will pour holy water over your naked bodies. God bless."

While the porters were leaving them in this well-used spot, Yeshi's mind was stuck on one word the porter said and that word was "naked." She looked to her right and left and she saw large groups of naked women. She assumed there were throngs of naked men some distance from them on the other side of the long ravine.

Instantly, she knew she had to undress completely and remove all of Alya's clothing. She struggled with Alya's clothing, but she knew that this was no time for any modesty. Their clothes were placed on higher ground next to the other women's' clothes. Another stark-naked woman helped her move Alya into a crevice in the ravine where holy water would fall abundantly on her. They were all in this together, fervently pursuing a cure.

When the first rays of the sun peered over the mountain, the priests began pouring ample quantities of holy water from their elevated position onto the hundreds of naked bodies below. The monks handed full plastic buckets of holy water to the dozen priests who showered the naked people below while chanting verses of the Bible. They did not stop until all the people below them were soaked.

The people tarried as they wanted to receive all the blessings of the holy water. When the water had evaporated from their bodies, they began to dress again. Many of the people had come daily for months to receive the baths with holy water and they would continue to come until they were cured and all demons were expelled from their bodies.

Yeshi copied the people around her and dressed herself and Alya. Then she waited for the porters to return to take them to the church, which is where she saw all the people going. Before the porters arrived, she filled one of her plastic bottles with holy spring water that was dripping from the top edge of the ravine.

After she filled her bottle with holy water, she held her wide open mouth beneath the drops to get and swallow a few mouthfuls of this holy moisture. She placed her hands under the dripping spring so she could carry some of its blessed moisture to place on Alya's lips. To her profound surprise, she found Alya with her eyes open.

Yeshi immediately dropped to her knees and thanked God for this sign of life. The porters arrived at this emotional moment and observed quickly why Yeshi was praising the Lord. The head porter said, "You must go now and pray in the church so you can preserve any gains that have occurred by bathing in the holy water."

They trotted toward the church with an Alya who was becoming increasingly alert. Alya could hear the people around her speaking in

Amharic. It was only upon hearing her native language that she knew she was home and in benevolent hands. She did not know where she was, but she did know that a life-saving miracle was starting to occur.

As Alya began to see the blue sky above her, she wanted to smile and say, "Amen," but she could not. Out of the corner of her right eye, she could see an ecstatic Yeshi. More than anything else that told her she was on the road to a miraculous recovery. Truly, in her case there was life after death.

CHAPTER TWENTY-EIGHT

Turkey or Bust

ALYA WAS HAPPY TO BE alive and at home after spending several weeks in Entoto for her miracle cure. She concentrated on getting better and spending as much time as she could with her family, particularly her daughter. At the same time, she stayed in touch with her next-door neighbor, Tigist, to see if she was making any progress in arranging their dream trip to Turkey. Alya did not want to leave her family again, but she was concerned about their mounting debt situation. If she did not make money, they were as good as dead. The moneylender only loaned Yeshi money because he had been told that Alya was going again to work abroad and he would get the amount lent back with a hefty sum of interest.

Tigist asked when Alya thought she would be ready to depart. Alya responded that she was feeling much better after her long stay in Entoto but would like to stay to celebrate Meskel with her family. Tigist understood that Meskel (the day of the cross) was Ethiopia's biggest religious festival and therefore staying in Ethiopia to celebrate this day made a lot of sense to her. She suggested to Alya, "Our families should go together to the bonfire (demera) that is lit in Meskel Square at dusk on this auspicious day."

"Yes, for sure. That's a wonderful idea. We should all go and join in with the drumming and dancing. Meskel is only a couple of weeks away, so we should confirm our plans with our families."

"Of course, let's plan on it. Hopefully, this festival will complete your healing and you'll be able to declare that you are physically fit to travel to Turkey."

Alya laughed and replied, "I already feel like I'm nearly my old self and I'm sure that the Meskel festival will complete my cure."

The next couple of weeks passed quietly. Everybody was looking forward to celebrating Meskel. The vast majority of Ethiopians are Orthodox Christians and they were elevated to a high religious pitch. The crescendo of their daily prayers in the church and at home grew in fervor as Meskel approached. As the day to celebrate the finding in the Holy Land of the true cross upon which Jesus was sacrificed got close, everyone became silenced by spiritual exaltation they felt within the deepest part of their souls.

The night before Meskel Yeshi gathered her family together in her modest sitting room to tell the story behind the discovery of the true cross before praying. She began by asking for the blessings of Saint Helena, the mother of Roman Emperor of Constantine the Great, who was the one who discovered the true cross during her fourth century journey to Jerusalem. Yeshi told how Saint Helena dreamed about how to find the cross.

Yeshi recounted, "Saint Helena dreamed that if the people lit a bonfire, the smoke from the fire would go up and descend to the Earth at the exact spot where the true cross was located. The following day she called on the people of Jerusalem and instructed them to gather wood to make a large fire in a location that was rumored to be the place where the remains of the true cross were buried. The fire acted just as she saw in her dream. Saint Helena added some frankincense to the fire. She asked the people to dig at the spot where the smoke entered the ground. To the loud acclaim of all, the holy cross was uncovered for the first time in centuries."

Yeshi finished her monologue by saying, "This story was told to me by my grandmother and it was told to her by her grandmother. I repeat it today on the eve of this holiest of annual religious festivals in the hope that you will repeat it to your offspring."

When Yeshi stopped talking, all fell to their knees to pray. They prayed with more seriousness and longer than usual. Tomorrow they would fast from eating any food until after the bonfire was lit at dusk in Meskel Square and had burnt itself into a smoldering heap. To prepare themselves for the big day, they slept late and spoke little to each other in order to preserve their religious energies and the strength of their beliefs in Jesus Christ their Savior on this holiest of days.

Late in the day Tigist arrived and asked, "Are you ready to join my family for our long walk to Meskel Square? We want to get there early so we can be near the demera when it is lit and not in the back of the crowd of thousands. Here, take this chibo torch I bought for you. We can relay our prayers as we use them to help light the bonfire. It's always a great sight to see the monks come with truckloads of huge stacks of firewood decorated with yellow daisies."

Alya took the straw chibo torch from Tigist and said softly, "Thank you. Give us a few minutes to join you in the courtyard."

Then Alya turned and said to her family, "You heard Tigist. Time to go."

Hiyab took her mother's hand and said in a squeaky toddler voice, "Let's go. I can't wait to see the bonfire."

The streets were full of people and the solemn crowds were quiet as they shuffled forward together in the same direction. Thousands of people were in a full state of reverence as they moved toward Meskel Square to celebrate the day of the cross. Many had participated in this holy religious occasion before but all acted as if this were the first time. Many were expecting miracles, while for hundreds of people a miracle was already occurring.

Hiyab was the first to see the trucks piled high with firewood and people running along the side of the trucks throwing yellow daisy flowers onto the jagged splintered branches. Hiyab pointed and said, "Look at the pretty flowers."

In front of the cortege of trucks were men beating big drums. The drummers led the trucks to the center of the gigantic square where groups of men began unloading the firewood and stacking it in layers to make an enormous, towering pile. Standing at the ready were a group of abunas dressed in their priestly regalia. These priests held unlit torches and were waiting for darkness to arrive to bless the crowd and light the glorious huge bonfire. They were already praying aloud in the ancient Ge'ez, the liturgical language of Ethiopia's Tewahedo Orthodox Church.

As the last rays of the sun disappeared on the western horizon, men with smaller torches lit them with burning candles. When the head priest deftly gave the signal, the men stepped up and lit the larger torches carried by the priests who spread themselves around the mountain of wood and when the head priest finished praying they stepped forward and lit the base of high stack of firewood. At that moment, everybody with a chibo torch lit it and rushed ahead to throw it on the Meskel bonfire. Alya and Tigist ran with hundreds of others to throw their torches on the bonfire. They and others wanted dearly to add to their blessings by contributing to the gigantic blaze.

The abunas stepped back and as the flames grew the people shouted their blessings. Some people in the crowd became overwhelmed with the

Holy spirit and fainted. The drummers pounded their drums as loud as they could. Some drumhead goat hide membranes were broken by the force at which they were being pounded. The blaze rose high into the dark sky and cast a flickering light on the dense crowd. All who felt the heat of the fire and breathed its smoke felt truly blessed. Alya held Hiyab high above her head so she could see the bonfire and be blessed by the light cast by its saintly flames.

Hiyab was uncharacteristically quiet for a toddler. Her family interpreted this as a sign that God was touching her with his holy presence. The bonfire flames began to die down and the crowd began to disperse. The families of Alya and Tigist were reluctant to leave even though they were hungry and bone tired after spending several hours celebrating the Meskel bonfire.

Yeshi finally said, "Let's go. Half the people have already gone. I'm tired and Hiyab is ready to sleep."

Alya whispered to Yeshi, asking her, "Do you want a piece of charcoal residue from the holy bonfire? Tigist and I plan to stay to collect a few pieces of charcoal when the remains of the bonfire cool down."

"That's good of you my daughter. Of course, I will want to use a piece of charcoal to mark the sign of the cross on my forehead and on the foreheads of all members of our family. This sign will keep us blessed in the days ahead."

Tigist and Alya found a place to sit on the ground among hundreds of others to wait for the smoldering remains of the giant bonfire to cool down enough to allow them to grab a few pieces of charcoal. Some boys picked up pieces of charred wood to see if they were too hot to handle. At first, they would juggle a piece of charcoal in the air and drop it if were too hot to hold. Eventually, these charcoal heat tests would demonstrate that some pieces on the periphery of the former bonfire were cool enough to hold.

Upon observing there were cool pieces of charcoal, the crowd scrambled to collect precious charcoal fragments of this year's Meskel bonfire. Tigist scarfed up a piece of charcoal and asked Alya, "Please turn around so I can mark the sign of the cross on your forehead?"

Alya did as Tigist requested and then took a piece of charcoal and did the same holy mark on her forehead. They entered the melee of people to collect a few more pieces of charred wood and placed them in a flimsy cloth bag that Tigist had brought for this purpose. It was late at night before they started walking home.

They walked slowly with heads bowed. When they were a good distance away from Meskel Square, Tigist broke their silence by saying, "I don't want to spoil this special religious moment, but I must tell you that I've been in contact with a man who says he can arrange our travel to Turkey and his connections have lined up jobs for us in this country. He wants to see us next week."

Alya raised her head and replied distinctly, "That's good news. I'm ready to go and make money so my family can pay off their debts and get on with their lives. Going to Turkey for me is like a dream come true."

When they were almost home, Tigist said, "I'll go see my Turkey guy tomorrow and when I get back, I'll tell you what he says."

"Well, let him know I'm fully onboard. Good night my dear sister. Can't wait to accompany you on our great Turkey adventure."

After she took her share of the Meskel charcoal, she entered her house to find everyone asleep. She placed the charcoal bits near Yeshi and donned a sleeping robe so she could lie next to Yeshi as she had always done. Yeshi heard her lay down next to her and said, "Glad you're home safe. We'll talk tomorrow. Good night."

Daylight drifted through the cracks in the walls and roofing of their humble abode, waking Alya with a start. She had slept more soundly than usual. Yeshi's place was vacant. Alya found the house eerily empty.

Their front door was wide open and nobody was to be seen in the courtyard. She hurried to the street and there she found her entire family parading about to show the holy charcoal sign of the cross on their foreheads.

This sight pleased Alya and she joined in the clapping and the praise everyone in the street was heaping on those with the cross inscribed in the middle of their foreheads. Yeshi gravitated to Alya's side and said, "We need to talk."

Alya followed Yeshi back to their sitting room. After they both sat down, Yeshi cleared her throat and said, "Tigist's mother tells me you are planning to go to Turkey. The good Lord knows we need you to work so we can get some money, but are you sure you have recovered enough to go abroad to work?"

"Dear mother. Please don't worry about me. I'm ready to go to my dream country, Turkey. With any luck, I'll have a good paying job in Turkey and be able to send money back to you. Everything I've heard about Turkey is positive and I know it's the gateway to Europe."

Yeshi was at a loss for words and leaned toward Alya to hug her while thanking God for such a brave daughter. Alya was of a small stature but she possessed the heart of a tiger. They sat quietly until the rest of the family came joyfully prancing into their small sitting room. Nobody wanted to talk but Hiyab could not contain herself and said loudly, "I'm hungry."

"She's right," Yeshi said forthrightly. "Let me go and buy something to eat."

Alya knew this meant that Yeshi had to go see the neighborhood moneylender first to get him to loan her more money. She would be able to say that her daughter was leaving soon to work in Turkey. This meant the whole neighborhood would know of her going to Turkey even before she knew anything about her trip to Turkey. She told herself, "I need to see Tigist as soon as possible."

Tigist was not at home. Alya assumed that she was out seeing her man who had the Turkey contacts. She sat on her front step so she could see Tigist as soon as she entered their shared courtyard. After a wait of a couple of hours, Tigist entered the courtyard in a quick-stepped hustle and spied Alya, who stood up to extend her usual greetings. Tigist was out of breath but she managed to utter, "It's all arranged. We'll be going to Turkey in less than two weeks."

Alya hugged Tigist and said in a grateful voice, "God bless you for making my dream come true."

While Alya was singing the praise of Tigist, a smiling Yeshi entered the courtyard with a basket of food and pulling a sheep tied on a rope leash. Alya knew she had borrowed money for food but not to buy a sheep. Yeshi noticed Alya's inquiring eyes and was happy to say, "When I was borrowing money, a man was standing nearby with this sheep and he overheard me say you were going to Turkey to work. He handed me this sheep. I asked him why he was giving me this sheep and he said, 'I brought this sheep to Addis to sell to someone to roast in celebration of Meskel, but I found no buyers. So, you take it. I know you will pay me when your daughter sends you money from Turkey. You can ask your moneylender how to find me.'"

Yeshi continued by saying, "We'll butcher and cook this sheep to celebrate your departure for Turkey. Now, please take this sheep and food basket while I go out to find something for the sheep to eat. God is good."

Alya and Tigist answered in unison, "All the time."

CHAPTER TWENTY-NINE

Unknown Lands

HIYAB BEGAN TO CRY. YESHI rushed to see what was causing Hiyab to bawl in such an odd manner. When Yeshi hurried to Hiyab's side, she pointed a finger at what Alya was doing. Yeshi took Hiyab in her arms and whispered into her ear, "Yes. I'm sorry, but mommy has to go to work so we can have everything we need."

In spite of Hiyab's tearful wail, Alya had to continue packing a few items in her battered suitcase. It was dreadful for her that she was obliged to leave her little daughter behind, but she did not have any other options. There were no jobs available in Ethiopia that paid a livable wage. It was a crying shame that she had to go abroad to earn a decent salary so she could support her family.

Their small house became deathly silent. Alya finished packing and entered to find all her family holding back their tears so they could say another goodbye to Alya. They all knew why she had to leave, but at the same time it was exceedingly difficult to accept she had to go for the good of all of them all. The worst for them was they did not know when she would be back.

Alya kissed all her family members goodbye while she held Hiyab in her arms and said with tears streaming down her face, "I'm going now. I'll miss all of you dearly. It is for our good that I have to go. Please pray for my safety and getting a good job in Turkey."

Belkis could not help herself and burst out loudly a stream of words. "It's not fair. We stay here like bumps on a log while you sacrifice for our welfare. You came back from the dead only to put your life on the line again for us. It's not fair."

Alya did her best to try to calm Belkis by patting her shoulder and saying tenderly, "You have said the truth my dear, but necessity doesn't care about the truth. I don't do this because I want to. I do it because we don't have any other choice. All I ask from you is to pray for me."

At that moment, Tigist appeared outside their front doorway. Alya knew that this signaled the taxi had arrived and was ready to take them to airport for their nighttime flight to Turkey. Alya set her daughter down, kissing her face several times, and embraced each of her family members, saying, "Please don't see me off. Seeing you wave goodbye to me will break my heart."

With those words, Alya abruptly turned and joined Tigist outside and simply said with her head high and a stiff upper lip, "Let's go."

Alya dared not to look back or even think of her family. She forced herself to think only of all the challenges that lie before her and Tigist. The taxi wove through rush hour traffic and arrived at the airport just as the sun was setting. Tigist paid the taxi man while Alya collected their suitcases.

A strange man appeared from the shadows and asked, "Are you Tigist?"

"Yes. That's me."

"Follow me."

The man led them to a dark part of the airport and told them, "Wait here."

Alya and Tigist stood quietly. They were afraid to speak but both knew that being placed in this old and dark part of the airport was very unusual. Their suspicions were curbed by the abrupt arrival of a jovial Habesha man who said clearly, "Please don't be afraid. Going to Turkey is tricky business, but don't worry. The plane is ready and waiting. All we're waiting for is the other Habesha women who are traveling with you."

This man stayed with them while they waited for other women to join them. Alya and Tigist felt comforted and breathed a sigh of relief. Other women were escorted to stand beside them and when their number had grown to seven the jovial man said, "Follow me."

They were guided through the dark abandoned hangar that was cluttered with construction debris by the jovial man who used his flashlight to illuminate their way. When they exited the terminal hangar, the man said, "Wait here."

The group of women halted and huddled silently as they waited for the word to go forward and board their plane. They all knew that going to Turkey was illegal and women like them were being smuggled to Turkey all the time because of the high demand in that country for domestic servants. They also knew that when the signal was given they should rush across the shadowy tarmac and board their plane as quickly as possible. The airport officials had been bribed to look the other way for a few minutes.

The jovial man turned and pointed to a distant plane sitting in the dark on the tarmac and simply said, "Run."

The women did not need to hear any more and sprinted toward the plane the best they could with their bags. Alya and Tigist were caught up in the moment and ran like mad with their group. When they arrived at the distant corner of the airport property where the aging plane was parked, another man stood at the short plane stairs and urged them to get onboard, "Be quick. Get onto the plane and find a seat. There is no time to lose."

Alya noticed as she was climbing the makeshift ramp to the plane's open door that it had propellers and they were already turning. No sooner had they entered the plane when its door was noisily slammed shut behind them and a man stood in the aisle and said loudly in Amharic, "Sit down and fasten your seatbelts. Keep them on until we get to Turkey."

They sat in the dark as all the lights in the interior of the plane had been turned off. The plane taxied at a high speed to an abandoned runway and took off. The frightened group of women were deep in prayer. It was not until the plane was out of Ethiopian airspace that the cabin lights were briefly switched on. At that moment, the Habesha man on the plane said, "Get some sleep. This flight will take the rest of the night."

Alya whispered to Tigist who was sitting in the seat next to hers, "I never been in a plane this small with those twirling things."

Tigist replied in a low voice, "I think those twirling things are called 'propellers.' They are a clear sign this is an old plane that is only used to smuggle people into Turkey. I counted twenty-two seats with two on each side."

A woman sitting behind them overheard their conversation said, "My brother is a pilot. This is an old DC-3 that has been junked."

After the woman spoke, the cabin lights were again turned off and they sat in the darkness. Alya held tightly Tigist's hand and said ever so softly, "Nothing to do but sleep and pray to God and all the Saints for a safe and uneventful flight to Turkey."

All the women onboard drifted off into a half-sleep state, reclining their upright seats. After a few hours in this semi-state of consciousness,

Tigist suddenly opened her eyes. She felt the plane rapidly descending and around the edges of the thick curtains that closed the windows she could see some daylight piercing the obscurity of the plane's cabin. She nudged Alya and said softly, "Wake up. The plane is going down. We must be almost there. I guess this aging plane can fly smoothly for hours."

Alya immediately sprang to life and became excited about their possible arrival. She turned her head and said to Tigist, "If we are landing soon, I should go to the toilet."

"You are first. I've got to go too and I'm sure all the women want to use the toilet. Get up and go to the back of the plane. That's where the WC should be located."

Alya unfastened her seatbelt and headed down the aisle to the back of the plane, but she only took a few steps when the man in the front of the passenger cabin rudely gripped her shoulder from behind and said firmly, "Sit back down and fasten your seatbelt. You can do your business after we land."

The other women observed what happened to Alya and changed their plans to relieve themselves. They wanted to slide the heavy fabric curtains so they would not block the light from passing through the seven small windows on each side of the plane. They wanted to see out and make it so the daylight could illuminate the interior of the passenger cabin, but they were scared of the reaction of the man overseeing them. No one made a move and waited to land. Tigist was smiling when she said to Alya, "Looks like you'll have to wait and baptize the ground in Turkey with your urine. I hope you can hold it for a little while longer."

Alya was not amused. She really had to go. Adding to her challenges were her growing hunger pangs. Under her breath, she whispered to Tigist, "We should have brought something to eat and drink. I don't know why we didn't think of that. I'm hungry."

Tigist was quick to answer, "Don't worry. I'm sure they will offer us some food and drinks when we arrive. It's a good sign that we are landing in broad daylight."

The plane swooped downward and landed smoothly. It taxied to an obscure corner of the airport and came to an abrupt halt. Their overseer lost no time in standing up and saying to the famished women passengers, "Sit still until I say get up. You have to get off while we refuel. Old faithful brought us this far and we thank God for that. Let's pray that it can take us the rest on the way without mishap."

The women sat as quiet as stones and did not make a move. After about fifteen minutes, the man did not mince his words and said, "Get ready to get off the plane. I'll open the door for you. A ladder will be brought for your descent. Wait for me on the tarmac next to the plane."

With a firm grasp on their handbags, the women bunched up in front of the plane's door. The man opened it and instructed, "Go down the ladder one at a time."

The women lined up in no particular order. Each was wondering about the use of a ladder, but they dared not say anything. They acted as docile sheep being herded off the plane. Once one woman was on the tarmac below, the other women tossed their handbags to her. Without the hand luggage and purses, it was easier to turn around and step on each rung of the short ladder.

They cowered in the shade of one of wings of the plane, waiting for the man in charge of them to tell them what to do next. The man suddenly descended from the plane and said, "Follow me. Don't worry about your suitcases. They're safely in the plane's baggage compartment. You must get away from the plane while it is being refueled. Follow me to a nearby lounge where you can wait."

They had no choice but to follow the man. Their surroundings were void of any human life. Alya was happy to know they were going to a lounge because she was thinking there would be a shop selling snacks. Her hunger was making her weak and she needed something to eat to maintain her strength. Therefore, she was disappointed when she saw the lounge where they were ordered to stay. The man locked them in an old, shabby unused lounge full of trash. There were old plastic molded seats covered with dust. They looked about the cramped space and began to wonder what was going on. One woman discovered on the fringes of the lounge a restroom and said, "I don't know if it works, but I got to use it."

This woman exited the restroom coughing and saying, "The restroom is dirtier than the filthy lounge. No human should be obliged to use such a place."

One woman pulled out a shemma scarf from her handbag and said, "We can use this scarf as a cleaning rag and wipe some seats clean enough for us to sit down. We should not be here long, but we should sit down and conserve our energy."

As the time drugged on, the hunger and thirst levels of the women rose. They had not eaten and drank for almost twelve hours. They were expecting to be brought food and water, but they sat in a stifling atmosphere with the temperature rising in a state of inanition. Tigist said to Alya, who was sitting next to her, "This is not right. We should be cared for and given some sustenance."

A woman sitting nearby said aloud, "Okay. I have to admit. I've some ambasha (Ethiopian traditional flat bread) and a plastic bottle of water."

Immediately, the women got up and encircled the sitting woman who said she had some bread and water to share. The actions of the women, prompted the woman to say, "Give me a couple of minutes to dig the bread and water out of my bag."

The woman with the large slice of a round bread loaf tore off pieces and handed a piece to each woman. Alya and Tigist savored the taste of the bread in their mouths before chewing and swallowing it. It was very tasty. I had been made with a cardamon spice and topped with sprinkles of sesame seeds. They washed the big piece of bread down by taking swigs from the water bottle that was passed around. It did not take long before the group finished the bread and water that was intended as a snack for one woman. They wanted more of this delicious food but there was no more.

They sit back down. More time passed and Alya became hyper concerned about their abandonment. She felt like a prisoner locked in a scummy plate glass-walled prison from which there was no escape. For sure, this was not normal and increasingly she wanted to know where they were. They had been kept in isolation in a desolate land and she had not seen one person. She prayed to see outside at least one other living person.

Alya was about to pass out when she spotted a man walking by outside of their containment lounge and she got up and ran up to the glass enclosure, using the last of her energy, and pounded on the glass door to get the man's attention. The man approached the other side of the door and Alya screamed in the Arabic she had learned in Dubai, "Where are we?"

The man answered, "This is Jordan."

Their caretaker man came running toward them, yelling at the man in Arabic, "Go away. I'm in charge here."

The Jordanian man quickly fled the scene. He did not want any trouble and realized he should not be sticking his nose into a business where it did not belong. The Ethiopian caretaker man was clearly upset. He quickly took a key from his pocket and unlocked the padlock on the chain wrapped around the handles of the grubby lounge glass doors and stepped inside the lounge to say loudly in Amharic, "I know that man told you we're in Jordan. Yes, I confirm that we're in Jordan because we have to take a deceptive route to Turkey. And, we have to arrive at night. Therefore, we got to stay here until nightfall."

The man turned around to exit the lounge, trying to ignore the calls from the women for food and water. Heeding these calls, he turned around and said tersely, "There will be plenty of food and water waiting for you on the plane."

He locked the chains on the outside door handles and disappeared in the direction of where their plane was parked. The women looked at each other with eyes full of doubt. Tigist said so all could hear, "Our fate is in his hands. We have no choice but to believe what he says."

CHAPTER THIRTY

Tricked or Trafficked?

THE SCUM-LADEN TOILET WOULD NOT flush. The white porcelain toilet was deeply corroded by black filth and it smelled like it was rotten from the piles of human excrement it contained. There was no way that Alya could urinate in the slimy bowl and she could not breathe in the putrid toilet stall. She ripped off some small pieces of her tissue paper and soaked them with drops of cheap perfume from the small bottle she always kept with her. It was only thanks to the pieces of tissue soaked with perfume that she stuffed up her nostrils to prevent smelling the foulness of the long-abandoned restroom that she could use the toilet. But still she did not urinate in the toilet stall, but in an obscure corner of the restroom.

Alya quickly hoisted up her panties and straightened her outer garments while she was hustling out of the grimy excuse for a restroom. She went to her seat next to Tigist. They had been locked in this dingy waiting room for hours. Alya was weakened by hunger and was on the verge of being deathly ill. The shadows were growing long as darkness approached. Alya was about to give ups on all her hopes and in a low voice said to Tigist, "I don't think I can hold on any longer. I guess I'll never see Turkey. Please tell my family that I tried."

An alarmed Tigist said briskly, "Buckle up. We'll soon re-board and eat and drink our fill."

Just as Alya was thinking she was about to fall down again; she was lifted by the joyous shouts of her fellow captives. Their caretaker man was running toward their awful confinement in this stinking old airport lobby dungeon. He rushed to untangle the heavy chains looped around the outside handle of the exterior doors of their glass prison and unlock the big padlock holding them firmly shut.

As the sun was setting, their overseer yelled for them to get aboard the plane as quickly as possible. They could hear that the plane's noisy engines had already been started and its propellers were whirling at top speed. The women were excited to by the prospect of continuing their journey, but they could not run as fast they would like because of hunger-induced weakness. But thoughts of satisfying their hunger with the food that would be provided once the plane was airborne kept them going.

They all boarded safely and sat in their same seats. They dutifully fastened their seatbelts and waited a few minutes for the plane to taxi to its take off from its clandestine point. When the plane rose from the unlit runway, all the women crossed themselves and kissed the small wooden crosses that dangled from their necks by a single thick black thread. These crosses hung on necklaces that all firm Orthodox Christian believers wore. Alya was the exception because she did not have the energy to make this holy gesture.

Tigist looked intensely at Alya and became alarmed as Alya had passed out. The unconscious state of Alya prompted Tigist to say as loud as her weakened body would allow, "Where's the food and water you promised us?"

Other women sitting behind joined her plea for nourishment by shouting repeatedly in a loud chorus, "Where's our food?"

They all called for food and water until they were drained of the energy needed to make their pleas. Their feebleness made them more docile. Although their minds were not functioning correctly, it did dawn on them that their caretakers wanted them weak so they could easily be managed. For sure, all their pleas had fallen on deaf ears, and nobody came to their aid.

Soon they passed out and all was quiet in the passenger cabin except for the grinding hum of the plane's engines. After a while, the caretaker man got up and walked down the aisle to see if all the women had passed out. He was pleased that things were going as planned and he was looking forward to landing at their destination and ridding himself of this female burden in the next couple of hours. He knew what he was doing to his fellow Ethiopians was wrong, but it was profitable, and for him money talked louder than anything.

The caretaker went into the pilot's cabin in the front of the plane. The pilot was the boss of the operation and asked in stilted-English in a heavily accented Arabic tone to the caretaker, "How's our merchandise? Soon it will all be over and we collect our payment. I'm looking forward to the return trip."

The dour caretaker replied in the best English he could muster, "They all have passed out from hunger."

The surly pilot quickly responded, "Good. When we're about to land, give them some bread and water so they will be presentable and not suspect anything. We should be landing in about thirty minutes. It will be tricky landing on an unlit airfield at night, but we should be all right."

The caretaker sat down and waited for the pilot to give the landing signal. As soon as he got the signal and felt the plane in a steep decline, he grabbed in a side closet a big clear plastic bag full of stale bread loaves and another bag full of plastic water bottles. He lugged the bags down the plane's center aisle to where his Ethiopian sisters were in a deep involuntary sleep. He shook the shoulder of some women and said blankly, "Wake up. We're nearly there. Here's some food and water."

His mention of food pricked the ears of the women in a semi-conscious state and the smell of bread served to wake up the others. The women all began munching on the old bread loaves and washing down the mouthful of bread bites with water. They did not care that the bread was molded. For them it was truly manna from heaven and they could not thank God enough.

No sooner than they had ate their fill of bread, the caretaker said, "Get ready for landing in a few minutes."

The women were happy that the landing was smooth, but they were worried that the plane landed in darkness. They could not see anything but felt the plane come to a jerky stop. The caretaker announced. "We're here. Sit still until we're told to disembark."

Tigist whispered to Alya, "We finally made it to Turkey. We'll see what happens next."

Alya replied almost inaudibly, "We're in God's hands now."

The caretaker said loudly, "Get up quickly and get off the plane. Follow that man on the tarmac."

All the women grabbed their handbags and hustled down the narrow and short staircase and followed at a gallop the Turkish man the short distance to some rooms on the edge of the plane parking area. The day was about to break. Alya looked back over her shoulder to see their plane taking off. She turned her head toward Tigist and said, "Our plane is taking off. What about our suitcases?"

Tigist was out of breath but managed to utter, "Forget them and worry about what comes next for us."

Alya replied, "You're right, but I'm sure wish I hadn't put my cell-phone in my suitcase. But what is done is done."

The presumed Turkish man herded them into a bare small room and said in halting English, "Here you stay."

A hush fell over the nine women. Their circumstances had made them speechless. They wanted to scream, but they are in a quandary of uncertainty. None of them had expected things to unfold as they had. Tigist was particularly concerned, but she was not willing to give up on her Turkey dream. Her immediate concern was they were locked in a vacant room with no windows and a door shut and locked from the outside. After about an hour, they tired of standing up and sat down on the floor in a crowded fashion, some laying partially on the others. They were worried that the dust on the tiled floor would dirty their clothes, but they had to sit down.

Tigist took a place next to the door because there was some fresh air coming in at the bottom crack of the thick wooden door. She could also see some daylight filtering beneath the door.

Several hours passed. The exhausted group became increasingly alarmed. They were beginning to think they had been forgotten about. Some of the women began to hear voices. Tigist's position near the door allowed her to hear voices distinctly. She did not understand a word because it was in a language she had never heard. Suddenly, the door was opened and the women felt refreshed by the cool breeze that wafted into the room. The same man who had placed them in the dank room said in the best English he possessed, "Out. People here to see you."

The women gladly exited the room and were pleased to see the early morning light. They were surprised to see so many people, men and women, standing in front of the cement, narrow-covered terrace. Their Turkish man spoke loudly to the crowd in his language and they began to raise their hands and point to the women. Members of the crowd started jostling each other as they tried to outbid the others and buy the woman of their choice. It became apparent to Tigist that they were being auctioned off like she had once seen in an open livestock market. She felt helpless and there was nothing she could say or do. All the women resigned themselves to a situation over which they had no control.

They felt like lambs being led to the slaughter. They had no choice but to submit to their fate. As part of the women in their group began to be led off by a local family, Tigist was thinking, "At least we're in Turkey and at the first opportunity we can run away to better life." But she did worry that they had been trafficked to another country. She was deeply saddened when they came to take away Alya, her close friend since childhood. Alya was crying when she was rudely separated from Tigist. She wondered if they would have some contact after they were established in their new jobs as domestic servants. While she was being pulled off by a man, she cried out, "Stay safe Tigist. We'll meet again."

The man grasping Alya's left arm said sternly, "My name is Royan and this is my wife, Rozerin. You now work for us as our house servant." Alya timidly replied, "My name is Alya. Pleased to meet you and to know that you speak English as well as Turkish."

Both Royan and Rozerin laughed aloud at Alya's words. Rozerin said, "This is Kirkuk and we are proud Kurds living in the Kurdistan, an autonomous part of Iraq, Yes, we speak English but our native tongue is Kurdish, but we also speak Arabic, which is the national language of Iraq. There are, however, many people here who speak a variety of Turkish." Rozerin continued by saying, "My name in Kurdish means 'where the sunrises.' The name, Royan, is a boy's name which means the same. If you like, you can call me Roze."

Alya wanted to explain what her name means in Amharic, but she felt like someone had punched her hard in the gut. In one instant, her dream of going to Turkey was shattered. She never expected to find herself in Iraq, a country she knew nothing about. She was in unfamiliar territory and she was deathly afraid of living the life of a house servant in a strange land. Her head was spinning and she wanted to flee but there was no escape.

Alya tried to look out the car window and digest all that she observed, but she was tired and her mind was cluttered with thoughts about what was happening to her. She noticed that the vehicle she was riding in was big and new, so she assumed that its owners were wealthy. This was definitely an alien world for her. She knew she would be challenged to put on a happy face and to survive.

All that counted was that she could do the work required of her to the satisfaction of the middle-aged couple sitting in the front seat, get paid a good salary, and send money to her family in Addis. She was prepared to sacrifice herself for this achievement. This was not the time—and she was not in the position—to talk about such things. She was counting on her new bosses to pay her a decent wage and to show her where she could send money home. For her, this is what were necessary elements of her lonely situation in a strange land far from home.

They parked in front of a huge mansion on a paved road in a new neighborhood on the outskirts of Kirkuk. Alya did not move a muscle until instructed to do otherwise. She sat stiffly in the backseat until Rozerin opened the car door and said, "Here's our home. You can get out now."

Alya did as asked and when she had her wobbly legs firmly on the ground,

Rozerin asked her, "Where's your suitcase?" Alya looked at the ground when she said meekly, "They took it."

She did not need to say more. Rozerin reacted immediately by saying in a kind tone, "No worry. We'll buy you new clothes."

For the first time, Alya looked directly into Rozerin's face and said softly, "That's truly kind of you madame. The only clothes I have are the ones I'm wearing."

Rozerin was quick to say, "I said don't worry about anything. We'll take good care of you as long as you take good care of us. We'll go to our tailor tomorrow and have a couple of maid's uniforms made for you. Let's go into the house now."

Alya dug into her energy reserves and walked up the three steps leading to the main entrance to the gigantic house. She looked up at the three-story ornate house and told herself, "I've never seen such a stately house—so big and fancy. If anyone in my country had such a house, they would either be a top government official or a successful businessman."

These thoughts prompted her to think that Royan was a rich and powerful man who deserved her highest respect. Definitely he was someone to fear. Alya was happy to be with Rozarin and was thinking that she was at the start of establishing a fruitful relationship with her.

This line of thinking was interrupted by their entry into the spacious and well-furnished house. It was like Alya imagined a royal palace to be. Her mind started racing with ideas on how she would clean this house. And this was only the ground floor. Her views of the house led her to ask Rozerin, "Surely, you have other maids besides me?"

"No. Just you and our mute local cook. And we paid top price to your broker for you."

Alya mumbled, "What's a broker?"

"That's the man who took our money and who retains your passport. If you cause us too much trouble, we take you back to him for a partial refund. That's how it's done here."

Alya devoured this tidbit of vital information. She had forgotten where her passport was located. Now she knew how things worked here and her heart sunk to have it confirmed that she and her services had been paid for. Maybe she was a notch above being a slave but not much higher. Time would tell if this was a good or bad thing in terms of earning the money and sending most of it to her family in Addis.

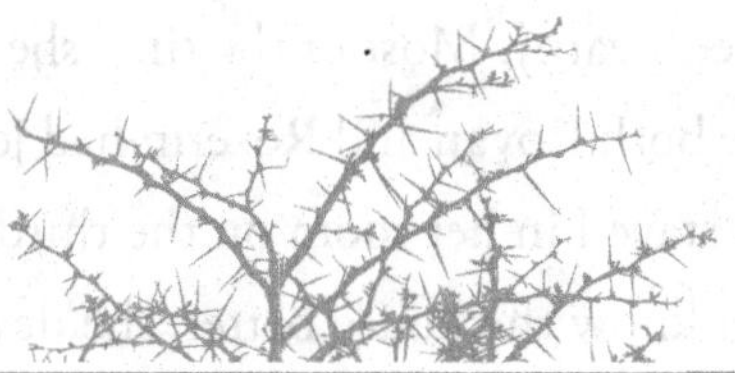

CHAPTER THIRTY-ONE

No Future

HER WORLD WAS THE BIG house. She had no knowledge of the world outside the house. The local society and language were unknown elements. The rise and fall of the sun were her main coordinates. The seasons were changing, as she noted it was getting cooler. Her circumstances were like a rudderless ship in uncharted waters. There was no doubt in her mind that she had no future. Her only hope was to stay alive to see her family again. Without that hope, she had no reason to live.

It had been a month since she was confined to the big house. The mute cook always left a plate of food for her on the kitchen counter. She had her own room with a small bathroom on the third floor. She rose before sunrise and worked until past sundown. Roze treated her kindly but avoided talking with her about subjects unrelated to her work. Alya sensed that she wanted to avoid any conversation that would imply that she was part of any conspiracy.

Alya did learn that Royan and Rozerin had three sons in a boarding school. It was only her and the Kurdish couple who occupied the house. The cook came early every morning on his bicycle and left every evening.

Alya assumed he lived nearby. Most of the time she found herself alone in the house because both Royan and Rozerin had jobs. And even when they were there, she stayed in her room on the third floor.

As Alya came to know the house better, she developed a work routine. She would clean from top to bottom one floor each day. She would take breaks to collect dirty clothes in Royan and Rozerin's master bedroom, and wash and dry them in the machines in the laundry room next to the kitchen. She would then iron the clothes and hang them in their places. She ate sparingly the plate of food always left by the cook and drank water from the kitchen sink faucet. She rarely saw the cook and did not know his name.

Loneliness enveloped Alya. She was brought up in a communal society and was from a close-knit family. Never in her life had she been so alone. Usually, in such solitude, she would find time to read her Amharic Bible, but she did not have access to a Bible. She did pray at length each night to her preferred Saint Mariyam, and to Jesus, and His Holy Father.

At the end of her first thirty days of lonely servitude, Alya made it a point to cross Roze's path before she left the house and went to work. She cleared her throat loudly so Roze would take notice of her. Roze approached Alya and said, "I suppose you are wondering about your pay. I guess it has been a month since you started. Royan and I have agreed to pay you $300 per month. How much of that do you want to send home?"

Alya's was pleased that her monthly salary expectations had been met and she hesitated to answer, "$200."

"Okay. Give me the name and the country you want to send that amount to and we'll go to the nearest Western Union office to send your money. I can do this on my own but you can come with me because we need to pick up your uniforms and other clothes that I've bought for you."

"Sorry to take so much of your time. I can do this myself if you'll just show me where to go."

"No you can't. You can't send money without your passport. And your foreign look will subject you to being stolen by traffickers. It's a dangerous post-war world out there and you shouldn't go out of the house."

Alya did not know what war she was talking about, but she was wary of being trafficked again. She wanted to ask Roze for more information, but she assumed that Roze believed the less she knew the better. Roze wanted Alya to focus on her work and stay far away from knowing anything about life outside the house as possible.

Roze said abruptly, "Let's go. Take the house keys and make sure all the doors are locked." Roze then told Alya, "Sit in the back seat and cover your head with your shawl."

The car smelled as if were new. Alya noticed it had white leather seats and was a luxury model. This was in addition to the car they used to transport her from the airport. Alya covered her head as Roze had instructed. She thought she had asked her to do this because she didn't want anyone to see that she had a foreign house servant. But the truth was that Roze was doing this for Alya's protection from those who may do her harm. She could not know that because she did not know anything about post-war conflicts and ethnic complexity of Kirkuk.

Roze screeched to a halt in front of a sign that said this was a Western Union office. She handed Alya a slip of paper and a ballpoint and asked, "Write down in English the name of the person you want to receive the money and the country and city the person resides in."

Alya placed the paper on her thigh and quickly wrote down the information Roze had requested and handed the paper and pen back to Roze. After reading aloud what Alya wrote, she asked for verbal confirmation, "Correct. At least now I know where you come from. Wait here. This should take only a few minutes."

Roze entered the dark office and made sure all three people present knew that she was there as she spouted off her needs. The chief agent served her in the royal manner that her high status commanded. She approached the worn wooden counter and rattled off a torrent of Kurdish words, describing what she wanted done. Then she slapped the slip of paper on the countertop and the money required to do her transaction. The agents obeyed her and dared not to say anything.

Her demands were quickly met and she was handed a receipt and profusely thanked for her patronage and the honor of serving her. Roze swept through the front door that was held wide open for her by office staff. She entered the car and tossed the receipt back to Alya who grabbed the receipt and said, "Thanks. It looks good. That was so quick."

"Let's go now to the tailor. When we get there, you get out quick and go straight into the tailor's job. The tailor is a trusted man, but we should get in and out of his place as soon as possible."

Alya hustled from the curb to the open front door of the tailor's roadside shop. Roze closed her car door quietly and followed Alya into the shop. Alya was puzzled by Roze stopping and turning around and looking behind her. It was as if she was checking to see if she were being followed or observed. She turned back to Alya and said, "You can never be too careful and you got to always watch your back."

The tailor was an old Kurdish man of few words. His mantra was not to take sides and say as few words as possible. He handed the two maid's uniforms to Alya and said, "If you want to try them on, go behind the curtain."

Alya looked at Roze to see what she wanted her to do. She pointed with her lips toward the thin flowery curtain hanging from the ceiling in the corner behind his Chinese-made sewing machine in the cramped tailor's shop. Alya went behind the curtain and undressed so she could try on her new uniform. She put on one uniform and stepped out from behind the curtain so Roze could see her. Roze looked at Alya and told her to step forward so she could walk around her. Roze was smiling when she said, "Perfect. I'm sure the other uniform is a duplicate. Take your clothes and the other uniform and get in the car. I'm in a hurry to get to work."

Roze did tarry a bit to exchange some words with the elderly tailor. As a secret senior member of the Kurdish network, he was a font of information and Roze wanted to hear the latest news. The tailor was as brief as he was blunt. He told Roze he had no news that would change anything.

Before the old man had said his last word, Roze rushed to her car and hastily opened the front car door and sat behind the wheel, losing no time to start the car and leave in a roar. She said to Alya, "I'll drop you and go to work. When I return, I'll bring some more clothes for you."

Alya said, "Thank you."

Clutching her uniform and clothes, and with a copy of her Western Union receipt in her hand, she got out of the car just as Roze was gunning the car to speed off. She unlocked the thick carved wooden front door and entered the cavernous house, locking the door behind her and leaving the keys on the stand near the door. She breathed a sigh of relief. This was her domain and she thought she had successfully transferred money to her family.

The house was all she knew. She knew nothing of the world outside of the walls of this gigantic house. The months passed as she followed her daily routine ... one day she would clean every bit of a floor of the house and on another day she would occupy herself with another floor. The washing, drying, and ironing was done on what she called her breaks. Special care was taken to make the bosses' bed and their bedroom clean and tidy.

Alya rarely saw her bosses, but she assumed they were pleased with her work, and if they were not, she would hear about it. After the passage of each month, she would get up earlier than usual to cross the path of Roze as she was about to leave the house. When Roze saw her, she knew she was to go to Western Union to send $200 to her home and give $100 to Alya. Roze always carried wads of U.S. dollars and Iraqi dinars in her large handbag.

When Roze saw Alya next, she would give her the Western Union receipt, confirming that the monthly payment to her family had been made. Alya always thanked Roze on her behalf and that of her family. She thought, "At least my family can satisfy their needs with these monthly payments and know that I'm alive. Yet, they must be surprised that these money transfers are coming from Iraq instead of Turkey." She assumed that Yeshi was checking her local Western Union office regularly.

It was a lonely existence for Alya. She had gained weight and her health was restored, but she found the absence of any interaction with other humans unbearable. Having a cellphone and phone credit card weighed heavily on her mind, but she never went out so she could not buy these items. Also, she was sure her bosses did not want her communicating with the outside world.

Often, she would play mind games with herself to pass the time, but her humdrum existence extinguished any hope of a better future. She would act like a princess and refer to the house as her palace, but with the passing days she clearly saw a dark future in front of her. The constant refrain revibrating in her mind was, "Is this my life?"

One day her routine changed with Roze's announcement that she and her husband would be going to Bagdad to get their sons and bring them back for the New Year's holidays. Alya was happy to see that her routine would be interrupted by the school holidays. As she did not have access to any calendars, she had no idea that the end of the year was approaching. Her first question when learning of her bosses' trip to Bagdad was, "Are you going to leave me alone in this house? How many days?"

Roze snapped quickly, "No. My husband's younger brother, Ejder, will be coming to stay in the house while we are gone. Our cook will continue working. Nothing will change as far as you're concerned. We expect to be gone for three days. We leave the day after tomorrow."

Alya meekly replied, "Thanks for telling me. I look forward to seeing your sons. Please tell me if there is anything you want done in the house before your return."

Roze nodded that she had heard Alya and went on her way. Alya turned and continued mopping on her knees the decorated glassy smooth granita floor of the vast living room. She could not wait for the three boys to arrive. Their arrival meant all had to be in shipshape in their rooms on the second floor. Alya was hoping she would be able to have a conversation and play with them. She loved children and now considered herself a childcare specialist in spite of her past difficulties with caring for children.

The day finally came for Roze and Royan to depart in the early morning. Royan's brother arrived with his suitcase and Roze called Alya for their perfunctory introductions. Alya kept her head bowed while they were being briefly introduced. When she raised her head, she noted the man, Ejder, staring at her and moving his eyes to check out her body. Perhaps he did not realize it, but he was communicating to Alya unwanted lustful desires. Alya decided firmly at that moment to stay as far away as possible from him. She looked at Roze with uneasy eyes and said softly, "Have a good and safe trip. May I now be excused?"

Alya walked quickly up the wide stairs to her third-floor bedroom. She locked her door behind her. Her mandated co-habitation with Ejder was filled with fear. She was determined not to have any contact with him and if need be she would stay in her room until her bosses returned. The only place to sit down in her room was on her twin-sized bed. She sat on the edge of the bed to collect her thoughts and decide a course of action.

While Alya was thinking about her next move, she heard steps down the hallway leading to her room. As the sound of the steps got closer to her door, her fears grew by leaps and bounds. She listened to the steps and then came an alarming knock at her door and Ejder saying, "Don't you have work to do? You better come out if you know what is good for you. If you want, I can tell you some secrets about Roze and Royan."

His last sentence gave Alya second thoughts. She was trapped. She knew she had to play her cards right to avoid being raped by Ejder. She decided to timidly open the door and assert herself with a charming smile by saying, "Let's go down to the living room to sit and talk so we can get to know each other."

Ejder was flattered. He did not want to take advantage of Alya so soon, but he could not pass up this opportunity to have sex. It would be good for them to know each other better before having sex. He was stimulated, but he was in no hurry. He had all day to complete his goal of having sex with Alya. He knew that is what all his friends expected of him. He was super horny. She was free game. He had nothing to lose.

It was good that Ejder did not know what Alya was thinking. She had decided that she would rather die than have sex with Ejder. Her idea was to cajole Ejder in a romantic way, then flee at the first opportunity. She did not know where she would go, but she would rather die at the hands of the townspeople than submit to Ejder's sexual desires.

CHAPTER THIRTY-TWO

Facing Death

ALYA DEFTLY DEALT WITH EJDER in spite of what he called "getting down to business." She knew what he meant, but she did not want anything to do with this skinny, greasy man who towered over her miniature physical frame. He thought he could do with her as he pleased. She tried to stay calm and come across to him as agreeable, but deep down she was mulling over her escape plan. Her choice was to keep him off balance by exhibiting an excess of fake charm. She edged closer to him on the living room sofa when she said, "You said you were going to tell me some secrets."

"Yes, but you excite me in a way that I've not felt in a long time, it's hard for me to think straight. But I'll try, but you have to promise to keep all I say between us. Okay?"

"Of course."

"Your boss couple are high-ranked Peshmerga officers. They both are officials at the Ministry of Public Affairs. But factionalism has torn the Peshmerga apart and created two strong political parties. These parties spy on each other all the time. Royan does not know if he will spend the night at home or in prison. Of course, they could kill him any time."

Alya was having difficulty digesting the sensitive information being told her by Ejder. She really did not understand anything. She interrupted Ejder by saying, "But where do they get all their money?"

Ejder smiled because he thought by revealing this information he was reeling Alya closer to him. He replied, "That's an easy question to answer. The Peshmerga helped the American soldiers win the 2003 war and it now is the military force for Kurdistan. Royan played a big role in getting Kirkuk's rich oil fields repaired and producing again. His work with oil made him a wealthy man."

"Let me see if I've got this straight. If the Peshmerga is the military for Kurdistan, what about the Iraqi army?"

"The Iraqi army would never dare enter Kurdistan. They fear the Peshmerga. And besides, Kurdistan is autonomous. Do you want to know what Peshmerga means in our language?"

"No. Tell me."

"It means 'those who face death'

Alya thought these words were appropriate for her personal motto of the moment. She reminded herself that her immediate goal was extricating herself from her dicey predicament with Ejder. Fleeing would mean certain death for her, but that is what she had made up her mind to do. She wanted to flee to the office of the man who kept her passport. There was no returning home without a passport. But she did not know the way there. Maybe she could get some basic information about the location and name of the office from Ejder.

Her thoughts were interrupted by Ejder who said, "They told me they were going to bid on one of the women in the next shipment. I'm glad they did and they chose such a well-shaped woman. You should be proud that you got all the round parts of a fully developed woman."

Alya was not sure she understood what Ejder was saying, but she tried to wedge into their conversation words that may be of use to her. So, she said, "You get regular shipments of women?"

"About every few weeks the word goes out on the grapevine that a plane is arriving with women smuggled from Africa. Anyone who's interested can go to the office and place a bid. This is always done in a hush-hush manner because smuggling is illegal, particularly the trafficking of people."

Alya found this information of interest and could not wait to ask, "What do you call the smuggler's office."

"The people in the street quietly whisper his name. They say under their breaths, 'sef kacakci.' I'm sorry I don't know how to say that in English. But that is what they say in Kurmanji, which is how we say Kurdish in our language. One thing that you have to understand is that smuggling of people and goods is a major market system here and much money is made by corrupt activities."

Alya got what she wanted—the name of the smugglers' office in Kurdish. She kept running through her mind, 'sef kacakci.' She knew she would need those two words when she fled into the city. With those two words, and the knowledge that an airstrip had to be near the office of the man who had her passport, she thought she could find the location of the chief smuggler's office. She did not know what her next move would be, but she knew having a calm demeanor was necessary. The main question rolling over in her mind was, "How can I get away from Ejder?"

While feigning some affection for Ejder, she spontaneously asked, "Would you like a cup of tea?"

Ejder was pleased. The modicum of affection that Alya was showing him fed his inflated ego and told him he was on the right track to having the first of many gratifying sexual experiences. He fantasized over how many times he could have sex with Alya before his big brother returned.

Lost in his thinking, he replied to Alya's question, "Yes, my dear. I would love a cup of tea prepared by you."

Alya stood up and said, "Excuse me while I go to the kitchen and make our tea."

While in the kitchen, Alya rattled teacups and placed the kettle on the gas stove to boil water. She found a tray and placed two teacups on it. She opened and closed kitchen cupboards to make noise to cover up turning the key to unlock the exterior kitchen door and opening it a crack. She carried the tray with the two teacups and set it gently on the coffee table in front of Ejder, saying, "Give me a minute to see if our tea water is boiling and then I can return with our tea. Do you take sugar and milk?"

"Two sugar cubes, my sweet one," said Ejder who was completely unaware of the deception that Alya was playing on him.

As soon as Alya returned to the kitchen, she quietly opened the door and fled down the street. She ran as fast as she could. Passerby's concluded that she was another abused wife running away from home. She continued her panic run until she came to an intersection. She stopped as she was short of breath. The only thing keeping her going was a strong flow of adrenalin. She spotted an elderly woman next to the street and said the two words in Kurdish about the boss smuggler, and the grey-haired woman did not respond but pointed in the direction she should go.

Alya knew that as soon as Ejder discovered she had fled, he would be enraged at being duped and fearful of losing his older brother's property. He would immediately begin to look for her and would not stop until he found her. She continued to run as fast as her feet could carry her. There in front of her was a building next to an airstrip. Then she saw the spot where Rojan and Roze took her first away.

A thoroughly exhausted Alya arrived at the office building and threw open the front door which she quickly closed and tried to lock but the key was absent. She turned and recognized the man who was coming out of an adjoining office and immediately dropped to her knees and begged him to help her. Tears were rolling down her cheeks when she said, "Please you have got to help me. Do you have my passport?"

The dowdy, rotund old man calmly said, "You have to go back to your house. Those people paid me for you and they have full rights over you. Besides, I'm keeping your passport until someone pays me for it."

These discouraging words were enough to oblige Alya to take her own life, but she asked, "How much do you want for my passport?"

The man clearly said in a cruel tone, "My price is one thousand U.S. dollars. Take it or leave it."

Alya bawled loudly, "What am I going to do? I have little money and a man is following me to kill me. Do you want my blood to be on your hands?"

At that moment, Ejder busted into the front door and came up to Alya and slapped her in the face with the back of his right hand as hard as he could. As Ejder was getting ready to clobber her with more blows to her body, Alya crawled to take refuge beneath a table. Blood was dripping from the wounds on her face and nose caused by Ejder's well aimed blow.

He pursued her under the table but was stopped by a torrent of Kurdish words directed at Ejder, who had a poor reputation when compared to his brother. He reminded that he had confided this woman to Rojan and he would do all in his power to protect her from any damage he would cause to her. Once Ejder was reminded of his low station in life, he swung around and stomped out of the office, saying, "No matter what, I'll be back with my friends to finish her off."

The old man quietly walked up to the front door and locked it with a key he had in his pocket. He retrieved some tissues from his desk and handed them to Alya who was still under the table. After a few moments, the boss of the smuggling ring said without any emotion, "You have to leave here. He'll come back as he said and he'll kill you and dump your body in the desert. Nobody will care or ask questions except Royan and Roze. They will ask what happened to their maid. I suppose I'll have to give them a refund of the money they paid for you. To stay alive, you got to disappear."

Alya was in pain and did not know what to do. She was thinking that she was better off dead. The kingpin of the people smuggling ring took exceptional pity on Alya and said, "Get up and follow me."

Alya struggled to get to her feet and limped behind the old man. He led her to a side door that he opened and said, "See across the open field that house about one hundred meters away? Get there and ask for refuge. An international non-government organization (NGO) operates that house for abused women. Get there and you should be safe."

His words were confusing her, but when Alya realized he was allowing her escape to safety, tears swelled up in her eyes. This sounded too good to be true, particularly as this option was unexpected. Alya thanked the old man and took off running toward the safe house as fast as her injured leg would allow her. Getting to that house was for her a life and death matter. Besides, it was the only option she had. It was either that house or death.

When she was almost at the front gate of NGO house, she stopped to look behind her. Nobody was following her. She thought that the smuggler boss would tell Ejder and his band of bloodthirsty thugs that she had left and he had no idea of where she went. She walked slowly up to the outer metal gate and was asked in English by the armed guard in front of the gate, "State your business."

Alya replied in a voice laden with misery, "I need help. I was told I could find safety in this house."

The uniformed guard looked at her from head toe. He then turned around and pushed a button which rang a bell inside the house. The sound of bell sent a woman scurrying out of the house to see what the guard wanted. Immediately, she saw the bloody and injured Alya standing forlornly with her head bowed and ordered the guard to open the outer iron gate so Alya could advance to the inner iron gate. When Alya was in between the two gates, she could have a private conversation with the woman who came from the interior of the house.

"Hello, my name is Doris Hines. My NGO runs this house for abused and abandoned women. What is your name and what is your problem?"

"My name is Alya. I'm from Ethiopia. I ran away from my job as a trafficked maid in the house of a prominent local couple. I was told I could get help here."

Doris hesitated a moment but as she unlocked the outer metal gate said with a big smile on her face, "Welcome. You'll be safe here."

Alya was about to express her thanks when the white woman embraced her. This middle-aged foreign woman was evidently full of compassion and felt that the thing Alya needed the most was comfort. She tenderly held Alya's hand as she guided her to the front door of her house. Doris' intent was to put Alya at ease in her new surroundings. She led Alya to a bedroom occupied by several other women and said in broken Kurdish, "This is Alya. She has come to stay with us. Please help her get cleaned up while I bring a set of our house clothes and a first-aid kit to doctor her wounds."

Immediately, the women hovered over Alya and guided her to an adjoining bathroom where she could shower and arrange herself. Alya could not believe her good fortune. She stripped down and stepped into the shower stall and turned on the warm water to relax and wash herself. The soap she used to wash her entire body had a sweet smell. After her shower, she dried off with a big towel, which she wrapped around herself and entered the large bedroom.

As she made her appearance, the other women clapped their hands and sung a local spiritual tune. One woman handed her house clothes to dress in. Alya returned to the bathroom to put on these clothes and then returned to the bedroom where the women again applauded and sang their song. This time Doris was there and she kindly requested, "Sit down on a bed. I want to look at your wounds and apply antibiotic cream and bandages that might be needed."

Doris dressed her wounds and hummed her own version of the tune the local women had sung before. Alya remained silent, but she did have questions for Doris, "Where are you from and where did you learn to speak Kurdish?"

Doris laughed lightly and said, "I'm American. My Kurdish is very poor, but the little I know I learned here where I've worked for several years."

Alya softly replied, "Thank you."

Doris' calm and poised manner helped settle Alya's frayed nerves. Doris finished doctoring and looked into Alya's face with loving eyes and said, "I'm sure you're hungry. Let's go to the kitchen where you can eat and we can talk in private. Please let me know if you have any trouble understanding my English, as I can speak in other languages I know."

"English is good for me. In my country, English is the language of instruction from the 7th grade on. I have worked in Dubai where I got to practice my English and learn some Arabic."

"You may use your Arabic with some of the women here, but Kurdish is the main language they speak."

The kitchen was filled with a table covered by cheap blue plastic sheeting with many chairs along its sides. Doris said in her mild-mannered way, "This is where we eat three meals a day. The times of our meals are posted on the door. Let me warm up some food for you and find you a cool glass of water."

Doris warmed up a plate of food in an old first-generation microwave. She placed the plate on the table in front of Alya with a glass of cold water. She then sat down beside Alya at the corner of the table and said, "Please tell me your story, especially how you got here."

Between bites and swallows, Alya told her story. Doris listened intently, without interrupting, but she made gestures to help keep Alya talking. Alya opened up and told her all she thought was important for Doris to know about her case. Alya looked at Doris and said, "I guess that's it. Please feel free to ask me any questions."

Doris thought for a moment and then said forthrightly, "You came to the right place. I'll need to see the smuggler man. We may have to move you to a safer location in Erbil. We'll talk more tomorrow. Now go rest and don't worry about anything."

Alya was reassured, but she had never heard the word, 'Erbil,' before. She imagined that was another city, but where was it, and why would she be safer?"

CHAPTER THIRTY-THREE

Safety First

"Wake up. We've got to go now," yelled Doris at the sleeping Alya who crawled into bed the evening before and had slept soundly all night long. The four other women sharing her bedroom had gone to bed hours after her and were already up. All Alya could remember was speaking to Doris and then coming to her bedroom, shown vacant bed and being offered a sleeping gown.

Doris shook her and again said, "Wake up. We have to go. It is not safe here for you."

Alya felt like she had been drugged, but she sat up and said after rubbing her eyes, "Okay, let me get dressed."

Doris said, "Good. I'll be in the car waiting for you with the driver. Hurry. I'll explain more in the car."

Alya dressed quickly and washed her sleepy eyes by holding water trickling out of the bathroom faucet in her cupped hands. She waved goodbye to the other women and all responded in languages she did not understand, but she assumed they were wishing her good luck. Alya ran out of the house and jumped into the back seat next to Doris. The car had already started and as soon as the guard opened the metal car-gate, the driver gunned the car and zoomed down the road.

After the car was well on its way, Doris said softly to Alya, "We got to go to our safe house in Erbil. I went to see the smuggler chief and he said men were coming to kill you. The sooner we get you out of Kirkuk the better."

Alya swallowed hard, but she did not really know what was happening to her. She wondered if she could get a job in Erbil so she could send money to her family. Of course, she wanted to stay alive, but she had to work or other lives would suffer. After thinking about Doris' words she asked, "Why won't the men who want to kill me come to Erbil?"

Doris was quick to answer, "They won't dare come to Erbil. There's another Peshmerga faction which controls Erbil and they're too afraid of being killed or detained in a prison."

Alya thought she again was in a situation over which she had no control and was restricted to moving with the moment. The car had made its way through Kirkuk and was on the highway leading to Erbil. Doris told the driver in her Kurdish, "Go as fast as you can. We've no time to lose and there may be roadblocks ahead. Our organization's logo painted on both sides of our car and our license plates should ease our way through any roadblocks. Also, I've been to Erbil many times. When those who are manning the roadblocks see me, they should wave us through as if I'm doing my usual business."

Alya was lost and did not know what to say. After they were well on their way, She asked, "How long will it take us to get there?"

"It should take a little over an hour, but much depends on how many roadblocks and how long it takes for us to get through them."

It was all unknown territory, but Alya had to verbalize some of her concerns and she wanted to converse with Doris, so she inquired, "When we get to Erbil, where will I stay? Will you stay with me?"

Doris told Alya, "Don't worry. You will be well taken care of in Erbil. My organization also has a house there and my Norwegian colleague, Ada, will take good care of you. I'll need to return to Kirkuk today."

Alya was taken back by Doris' good cheer and all the time she devoted to her. She could not help but say, "I want you to know that I appreciate so much all that you have done for me. Someday I hope to be in a position that allows me to repay you. I owe you my life."

Doris knew how hard it was for Alya to say these words and tried to tamp down the emotions of the moment by saying, "Please don't let anything I do for you be considered exceptional. It's all part of my job. I just want you to be happy and safe. I'll deal with the men who are looking for you. They won't know where you've gone."

The driver said something in Kurdish and Doris answered. The driver turned into another road leading deep into Erbil. Doris turned her head and said to Alya, "We're almost there. I'll introduce you to Ada, explain your case, and then I'll return to Kirkuk. Anything you have to say before I turn you over to Ada?"

"I can't think straight right now. I'm sure there are plenty of questions I could ask, but I have nothing to say right now. Can you tell me if there are any other Ethiopian women in the Erbil house?"

"I don't think so, but that's a question you can ask Ada."

The car came to a sudden stop. Alya looked out her window and saw a two-story house with the same guarded metal gates as the NGO house in Kirkuk. Also, there was a car with the same organization logo painted on its sides. A blond-headed mature white woman came running out of the house and instructed the front gate guard to hurry to let her colleague into the inner yard.

As soon as they came in contact, the woman embraced Doris and said, "This is a pleasant surprise. What brings you here?"

Doris unabashedly said, "It's to find a safe place for this Ethiopian woman to stay. I present to you Alya. I hope you have room for one more because she has to stay here. I'll explain later."

Ada who appeared to be cut out of the same cloth as Doris, embraced Alya and said, "Welcome to our house. There is always room for one more."

For her part, Alya said, "Thank you for your warm welcome. Do you have any Ethiopian women here?"

Ada replied, "No, no Ethiopians. But I'm sure our women will welcome you with open arms. We have Kurdish, Turkish, Arab, and Assyrian Christian women."

Alya got the impression that the abuse of women was a common thread to all the ethnicities in this region. It did not matter which cultural group you belonged to—wife-beating was common. Alya wondered about which category she would be placed. All she wanted was to be free and allowed to work to make money to send home. Alya was curious so she asked Ada as they stepped up to the front door of the big house, "How long does a woman stay here?"

Ada smiled and said, "As long as it takes for them to stabilize and learn the skills they can use to survive in the outside world. Each case is different. Some have children and return home. Others go to their family's village and live with relatives. There are some women who have been here more than once. We find that the thing these women need the most is a safe place to stay until they can get back on their feet. The residents of Erbil know that this is a safe house for abused women." Ada continued, "Why don't you go in the house while I chat with Doris. The women are waiting to see the newest member of their group."

Alya thanked Doris again and timidly stepped through the front door to be greeted with clapping and singing by about a dozen women of all ages, shapes, and sizes. Alya had never been received in such a joyous manner and she could not hold back tears of happiness. They all welcomed and hugged her. She did not understand their words, but she felt their warmness and sincerity. She gravitated toward the few Arab women because of the Arabic she had learned in Dubai, even though the Arabic they spoke was different than the dialect spoken in Dubai. She was also glad to see the Christian women wearing crosses around their necks and showed them her cross necklace. All the women wanted her to feel at home. And in doing that they succeeded.

Ada entered the house and in Kurdish thanked the women and asked them to go back to their duties. For most of the women that meant returning to the sewing room where they were learning to design and sew clothes. With this sewing skill they could support themselves. The room was chock full of Chinese-made treadle sewing machines and overseen by an elderly local woman.

Alya stayed behind while the other women returned to their assigned tasks. Ada took Alya's hand and took her into her small office. After they were seated, Ada said, "I hope you'll learn to like it here. Doris explained why you were brought here. You're an unusual case and I'm not sure what to do with you. Just relax and we'll figure things out as we go. It's important for you to be safe and in possession of your passport. Right now I'm thinking that at the first opportunity you should get on a plane and go back to Ethiopia. What do you think?"

Alya wasted no time in replying to Ada's question by saying assertively, "I want a paying job so I can send money to my family. Please help me do that. By the way, you said I was in possession of my passport. As far as I know, my passport is still with chief people smuggler in Kirkuk."

"Well we're not a hiring agency and I'm afraid to release you to fend for yourself in this foreign environment. As for your passport, Doris did not give it to you directly because she didn't want you to know she paid the smuggler chief for it. I can give it to you at any time. I recommend that you use it to travel home as soon as you can."

"I'm thrilled to know you have my passport, but I don't know if I'll ever be able to pay Doris back. I'll be forever indebted to her."

At that moment, a woman interrupted them. She spoke in Arabic and she could see that Ada did not understand her so she answered in her Dubai Arabic and the woman left. Alya asked Ada, "You don't understand Arabic?"

Ada chuckled and said, "No, I don't, but I see that you do. So, you're hired as our Arabic interpreter."

"What do you mean?"

"We have a budget line item for an Arabic translator and you are it. This job doesn't pay much, but over time it can add up. Okay?"

Alya was feeling much better now, having learned of this job and happily said, "This is good for me and I'll do my best to make it good for you too. Well, I guess I should get to know the Arab women and practice my Arabic."

The pay for translating was small, but it was a gratifying job, especially as it got her close to the Arab women and she was doing something useful. Free room and board made up for the low pay. Alya had no complaints and after some months the hundred dollars a month did add up. When she had $500, she would ask to be taken to the nearest Western Union office. And she was always paid on time at the end of each month. At the same time, she enjoyed the camaraderie of all the women. She really felt at home, but she knew that her situation was not forever. Some women came while others left.

Six months passed quickly. Alya joined in the warm welcoming of each new woman. She became a leader and Ada talked to her about becoming a staff member. She was agreeable as long as it paid more and she would have the opportunity to send money home. She was now making $200 a month. She kept all her money folded inside her bra and only took it out when she was alone in a locked bathroom. She was waiting for Ada to take her to Western Union.

One day Ada called on her newest staff member, Alya, who thought this would be a routine talk about her job but she was surprised when she said, "Today, when I was in the open market, I saw a foreign woman and asked her if she were Ethiopian. She said yes and I told her that I had an Ethiopian woman working for me. She asked where my house was and promised to visit someday to meet her Ethiopian sister. So, you may get a visit someday.."

Alya was delighted about the prospect of meeting another Ethiopian with whom she could speak to in her own language. She responded to Ada by saying, "That's interesting. It'll be a good day for me to meet her and converse in Amharic."

Weeks passed and Alya occupied herself by assisting Ada manage the house. It was a good time for her and allowed her to expand her horizons beyond the tasks of being a domestic servant. The front gate guard rang the doorbell and Alya hustled to see what he wanted. She could not understand the guard, so she called Ada who listened to what the guard had to say and then turned to Alya to say, "I think it's the Ethiopian woman I met in the market. Go see if she is the one."

Alya went to see the woman standing at the front gate and she could not believe her eyes—it was Tigist. She ran to unlock the gate, sobbing as she went to embrace her closest friend from home. She was so excited to see Tigist, she could not talk. Tigist was also tongue-tied. She could not believe that her long lost sister was right here in front of her. When Alya finally loosened her grip on Tigist, she called to Ada, who came quickly to hear, "This is not only an Ethiopian, but also my sister who I have known my whole life in my housing compound in Addis Ababa. We arrived in Kirkuk on the same plane. We have a lot to catch up on. Can you excuse me for an hour or two while we talk?"

"Of course. I'm so glad you two got together. Come on in and have the kitchen table all to yourselves. Talk as long as you want."

Alya and Tigist sat at the corner of the table, holding hands. They sat quietly for a long time, trying to absorb the moment of their unbelievable reunion and think of where to begin and what to say. Suddenly, they both started jabbering in rapid fire Amharic at the same time. The spontaneity of their words caused them to laugh at length. When they settled down, Tigist said, "You first."

Alya told her sad story and all the important events that had happened to her since they were separated almost a year ago at a dismal old part of Kirkuk airport. Then Tigist told her story of how she got to Erbil. Her story was less eventful and happier than Alya's. She worked for a good and wealthy family in Erbil and they had rented her an apartment.

They talked for a couple of hours and wanted to continue enjoying their time together, but Tigist had to go. Her final words to Alya were, "You must come live with me. If you do that, I have a big secret to tell you. If you want, I can also find you a job, but wait until you hear my secret."

Tigist's words made Alya's head spin. She did not know what to say to Tigist. All she knew was that she had to join her as soon as possible. After a pause of a few minutes, she said to Tigist, "Come back in a month and I will go with you to your apartment. I will give Ada one month's notice now and explain to her why I'm leaving. She has been really good to me."

Tigist said, "I got to go now. I don't want to leave you but I have to. I'll be back in a month. Be ready to go with me. Tell Ada goodbye for me."

Alya did not want to see Tigist go but then she reminded herself that she would see her again in a month. At that moment, Ada appeared and asked, "Did your friend leave?"

"Yes, she left. Ada, we have to talk."

CHAPTER THIRTY-FOUR

Turkey Trap

"WELL, WHAT DO YOU WANT to talk about?"

Alya heard Ada's words and felt like she needed to stand in front of Ada's desk to tell her what she had decided, but she could not say her words to Ada because she had been so nice to her. There was no nice way to say what she had to say. After a long pause, in a barely audible tone she said, "I'm sorry. I really love this place and you have been very good to me, but I must go to live with my sister."

Ada could see how nervous Alya was and tried to ease her tension by saying in a compassionate manner, "Please sit down and take it easy. I know this is a hard decision for you. I always knew the day would come for you to go your own way. All I want is for you to be happy and safe. Please share with me your plans."

Alya felt some relief and sat down and explained to Ada, "Tigist and I grew up together and we arrived in this country in the same plane. We got to be together. Our desires and destinies are the same. We always knew it was only a matter of time until we would be back together again."

The sympathetic Ada smiled and said, "It's true you've your own life to live and I understand more than you can imagine about your need to go live with your sister. My only question for you is when do you plan to leave?"

Alya was feeling more relaxed now and answered Ada straight forwardly, "In a month's time my sister will return, and we'll go together to her place. By then, she hopes to find a job for me."

Ada said in a good humor fashion, "Well, that's that. I wish you the best. Feel free to visit me anytime. You're always welcome here. And I guess you'll want me to give you your passport."

Alya touched her eyes to prevent tears from rolling down her cheeks and asked, "May I be excused now? I've a lot to think about. Of course, if you've got more to say, I can stay."

Ada stood up and said loudly, "Go now before you make me cry."

Alya left Ada standing in her small office and went straight to hide her face in the pillow on her bed. Ada turned around her large female body and bawled like a baby, repeatedly saying to herself, "I really liked Alya and now it has come the time for her to leave."

The days whizzed by. In an effort to please Ada, Alya did her job to perfection. Deep down she was aware that the other women felt something was off with her, but she preferred that Ada announce her departure. All the while she looked daily out the front of the house because she did not want to miss the arrival of Tigist.

After about a month had passed, Ada gathered the women together and informed them that Alya was leaving, and they should all wish her well. When they heard the news, they all started undulating loudly as if a member of their families had died. Ada raised her hands in an attempt to quiet them down and say, "We need to have a going away good luck party for Alya."

A month had nearly gone by, and the seasons were changing. Cooler temperatures were progressively invading the lives of the women and all that they did. But the onset of winter did not obstruct throwing a big going away party for Alya. The women decorated their dining hall with paper red flowers and baked a big cake with Alya's name etched with blue icing on its top. They collected money to buy a sheep to butcher and a super going-away gift. They all loved Alya and hated to see her leave.

They laughed, sang, danced, ate their fill, and cried during Alya's going away party. There was a cornucopia of languages, but they were all singing the praises of Alya. Amidst the tower of babble, the oldest woman stepped forward with a beautifully wrapped package to offer Alya. There was a sudden hush while the elderly woman handed the gift package to the tearful Alya.

Alya did not know what to say or do. Never in her life had she had a party dedicated to her honor and been given a present. The women gathered around her, and she could see on their faces that they wanted her to open the package and see what they had gotten her. Alya was speechless as she tore gently the wrapping paper to reveal a nicely embroidered long yellow traditional Iraqi dress.

Alya could see by the hand motions the women were making that they wanted her to try it on. Therefore she proceeded awkwardly with the help of a couple of Arab women to put it over her head and clothes she was wearing. Once the dress was covering her completely, the women all clapped and said among themselves that this dishdasha dress fit her perfectly. Alya displayed the dress with a dramatic flair and said repeatedly, "Shkran lak." (All the women understood that she was saying 'thank you' in Arabic.)

The party continued with much gaiety well into the night. Ada joined in on the festivities but was the first one to leave. They consumed big slices of chocolate cake and drank their fill of lemonade punch and ginger tea. Alya was among the few women left when she said in Arabic, "Thanks for giving me such a wonderful and memorable party. I'll always cherish the time I spent with you. Allow me to bid you farewell now."

With a strange feeling in the pit of her stomach, Alya went to bed thinking that Tigist could show up any day to whisk her away from a place that had been her home for many months. She slept soundly until there was a soft knock on her bedroom door. It was early in the morning and a new day was dawning. She got up and opened the door a crack to see who it was. It was Ada and she whispered, "Your sister is here. Get ready to go. Here's your passport."

Alya nodded and closed the door softly as she did not want to disturb the other women sleeping in her room. She quietly did her toiletries as fast as she could, stuffing her few belongings and her new dishdasha dress in an old pillow slip, folding a handkerchief over her passport and slipping it into a special spot within her clothing. She wrapped herself in a blanket and tiptoed out of the room. She rushed downstairs and embraced Tigist, saying in Amharic, "I thought you would never come."

Tigist replied, "Silly girl. I'm here, aren't I? I came early so I would not be late to work."

Ada was standing next to them, admiring the close connection between the two. She had her faded bathrobe on and a white business envelope in one hand. She held out the envelope to Alya and said, "Here's your pay and a little something from me. I wish you the best of luck."

Alya lost no time in embracing Ada and telling her, "I can't thank you enough for all you have done for me and your deep understanding of my situation."

Ada's last words to Alya were. "You can keep the blanket. You'll need it to ward off the winter cold. I hope our paths cross again under better circumstances."

Tigist took Alya's hand and they exited the house that had been the home of Alya for almost a year. Neither of them looked back as they walked a long way in silence to Tigist's apartment. A few people passed without saying a word. They entered a new part of Erbil and after a few more blocks came to a new, twelve-story apartment building. As they approached the building, Tigist said, "My one-bedroom apartment is on the fourth floor. We can take the lift."

They took the lift without incident and got off on the fourth floor. Tigist's apartment 401 was not far from the lift. Tigist dug a set of keys out of her handbag and opened the door to her apartment. Alya was impressed by the modernity of the place and that it was well furnished with the latest furniture and appliances. It was a dazzling experience that took Alya's breath away. Tigist noticed the look of amazement on Alya's face and said, "My boss is one of the wealthiest men in Erbil and he owns this building."

Alya kept her thoughts to herself but she wondered if Tigist was not serving her boss in ways she could not mention. Alya did not like to think of Tigist in this way but how else could she be living in such luxurious surroundings? She did not know what to say but said the following, "You have it so good. Your boss must pay you well."

Tigist was quick to answer, "Yes, he pays me well for cleaning his house and washing his clothes, and he gives me this furnished apartment free of any rent. Thanks to him, I've been able to save up a lot of money. I have not sent any money home because I want to continue the pursuit of our dream."

"What do you mean? We're trapped in this part of Iraq," blurted out a perplexed Alya.

Tigist continued, "Our dream was to go to Turkey and we can still go if you want."

Alya almost screamed, "Our dream was shattered when we got off the plane in Kirkuk."

Tigist was ready for this conversation and said firmly, "No it wasn't. Going to Turkey is still possible and now that I have you with me, it is more possible than ever."

Tigist's words prompted Alya to say one word, "How?"

Tigist invited Alya to sit down beside her on the sofa so she could explain, "You know it's a big business here to smuggle goods and people to Turkey. We're not that far from Turkey and in one night's drive we can start a new life in Turkey. All we need to do is pay a contact of mine some money and he'll tell us what night we can go."

Alya hesitated to say, "So that's your big secret? Why not just stay here? Looks like you have it pretty good."

"Yes, but Turkey is where we planned to go. People like us are being smuggled into Turkey from here every night. And, from Turkey we can go to a European country and find a life worth living."

Alya thought a moment and said, "When do you plan to go?

"As soon as possible … now that I have you with me. I'm ready to go. You must go with me. You don't have to pay for a thing. Just come with me so we both can see Turkey together."

Alya's was in a state of shock and took a long pause before responding, "Alright. I can't let you go alone. Besides, there's nothing here for me."

Tigist hugged Alya and excused herself, "I must go tell the man that we're ready to go any night."

Alya used the time Tigist was away to look at every crook and cranny in Tigist's spiffy apartment. She opened her closet to see more clothes than she had ever seen for one person. She could not believe that Tigist would leave all these clothes behind. Then she heard the front door being opened and quickly closed the bedroom closet and ducked into the adjoining bathroom.

Tigist called out, "Alya, where are you?"

Alya stepped out of the other bathroom door leading to the living room and said, "I'm here using the toilet. You're back fast."

Tigist was breathless when she said, "Is tonight too soon for you?"

That was quicker than Alya wanted, but she answered, "No, but I'm surprised that we can leave so soon. What about all your stuff?"

"Forget everything. We must sneak out and nobody can know what we are up to. The man said meet him at a place I know at midnight."

Alya was curious and asked, "What's the man's name?"

"No names. I don't tell him our names and he doesn't tell me his. He said only bring what we can carry. The only language he understands is money."

Alya was not in the mood to start a nighttime journey to Turkey, but she started running through her mind all she wanted to do before they took off at midnight. She tried to get herself ready mentally on short notice and said to Tigist, "I guess I'm ready to go because all I possess is in this bag and all my money is tucked away in my bra. I suggest we eat and drink. By the way, how long will it take us to get to Turkey?"

"The man said it would take two to three hours to get close to the Turkish border with Syria. He said he had traversed this short leg of Syria's far northeast part many times. He emphasized that this is where Iraq, Syria, and Turkey came together along the Tigris River. For years, he has smuggled people to Turkey successfully."

Alya was in a more cheerful mood, having accepted being smuggled to Turkey. She said, "Sounds like he knows what he's doing. Incidentally, how much did you have to pay him?"

"$1,000 for each of us. All up front."

Alya raised her eyebrows and thought, "That's about how much money I have. I'm sure glad Tigist paid for me. I'll keep my money safely tucked away in my left bra cup and my wrapped passport in my right bra cup."

Tigist fixed food and set it on the kitchen bar with big jugs of cool water. They ate and drank their fill. Alya washed and dried their dishes while Tigist decided which clothes she wanted to stuff in her carry-on bag. Tigist told Alya, "Get some rest. I'll stay up because I don't want to miss our rendezvous at midnight with the man. It's a short walk to our meeting place. We should leave thirty minutes before meeting up with him."

Alya went to sleep on Tigist's wide king size bed. The next thing she knew was Tigist saying in her left ear, "Get up and ready. It's almost time to go."

With a heavy head, Alya grudgingly got up. The depth of her drowsiness was surprising. At the very moment she needed to be the most alert, she was weighed down by a sleepy head. She shook off her sleepiness and as usual followed the lead of the energetic Tigist. There was nothing that could stop Tigist—it was Turkey or bust.

They quietly slipped out of the apartment. Tigist locked the door and slid the keys underneath the door, marking her permanent departure. They took off their shoes and tiptoed down the hallway and stepped lightly on the stairs, descending to the ground floor. They walked to the front glass doors of the apartment complex and opened them as quietly as they could. Alya followed closely Tigist into the chilly dark, moonless night.

It was an eerie walk for Alya. She was already scared and their clandestine journey into the unknown was beyond anything she could imagine. Tigist led her to what appeared to be a wide spot in the road. Tigist stopped and as soon as she did a four-by-four pickup roared toward them and came to a halt a few feet in front of them. The man driving flung open the door and motioned them to climb in and sit in the front seat beside him. As soon as they were seated and the car door was shut, the man gunned the car and took off into the night with no headlights to guide him. He said in broken English, "Make yourselves as comfortable as you can. It'll take a couple of hours to get to and through Syria to a place near the Turkish border. Don't worry. I've done this many times."

After he said these words, the man laughed joyfully as if this was just another night for him to do his lucrative business. Alya and Tigist laid their heads on top of their bags, which they clutched on their laps, trying to get some sleep and prepare themselves for the trials ahead. After a while, the man told them to wake up and be alert as they were crossing into Syria. After driving a ways, the man said softly, "See those lights? They're on the Turkey side of the border. Soon I'll let you out and you'll have to go into Turkey on foot. If you hear water running that is the Tigris River, and that means you have gone too far east and need to take a more westerly direction."

When the man said these words, he had a confident tone and his English was much better. Alya and Tigist assumed he had practiced saying these words with the many people he had smuggled into Turkey. Suddenly, the car stopped and the man said, "Get out quickly and quietly. Head for the lights. I got to return the same way I came before the Syrian military patrols get me. Good luck."

Alya and Tigist were in the middle of a desolate terrain covered by thorn bushes. They did not dare say a word. Tigist led the way. She attempted to follow a path which took them closer to the border lights. They were making good time skirting the thorny bushes. All of sudden there were beams of flashlights shining on them and Arabic words ordering them to stop. In a panic, Alya jumped into the bushes to hide. Tigist did the same on the opposite side of the path.

When Alya jumped into the bushes, a thorn ripped her upper arm and left a bloody, jagged cut. The blood smeared on the bushes led the Syrian military troops to Alya's hiding place. A solder said in a strangely accented English, "Come out."

At that moment, Alya rose slowly from the bushes, telling herself that she had no choice but to accept her fate. She expected to be raped and then killed.

CHAPTER THIRTY-FIVE

No Place Like Home

ALYA HELD HER LEFT HAND over her bloody deep wound on her upper right arm while she was led by two soldiers at gunpoint along a barren dirt path. She had no choice but to leave her bag behind. Her tears elicited no mercy from her captors who were emotionless. For her captors, this was a routine nightly capture of a smuggled foreign woman trying to cross into Turkey.

A dusty path led to a lone, shabby house and Alya was thrown into a room full of other women as the door was latched behind her. There was no light so she could not see her fellow captives well. She touched the clammy plastered wall until she came to an empty space and sat down against the wall. There was nothing to do except wait until daylight revealed her surroundings.

She tightly wrapped part of her shawl around her wounded upper arm. She softly called out to Tigist. There was no answer, so she concluded that Tigist was not in the dark room where she was being held. Maybe she escaped and was now in Turkey, or worse, she had been killed. Alya's mind was a blank except for the pain caused by her deep wound.

The excruciating pain caused by her wound kept her from sleeping. She knew she was in a room with other people, but she could not see them, so she could not ask for help. She suffered alone and tried not to moan because she did not want to disturb the others.

When the sun began to rise, she began to get an idea of the others with her in their barren concrete confines. She noted that all her fellow captives had a much darker complexion than her and were sleeping the best they could with their backs against the wall or on the hard cement floor. She counted nine women and assumed this was just one night's catch.

Alya waited for more daylight to filter into the room so she could see more clearly. The woman nearest her stirred and sat up. In an almost inaudible voice, Alya greeted her and said in English, "My name is Alya. How long have you been here?"

The woman answered with a sort of English that was unintelligible to Alya who deduced the woman was from West Africa. The woman did notice Alya's bloody arm and called to one of her companions in a language Alya had never before heard. This woman staggered to a place next to Alya and said in easily understood English, "My name is Abassi. I'm a nurse. Let me see your wound."

Alya removed her hand and allowed Abassi to see her where she had been deeply penetrated by a thorn. Upon seeing the wound, Abassi called to another woman in a strange language. This woman brought a metal bucket of water from the other side of the room. Abassi took another part of Alya's shawl and dipped it into the water. Then she proceeded to cleanse Alya's wound the best she could, saying, "This is a deep wound. You need antibiotic pills or injections, and the application of an antibiotic ointment. But you'll get none of that here. As long as I'm here, I will tend to you."

Almost overcome by pain, Alya used much of her energy to say, "Thank you. Where you from?"

Abassi was quick to reply, "I'm a Yoruba from Nigeria, so are my sisters. We were captured together last night as we headed toward Turkey. We left home a couple of months ago. How about you?"

Alya weakly replied, "Ethiopia. I came from Iraq last night with my sister. I don't know where she is."

Abassi said forthrightly, "She's either dead or in Turkey."

At that moment, there was a rustling sound at the locked metal door and then it was opened and a plastic bag full of bread loaves was set inside along with ten bottles of water. Abassi immediately took control, shouting at her compatriots in their language. She gave a loaf and a bottle of water to Alya then passed out the same to each member of her group.

Alya felt an odd kinship with this group. They were all in the same nasty fix. After she ate her loaf of bread and drank some water from her plastic bottle, she asked Abassi, "There's no toilet?"

"There's a pit latrine in the back of the room. Be careful not to fall in."

The day wore on and they did not know the name of their location nor what would be done to them. The room became dark again with the arrival of nightfall. Some of the women started to lament staying another night in this small old house with stale air but Abassi told them, "Be quiet. We're lucky to still be alive. We knew we were taking a big risk. Stay strong no matter what happens. All is in God's hands, so pray to Him."

Alya was about to drift off into a semi-sleep when there was a loud knock on the door and then it was flung open and flashlight beams danced about the room. A loud voice said in a Syrian Arabic dialect said, "Get up and come out."

Although it was clear what the armed soldier wanted, Abassi asked one of her comrades what he said and she said in Yoruba, "He wants us to go out."

Alya was to learn later that woman was Leila and she was Muslim who learned Arabic studying at Koranic schools (Madrasahs) in her hometown in Nigeria. Once outside, the soldiers lined them up and shackled a chain around their ankles. They then walked them haltingly a few paces and they were roughly loaded onto a truck. It was evident they were moving them, but was it to a place of execution or to another prison? And why was all their work done at night?

They did not know where they were going, but after a couple of a couple hours on the road they knew that their next destination was not close by. The truck they were in had a canvas cover so they could not see out. They were on a smooth highway and the truck moved along at a fast speed. The drive lasted all night and the truck finally came to an abrupt stop at dawn.

The women were herded off the truck and in locked step they were walked toward a huge prison and shoved into a large jail cell. Only then were their shackles removed and they were free to pace in their cell. Alya asked Abassi, "Where are we? What will they do with us?"

Abassi said, "I don't know, but I'll ask Leila to ask those in the adjoining cells."

"Never mind, I'll ask myself. I can speak some Arabic."

Alya asked in Arabic a woman in the neighboring cell, "Where are we?"

The woman laughed like she was mad and said, "This is the Sednaya military prison near Damascus. You'll be lucky to get out of here alive."

Alya swallowed hard after hearing the diabolic voice of this scary woman in the next cell and quietly told Abassi what she said. She then checked her bra to see if her money and passport were intact. She knew she would need her money to bribe her way out of this human slaughterhouse. She moved her passport to a securely knotted compartment in her skirt. She could make do without her bag which was dropped when she was captured, but she was good as dead if she did not have money and her passport.

Abassi said to Alya, "You need medical attention. Maybe the guard outside of our cell can help if you show him your wound."

Alya uncovered her wound and whispered to the guard to come and see. The guard looked at her festering wound and said, "Wait."

After a while, the guard returned with another man dressed in a white coat who looked through the bars at her wound and said, "Wait for me."

The medical man returned with a first aid kit and gently doctored Alya's infected wound through the bars of the cell, applying generous amounts of antibiotic ointment and giving her a couple of packets of antibiotic pills and a small plastic bottle of water to take them. Alya did not know if he were a doctor or a nurse, but she thanked him profusely. His good treatment and manner gave her a glimmer of hope.

Abassi, who was standing beside Alya, was amazed at how efficient and kind the medical man was and said, "Maybe there is hope that we can get out of here alive."

They were surprised that they were fed decent food and given plenty of drinking water every day. Also, the two toilets in their cell were functioning properly. They were taken every few days to wash themselves and their clothes in a cold-water group shower room which was located a short distance down the corridor. The days of their confinement turned into weeks which turned into months.

During this time Alya tried to make friends with the man guarding their cell. He was responding favorably to her sweet talk in Arabic. Leila overheard their conversation and when she saw the lust in the man's eyes she reminded him in Arabic that it was haram for a man to touch a woman. Upon hearing Leila's words, the guard backed off.

Nonetheless, Alya kept speaking to the guard. She wanted to know from him when, if ever, they would be released. The guard replied, "Many more months but exceptions can be made."

Alya calculated they had already been in this prison for three months and she was eager to get out and catch a flight to Addis. She told the guard that she trusted him to get her out of there as soon as possible. The guard said, "No problem if you got some money and passport. I could let you out and get you a ticket. Pay me $500 dollars and give me your passport and I'll arrange everything. But you'll have to pay me another $500."

Nobody could see Alya giving her passport and money to the guard and she said, "Okay. I have nothing to lose, but I don't want anyone to see our business. Come back when your shift is finished and the other women are asleep. I'll prepare everything so our transaction is fast and secret."

The guard came as instructed and Alya quickly passed her passport and the money through the bars. The guard was gone in a flash and Alya felt like a fool. She had just given away her lifeline to a foreign stranger. But she told herself that she had to do something, otherwise she would rot forever in this jail.

The days went by and Alya increasingly fell into the dumps. Abassi and the other women in her cell asked what was wrong with her. It had been several weeks since she had seen her guard friend. She had given up all hope of ever seeing him again. She resigned herself to spending her life in this prison or until she was taken out to be executed.

One early morning she heard somebody who was outside her cell clearly calling her name. She rose to see at the front of her cell her guard friend with a big smile. He said, "Come fast. I'll let you out. There's a car waiting to take you to the airport."

Alya could not believe what she was hearing. She hurriedly tiptoed around her sleeping cellmates and by the time she got to the front of her cell, her guard friend had opened the front gate which he rapidly shut after Alya exited. The guard friend said, "Here's your passport and ticket. Where's my $500?"

Alya reached into her bra to retrieve $500 and handed it to him. She felt like hugging him but that would have been wrong. The guard said, "Hurry, the car is waiting for you. Go well. I wish you all the best."

The waiting car was already running and took off as soon as Alya got in the backseat. The main gate of the prison opened as soon as the car approached. It appeared that everybody was involved in her escape caper. She knew the airport was some distance away so she tried to relax and watch the outskirts of Damascus flash by. She had been in the car about thirty minutes when the car came to a screeching halt and the driver said harshly in stilted English. "Get out. There's the airport."

Alya got out and the car sped off. She clutched her passport and ticket as she walked on the pavement toward the distant airport terminal. She was certain that something would prevent her from boarding the plane. There were security forces at the departure terminal gate. These forces looked at her documents and she expected to be taken back to prison. To her great surprise and relief, they waved her through. She went directly to the Ethiopian Airlines counter and was happy to speak in Amharic. As she did not have any baggage to check, she was given her boarding pass quickly and swiftly went through additional security checks.

It was only when she was in the waiting lounge at her flight's assigned gate that she started thinking that she was truly going home. As she boarded her flight and found her assigned seat, she could not suppress her giddiness. She could not believe that she would be home in a few hours. Her family would be surprised to see her. She knew it would be difficult to explain her adventures to them.

The plane arrived at the international airport in Addis late in the afternoon. She did not want to go home in the daytime because she did not want the neighbors to know that she had returned. She sat for a long time in the outer airport lounge. The $200 that remained hidden in her bra she changed into Ethiopian birr.

She waited until well past nightfall to take a taxi home. Alya had the taxi let her stop and let her out a block from her house. It was late at night and there were no people on the street leading to her house. She entered her empty compound and softly knocked on her front door. Yeshi said on the other side of the door, "Who is it?"

"It's me. I'm back."

Yeshi slowly opened the door and said softly, "Where have you been? You must have been hiding somewhere in Addis because we're dying under a heavy load of debt."

Alya was not surprised to hear such words from Yeshi, from whom she did not expect a warm welcome. Yeshi would never believe her true story. Alya knew it was useless to try to convince Yeshi of the truth and simply said, "I'm tired. We'll talk tomorrow."

Yeshi grabbed an envelope from the coffee table and said, "Here. This came for you a few days ago. I'm going back to bed now. You can sleep on the couch."

Alya snatched the envelope from Yeshi's hand. She had never received a letter before and was eager to see who would write. The light from the flickering candle was poor, but she did her best to read the letter which was handwritten in a beautiful Amharic script. She saw immediately that it was from Tigist and thanked God she was still alive. The letter was short and read as follows:

"My Dear Sister Alya, (I hope you are alive to read this.)

First, I want to thank you for saving me from being captured. The soldiers were occupied with you and that allowed me to escape to Turkey where I stayed in difficult conditions for a couple of months before making my way to France. I'm now planning to go to England. I hope you are able to read this someday and we meet again. Always love, Tigist."

The tears rolled down Alya's cheeks. She was happy that Tigist was safe and she was back home. She did not care about Yeshi's disbelief of her true story and her cantankerous ways—she would eat dirt before she ever again ventured abroad to work. She would not fall down again.

ABOUT THE AUTHOR

Mark G. Wentling has 50 years of humanitarian service that began in 1967 as Peace Corps Volunteer for five years in Honduras and Togo. He has visited over the past half century all 54 African countries. He says he was born and raised in small towns in Kansas but made in Africa.

He resides in Lubbock, Texas with his Ethiopian wife. He wishes to be known as a good father, humanitarian, an author, a teacher and as someone who has a good and generous heart.

Printed in the United States
by Baker & Taylor Publisher Services